C0-AQH-153

Praise for Deathmark

Jann Arrington-Wolcott is a powerful storyteller and first-rate writer. I was so impressed with her thriller, Brujo, *that I optioned the movie rights and produced it as a television film titled,* Seduced by Evil. *After reading her latest,* Deathmark, *I said, "She's done it again!"*—Martin Markinson, Producer/Theatre owner, including the Helen Hayes Theatre, New York.

Deathmark *sizzles with sexual tension, supernatural intrigue, and the glittering world of professional art. Jann Arrington-Wolcott's new thriller takes the reader on a wild ride filled with deception, murder, jealousy, shamanism and fact-based Native American history from the time of the buffalo. I couldn't put it down!*—Anne Hillerman, author of *Spider Woman's Daughter*

A first-rate novel, stunning, sensitive and suspenseful, with characters you root for and a deadly twist you won't see coming. Jann Arrington-Wolcott is a gifted storyteller. I look forward to reading more of her work.—Margaret Coel, author of the Wind River mystery series

Deathmark *is a sexy tale that unfolds in dreams, crosses lifetimes and cultural boundaries, erupts into mystery, and reads fast and fun right up to the last line.*—Sandi Ault, Award-winner of the *WILD Mystery Series*

SENSATIONAL! Jann Arrington-Wolcott delivers another gripping, glue-you-to-your-seat thriller! I had a ball staring in the film version of her previous book, Brujo. *Let me tell you,* Deathmark *is every bit as mesmerizing.*—Suzanne Somers

I one-hundred-percent recommend reading Deathmark*!
Based on tenets of shamanism, this is an exquisite and gripping
story that blends ordinary reality with surreal phenomena. Whether
you believe in reincarnation or not, Arrington-Wolcott's weaving of
two vastly different worlds results in a thriller that is very hard to put
down!*—Jeannette M. Gagan, PhD. Author of *Journeying: Where
Psychology and Shamanism Meet,* and *Grow Up Your Ego: Ten
Scientifically Validated States to Emotional and Spiritual Maturity.*

Deathmark *is a memorable, exciting book. Arrington-
Wolcott's depiction of shamanism is well researched and the
theme of her story is inspirational.*—Barbara Tedford, Ph.D.,
professor and shaman, author of *The Woman in the Shaman's Body.*

*Keep-you-up-all-night suspenseful, this cross-genre nov-
el set in Santa Fe and San Francisco is as seductive as they come,
and as dangerous. Unpredictable and compulsively readable!*
—Wolf Schneider, *ABQ A&E*

For Selena &
George
with
admiration &
love
Jann

Deathmark

Jann Arrington-Wolcott

2014

Copyright 2014   Jann Arrington-Wolcott

ISBN# 978-1-941052-03-7 Trade Paper
ISBN# 978-1-941052-04-4 e-Book

Library of Congress Control Number:
2014939998

Cover Design: David A. Szalay

All rights reserved.
No part of this book may be reproduced or
transmitted in any form or by any means,
electronic or mechanical, including photocopying,
recording or by any information storage and retrieval
system without written permission from the publisher.

This is a work of fiction. Any references to places, events or people living or
dead are intended to add to a sense of authenticity and to give life to the story.
Names, characters and incidents are products of the author's imagination and their
resemblance to any real-life counterparts is entirely coincidental.

Pronghorn Press
pronghornpress.org

In memory of my beloved son
David Andrew Szalay (1968-2006)
Artist, humanitarian, comedian, spiritual guide.
You were and still are such an inspiration and part of this story.
We know, my darling, that Love Never Dies.

Everyone dies, but no one is dead.
—old Tibetan saying

Deathmark

1

They return! *The lookout's voice rang from the top of the ridge.*

She dropped the moccasin she was repairing and hurried to the edge of the encampment, just as the hunting party broke through the woods and came into view. Her smile faded. Eight horses—two of them laden with venison, deer hides, and antlers—but only five riders. Beneath the sound of excited voices and yapping camp dogs, she heard the approaching warriors' chant. The sound was chillingly familiar—the ancient song of grief. She'd heard it often enough in her young life.

"No! It cannot be. One Above, do not let it be." She ran to meet them, frantic and half-blinded by tears.

The body lay tied across the back of a white stallion.

"Running Wolf!" His name tore from her throat.

The riders came to a stop and dismounted. She stared in horror as they untied *Running Wolf's* body and lifted it from the horse's back. Jagged wounds ripped across his right shoulder and down his chest. Claw marks! His head hung at an impossible angle. Dark blood caked his skin like war paint, his glazed eyes were open, pupils dilated.

Screaming Eagle, wearing three eagle feathers in his hair and black stripes of command across his cheeks, approached her. He spoke in a voice heavy with grief.

"Your husband met his death with honor, as befits a warrior. He died with the mark of the bear."

She walked, half-stumbling in shock, beside the body as it was carried into the hushed camp. A buffalo robe was spread on the ground in front of the lodge she had shared with *Running Wolf* for such a short time—only seven moons—and his body was gently laid upon it.

The tribe gathered close, many of them wailing their grief. She dropped to her knees, sobbing, beside him. Cradling his head in her lap, she felt the child in her womb stir against her husband's cold cheek. A son. She felt certain she carried a son, the eagerly awaited child of their happy union.

Her eyes were drawn to the bear claw amulet hanging from her beloved's neck, the leather cord now stiff with blood. Pulling him closer, she tried desperately to warm his cold skin with the heat of her love. As she slid her hand under his mutilated shoulder, her fingers touched a deep, blood-crusted wound on his upper back.

She withdrew *Running Wolf's* skinning knife from the scabbard around his waist and—with a primal scream—hacked off handfuls of her long, black hair. She ripped the blade down the length of her left arm—once, twice, three times. Ignoring the stinging pain and flowing blood, she did the same to her other arm. Then she stood and sliced the backs of her calves. Finally, she raised the blade to her face and slashed it hard across one cheek... and then the other.

Callahan bolted awake in the darkness, heart pounding, body drenched in a cold sweat. Shivering, she pulled the covers over her shoulders and peered at the luminous dial of the clock on the

Deathmark

nightstand. *Five-thirty. Time to get moving.* She had a plane to catch.

As she switched on the bedside lamp, she heard the familiar thump-thump-thumping of her Great Dane slapping his whip-like tail on the brick floor. He groaned as he stood, yawned, and stretched his long frame. From her position, Callahan could see only his black hips and tail angled toward the ceiling. The comical sight helped to buffer the anxiety caused by her dream.

"Come here, Mucho."

The dog padded over, greeted her with his distinctive, back-of-the-throat *rrrrrumph* sound, and rested his chin on the mattress beside her. "I have to leave you for the weekend." She scratched the top of his broad head and his big, floppy ears, as she spoke. Mucho whined, as though he understood her words.

"I know, my big sweet baby. I'll miss you, too. But Mommy has to sell her paintings."

Callahan gave his head a final pat before getting out of bed. Mucho trailed after her as she hurried into the bathroom and turned on the shower. She stepped in, closed her eyes and lifted her face to the spray, enjoying the warm water as it ran through her short red hair. Reaching for the shampoo, she was jolted by vivid scenes: *a campsite with colorfully decorated tipis, shouting children, barking dogs, women singing and scraping hides, half-naked men on horses, grim painted faces, the lifeless body of a young man...*

The shampoo slid from her hand and struck the tile, dispelling the last terrible image. She took several deep breaths, fighting a wave of nausea. The dream was more gut-wrenching each time it occurred. And lately that was at least once a week. *Why? What's happening to me?* She lathered and rinsed her hair. *I can't think about this now.* But the dream continued to circle in her mind as she dressed and did some last-minute packing.

"A male escort?" Callahan stared across the table in the restaurant of her hotel at the owner of Gallery on the Bay, the San Francisco showplace that handled her work. The stress of traveling—something she hated—combined with that devastating dream had left her feeling edgy. "You're suggesting I hire a male escort? Come on, Leda. You've got to be kidding."

"It's the perfect solution. You just said you dreaded the party. A date would make it fun."

"A paid escort? No way."

"Why not? Lots of women are doing it."

"No one that I know."

"That's because you spend all your time working, locked away in that backwoods hideaway of yours." Leda paused to take a sip of wine. "Not that Santa Fe isn't charming. But, frankly, I don't know how you stand the isolation."

"It suits me just fine." Callahan would choose her rural home over the ornate Fairmont Hotel any day. And she would definitely choose Mucho's company over Leda's. *I wish the show could have been postponed. I'm just not up to this.*

"Now, about tonight..."

"Look," Callahan interrupted, "what if I just skipped this party? Would it really matter that much? These people know my work. You could say my flight was delayed or something."

Leda put down her wineglass and leaned forward. "You can't be serious. This is the Beckworths' annual art gala, darling. It's been planned for months, and it coincides perfectly with the opening of *The Callahan O'Connor Exhibit* tomorrow night. You're the guest of honor, my shy *artiste!*" She paused for effect. "I shouldn't have to remind you that Howard and Adele Beckworth are major collectors of your work."

"I appreciate that."

"Then I'm sure you understand why this party is important." Leda's voice softened slightly. "We keep our clients happy. Besides, it's going to be a very posh affair. The society editor of the *Chronicle* just called; they're sending a photographer to cover it. It's great exposure and good politics."

"I know." Callahan sighed. "Forgive my lack of enthusiasm. I'm not exactly a party girl under the best of circumstances. And these days... "

"I understand. You've been through what my therapist calls 'a transitional time.' Is the divorce final?"

Deathmark

"Three months ago." The thought of her ex-husband left a bitter taste in Callahan's mouth. She nodded at Leda and glanced at the laughing couple at the next table.

"Are you taking anything for depression?"

Callahan shrugged. Low-level depression had been a problem for most of her life. "My doctor put me on one of those daily happy pills about six months ago." She was glad she'd also remembered to pack some Xanax, to take the edge off her social anxiety. One-on-one or small groups she could handle just fine, but the three-ring circus of a party, followed by the opening of her exhibit…crowds of strangers… She gave a small shudder.

"Is it working?"

"What?"

"Your anti-depressant. I've been taking Pristiq—I call it 'Vitamin P'—every morning for over a year. I absolutely swear by it."

Callahan shrugged. "I can't tell if it's making a difference, or not. Anyway, I don't like taking pills on a daily basis, and plan to wean myself off of it. Who knows what those things really do to our brains? I'd rather just stay focused on my work. That's the best medicine for me."

"What about sleeping pills? I just discovered the best…"

"No," she insisted, hoping to change the subject. "I don't have trouble sleeping." *Except for those dreams.*

"Well, my diagnosis is that you are *way* overdue for some fun."

"Maybe… but paying some stranger to take me to a party isn't my idea of fun."

"Don't knock it 'til you try it." Leda's glossy red lips twisted into a smug smile. "Trust me. A night with the right escort would do more for you than a week of spa treatments." She patted her cheek. "This glow doesn't come from makeup alone, darling."

Callahan took a sip of mineral water and studied the gallery owner's face. Leda did look good. She had to be in her early fifties, but thanks in part to excellent surgery, she could pass for ten years younger. Of course, she also worked out with a personal trainer several times a week.

I've got to start exercising, Callahan resolved. *Buy a treadmill. Go on a diet....*

"Besides," Leda pressed on, "an escort would offer protection from any unwanted attention. Remember that jerk from Atlanta who was all over you at the reception in January? Farley something-or-other."

"Farley Simms. How could I forget? The second time he patted my butt, I stomped my boot heel into his foot."

"Well, apparently pain turns him on. He was back in town and at the gallery the other day, asking about you. Referred to you as a 'spitfire' and made a point of saying that he'd be at the party tonight."

Callahan groaned. "Heaven help me."

"I wouldn't count on heaven, darling, but a nicely muscled escort would do the trick—no pun intended. Let's consider it settled; I'll call the agency this afternoon. The standard rate is three-fifty an hour. I'll arrange to have it charged to the gallery. We can settle up later."

"Hold on a minute! No way am I hiring a male prostitute."

Leda rolled her eyes. "Oh, don't be so provincial, darling. It's perfectly legal. You're paying for the escort's time. As consenting adults, what the two of you do during that time is nobody's business. Think of it as hiring a bodyguard, if that makes you feel better."

Before Callahan could come up with a response, Leda continued, "You know, I understand why you're keeping men at a distance right now. I went through a celibate time myself after Victor and I called it quits. I'd wasted three years on that two-timing bastard. I wallowed around in bitterness and self-pity for almost two months. Then one morning, after a long, lonely night, I realized I'd had enough. I decided to take care of *my* needs, on *my own* terms. That's when I discovered Dream Dates." She reached for her nearly empty wineglass.

Callahan's eye for color couldn't help noticing that Leda's perfectly groomed fingernails were the same blood-red shade as the Bordeaux she was drinking. In an instant, she was back in the dream, wailing in grief, throwing herself across her husband's mutilated body. *Running Wolf...marked by the bear....*

16

Deathmark

Leda's voice yanked her back to the present.

"Callahan! Are you okay?"

"I'm… sorry. What did you say?"

"I asked if you're feeling all right. You just went pale as a ghost."

Callahan took another drink of water to wet her dry throat. She felt a little disoriented.

"I… I'm just tired, I guess. It's always a big push to get ready for a show."

"Well, your hard work will pay off. These latest paintings are spectacular. What with the press the Beckworths' party should generate, I expect a wall-to-wall crowd for the opening tomorrow. So be sure to wear something smashing tonight, something that will photograph well. I did mention it's black tie, didn't I?"

"If you did, it slipped my mind." Callahan shifted in her chair, wishing again that she'd never left Santa Fe. The outfit she'd brought to wear to the party would hardly qualify as "smashing." A simple black wool dress with a matching jacket, chosen to hide the extra ten pounds she'd put on during the past few months. *To hell with it. I'm here to sell my work, not make a fashion statement.*

She picked up her menu and began reading. Perhaps some soup would settle her nervous stomach.

"Dream Dates is the best escort service in town." Leda was apparently returning to what was obviously a favorite topic. "I've personally done the research."

Callahan put down the menu. "I'm not making any judgments here, but I have to say I don't get it. Why would you pay some guy to have sex? Seems like there are plenty of volunteers out there."

"Like Farley Simms?" Leda snickered. "The great thing about hiring an escort is that you're in control. You get what you pay for. No strings attached. No hidden agendas. It's a business arrangement, period."

"What about disease? My god, Leda, especially in this city…"

"You'd probably be safer with a high-class escort than with some guy you met socially. An escort would be just as concerned about safe sex as you are—he couldn't afford not to be. But hey, if you're not comfortable with the idea, don't sleep with him. Just enjoy his company. As I said, these guys are pros. They really know how to treat a woman."

That would be a refreshing change. Callahan couldn't avoid the unwelcome image of Brad's angry face. She took a deep breath and pushed the memory of her ex-husband away as Leda polished off her wine and caught the eye of a waiter.

"All of this talk has given me an appetite. Ready to order?"

"You better dash up to your room," Leda said, as they walked from the dining room into the hotel lobby. "You've got a phone interview with *Art Scene* magazine in twenty minutes. Be your most charming, darling. I had to pull some serious strings to make sure the article comes out before the big Tucson retrospective this February. See you tonight."

Callahan stood watching Leda's slim, retreating figure and then headed for the elevator. *A "date" that charges by the hour. Well, Dorothy, you aren't in Kansas anymore!*

Moments later, she opened the door to the eighteenth-floor suite reserved for her by the gallery. She appreciated the VIP treatment: cozy rooms, elegantly decorated, with a gorgeous view of the bay. *Too romantic.* A familiar wave of loneliness washed over her.

Fifteen minutes later, the phone rang and a reporter with a no-nonsense approach was on the other end. After the usual background questions, he got to the focus of his story. "Do you have any response to the perception that you are an Anglo capitalizing on the current fascination with American Indian culture?"

"That used to be a concern," Callahan admitted. "Then a close friend who is Native American set it straight for me."

The reporter interrupted before she could explain.

"Are you talking about Doctor Russell Gautier—the psychologist/shaman who's written extensively as Red Feather? I saw a photo of the two of you together at a Santa Fe charity event in *Cowboys and Indians* magazine."

"That's right. Red Feather told me years ago that artists have

Deathmark

only one obligation—to follow their heart. That rang true. From that moment on, I began trusting that my work has its own truth and direction."

"Your *Lakota Land* and *Fallen Hero* series have been snapped up by top collectors, and your dedication to your work is well known. What fuels that dedication?"

"I love my work. In fact, I'm happiest when I'm painting. I've switched from oil to acrylics because I like the drying speed. The images grab me and I paint my way in. Each one is a discovery for me, unknown until I see it. As the great Spanish poet, Antonio Machado, wrote, 'I find the road by walking it.'"

"Interesting. You were classically trained, hold a degree in fine art from UCLA, started off in portraiture, and have now won acclaim for your paintings of early American Indian life. Your work has remained fundamentally figurative. Do you use models?"

"Not anymore. Models—anyone at all in my studio except for my dog—would be a distraction to me. Break my concentration. I live a rather secluded life, and solitude is essential to my work process. In fact, I can disappear for days in my studio without being missed."

"A recent article in *Southwest Art* described your art as 'mythic, yet sensual.' Would you agree?"

"Yes, it feels sensual to me." *Far more than I'd ever admit to in print!*

"Who are your major influences?"

Callahan repeated her practiced answer.

"I absorbed technique from the European tradition—Michelangelo for the figure, Vermeer for the light, Bosch for detail, Sargent, El Greco, and Dŭrer for portraiture." She paused, and then opened up a little more. "That training taught me *how* to paint, but not what I *needed* to paint. Once I started the *Lakota* series, everything shifted. Red Feather helped me turn my energies inward and really see."

"See what?"

"What lies beneath the surface. The soul of my work."

19

Exhausted after the interview, Callahan undressed and slipped naked between soft cotton sheets for a short nap. She was almost asleep when the phone rang.

"Hi." It was Leda. "How'd the interview go?"

"I did my best to make you proud."

"Great. We'll schedule a photo shoot with them later. As for the escort, it's all set. He'll pick you up at seven-thirty. His name is—just a minute, I wrote it down—Luke Bennett. And from his description, you're in for a *real* treat."

Callahan fought through her grogginess. "Listen, Leda... I'm really not comfortable with this. I'd rather just go by myself."

"Too late. I waved my magic wand. It's done. See you at eight." The line went dead.

Damn! What a pushy pain in the ass. Good thing I don't have to socialize with her more than a couple times a year.

Callahan closed her eyes. An instant later, she was spiraling into another dream.

The sound of drums, soft and steady as a heartbeat, filled the warm, summer air. She watched, half-hidden behind a tree, as a group of warriors filed past, heading for the council lodge. He stood out from the rest. So tall and handsome! It was the confident way he carried himself, as well as the eagle feathers fastened in his hair, that marked him as a leader.

"Running Wolf." Although his name was but a whisper on her lips, he seemed to hear. His dark eyes found her, and she saw the corners of his mouth lift in a slight smile. She read the promise in his glance: Tonight. I will come to you again, tonight.

Callahan moved in and out of a deep sleep before coming fully awake. She stared at the clock on the nightstand—quarter to seven! Her muddled brain tried to recall what time Leda said the escort would arrive. *Seven-thirty?* She threw the covers back and headed for the shower.

Deathmark

Dream images of a muscular, bare-chested man flashed through her mind as Callahan toweled off. She took several deep breaths, trying to focus her attention on the here and now, quickly blowing her hair dry. She'd cut her shoulder-length hair after the divorce, realizing it was an act of hostility toward Brad. He'd liked her hair long. *Screw Brad.* Her new style, layered and short, suited her—low maintenance, no fuss. She smoothed a thin covering of makeup across her nose and lightly freckled cheeks. Leaning closer to the mirror, she examined the fine network of lines radiating from the outer corners of her eyes. They'd gotten deeper lately, no doubt about it. *Face it, O'Connor, you're pushing fifty. The wrinkles are just going to get worse. And so are those gray hairs you're calling 'highlights.'*

She applied a quick smear of color to her lips, then turned away from the mirror and zipped herself into her dress. The fit was a little snug. *When did I last wear this?* Then she remembered. The Christmas party at Brad's real estate office, almost ten months ago. He'd gotten drunk that night and they'd quarreled bitterly as she drove them home. Once inside the house, he gave her a push that knocked her against a bookshelf and left an ugly bruise on her shoulder.

Callahan shook her head, in an effort to dislodge the memory. *It's in the past. Leave it there.* She slipped into the jacket and added a pair of silver hoop earrings that had belonged to her mother. Crossing to a full-length mirror, she checked the rear view. *Not exactly smashing. But it'll have to do.*

She put on seldom-worn high-heels, hoping she could get through the evening without her feet killing her—or tripping and falling flat on her ass. Sitting on the bed, she swallowed half a Xanax. *Why did I let Leda bully me into hiring the escort? It's just an added pressure I don't need.*

A soft rapping on the door interrupted her thoughts and brought her to her feet. *Oh hell, he's here. What's his name…?* She looked through the peephole of the door at a dark-haired man dressed in a tuxedo. After a moment's hesitation, she opened the door.

"Ms. O'Connor?"

She stared up at a tall, strikingly handsome young man.

Young was certainly the word. *I don't believe this! How old is he? Twenty-five?*

"I'm Luke Bennett." He smiled, showing perfect white teeth. "I was told you'd be expecting me."

"Well, I… "

"You are Callahan O'Connor, aren't you? I hope I have the right room."

"You've got the right room." She hesitated, trying to compose herself. "Luke, did you say?"

"That's right."

"Well, come in. I'll just need a minute to get my things together." She walked into the dressing room and closed the door behind her.

Damn you, Leda. What were you thinking? I'll feel like a fool tonight. Maybe I can pass him off as my son. Then she realized that he was probably younger than Patrick, who had just celebrated his twenty-eighth birthday. She grabbed her purse and a lightweight shawl. Spotting the other half of the Xanax on the bathroom counter, she swallowed it—before rejoining her "date."

Callahan couldn't help but be impressed by Luke's looks. His dark brown hair had a slight wave to it and was stylishly cut to emphasize a well-shaped head. Strong, square jaw. Nice nose above full, sensuously curved lips. Something about him struck her as vaguely familiar. *He's good-looking enough to be a model. Maybe I've seen him in a magazine ad.*

He held her gaze for a moment, and she noted how striking his eyes were—*steel blue, with soft aquamarine under-tints.* Emphasized by thick black lashes and brows. But there was something very mature about the way he was looking at her, studying her, with the outer corner of his left eyebrow raised slightly. *Not quite so young,* she realized. *Closer to thirty.*

"I read about you in today's paper, about your exhibit," he said. "Congratulations on your success."

She took a deep breath. "Thank you. Are you interested in art?"

"I took art appreciation in college, but it met at eight in the morning. I'm afraid I slept through most of the classes." He flashed another dazzling smile. "But don't worry, I can fake it tonight, if I need to."

She believed him. "That won't be necessary. Just be the strong, silent type."

"Whatever you want."

Again, Callahan found herself staring into his eyes. With an effort, she looked away. "Well, I'm told that I'm the guest of honor at this shindig. Bad form to be late. We'd better get going."

"You don't sound very enthusiastic."

"I hate big parties; crowds make me nervous. But I remind myself this is business."

He nodded. "We do what we have to do." He moved closer and draped the shawl around her shoulders. "You know, Ms. O'Connor..."

"Please, call me Callahan."

"I was just going to say, Callahan, that you're not what I expected. I mean, after reading the newspaper article, I didn't expect you to look so young. Or to be so pretty." He paused. "I hope that doesn't sound too forward."

She couldn't help but smile at what was probably a practiced line. "Frankly, I didn't expect *you* to look so young either."

A slight frown creased his forehead.

"I'm sorry if you're disappointed."

"Oh, I'm not disappointed." She was surprised to realize that was true. "I think some youthful energy is just what I need to get through this evening."

His confident expression returned. "Well, I'm here to provide whatever you need."

Callahan groaned inwardly. *What I need is to have this party behind me. I'll have to set him straight if he thinks he's been hired for any other "services."*

"Shall we?" He held out his arm.

She hesitated for only a moment before taking it.

During the taxi ride, Callahan began to relax a little as the medication kicked in. In addition to being charming, Luke was surprisingly easy to talk to. *He may be young, but this guy has been around.*

"How long have you been in the escort business?"

"About six months. I just do it on the side. Actually, I'm a law student at Hastings." He paused. "I'm in my last year. But now, all of a sudden, I'm having second thoughts."

"Like what?"

"Like shucking the whole thing, getting out of this crazy city and heading to Wyoming or Montana. Leading a simple life. Maybe working on a ranch."

"I grew up on a ranch in West Texas."

"No kidding? That must have been great."

He shifted his weight, turning toward her. Suddenly, Callahan found herself acutely aware of the closeness of his body and the cologne he was wearing—a subtle, masculine scent. *Very nice.* She drew back.

"Do you still have the ranch?" he asked.

"No. It was sold when I was a teenager, after my father died."

"That's too bad. Where did you go then?"

"Dallas. My mother had had enough of country life."

"But you hadn't. Now you live on several acres outside of Santa Fe, New Mexico."

She shot him a surprised look.

"To quote that nice write-up in the paper: 'O'Connor's haunting, mystical images of Plains Indians have a mesmerizing power that grabs the viewer and doesn't let go.'"

Callahan gave a little laugh. "You certainly did your homework. I'm impressed."

"It's part of my job."

Of course. This is just another job to him. And, from what I've seen so far, he's good at it.

"But I have to say," he continued, "I'm the one who's impressed. It's an honor to be your escort tonight."

"Thank you." *Saying nice things is also part of the job.* She felt her apprehension return. What if someone at the party recognized Luke, knew that he hired himself out? *Don't be so provincial.* Leda's voice echoed in her head.

Deathmark

"I like your name," Luke said. "*Callahan*. It feels nice on my tongue."

She tried to ignore the erotic image his words evoked.

"It was my paternal grandmother's maiden name. My parents expected a son when I was born. I got the name anyway."

"It suits you," he said, as the taxi pulled through an open gate onto the circular driveway of an impressive, Tudor-style mansion. "An unusual name for an unusual lady." He paused. "How do you plan to introduce me tonight?"

"As my friend, Luke. That's all anyone needs to know."

"That works."

They stopped near the massive front door, and a uniformed attendant opened the door for Callahan and helped her out of the taxi as Luke paid the driver.

"Wait," she said, feeling awkward. "Shouldn't I get this?"

"All expenses are billed to the gallery." His hand lightly touched her waist. "Ready to make a grand entrance?"

She took a deep breath. "Ready as I'll ever be."

2

My dear! Adele Beckworth, her ample frame encased in flowing gray silk, rushed forward to grasp Callahan's arms and kiss the air near her cheek. "I'm delighted you could be here," she said, pulling back to beam at her. "Everyone's *dying* to meet you."

Callahan responded with her best public smile. She was about to introduce Luke when Adele turned her toward a tall, silver-haired man who was closing in on her left side.

"Henri LaPoint," Adele said, "I want you to meet Callahan O'Connor, our guest of honor. We have a wonderful collection of her paintings."

"Nice to meet you."

"And Henri's wife, Bettina," Adele added.

"Hello…"

Callahan shook hands with a blade-thin woman whose off-white cocktail dress perfectly matched her upswept hair. Diamonds dangled from her ears and around her neck.

Deathmark

"Your work is so narrative," the woman was saying. "It has such a haunting quality. Of course, Native Americans are quite the subject *du jour,* aren't they? I was just reading…"

"Excuse me, dear," Adele interrupted, "but Callahan must meet Nicole Peterson, who's visiting from Boston."

"Hello." Callahan's smile was already feeling forced. *Good thing I took a whole pill.* She looked over her shoulder and caught Luke's eye. He winked at her. Hired or not, she appreciated his support. An unexpected warmth gathered in her chest.

"I'm curious," Nicole-from-Boston said. "Why are the faces in your paintings always blurred or hidden?"

Callahan tried to focus on the question. "I think of my images as representing emotional states and stages of Native American life. They aren't meant to be portraits…"

"Howard," Adele's high-pitched voice interrupted, "look who's here."

Callahan turned to shake hands with her elderly, slightly addled host.

"A pleasure to see you again, my dear. How are things in Arizona?" he asked.

"Actually, I live in New Mexico. And things are fine there. Very peaceful."

"Well, you must come to the city more often for a little excitement. Oh, here's someone you'll enjoy talking to. Claude Griswold, meet Callahan O'Connor. Claude spends a lot of time in your neck of the woods. He has a home in Phoenix."

Callahan abandoned the geographical distortion and just nodded as she shook Claude's hand.

"Claude is with the Heard Museum in Phoenix," Adele clarified, "but as an opera buff, he summers in Santa Fe."

"True." Claude adjusted the red and black silk ascot around his drooping neck and sighed dramatically. "Summers are absolutely divine in Santa Fe. And that beautiful open-air opera house! The setting sun striking the Sangre de Cristos while world-class opera fills the air. So, my dear, which operas inspire your art?"

"Well," Callahan responded, "none of them, actually. It's not that I don't appreciate opera, it's just that my images don't resonate to that European, three-quarter time."

Claude looked personally insulted. "Indeed? What music do you prefer?"

"Robby Robertson and his Red Earth Band really do it for me. And, of course, Carlos Nakai's flute and drum music."

"How...*interesting*." Claude's tone was anything *but* interested, and his attention shifted immediately to a plate of hors d'oeuvres being offered by one of the catering staff.

Suddenly, Leda appeared, grabbed Callahan's arm and hissed in her ear, "Play along with the old opera queen, darling. He's not only loaded, he's on the board of the Heard."

Adele resumed her hostess role. "Dear, you've met Farley Simms, I believe. He flew in from Atlanta just for your show."

Callahan stiffened as she was pulled into a unwelcome hug, pressed against the man's extended belly. "You're even better looking than I remember," Simms whispered, his mustache tickling her ear.

She freed herself from his embrace and glanced around. *Where's Luke?*

As if she'd conjured him up, Luke materialized beside her.

"I need to speak to you for a moment, Callahan. Excuse us, please." He took her elbow and quickly steered her to a quiet corner of the room. "I hope I wasn't being presumptuous. It looked to me like you could use a break—or a wide receiver in a tuxedo to run interference for you."

She grinned. "You read that right, and I appreciate it. I'm not very good at this, I'm afraid."

"I think you're good—terrific, actually. Especially for someone who hates crowds."

The intimate tone of his voice surprised her. If she didn't know better, she'd think he was flirting with her. *Don't kid yourself, O'Connor. He's just doing his job.*

"I'll bet you could use a drink... some Champagne?"

She almost agreed, but then thought better of it. *Not on top of the Xanax.*

Deathmark

"Club soda would be great."

He signaled a passing waiter and when their drinks arrived seconds later, Luke looked into her eyes before touching his glass to hers.

"Here's to finding what we're looking for."

She felt a little taken aback. *He's definitely flirting.* Before she could think of a response, they were joined by the ever-watchful Leda.

"What are you two doing over here in a corner by yourselves?" She gave Luke an appraising look.

"Just catching my breath. So… Leda, this is Luke Bennett. He just rescued me from Fat Farley Simms."

Leda's gaze lingered on Luke and then refocused on Callahan.

"Darling, *Mr. Simms* was in the gallery again this afternoon. I think he's going to buy *Calling the Spirits*. A little socializing at this point wouldn't hurt."

"He's buying my work, not my company," Callahan snapped.

Leda gave Luke a flirtatious little smile. "I adore Callahan, in spite of her artistic temperament."

"I admire her because of it," he said.

Leda looked amused. "Glad to see you two are hitting it off."

They were interrupted by a camera-toting young man who identified himself as a photographer from the *Chronicle*. He stepped back a couple of feet and snapped off a few quick shots.

"You'll want some of Callahan with the Beckworths, too." Leda went into take-charge mode, scanning the crowd. "There they are, over by the buffet table." She urged Callahan and the reporter forward. "Here," she said over her shoulder to Luke as she handed him Callahan's glass. "Hold her drink."

"Yes, *ma'am*," Callahan heard him reply under his breath.

After what seemed like an eternity of Leda-directed socializing, Callahan looked around for Luke. This party couldn't be much fun for him. Of course, she reminded herself, he *was* getting well paid for the evening.

He came up behind her. "How are you holding up?"

"My feet are killing me." She glanced at her watch. "We've been here two and a half hours. It feels a lot longer."

He gave her a sympathetic look. "You've been too busy to eat anything. The buffet is great. Let me fix you a plate."

She shook her head. "Thanks, but I'm ready to make my escape. I've schmoozed every prospective buyer and then some."

"I'll call a taxi. Be right back."

Callahan turned to Leda after Luke retired to a corner of the room to speak on his cell.

"I'm going to give my best to our hosts and sneak out of here."

Leda smiled knowingly. "Well, I can't say that I blame you. He *is* gorgeous. Those eyes! That chiseled jaw. Now, admit it. Wasn't my idea a great one?"

"Please. Luke's a very nice young man. And I'm emphasizing the word *young* here, Leda. Geez, I nearly keeled over when I first saw him."

"Twenty-nine isn't all that young."

"So you knew his age?" *At least he's a year older than my son!*

"Of course. They told me all about him. Let's see. He's six-two, a hundred and eighty pounds, strictly heterosexual—or so he maintains. That's unusual in this town. He's extremely bright, and in his last year of law school." She paused. "There were other pertinent details, too, if you know what I mean."

"No, I don't."

"Measurements, darling. Apparently, Luke is *not* your ordinary guy."

"They give out that sort of information?"

"If you ask for it."

"That's terrible, Leda. I mean, it's just demeaning."

"It's a business, darling. People want to know what they're paying for."

Callahan shook her head. "I've been on exhibit long enough for one day. I'm headed back to my hotel. And to bed. Alone."

Leda sighed. "What a waste." Then her expression brightened. "Tomorrow's reception is scheduled from five-thirty to seven-thirty, so plan to be at the gallery around five. Afterward, we'll go out for dinner and celebrate your sales. Sleep tight, hugging your pillow, you silly girl." She waved at someone and strode across the room.

Callahan said her goodbyes and made her way through the crowd toward Luke, who was waiting for her by the front door. Suddenly, she was again face-to-face with Farley Simms.

"I'm beginnin' to think you're avoidin' me, sweet thang." His southern drawl was slurred with drink.

"Actually, I'm just leaving."

"Nooo … we have lots of catchin' up to do, darlin'."

Not on your life, buddy. But before she could reply, Callahan felt a hand on the small of her back.

"You'll have to excuse us," Luke said to Farley, his voice pleasant but firm. "Our cab is here."

"Wait just a minute, young fella…" Farley's bushy eyebrows came together in a frown. "Who the hell are *you*?"

"I'm her *date*. Have a nice evening." Luke propelled Callahan past a shocked Farley and out the front door.

Once in the taxi, Callahan found herself at a loss for words. She shot a glance at Luke, wondering if he assumed that their evening together was just beginning. She felt compelled to clarify that point, and fast.

"You were a great help to me tonight, Luke. Thank you."

"My pleasure."

"Look, I feel awkward about this. But, as you've probably gathered, this is my first experience with an escort. Leda arranged it, pretty much against my better judgment."

"Are you regretting it?"

"Not at all. You've been a wonderful… escort. I just meant that I live a fairly simple country life. Far removed from big city doings."

"I envy you."

"What I'm trying to say is that I don't know what assumptions you might have about… my assumptions." She stopped, laughing with embarrassment. "That didn't make a lot of sense, did it?"

He sat quietly, watching her, his left eyebrow slightly raised.

"Okay, let me try again. Please don't take this personally, but

I'm just going up to my room now. Alone."

"I figured that. And I don't take it personally."

The taxi pulled up at the Fairmont. Luke paid the driver and escorted her into the lobby. "I'll see you to your room," he said.

"You don't have to do that."

"I insist."

They stepped into a waiting elevator. *Should I tip him? Probably so. How much? Twenty-five percent?*

When they arrived at her door, she opened her purse and took out her wallet. He shook his head. "No. Please. Don't spoil it."

Spoil it? "I'm sorry. I don't know the etiquette for this sort of situation."

"I know you don't, and that's refreshing."

There was something in his expression—an intensity that captured and held her. Before she could react, he raised his hand and gently touched her cheek. The unexpected gesture felt intimate and strangely familiar. She shivered as Running Wolf's image teased the edge of her mind.

"Good luck with everything, Callahan," he said. "I really enjoyed tonight." He turned to go.

"Luke. Wait." She hesitated, uncertain of what she wanted to say. "Take... take care of yourself," she managed.

His smile looked strained. "I've always had to." He stepped into the elevator, and she watched the doors close in front of him.

Deathmark

3

RUNNING WOLF *groaned and quickly pulled her body on top of his. His hands caressed her naked back beneath the heavy buffalo robe. Pushing her straight black hair over one shoulder and out of her eyes, she braced herself on one elbow and gazed down into his sleepy, smiling face. She could feel her nipples harden against his smooth, broad chest.*

Although it was still dark inside the tipi, she could hear the winged ones in the trees, singing their greetings to the dawn.

"Morning breaks, beloved," she whispered. "But I would have you stay here with me longer. Just a little longer." She lowered her face, kissed the scar above his left eyebrow, and opened her lips to his.

The hotel telephone broke into Callahan's sleep. She tried to ignore the sound and cling to the familiar, erotic dream. *Just a little longer...* The ringing continued, dragging her back to waking reality.

She fumbled for the receiver. "Hello?"

"Cal? Your cell is turned off, as usual—if you even remembered to take it. Don't tell me I woke you."

"Oh." She tried to focus on her best friend's voice. "Donny. What time is it?"

"It's ten-fifteen here in sunny Santa Fe, so it must be an hour earlier there. You're usually such an early riser I figured you'd already be out buying me trinkets. Just wanted to leave a message saying all's well on the home front."

She stifled a yawn. "Thanks. Glad to hear it."

"So, how did it go last night? Did you wow them at the party?"

"I don't know about that, but I managed to get through it."

"You sound tired. Was it a late night?"

"Not really. I was just sleeping hard." *And what a beautiful dream it was.* She sat up in bed, trying to shake a vague feeling of depression and loss. "How's Mucho?" she asked.

"Mucho poocho is in fine form. I read him the latest chapter of *Poisonous Passion* where my heroine, Fiona Fontaine, seduces the stable boy. And the pooch just yawned and walked out of the room. Exactly what I need, another literary critic."

Callahan had to laugh. "And how's he getting along with Martha Stewart?"

"I'll let her tell you, she's sitting right here on my shoulder. Martha? Martha! Come on, sweetbeak. Say hello to Cal."

There was an ear-splitting screech, and then Donny's beloved cockatoo began to chant: "I see London. I see France. Underpants." A short pause and then another raucous screech. "Underpants!"

Donny came back on the line. "She's in one of her moods. Do you suppose it's avian PMS? Just a minute, this little jailbird's going back in her cage." There was an outraged squawk in the background. "Actually, Mucho seems quite smitten with Martha, except when she lands on his back. He draws the line at playing horsey. The bad news is he's teaching her to bark."

"Oh, no. Are you getting any writing done?"

"After twenty-six bodice-rippers, I can write this stuff in my sleep. Actually, I'm thinking of working an amorous Great Dane into my next plot line. Don't laugh. It's not easy coming up with new twists." He sighed. "But it does pay the mortgage. Speaking of which, is Leda in full battle dress?"

"The opening isn't until tonight, but she's already salivating over sales. She's in rare form, overseeing everything like the ultimate cruise director."

Donny chuckled. "I trust she's taking good care of you? After all, you're the little goosey that lays those golden eggs."

"I'm being pampered in a lovely suite. And speaking of getting laid, wait 'til you hear what else Leda arranged—or tried to." She spent the next few minutes describing her evening with Luke.

"Don't tell me you sent the dear boy home after the party!"

"Of course I did."

"Oh, honey. What am I going to do with you? You can't continue living like a nun. It's not healthy."

She sighed, having heard this lecture too many times. "Please…"

"Okay, okay… I won't nag. When are you coming back to us?"

"My flight leaves around noon tomorrow. I'll be by to get Mucho before five."

"Perfect. I'll fix something special for us to nibble on while we catch up. Oh, I went by your house yesterday. Consuela was scrubbing the bricks in the entryway and jabbering away to herself. My Spanish isn't perfect but I think her husband is in *el* doghouse again."

"Oh, dear. At least we never have to guess what's on in Consuela's mind." Running her fingers through her cropped, sleep-matted hair, Callahan had a sudden flash of long, silky black hair. She could almost feel the weight of it against her bare shoulder. Her dream pulled at her and she closed her eyes.

"Anyway," Donny was saying, "everything looked under control. I told Consuela to call me if there were any problems." There was a pause. "Cal? You still there?"

"What? Oh. Yes. Thanks for checking on things."

"Don't worry about a thing. You're in the big city. Go shopping. Buy something slinky."

She sighed. "Not at this weight."

"What are you talking about? As long as you can zip that cute booty into size ten jeans, your weight is fine."

"How do you know what size I wear?"

"I have a genius for retaining details, my dear. But I swear— I'd like to take a whip to that damned Brad for what he did to your self-image. So you've put on a few pounds. Great! You used to be too skinny. I have a bulletin for you, honey. Most men—we're talking straight men here—like curves. They are *not* attracted to size six matchsticks, regardless of what works on the runway. That's the truth. *In Style* did a survey."

She couldn't help but smile. "Well, in *that* case, it must be true."

"Damn tootin'. Now, hit those shop-lined streets, Cal girl. Go wild. Indulge in something outrageous. Sequins! Feathers! You deserve it."

She hung up, silently blessing Donny. They'd hit it off from the moment they first met, at a Santa Fe Fiesta party almost ten years ago. He was always there for her. She loved him dearly and for many reasons, not the least of which was his ability—even during hard times—to make her laugh.

Callahan ran a brush through her hair and dressed hurriedly in a warm cotton sweater, slacks, and comfortable walking shoes. Donny was right, she had a whole day in beautiful San Francisco to enjoy as she saw fit. A walk to Union Square would do her good. Through her hotel window the late October sky was a cloudless blue, but she grabbed her trench coat, just in case.

Luke chose a chair in an out-of-the-way corner of the Fairmont lobby and slumped into it. He was determined to see Callahan again, and didn't want to wait until her show that night—if he'd even be free to attend. The agency could book a client for him at the last minute. Besides, she'd be surrounded by people. He opened the morning paper to the Arts section again and studied the photo of her taken at last night's party, with him in the background.

I want more time with her. Alone. It's early. She's probably

Deathmark

still in her room. I could call, tell her... what? That I'm down in the lobby? Careful, man, you're crossing the line here. And if the agency finds out, you're done. Impulse control, impulse control. Move too fast and you'll spook her.

At that moment, the elevator opened and she stepped out. His breath caught. He slumped down in his chair, holding the newspaper to shield his face, as she walked past him and out the front door.

Callahan strolled down Powell Street. The air felt crisp and smelled of the ocean. She breathed deeply and realized that she felt better than she had in some time. Almost relaxed. The exhibit was mounted and the stress of this trip would be behind her after tonight. But her spirits sagged a little as she walked past an affectionate couple, their arms around each other, their conversation punctuated with laughter. The sight triggered a feeling of emptiness in her.

There are worse things than being alone. Especially given my track record with men. Since banishing Brad from her life, she'd reminded herself of that on many occasions. That had been—she realized—exactly six months ago *today,* April twenty-fourth.

An unwelcome image of Brad, standing in the kitchen fixing himself the first of several martinis, invaded her thoughts. He'd come home from work in an especially black mood. Things hadn't gone well recently at the real estate company he'd been with for less than two years. Some big land deal had fallen through.

The scene replayed in her mind as she walked.

"Where the hell are the green olives?" Brad demanded as he searched through the refrigerator. *"I had them here, right here, on the top shelf. That goddamn maid must have eaten them."*

"Oh, knock it off!" Callahan snapped. *"Consuela wouldn't have done that. Besides, she doesn't even like olives."*

He glared at her. *"How would you know? You're up there in your studio playing Pocahontas with her paint box while Consuela's here—doing god knows what—all day long."*

She was tired, having put in long hours getting ready for a show in Dallas, and her outrage at his Pocahontas crack overruled *her better judgment.*

"My 'little paint box' keeps the liquor cabinet stocked, doesn't it? As for Consuela, she only comes in two days a week and works damned hard, picking up after you."

"Oh, fuck." He shoved the refrigerator door shut and stalked off into the den.

The evening had deteriorated from there, with Brad refusing the dinner she'd spent almost an hour preparing. He continued, instead, to drink.

Her appetite had vanished, as well. Shoving the beer-battered, chicken and chile rellenos *into the refrigerator, she shut herself up in her study to do paperwork. About an hour later, the door burst open. Brad's handsome features were distorted with drunken anger.*

"I'm sick of being ignored by you," he snarled.

She looked up and sighed. "These bills need to be paid before I leave for Dallas."

"To hell with the bills," he slurred. "Is it asking too much for the famous Callahan O'Connor to act like Mrs. Brad Hamilton once in a while? Pay a little attention to her husband? Maybe join him for a drink?"

"You don't need another drink. You're obviously way past your limit."

Brad's rage exploded, and he lunged toward her. Grabbing Callahan's arm, he yanked her to her feet. Mucho, who had been asleep on the floor behind the desk scrambled to his feet, watching Brad intently.

"Don't pull that high and mighty crap with me! Just because you're a hotshot artist you think you can treat me like dirt. I may not make as much money as you, but I'm still the man in this house."

"Then act like one. Let go of me." Her voice was low. She'd heard it all before.

"I'll let go of you, all right." He pushed her so hard she fell over her desk chair. As she lay sprawled on the floor, he continued to shout. "Don't confuse me with that dried up old Edwin. Or that fucked-up hippie who got you pregnant and took off. Admit it! You

don't know how to act with a real man."

"You're probably right," she replied in a soft, furious voice. "I'm not sure I've ever been with one."

Callahan knew she'd gone too far and in the same moment everything seemed to happen at once. The sharp toe of Brad's eel-skin boot connected hard with her ribcage, just under her left breast. She gasped for air, struggling to roll out of his reach. Just as he prepared to kick her again, Mucho growled and then attacked.

"What the...?" None too steady on his feet to begin with, Brad lost his balance, falling backward. He went down, one hundred and fifty-five pounds of Great Dane slamming him to the floor. "Get off me!" he roared. "Goddam dog...."

Something inside Callahan finally snapped. She crawled back to her desk and opened the bottom drawer, where she kept her loaded Smith & Wesson .38 Special.

"Move, Mucho," she yelled, pointing the gun at Brad, deadly serious. "Over here, boy!"

Mucho looked back and forth between them, growling deep in his throat. After a moment, he lifted his front paws from Brad's chest and came to stand beside Callahan.

"I'm not negotiating this time, you miserable bastard. I mean business. You're out of here."

Brad's flushed face had gone pale. He was well aware of her skill with a gun, having witnessed her blow the head off a rattlesnake that had slithered onto their property the summer before.

"Put that thing down, babe," he pleaded. "Look, I didn't mean..."

"Out!" She was barely aware of the tears—part pain, part rage—streaming down her face.

The barrel of the gun didn't waver as Brad rose on unsteady legs and staggered down the hall. Moments later, she heard the front door slam and his Volvo roar out of the driveway.

The assault left Callahan with a cracked rib and all illusions about her marriage shattered. The next morning, after her doctor had taped her up, she called her attorney, had Consuela pack up Brad's personal belongings, and changed all the locks in the house.

Now, half a year later, much of it spent in isolation, she looked back on her life, searching for pieces of herself that she'd lost along the way. *Two years.* Why had she put up with Brad's drinking and violent temper for that long? Mostly because she didn't want to face the fact that marrying him was the biggest mistake she'd ever made. Of course, he'd seemed wonderful in the beginning—good-looking, sexy, exciting. He'd made her feel desirable and more alive than she had in many years. But after a blissful honeymoon in Italy, and a few months of happiness, his dark side began to show. Increasingly, his attentiveness turned into unreasonable jealousy and his spontaneity disintegrated into erratic behavior, especially when he'd been drinking.

The physical abuse didn't start until near the end of the first year. And always, after each harrowing episode, he swore—so convincingly—that it would never happen again. Repentant, Brad would be more like his old self for several months, but it didn't last. Whatever demons drove him always resurfaced with a vengeance.

She shook her head to dislodge the painful memories and the self-recrimination that followed. Two divorces. More dead-end relationships than she cared to count. Not a good track record. One thing was certain: whatever she was looking for in a love relationship had always eluded her, except in her dreams.

She couldn't regret her first, brief marriage to Kevin, her pot-smoking, college boyfriend. He was nothing but a footnote, a youthful impetuosity in her life, except that he had fathered Patrick, her only child. After Kevin, for the next ten years, she was a single mother—working by day in a San Diego art gallery to pay the bills, painting at night after Patrick went to sleep. Long hours, living on coffee and nerves. Those had been rough years, a constant struggle to stretch time and money. The romantic relationships she'd fallen into during that period were inevitably disappointing. Her priorities had been Patrick and her art, and few men were willing to settle for third place.

She had finally stepped off the dating merry-go-round when her long-time friendship with Edwin, a retired investment banker almost twenty years her senior, deepened into love. Not the passionate, romantic love of her dreams, but a solidly stable relationship secured in enjoyment of each other's company, shared values, and mutual respect. They were comfortable together. When

Deathmark

he proposed marriage, she convinced herself it was the right thing to do. He was kind, considerate; she was lonely, tired of struggling. Most important to Callahan, Edwin, who had never had children of his own, was genuinely fond of her twelve-year-old son.

The three of them moved to Santa Fe, where Edwin had a second home, and Callahan finally had time to concentrate on her art. Her hard work gradually began to pay off. A prominent local art gallery began handling her paintings, and in the next few years she earned several awards and recognition as an important regional artist.

As the years went by, she told herself passion didn't matter; that her increasingly platonic relationship with Edwin was more important than sexual sparks. But although she'd done her best to hide it, especially from herself, she knew down deep that it was an uneasy compromise.

Edwin's sudden death from a stroke five years ago had left her feeling both grief-stricken and guilty. Had she not been in Chicago on a promotional trip, she might have gotten him to the hospital in time. The knowledge that Edwin had died alone had been a terrible torment. With Patrick away at college, her natural instinct was to handle her sorrow by withdrawing into herself. For more than a year, she did little else but work.

In retrospect, she hadn't stood much of a chance when Bradley Hamilton attended a local showing of her work and immediately set his sights on her. He'd come on strong—calling daily, writing love notes, sending flowers and little gifts—and Callahan had fallen hard. Emotionally needy and vulnerable, she'd convinced herself that here, at last, was a man who could inspire real passion, the same passion she found in her work and in her dreams. Ignoring a deep inner warning, she'd seen in Brad only what she'd wanted to see. *How could I have been so blind?*

As the sole beneficiary of Edwin's sizeable estate, supplemented by the income from her paintings—which by then were selling nationally—she enjoyed a very comfortable life. Her money, she finally came to realize, had been a magnet to a man of Brad's high-living tastes.

A clanging cable car went by, pulling Callahan back to the

41

present moment. She entered the nearest coffee shop, ordered a bran muffin and cappuccino, and settled into a booth with the morning paper. She turned immediately to the Arts section. *Nice photo!* There she was, looking a little self-conscious beside an absolutely beaming Leda. Callahan looked closer. In the background, slightly blurred but definitely recognizable, was Luke's handsome face. She stared at it for a moment, trying to decide how she felt. *Well, there I am, in the company of an American gigolo, for the whole world to see. Do I care?* She suddenly realized that she didn't. *What the hell. It'll give Donny a big laugh.* She ripped out the page and stuck it in her bag.

Callahan lingered over the rest of the paper and her breakfast, and then gathered her things. On the way to the counter, she spotted a display: "Authentic San Francisco Sour Dough Starter Kits." *Perfect gift for Donny.* After paying her bill, she continued down the hill toward Union Square. It was ironic, she realized, that while her professional life was undeniably successful—sometimes she had to pinch herself to believe her good fortune in that area—her personal life wouldn't win any awards.

She stopped to admire the window dressing at Saks, before going inside. Donny was right, a new outfit might perk her up. After twenty minutes, she was out on the street again, empty-handed. In spite of her friend's attempts to jazz up her wardrobe, the latest fashions didn't interest her. For Santa Fe social functions, she was comfortable in a denim skirt and blouse or one of her hand-tooled suede outfits, accessorized with turquoise and silver jewelry. Workdays were spent in paint-splattered jeans and sweatshirts.

Across the street from Saks was a bookstore. That was more like it. Books had always been one of her passions, constant companions when she was a child on the ranch. After browsing through the latest fiction and art books, she rode the escalator to the second level, where the metaphysical section was located. She was paging through a new, well-reviewed book on reincarnation when she heard a familiar voice.

"Callahan?"

She turned and found herself staring into a pair of startlingly blue eyes.

"Luke!"

Deathmark

"Well, this is a surprise—running into my favorite artist in my favorite bookstore."

"Yes, it *is* a surprise."

"Did you see the picture of us in today's paper?"

"I did." She couldn't help but smile at his pleasure.

"I guess that makes it official, we're an item." When she didn't answer, he laughed. "You should see your expression. I'm sorry. I was just kidding. Don't worry, my name wasn't even mentioned. I'm just another face in the crowd."

"I'm not worried."

"Anyway, it was a great write-up about your show. How does it feel to be a celebrity?"

"I don't think of myself that way." She deliberately changed the subject. "I was out for a walk, and I just wandered in here. Bookstores are my weakness. When I'm not painting, I'm reading." She looked away, unaccountably embarrassed. *I'm babbling....*

"I'm an avid reader, too. It's always been my escape. By the way, that's an interesting book." He pointed to the one she was holding. "I perused it a couple of days ago."

Perused? He certainly sounds like a lawyer. She met his gaze. "Oh, really? Do you believe in reincarnation?"

"I wouldn't go that far. But I try to have an open mind. How about you?"

"It's certainly an interesting philosophy." She hesitated, for her it was a very personal topic.

Luke shifted his weight, moving in a little closer, obviously not ready to end their conversation.

"This place is like a home-away-from-home to me. Actually, I live a few blocks away, in a studio apartment, not big enough to turn around in. On weekends, when I'm not with my study group at the law library, I'm here. Comfortable chairs and good coffee. That reminds me, I'm starved. How about joining me for lunch? There's a great pasta place across the street."

"I don't think so. I had a late breakfast."

"Please?' His smile was irresistible. "My treat."

She smiled back, noticing how his navy blue sweater accented his eyes.

"Okay," she heard herself agreeing. "Why not?"

Deathmark

4

They were seated at a corner table in a trendy restaurant with a cozy atmosphere. Callahan watched Luke examine the menu. *Why does this good-looking young guy want to spend time with me? He must have a girlfriend, some gorgeous twenty-something. In fact, he must be fighting off the women.* She looked at the menu in front of her. Resisting delicious-sounding pasta dishes, she reluctantly settled for a fresh arugula and mushroom salad. *This extra weight has to go, no matter what Donny says. I can barely breathe in what used to be my baggy Levis.*

Luke leaned back in his chair. "I can't help noticing that you don't wear a wedding band. I wondered last night if you were married, but that's not something an escort asks a client. Now that the occasion is different, I hope you don't mind the question."

She wasn't sure whether she minded or not, but she found herself answering. "I'm divorced, as of a few months ago."

His eyebrow shot up. "Your first marriage? Again, if you don't mind me asking."

She was a little taken aback by his forwardness. But then his eyes fastened on hers, and her normal reticence fell away.

"I've been divorced twice and widowed once. Obviously, I'm not so lucky in love."

"That makes two of us."

"Nobody special in your life?" *Hard to believe.*

"Not now." He picked up the wine list. "Do you want a drink?"

"No thanks, but you go ahead."

He shook his head. "I'm not much of a drinker, especially in the middle of the day."

After they placed their orders for iced tea, he gave her an appraising look.

"You're different from the women I usually meet. You've got so much going for you—talent, success, good looks—but it hasn't gone to your head. You seem very…real. As I said last night, that's refreshing."

Callahan offered a small smile, but had no idea where to take the conversation from there. She started to reach for a piece of delicious-smelling *focaccia*, but Luke was already ripping a piece. He dipped it into the little dish of olive oil suffused with rosemary and handed it to her with a suggestive smile.

"Some things in life are just too good to pass up."

Callahan gave in and took a bite. He was absolutely right.

During lunch, they talked mostly about her art. "So…what made you decide to paint Indians? Oh, excuse me, Native Americans is the politically correct term, isn't it?"

She smiled. "It is. As often as I'm asked about my subject matter, I've never come up with an easy answer. I can only say that the images I create seem to be a part of me, on a deep, subconscious level. I get most of my ideas from dreams." As she said the words, she couldn't help thinking of the erotic dream she was having when she woke that morning. Running Wolf certainly wasn't dead in *that* dream.

Luke's hand moved across the table and touched hers.

"Callahan?"

Deathmark

She jerked her hand back and stared at him, feeling a little disoriented.

"Are you okay?" he asked.

"I was just remembering...something." She took a deep breath and tried to focus on the here and now, on what this disturbingly attractive young man was saying.

"You must have fascinating dreams. I don't usually remember mine." He took a bite of his shrimp risotto and chewed thoughtfully. "Although—this is weird—sometimes I wake up knowing that I was having a powerful dream. It happened to me this morning. Even though I don't remember the dream, I still feel the *effect* of it."

"In what way?"

"It's a strange feeling, like I'm nostalgic for something I've never known."

His eyes again met hers, and she was struck, as she had been the night before, by the intensity of his gaze.

"Does that make any sense?"

Incredibly enough, he had perfectly described the yearning that both haunted her days and fueled her work.

"It makes perfect sense to me."

They shared another long look. *What's going on here? I hardly know him, but I feel as though...*

"I really liked seeing your paintings last night," he said. "Especially the one with the old man standing on a hilltop with his arms raised, like he was greeting the rising sun."

She smiled. "That *is* what he's doing. *Morning Prayers* is the title of that piece."

"I couldn't get over the colors, especially in that sunrise. It really affected me. I wished I could just step into the painting. I'm sure you hear that kind of praise all the time, but I mean it. I'm eager to see more of your work."

He took a drink of tea, and Callahan watched him lick his full lower lip. Suddenly aware that she was staring at him, she forced her attention back to her salad.

"I've always been interested in Indi...oops...*Native Americans*," Luke continued, "their culture and way of life. I'm supposed to have some Native blood, myself. My grandmother was half Cherokee. She grew up on a reservation in Oklahoma. At least that's the story my father told."

"You didn't know her?"

"She died right after my father was born."

"That's too bad—that you never knew her. There's so much wisdom in Native teachings. My friend, Red Feather, has been a strong influence in my life for many years. In fact, he's the one who suggested I start painting scenes from my dreams. I'm really indebted to him for that. It was a turning point in my career."

"So he's an artist?"

"No. Actually, he has a impressive background: a doctorate in anthropology and a master's in psychology. He's become a powerful shaman and believes in the holistic approach to healing, that our physical, emotional, and spiritual health are all connected. He's written several books on the subject."

"Hmm, sounds interesting. I've always wanted to meet an authentic medicine man."

"Red Feather is the real deal. He's helped me to understand that art, in its many forms, is really a spiritual practice, a way of connecting with our soul."

Luke's expression grew even more thoughtful.

"Do you really believe we have a soul to connect with?"

"Yes, I do. What about you? What do you believe?"

"Good question. I'm still trying to figure that out. I'd like to believe we're more than just these bodies. Otherwise, life seems pretty pointless."

She nodded. "According to Red Feather, realizing soul as our true identity is what the spiritual journey is all about."

He leaned in closer to her, elbows on the table.

"See, Callahan? You're different. I mean, here we are, talking about souls and the spiritual journey. I don't usually have this sort of conversation with women…with anyone, for that matter."

"What kind of conversations do you have?"

"Besides contract law, the latest celebrity trial, and the Giants?" He switched into a mimicking tone of voice and continued.

Deathmark

"What gym do you go to? Which restaurants are on the A-list this month? Do these highlights make me look younger? And the big one: what are the afternoon rates at the better hotels?"

She found herself laughing, really relaxing for the first time in a long while.

Luke finished the last of his lunch and leaned back in his chair, studying her.

"You, on the other hand, seem so grounded, so certain of who you are," he said.

"Do I? Actually, I doubt that any of us knows who we *really* are. I suspect we're much more complex than we realize."

"Yeah, I know what you mean. Sometimes I feel like several different people living in one body."

A waiter interrupted, collecting their empty plates. "May I interest you in dessert?"

Luke gave Callahan a naughty grin. "Let's share a *tiramisu*. It's sinfully good."

She smiled. *This guy is something else. Sinfully good, indeed.*

"And coffee?"

"Please. Black."

When the waiter was gone, Luke said, "Tell me more about yourself. Something I haven't read in the newspaper."

"Like what?"

"Let's see. What's your favorite color? Do you come from a large family? Did you have a happy childhood?"

They teach interviewing technique in law school, don't they? He gets an A+.

"Okay. As an artist, it's hard for me to pick a favorite color. But I guess I'd have to say the many shades of green…"

He smiled. "Green, like your eyes. But go on. Tell me about your family.

"Okay. I was an only child. And yes, I had a happy childhood on the ranch." She paused. "It was an idyllic time that ended the day after my fifteenth birthday, when my dad was killed."

"What happened?"

Callahan had a sudden flash of sitting on a fence post,

watching her red-headed father perched atop an enraged bronc he was determined to break.

"Hey, Daddy!"

He turned to give her a big smile. "Hey, yourself, honey girl!"

An instant later, he was lying in the dust with a fractured skull. She willed the traumatic memory away.

"A horse threw him…and then kicked him in the head. He died moments later."

"That's terrible. Were you close?"

She nodded. "Very close. He was a big-hearted Irish cowboy."

"Last night, you said you and your mother moved to Dallas. Is she still there?"

He pays attention. "Mother died of cancer ten years ago."

He covered her hand with his, an intimate gesture that both comforted and disturbed her. As though reading her thoughts, he moved his hand away.

"Do you have children?"

"A grown son. In fact, Patrick is just a year younger than you."

Luke didn't bat an eye, nor did he seem to question how she knew his age.

"He must be very proud of you."

"I hope so. I'm sure proud of him, he's the light of my life. We've always had a close relationship, except for a few years when he was a typically impossible teenager."

"What does he do?"

"He has a Masters in computer science and develops software for a company in Denver. In fact, my techie son is building a state-of-the-art website for his electronically challenged mom. He keeps trying to drag me into the modern age. According to him, I'm the only person in the civilized world who refuses to text. And I rarely have my cell phone turned on…or even remember where I left it. I basically just use it when I'm traveling. As an artist, I try hard to control my time and stay on schedule."

"And as a woman? Do you maintain such control in your personal life?"

Callahan looked away. Luke was immediately apologetic.

Deathmark

"Forgive me. That's definitely none of my business." When she didn't respond, he continued. "I'd just really like to know more about you."

"Why?"

It was his turn to look away.

"Good question." Then his eyes fastened on hers again. "I don't know. I just feel drawn to you" He hesitated. "Uh oh, you look a little alarmed. Please, don't be. It's just that sometimes my life feels so… lonely. Empty of real contact. As I said before, you're an unusual, interesting woman. Please, take that as a complement, nothing more."

"Okay." She smiled for him. "Thank you."

His own charming smile returned.

"So, except for your lack of interest in technology, you seem pretty modern to me."

She shrugged and took a sip of tea. *You should check out my dreams.*

"And independent." His left eyebrow lifted, slightly. "So, do you live alone?"

"Not quite. I have a dog—a really *big* dog." She laughed. "A wonderful Great Dane."

His expression became a little wistful. "I've always wanted a dog. But I've never been settled down enough to take care of one." He abruptly changed the subject. "Hey, do you like to dance?"

"I haven't been dancing in years, but I loved it when I was younger."

"The newspaper article said you're forty-eight. That's not exactly old."

"Forty-nine, actually. I had a birthday last month." She hesitated. "I'm not the kind of woman who tries to hide her age. In fact, I'm rather proud of it.

"Now, it's my turn to ask you something. Do you often invite older ladies to lunch?"

"I see several mature ladies, on a professional basis. But a lunch date like this? Never happens."

"Is that what this lunch is? A date?"

"Sure. Are you okay with that?"

She gave a little laugh. "I guess so. It's just that I haven't had a date, with anyone but close friends, since my divorce."

"I'd like very much to be your friend."

Before she could think of an appropriate reply, the waiter arrived with their dessert and coffee. Callahan, grateful for the reprieve, savored the first bite.

"You were right... "

"I'd never steer a lady wrong."

She tried to hide a smile. *Really? Not sure I'd bet the ranch on that.*

"Okay, I've done enough talking about myself. It's your turn."

"Not much to say. I grew up in the Midwest, just outside of Detroit. Got my B.A. in Criminal Justice from the University of Michigan. Bummed around for awhile and ended up out here in law school. That's about it."

"You aren't getting off that easy. Favorite color? What about your family? Did *you* have a happy childhood?"

"Red, for its stimulation and association with the life force."

His in-depth answer surprised her. *Hmm, this guy is full of surprises.*

Luke paused for a moment, his eyes darkening. "I was an only child, too. But I wouldn't describe any part of my childhood as 'idyllic.'" Another pause, as though he was debating whether or not to continue. "My mom deserted my dad and me, ran off with some guy when I was seven years old. I don't know or care where she is now. My dad...well, the less said about him the better."

"I'm sorry..."

He shook his head. "I survived it. What's that saying? 'That which does not kill us makes us stronger.'"

"I guess so." Callahan's interest in Luke was growing by the moment. *He's a real paradox: a philosophical law student-hooker who quotes Nietzsche. Obviously has a head on his shoulders, in addition to his other assets.*

"What drew your interest to criminal justice and law?"

"I've always had a fascination with the workings of the

criminal mind and the things people try to—and often *do*—get
away with."

She took that in, and then asked the question that was foremost
in her mind.

"How did you get into the escort business?"

He shifted in his chair. "Well, at first it was kind of a kick.
I met a guy at the gym who was escorting. As he talked about it,
what easy, fast money it was, I thought, hey, why not? It sounded
like the ultimate male fantasy." He switched again into his mimicking
tone. "Get paid for getting laid." Then his voice became confiding.
"Besides, I really needed money—to stay in school, pay my rent, just
to survive in this city. I was waiting tables at nights and on weekends,
working my butt off but just barely getting by. So I signed on with the
agency." He looked away and then back at her. "Do I lose points with
you for doing that?"

Lose points? He's talking like this really is a date.

"No. I've just never known anyone in your profession. You
said that it was a kick at first. And now?"

He shrugged. "I enjoyed it last night. Like everything, it has
its not-so-glamorous side. But the pay is good. And I figure I'm not
hurting anyone, except maybe myself sometimes."

There was an uncomfortable silence.

"If you'd rather not talk about it..." she offered.

"It's okay. Of course you're curious. Everyone is. A guy from
the agency was on *Jerry Springer*—you know, that tacky TV show—
last month. *Women Who Pay for Sex* was the name of the segment.
They invited me, but I said, 'No way.' I'm not exactly proud of what
I'm doing. It's just a way to get by while I'm in school."

She nodded, and decided to change the subject.

"You said last night that you were having second thoughts
about practicing law. Why is that?"

"I don't know. My heart just isn't in it. It's like something
else is calling me. I haven't figured out what it is." He shrugged then
studied her with that strange, unnerving intensity.

"Okay, now it's your turn again. You said your father was
Irish. So, is O'Connor your maiden name?"

She nodded. "I took it back after my first divorce. I decided that since I was born an O'Connor, an O'Connor I would stay. Besides, an artist can't keep changing her name." She glanced at her watch. "Speaking of which, I need to get back to the hotel and attend to a few things before tonight's opening. I'm due at the gallery by five."

He signaled the waiter for the check. "I may see you there. I mean, I'll try to. I really want to see your show." He shifted in his chair, looking uncomfortable. "I…I just don't know yet whether or not I'll be working tonight."

"I understand. Well, drop by if you can." She realized with some surprise that she really *did* want to see him again.

He started to say something and then stopped.

"What?" she asked.

"It's strange, but I feel like I've known you for a long time. Like you're someone I could actually trust. It's really been good spending time with you."

"I've enjoyed it, too."

Again, his eyes captured and held hers. Shaken by her physical response to him, she pushed her chair back. He was immediately on his feet to help her. And then he bent to collect her purse from the floor and carefully placed her trench coat around her shoulders. *A perfect gentleman. Damn! Do men like this come in an older version?*

Once outside the restaurant, he asked, "Do you want a cab? It's an uphill walk to the Fairmont."

"No. I can use the exercise." *And maybe the fresh air will clear my head.*

He glanced at his watch and frowned. "I'd walk with you, but to tell the truth, I've sort of lost track of the time. That's really unlike me. There's someplace I need to be in a few minutes. Good luck tonight, Callahan."

"Thank you. And thanks, too, for lunch."

He reached out and touched her cheek, letting his fingers rest against her skin for just a second. Then, without another word, he stepped onto the crowded sidewalk and disappeared.

Callahan stood still for a long moment, feeling the lingering warmth of his touch on her skin. *He did that last night—touched me like that.* She was aware of tears behind her lids and a completely irrational yearning.

Although the sky was still bright and clear, Callahan made her way back to the hotel in a fog of confusion.

What's the matter with me? I had lunch with a bright, attractive young man. Way, way too young. I'll probably never see him again. So what? Why do I feel so shaken?

5

The large open rooms of Gallery on the Bay were filling with people. Platters of *hors d'oeuvres* covered one long, linen-draped table, wine and mineral water were served at another. Callahan felt a little shaky, in spite of the pill she'd taken before leaving the hotel. She fortified herself with a couple of tasty miniature crab cakes. *All I had for lunch was that salad and three bites of tiramisu.* She helped herself to two more crab cakes.

The cream-colored walls were filled with Callahan's oversized canvases, a sight that never failed to thrill her. Each piece she painted was like a child to her, something that had come out of her and assumed a life of its own. Some of the paintings were especially hard to part with.

"There you are." Leda rushed forward, exuding her usual overbearing energy. "You look fabulous, darling, the epitome of Santa Fe style." She brushed Callahan's bangs back from her forehead.

Deathmark

"That great red hair should frame your face, not hide it." She went on to straighten some of the fringes on Callahan's tan suede vest. "Great outfit. Western, but not too Annie Oakley. Those ostrich cowboy boots are gorgeous! I must visit you and buy a pair just like them."

Callahan sipped her mineral water and didn't respond to the bait. Although she had a large house with two guest rooms, she would put up a barbed wire fence with her bare hands to keep Leda out.

Leda lowered her voice. "Two more paintings sold today, *Summer Encampment* and *Quiet Celebration*. Marc Sutton will be here tonight. He bought one of your pieces last spring and wants another. I think he's torn between *Daybreak* and *Song for a Dead Warrior.*"

Callahan stared up at the four-by-five-foot canvas hanging on the wall in front of her. *Song for a Dead Warrior* had almost not been shipped to the show.

"I hate to part with this one. It's special to me. If Sutton doesn't buy it, I'll take that as a sign that I should keep it for myself. Just put a 'sold' sticker on it, and I'll ship you a substitute."

"Darling, the way they're selling, I'm going to need half a dozen more ASAP, anyway." She waved a greeting to a well-dressed, elderly couple just coming in. "The Steinbergs," she said, in a lowered voice. "Big collectors. I was hoping they'd show." She grabbed Callahan's hand and led her toward them.

During the next forty-five minutes, Callahan answered questions about her work and made small talk with a steady stream of visitors. Every so often, she found herself glancing toward the front door, trying not to feel disappointed. *Luke has other plans. He's a working boy, after all. By now, he's probably...*

Leda's voice cut into her thoughts. "Well, well, look who just arrived." Her voice dropped to a whisper. "Is there something you're not telling me?"

Luke, dressed in a well-tailored, charcoal-gray suit, was scanning the crowd. When he spotted Callahan, he grinned.

She felt an undeniable thrill. *He did come, after all. He's so damned good-looking. If I were twenty years younger...*

She watched him walk closer to the wall to study a canvas. There was something about the way he handled himself. That confident bearing was eerily familiar. She had to pry her eyes away from him as another man approached her.

As soon as she could tactfully disengage herself from his conversation about visual language and color theory, Callahan glanced around and located Luke studying *Song for a Dead Warrior.*

She turned to answer an elderly woman's question about her technique.

"I work with acrylic on canvas, primarily. Acrylic dries faster and isn't as toxic as oils."

Moments later, Callahan noted that Luke hadn't moved. He was still staring, transfixed, at the same painting.

"Excuse me," she said to the woman who had been describing, in tedious detail, her grandson's artistic aspirations. She walked up to Luke, who seemed oblivious to her approach.

"Do you like it?"

He started, and then turned to her with a distracted look. "I…yes, I do. It's…amazing." He shook his head. "Listen, Callahan, there's something…"

"I'm sorry to interrupt you two," Leda said, gliding up beside them, "but, Callahan, I want you to meet some people who'll be joining us for dinner tonight."

Luke touched Callahan's arm. "I have to go." His voice was tense. "I…I'm sorry." He made a break for the front door.

Doing her best to respond to Leda's clients and friends, Callahan's thoughts kept returning to Luke's abrupt departure. *He was obviously upset. But why?*

Two hours later the crowd had thinned to less than a dozen people. Although pleased with the enthusiasm for her work, Callahan was more than ready for the show to end. She was tired of standing around in her new, not-quite-broken-in boots, talking to strangers.

Leda waved goodbye to a departing group then found her.

"What happened to lover boy? I thought he might be joining us for dinner. Off the clock, of course." She fluffed her dark hair from under her shirt collar. "He certainly dresses up a room."

"He had to leave."

"That's not surprising. It's Saturday night and I'm sure he's a busy boy. With that face and build he must be in real demand. I may have to request him myself one of these weekends."

Callahan looked away, trying to hide her irritation.

"Well, my dear, we made three, possibly four, more sales. All in all, a most profitable weekend. We're on a roll, so let's keep that art crating service busy. Get those new canvases here as soon as the paint is dry."

Callahan gritted her teeth. *Push, push, push.*

"What about *Song for a Dead Warrior*?" she asked, suddenly remembering Luke's apparent fascination with it.

"It's still yours. Marc decided on *Daybreak*. But I'd like to keep it hanging a while before shipping it back to Santa Fe. Now, let's gather everyone up for dinner."

"Everyone? How many have you invited?"

"There'll just be six of us. Very cozy."

Callahan breathed a sigh of relief. *Almost over.* She couldn't help thinking how good it would feel to be back in her quiet, provincial world.

Callahan's dinner—roasted quail on a bed of wild rice with cranberries and walnuts—was delicious and the conversation at their table relaxed and interesting. But the image of Luke, standing in the gallery, staring at her painting, wouldn't let go. The confident way he moved, the angle of his shoulders. The sense of familiarity.

I've got to stop this. I meet the most inappropriate man imaginable and start having obsessive thoughts about him. Leda's right, I've been in isolation too long

The telephone was ringing when Callahan opened the door to her suite an hour later. She checked her watch as she rushed to answer it. Ten-thirty, eleven-thirty Santa Fe time. No doubt it was Donny, who rarely went to bed before midnight, checking to see how the opening had gone.

"Callahan?" Luke's voice sounded tense. "I want to apologize for bolting out of the gallery like that. I need to explain. I'm downstairs right now, in the lobby. Would it be okay if I came up?"

Her stomach gave a little lurch. "Well, I don't know. I just walked in…"

"Please? It's important."

Against her better judgment, Callahan gave in. She hung up the phone, pulled off her boots and hurried into the bathroom. *I should have said I'd meet him in the lounge.* She quickly brushed her teeth and touched up her lipstick. *But I can't wear those damned pointy-toed boots another second.* A soft rapping at the door interrupted her thoughts.

He stood in the hall, a worried expression on his face.

"Come in." She closed the door behind him and waited with her arms crossed in front of her.

"I'm not sure how to handle this. I don't want you to think I'm some kind of freak."

"Why would I think that?"

"Because of what I'm about to show you." With that, he took off his suit jacket and draped it across the arm of a chair. Then he started unknotting his tie.

"Hey! What are you doing?"

He removed his tie and began unbuttoning his shirt.

"Now, just a minute…"

"Don't get the wrong idea. I have to show you something." He opened his shirt, exposing a well-muscled chest.

Callahan looked closer and gave an involuntary gasp. Beginning on the lower right side of his neck and fanning out across his shoulder and upper chest were four faded-red marks—like slashes—each about a quarter-of-an-inch wide. Farther down, just under his right nipple, were two more, slightly wider and more jagged than the others.

"Oh, my god…" She moved toward him. "Those look like… claw marks. Just like…"

"The wounds on the Indian in your painting. "

"*Song for a Dead Warrior.*" She reached out, running trembling fingers over the marks.

Deathmark

"How did you get these?"

"Birthmarks. They were a lot more noticeable when I was a kid, but they faded as I grew up. He took his shirt off. "There's another mark, much wider, on my back. See?" He turned around, exposing a six-inch-long, four-inch-wide jagged mark. "It looks like something tried to eat me, doesn't it?"

A rush of emotion took her breath away. *It's not possible!* His marks were identical to wounds she had seen in dreams for much of her adult life. *Deep, bloody gashes ripped through smooth bronzed skin. Fatal wounds inflicted by a grizzly bear.*

Roaring sound suddenly filled her head. Time shifted. *She flung herself across his cold lifeless body. Running Wolf... No!*

And then Luke's arms were around her, holding her against his naked chest, supporting her.

"Here," he said, easing her down onto the sofa, "lie down. I'm sorry. I didn't mean to shock you like that."

"I'm... I'm all right. I guess..."

Luke walked to the mini-bar and quickly returned with a glass of mineral water. "Take a sip."

Callahan slowly sat up and took the glass. Her eyes fastened on the marks. *Could he have drawn them—used some kind of paint?*

"I know what you're thinking," he said. "Be right back. He disappeared into the bathroom and returned with a wet washcloth and bar of soap. "They're real. Go ahead, try to wash them off."

She did, scrubbing hard. The skin around them reddened, but the marks remained. "I don't understand," she said.

"All I know is that they've always been there." He reached into his jacket pocket and removed several photographs. "I tore these out of an album—one of the few mementos of my early years. This was taken when I was about a year old, sitting in the sun on our porch. The marks are clearly visible. And here I was about ten, at the beach. And this was taken when I was a high school senior, on a volleyball team. Even though I was tanned, you can still see the marks."

Callahan took the photos, and examined them closely. Her hand was shaking.

"I...I don't know what to say."

"It's weird, for sure," he said as he sat down beside her on the sofa. "I couldn't believe my eyes when I saw that painting. I mean, they look exactly the same, right?"

She took another drink of water. *Can I believe him? But why would he lie about this?*

He stood and walked to the chair where he'd thrown his shirt. Even in her stunned condition, Callahan couldn't help noticing the broad expanse of his shoulders and the ripples of his flat abdomen. The muscles in his upper shoulders and arms looked almost sculpted.

"How do you happen to have these photos with you?"

"I no longer have a family. So, everything I own is with me."

"I could use a glass of wine," she said.

"Good idea. Me, too. Red or white?"

"Red, I guess. Whatever's there."

He put his shirt back on but left it unbuttoned as he filled two wine glasses from the mini-bar, placed them on the coffee table, and sat back down close to her. Callahan took a drink, and then another. She picked up the photos and examined them again.

"I need another look at those marks, to compare them to the photos, okay?"

"Be my guest." He opened his shirt.

She stared at his chest for a long moment. "They absolutely match the wounds I've painted—over and over. How can that be?"

"You've painted them in other pictures besides the one I saw tonight?"

She nodded. "I did a whole series called *Fallen Hero*. The final painting is *Song for a Dead Warrior.*"

"Where did you get the idea for his wounds?"

"I've seen them for years, in my dreams."

He stared at her. "Are you *serious*? When did the dreams start?"

"When I was about fourteen." She hesitated. Her dream world was intensely personal, and she was reluctant to share it. In fact, she'd never really opened up about it, except with Donny and Red Feather. But Luke was watching her so intently that she fortified herself with more wine and continued.

"My dreams have always been incredibly realistic. It's like

62

Deathmark

watching a TV series I've seen countless times, only I can't change channels. I'm part of the action. The dreams occur randomly. Most are reruns, but occasionally I have a new one. Sometimes when I wake up, I feel that the dream world I just left is the real world and my waking world is the dream."

His gaze never wavered from hers. "Please, go on."

"Well, in these dreams I'm a young Plains Indian woman, named Sun-in-Her-Face. From the research I've done, I'm pretty certain my tribe is part of the Lakota Nation. We live in tipis, moving from place to place, following the seasons and availability of food. It's not an easy life, in fact, it's often downright brutal. But, still, there are aspects of that existence that are appealing."

"Like what?"

"Living close to nature. The people I dream about live by a strict code of honor. Life is raw, but there's an order to it. Everyone knows what's expected of them." She stopped for a healthy sip of wine and to gather her thoughts.

Luke waited for her to go on.

"Most of my dreams are about a young warrior named Running Wolf. He's my lover, my protector...my husband. He's everything to me." She paused. "It's strange, but I've never been able to remember his face after waking—the others but not his."

"A faceless Indian lover that visits your dreams... and he's the hero in *Song for a Dead Warrior,* the one with the wounds?"

Callahan nodded. The wine was definitely taking the edge off her nerves. She drank a little more.

Luke stretched his arm out, resting it on the back of the sofa. She tensed a little as his fingers touched her shoulder, casually, as if by accident.

"How often do you have these dreams?"

"Several times a month. Although lately it's been more often."

His fingers moved slightly, and Callahan felt them brush against her hair. *Is he making a move here?* She leaned forward and took another sip of wine.

"Excuse me for asking so many questions. It's just that this is pretty mind-blowing."

"That's one way to put it."

"Do you mind telling me more?"

She leaned back. "Actually, it's good to be able to talk about it to someone who's really interested." Callahan was acutely aware of his closeness, the subtle fragrance of his cologne. She felt a sudden warmth suffusing her body.

"What killed this...what's his name, Red Wolf?"

"Running Wolf."

"What made those wounds in the painting?"

"A bear."

Luke winced. "That really gives me the creeps. I've always had this peculiar reaction to bears. When I was a kid, I'd go to the zoo and just sit and watch them. I was fascinated, but they scared the hell out of me. Still do. I saw a movie not long ago where a guy gets mauled by a bear, and I swear I could feel those claws ripping into me. I had nightmares about it for weeks." He gave her a half-smile. "Hey, maybe *that's* how I got these marks. Maybe I've been visiting your dreams."

His words caused Callahan's throat to close. She stared at him, unable to speak.

"Hey, no...I'm just talking crazy." When she didn't respond, he leaned in even closer. "Callahan...why did that upset you?"

"In...in one of my dreams, a band of hunters returns to our encampment with Running Wolf's body strapped to his horse, his neck obviously broken, those deep, bloody gashes across his shoulder and chest." She hesitated, and then plunged ahead. "But there's something else in the dream, something I've never painted. His upper back... it's torn open."

Luke looked genuinely shocked. "No way. That's...just incredible. And I have that big, nasty mark on my back. What the hell kind of coincidence is *that*?"

Coincidence? Is that all this is? Callahan's mind was reeling.

"Do you know what I think all of this could mean?" His voice was suddenly soft.

"What?"

He leaned in a little closer. "Maybe we were destined to meet."

Deathmark

Is he serious? Or is this just the world's weirdest come-on? Either way, it's about to get out of hand. She shifted her weight, putting a little more distance between them. His glass was almost empty. It was time for him to leave, to give her a chance to sort through her thoughts.

"It's late, Luke. I think you'd better go."

"Please, Callahan, not yet. I want to hear more. You said you're convinced that the tribe is Lakota. That's Sioux, isn't it?"

"Actually," she said, warming to one of her favorite subjects. "The word 'Sioux' evolved from an Ojibwa word, which was usually translated as 'Snake' or people from an alien tribe. French trappers spelled the word *Naudoweissious,* English speakers shortened it to Sioux. Lakota is a Siouan word meaning 'Allies' or 'Friends.'" She gave a little laugh. "That's no doubt more than you wanted to know."

"Are you kidding? This is fascinating. What time period are we talking about?"

"I can't know exactly, but I've pinned it down to the mid- or late-1700s The tribe I dream about has plenty of horses, so it couldn't have been earlier than that. But they still used primitive weapons—bows and arrows, spears. By the early 1800s, most of the tribes of the Great Plains had metal tools and guns."

"You've really researched this, haven't you?" Luke's fingers lightly touched her hair.

Callahan lifted her glass and swallowed the last of her wine. *I should make him go right now. I need to think this through. But I don't really want him to leave. This is crazy!*

"I've heard of realistic dreams," he said, "but nothing like this."

"I'm not so sure that's what they are." She didn't plan to say the words; they just came out. "They feel more like memories. I think I must have lived during that time."

He stared at her. "You're talking about reincarnation?"

"It's an explanation that makes more and more sense to me."

"You're serious." He studied her for a long moment, with his eyebrow raised. "How would my birthmarks fit in with your dreams—or memories, if that's what you think they are?"

"I don't know. I don't know what to make of them. Or of you."

"You don't know what to make of me?"

She heard a slight defensiveness in his voice.

"I don't know what to make of my reaction to you. Look… I've learned to be cautious about people. I don't trust easily anymore. And yet here I am, opening up to you, sharing extremely personal aspects of my life…" She broke off and put her empty glass on the table. "Sorry. I'm babbling. You must think I'm the one who's a freak."

"Not a freak." He touched her cheek in that strangely intimate way. "Do you really want to know what I'm thinking? I'm thinking how much I want to kiss you. And wondering what you'd do if I did."

More than his words, something in his touch and the tone of his voice—that odd familiarity—overcame the last of Callahan's resistance.

"I think I would kiss you back."

His lips were soft, and his first kiss was gentle. He cupped her face in his hands and pulled back to look into her eyes. Then he lowered his mouth to hers again, this time hard and strong, and they kissed with the urgency of long-parted lovers.

She pulled back. *What's come over me?*

He kissed her again, with an intensity that cut off her thoughts. She was shocked by the force of her response. His kiss melted something that had been frozen within her for a very long time. The rush of feeling, the depth of the need she felt left her stunned. She should pull away—knew she should—but felt powerless to do so. She gave a little gasp as he slid his hand under her leather vest and cupped her breast.

Yes. Oh, yes. Hot desire shot through her. She closed her eyes, pressed her lips against his neck. Moving down, she tasted the skin on his chest.

Luke groaned, but then pulled back and stood up, bringing her with him.

"You're sure about this?" His breathing quickened.

The only thing Callahan was sure of was her overwhelming need. Beyond that, she couldn't—wouldn't—let herself think.

Deathmark

"Yes…"

He slipped her vest off her shoulders and tossed it toward the sofa. Then he unbuttoned and removed her blouse, expertly unfastened her bra and kissed her breasts.

"You're beautiful," he whispered, his mouth warm against her skin. He drew his tongue across her nipples, took one, and then the other, into his mouth. Her body trembled and she felt a heat building deep within her. He continued kissing her breasts until she was shaking with desire.

As they moved into the bedroom, Callahan had the fleeting realization that she might really regret this. But when he pulled her into his arms again, she knew there was no turning back.

She unzipped her skirt, letting it slide down her hips and fall around her feet, pulled down her panties and kicked it all aside. Standing naked before him, she had a moment of self-consciousness—the extra weight on her hips…around her waist.

"You're so beautiful." He spoke softly, gently pushing her onto the bed. He began, quickly and gracefully, removing the rest of his clothing. *He's practiced undressing, for effect.* The realization broke through her mind-numbing passion, but didn't temper it. His erection was impressive beneath his white silk boxers, which were instantly on the floor, followed by his shoes and socks. His eyes held hers as he lay down beside her.

His mouth on her breasts, moving slowly down her body, awakened sensations that left her gasping with pleasure.

"Do you have…protection?" she asked, proving to herself that some portion of her rational mind was still intact.

"Of course." He reached for one of the several condoms he must have placed on the nightstand, beside his watch, while undressing.

Several? He's certainly prepared. Did he plan this?

He continued caressing, touching her at a level beyond her flesh. Moments later, she was frantic to feel him inside her.

"Now," she pleaded. "I want you now."

He entered her carefully, but with a sweet driving force. She arched her back to meet his movements. Everything felt so good, so natural, and suddenly she knew it was going to happen. She felt her

67

body tense, anticipating the sudden delicious rush of sensation. Her breath came in quick, short pants.

"Oh, yes…" she moaned, "I'm so close…"

He lifted his head. "Look at me. I want to watch your face as you come."

She held his gaze as long as she could, until her body shuddered and arched against his and she cried out and closed her eyes, carried beyond herself by the force of her orgasm. She was surprised to feel another orgasm build and explode right behind it. *I've… never… been multi-orgasmic.* He climaxed seconds later, his final thrusts reaching to her deepest core.

They lay still for a long moment. Callahan felt tears on her cheeks. Luke lifted his head, looked at her with concern.

"You're crying…did I hurt you?"

"No, you didn't hurt me. It's just that it's been so long. So long since I've felt…" *Smooth bronzed arms held her…long black hair brushed against her face and naked shoulders. They moved together on a bed of soft dark fur….*

Luke kissed her forehead, bringing her back to the present. She focused on him, willing the dream image away.

"For me, too," he said. "You get a little numb in this line of work."

She had to ask. "Was this work, Luke?"

"No." His voice went soft. "This was something I wasn't sure I could still do. This was making love." He rolled onto his side, close to her. They kissed again.

"Stay with me tonight," she whispered.

"You'd have a hard time making me leave."

Sometime later, Luke's breathing deepened. Callahan carefully disengaged herself from his sleeping embrace and went into the bathroom. As she removed her smeared mascara, she stared at herself in the mirror, at her glowing face framed by disheveled hair. *This is just freaking unbelievable. What is this strange connection between Luke and me?* She knew it wasn't just physical. Incredible as the sex was, this was more complicated. Much more.

Deathmark

She poured a glass of bottled water and swallowed a couple of aspirin to head off the throb beginning in her temples. *How many glasses of wine did I have tonight? Don't blame the wine, O'Connor. Admit it. You had sex with him because you wanted to. And the experience was fabulous—not to mention way overdue.* She flipped off the overhead bathroom light.

Suddenly, out of the corner of her eye, she saw a slight movement in the mirror. She gasped as a faceless image came into sharper focus. *A tall, bare-chested man, with thick, straight black hair hanging past his broad shoulders. He wore a loin cloth and leather leggings. A large claw hung from a strip of braided leather around his neck. A bear claw. Running Wolf!*

The image in the mirror moved closer, his hand outstretched, reaching toward her. The water glass slipped from Callahan's fingers and shattered in the sink. She whirled around and found herself face to face with…Luke. With a soft, strangled cry, she turned back toward the mirror and stared at Luke's reflection, at his concerned face and short, tousled brown hair.

"I'm sorry," he said. "I didn't mean to scare you."

She sucked in a deep breath, trying to slow her pounding heart.

"Did you cut yourself?"

"No…I don't think so."

A moment later, he filled another glass with water and turned to her.

"You're shivering." He put his arm around her. "Come on. I'll warm you up."

Wordlessly, she allowed him to lead her back to bed. Before joining her, he turned off the lamps in the sitting room. Then he slid beneath the covers, hugging her close and stroking her back. Before long, he dropped into a deep sleep.

Callahan continued to stare into the darkness, trying to make sense of what she'd seen in the bathroom mirror. And then Luke mumbled something in his sleep and pulled her closer. It felt good to be held. So good. Closing her eyes, Callahan surrendered to the darkness.

6

Sharp pebbles dug into her bare knees as she knelt on a lonely hill some distance from the encampment. She ignored that discomfort, as well as the constant throbbing pain in her slashed calves, arms, and cheeks. Physical pain could not compete with the agony in her heart.

Her vision blurred with fatigue as she stared up at the scaffold where Running Wolf's body lay. How many days had she spent wailing her grief song and stumbling back to camp only when night fell? Four days? Five? She had almost no voice left—her throat was raw from lamenting. As she stared with unseeing eyes at the burial scaffold, painful scenes replayed in her mind.

She had washed and prepared Running Wolf's body for burial, refusing to allow any hands but hers to touch him. She had brushed and braided his hair and tied two golden eagle tail feathers into them. After smoothing a thin layer of warm buffalo fat on his face—still

Deathmark

handsome in death—she painted it with red ocher to symbolize eternal life. On his right cheek she carefully drew a black bear paw, symbol of bravery and strength and the emblem of his medicine clan, while sending a prayer that it might offer protection in the spirit world.

She had cleansed the terrible, gaping wounds on his chest and shoulder, the voice of the war chief, Screaming Eagle, echoing in her head. "The mark of the bear...he died with the mark of the bear, with honor, as befits a warrior." The words were cold comfort to her shattered heart.

After dressing her husband in his finest clothes—a shirt of softest doeskin, which she had lovingly tanned, stitched and decorated with an intricate pattern of porcupine quills for the Sun Ceremony three moons ago, fringed leggings, and his best moccasins—she tied his bear claw amulet around his neck.

"My heart is yours, for all time," she sobbed, kissing her beloved's cold lips for the last time. "For all time. This I swear."

Spotted Elk, Running Wolf's younger brother, was allowed to help with the final preparations, wrapping the body in a red burial robe and then binding it tightly in two layers of water-softened buffalo hides.

At daybreak, the entire camp—almost one hundred people of all ages—had formed a procession behind Running Wolf's body as it was carried by his favorite horse, Stands Firm, up the hill to where four tall poles had been raised to support the burial platform. The white stallion's face and body were painted with red spots of mourning.

The People, many with faces blackened with ashes and hair hacked off to express their grief, walked slowly, singing Running Wolf's praise song. They lauded him as a brave warrior and skilled hunter. They sang of his generosity, his fearless nature, and of his last challenge—confronting the giant grizzly that had come to claim the deer Running Wolf had killed.

After the bound body was lifted to the platform and secured with rawhide ropes, the wailing crowd had fallen silent. Screaming Eagle stepped forward and attached to the scaffold those items Running Wolf would need on his journey to the Spirit World—his shield, painted with symbols of the bear, his lance, decorated with *three enemy scalps, his war club, a knife, a bow and quiver of arrows, a bag of dried buffalo meat, and a container of water.*

Facing the burial scaffold, Screaming Eagle raised his right hand in a gesture of farewell.

"Ride with the wind, my brother."

Other warriors had come forward, one by one, to face the scaffold and speak final words to their fallen friend.

A gust of freezing wind yanked her from her reverie. Her ears, exposed by her chopped-off hair, burned with the cold. "Mita'wa higna, my husband," she wailed in a hoarse voice. "Did you have to be so brave? I would rather you had dishonored your name and run from the long claws. You could have returned safely to me and seen our son's face." She wrapped her arms around her swollen belly and rocked back and forth in her relentless grief. "Soul of my soul, can you hear my voice? Can you hear my heart crying your name?"

As though from a great distance, she heard his voice.... *Whose voice?*

"Hey, are you all right?' Luke turned on the bedside lamp.

She was disoriented and shocked by the sudden light. *Where... where am I?*

"Callahan?"

San Francisco. I'm in San Francisco. With Luke. Not with...

"What's the matter? Are you sick?"

"I was dreaming."

"You were crying out in your sleep, strange words. Was it one of your Indian dreams?"

She nodded, trying to calm her breathing.

"Were you dreaming about the one with my scars?"

"Yes." Her voice was shaking. "It was so real. It's always so real. I washed his wounds and prepared his body…"

"Okay," Luke cut her off. "Okay. Calm down. You're awake now. You're here with me." He drew her into his arms. "Wow. That must have been some dream. Those sounds you were making…" He took in a deep breath and slowly let it out. "This is a really weird

Deathmark

scene, isn't it? Beyond weird. I meet you and feel this really strong attraction. I just have to see you again, figure some way to spend time with you. Then I find out you've been painting my birthmarks—my exact marks!—on an Indian you believe you were married to *in another lifetime*. Whew…I don't know how to wrap my mind around this, Callahan."

She spoke the words against his chest. "I don't either."

"You're still shaking."

"I'll be okay. I just need a few minutes." She held him tightly.

He stroked her hair as Callahan took deep breaths, trying to regain her bearings.

After a few minutes, Luke began to untangle himself from her. "You'll have to excuse me," he said, his voice sounding strained. "I need the bathroom."

"Mita'wa higna... mita'wa higna..." The sound echoed in Luke's head. He splashed cold water on his face and stared into the bathroom mirror. *She's talking gibberish in her sleep. I was only half awake, but for a minute there I swear I understood…impossible!*

He splashed more water on his face and gripped the counter to steady himself. *Hold on here, stud. It's not like you're a stranger to kinky scenes in hotel rooms. You like risky business and the high-stakes game. And you really like this lady. You thought maybe your luck could change. You scoped her out, read up on her, thought you knew what you were going after. But there's more going on here than you bargained for. Way more. Shit. It's time to split.*

He walked out of the bathroom and silently began pulling on his clothes. His face, visible in the soft light, looked different to Callahan, closed off and defensive.

She sat up in bed. "Wait. Luke. Are you leaving?"

"I'm sorry, Callahan, I really am. But I have to go. I'll call you later."

Before Callahan could react, he was out the door. She leaned back on her pillow, eyes filling with tears. *I don't believe this. Here I am, crying about yet another man.*

A sharp knocking propelled her from bed. She slipped a robe on as she hurried to the door. After a quick glance through the peephole, she yanked the door open.

"I can't," Luke said. "I don't know what the hell's going on here. But I can't leave you."

She closed the door behind him and melted into his arms. They held each other until she whispered, "Come back to bed."

He quickly undressed, slipped under the covers, his body tense. "I'm sorry I reacted like that. I don't understand it. I don't scare easily, but your dreams scare me. Your paintings scare me. But there's something about you…" He left the sentence unfinished. "Let's not talk about it anymore." He pulled her close. "Not now." He ran his hand along her hip and thigh. "Let's just be together."

Callahan buried her face in the warmth of his neck. She clung to him, lost in a need that went far beyond the physical and feeling an emotion that touched her in the deepest, loneliest part of her soul.

She woke slowly, floating on the surface of the familiar dream. *Lying on soft fur…locked in his warm embrace, her head resting on his shoulder, her body pressed against his. Familiar.* Reluctantly, she released the dream images and let herself come fully awake.

A hotel room. Not a tipi. Beside Luke. Not Running Wolf.

Turning her head, Callahan peered at the clock on the nightstand. A little after eight. Luke was still asleep, stretched out on his back. She studied him, admiring his handsome profile, his strong, beard-shadowed jaw, the way his hair was cut around his ears. Suddenly, a vivid flash—*long black hair, hair with a pleasant odor of smoky campfires, a bare chest, broad and hairless, sun-bronzed skin…*

Callahan pulled back from Luke and the dream images. Silently, she slid out of bed and went into the bathroom. As she brushed her teeth, she realized that she was no longer eager to get

Deathmark

home. *A few hours won't make any difference. I need to spend as much time with Luke as possible—find out as much about him as I can.*

She located the number of the airline and rebooked on a late afternoon flight. Then she walked back into the bedroom and sat on the edge of the bed, watching Luke while he slept.

As though sensing her presence, he opened his eyes. "Ummm. Hi…" He rolled toward her. "Do you always look so incredible in the morning?"

"Only after an incredible night."

"And now it's morning."

She was moved to see what looked like genuine sadness in his eyes.

"When does your flight leave?"

"Not until three-thirty this afternoon. I just changed it."

"That's good." He drew her down onto the bed, untied her robe and opened it. "I want to see you in the daylight."

Callahan cringed inwardly, uncomfortable about exposing her less-than-toned, middle-aged body in broad daylight. Before she could protest, he gently cupped her breast.

"I love the way you're built," he said. "Rounded and feminine."

Her grateful smile faded with a sudden memory of Brad, slapping her on the hip. *"What're you packing in those saddlebags, babe?"*

Luke's voice interrupted the memory. "Callahan?" He propped himself up on one elbow. "You look upset. Did I say something wrong?"

"No. You've said everything just right."

Although there were a lot of unanswered questions, she knew that her earlier impressions of Luke had been correct. He was someone special. He had proven that, in more ways than one. Moments later, he was proving it to her again.

Callahan watched Luke walk naked into the bathroom. Her eyes traveled from his tight, muscled buttocks up to his upper back, fastening on his birthmark. *The open wound on Running Wolf's back, in exactly the same location! How can that be?*

She took a few deep breaths to center herself in present time. Realizing that Luke was in the shower, she grabbed her cell, turned it on and punched in Donny's number in Santa Fe. His answering machine picked up after the first ring.

"You've reached the Denton residence. I'm screening my calls. Leave your name and number. If you sound interesting, I'll get back to you. Otherwise, have a nice life."

"Donny? It's me. If you're there, pick up. Donny…"

"Hold on. I'm in the middle of a very sensitive scene here." She could hear the click of his computer keyboard. "Let me save this. It's a fucking masterpiece, literally. Okay, Cal. What's up?"

"I just wanted you to know that I'm taking a later flight. I don't get into Albuquerque until six-thirty tonight. So I'll probably get to your house after eight."

"Fine. Make the most of your time there."

"I…am."

"What's going on? You sound a little mysterious."

She hesitated, and then decided to tell him. "I can't talk long. He's in the shower."

"*What*? Who's in the shower? Come clean, girlfriend! You have my full attention now."

"The water just turned off. I have to go."

"No! You can't just leave me hanging like this. It's too cruel!"

As Donny continued to protest, the bathroom door opened and Luke came out, his hair wet and a towel draped around his narrow waist.

"I have to go. See you tonight." She hung up the phone.

"Excuse me." Luke's voice sounded a little cool. "I didn't mean to interrupt a personal call."

"It's okay. I was telling a friend in Santa Fe that I'll be on a later flight. He's keeping my dog."

A muscle twitched in Luke's jaw. "I see."

"I don't think you do. Donny's my best buddy. He writes romance novels, offers me fashion advice, cooks comfort food for me when I'm down."

Luke plopped down on the bed, a sudden grin on his face. "All

76

right. You don't have to spell it out for me. But, hey, speaking of food, I'm starved. Let's call room service."

They ate breakfast in robes at a small table set by the window. Callahan was thoroughly enjoying her eggs Benedict. *To hell with the calories, he likes my "roundness."* She looked up from her almost-finished plate to see Luke studying her.

"You don't speak that Indian language when you're awake, do you?"

She shook her head.

"Then how can you understand what's being said when you're dreaming?"

"I don't know. I guess my subconscious translates it for me, somehow."

He was quiet for a minute. "What convinced you that these dreams are actually memories?"

"Things that have happened, through the years."

"Such as?"

Callahan hesitated, wary about exposing any more of herself than she already had.

"Come on," he urged. "Don't you trust me?"

"I want to," she replied honestly. "It's just not easy to talk about. And, I have to warn you, it gets stranger yet."

"It's *already* strange as hell. And I'm still here, aren't I?'

She met his eyes. "Yes, you're still here. Okay, here goes. I told you that the dreams started in my early teens, becoming more frequent the older I got. Then, during the birth of my son, I had a bizarre experience, something that went way beyond a dream." She fortified herself with a sip of coffee.

"As my labor pains got worse, I remember thinking *I've done this before! I've been through childbirth before.* And then, bizarre as it sounds, I slipped into another reality. I was no longer in the hospital room, I was in a tipi. And I was having a baby."

Just talking about that experience of being herself and Sun-in-Her-Face, at the same time, brought back all the feelings—the pain, fear, and disorientation of two very different lifetimes colliding.

Pain ripped through her belly, spreading across her lower back with each contraction. Sweat ran down her neck and between her bare breasts as women's voices chanted in rhythm with her panting breath. She could smell the damp fur on which she'd been squatting, naked and supported by two older women. One of the women slipped a thick piece of dried buffalo hide between her teeth as the pain and pressure intensified.

"Bite down, daughter," she instructed, "and pray to the One Above for strength."

But no one could help the baby son she finally delivered, well formed but much too small. He gave one feeble, heart-rending cry, as though protesting the fate that robbed him of his life. The only other sounds in the lodge that long night were her own anguished cries as she rocked the tiny, cold body.

Luke's hand was warm on her arm. "You don't have to talk about it, if you don't want to."

But Callahan felt strangely compelled to continue. "In the hospital, I slid in and out of that other reality during the last stages of my labor. I was in a state of complete confusion after Patrick was born. The doctor assumed that I was having a reaction to the pain meds. Later that night, a nurse shook me awake. She said that I had been screaming—words she couldn't understand. I remember clinging to her, insisting that my son was dead—as he had been in the tipi. She brought Patrick into the room to prove that he was alive. Even as I held my perfectly healthy baby, I felt agonizing grief and confusion."

Luke shook his head. "Wow." He paused. "That language you spoke in your sleep last night... I can't get it out of my head."

"Apparently, I do that on a pretty regular basis, especially in the last few years. Brad, my ex, complained about my 'crazy sleep talk,' as he called it. It annoyed the hell out him."

Callahan poured herself more coffee, holding the cup in both hands to warm her cold fingers. She swallowed hard, and then she continued.

"It's taken me a long time to piece the story together. Each time I dreamed about holding Running Wolf's body, I was vaguely aware of my swollen belly. Later, as I had other dreams, I realized that I was pregnant when Running Wolf was killed. The shock of his death caused our son to be born prematurely. He didn't have a chance."

A moment passed before Luke spoke. "You're really convinced that you've lived before, aren't you?"

"I still have questions and occasional doubts. But it would explain why I keep having these dreams. I'm telling you, they're as real as the conversation we're having now."

Luke pushed away his empty plate. "You know, until I met you, reincarnation was just an interesting theory, an odd shelf in the bookstore. I didn't give it all that much thought. *Now*? To tell the truth, I'm not sure I *want* to believe in it. This life is about all I can deal with. More than I want to deal with, sometimes."

She responded to the confusion and something else—pain?—in his eyes and laid her hand on his.

"This has really upset you."

"Forget it," he said, with a tight smile. "I'm fine." He stood, came around the table and lifted her gently to her feet. "Why wouldn't I be?" He untied her robe, slipped his hands inside. "I'm here with you, and there's no one I'd rather be with." Cupping her naked bottom, he pulled her close against him.

Callahan opened his robe and put her cheek against his chest, ran her fingers gently over one of the reddish marks. Then she pressed kisses along its length, caressing it with her tongue.

Luke groaned and led her back to the bed.

"I'm going to miss my plane," she said sometime later, lying exhausted in his arms.

"Do you care?"

She gave a soft laugh. "Not at the moment. But they're going to kick us out of this room. I already asked for a late checkout. Two o'clock was the best they could do. What time is it now?"

"One forty-seven."

"We've got to get moving!" She forced herself to move away from him.

"No." He grabbed her, nuzzling her neck.

"Seriously. I've been gone for three days, and I'm behind in my work schedule. Hard as it is to leave you, I need to get home." She gave him a lingering kiss and managed to get out of the bed. Hurrying into the bathroom, she quickly touched up her face and hair. Fifteen minutes later she was dressed and packed.

Luke stood with his back to her, looking out the window.

"I can't let you just drop out of my life. How can I reach you?"

She opened her purse and took out a business card with her name and web site address. Luke offered a pen and she added her land line number before handing it to him.

He studied it with a wistful expression on his face.

"Tesuque, New Mexico."

"It's a small village on the outskirts of Santa Fe. You probably won't believe this, but it's named after a nearby Indian pueblo."

He smiled, shaking his head.

"I believe it. It sounds like a perfect place for you—in *this* lifetime." He tucked the card into his pants pocket and picked up her two bags. "Come on… I don't want you to blame me if you miss your plane."

Outside, as the doorman hailed a cab, Callahan turned to Luke. She was close to tears.

"Goodbye, dear Luke. Stay safe." She got into the taxi and looked at him through the window.

He motioned for her to roll the window down and then leaned in to give her one last kiss.

"You haven't seen the last of me, Callahan O'Connor." He traced his finger lightly over her cheek. Then he stepped back as the taxi pulled away from the curb.

Deathmark

7

The Flight to Albuquerque passed in a haze. Callahan kept reliving the past few days, trying to make sense of them. *I must, somehow, explore this connection between Luke and my dreams. Otherwise, it's going to haunt me for the rest of my life.* There was only one person who might be able to help. She had to see Red Feather.

After the plane landed, she collected her bags and retrieved her white Jeep Cherokee from the parking garage. Soon she was on the interstate, headed north to Santa Fe. As she left Albuquerque behind, the sun was just setting, blazing the western sky with shades of fuchsia, orange and gold. Callahan made a mental note to reproduce that blend of colors on canvas.

Forty-five minutes later, she topped the summit of La Bajada Hill and saw the lights of Santa Fe nestled in the foothills of the Sangre de Cristo Mountains. She felt the familiar relief of coming home. The beauty and vastness of the high desert landscape never failed to comfort and inspire her.

There was little traffic along the narrow streets as she passed through the historic center of town. Native Americans who sold their wares under the portal of the Palace of the Governors had packed up for the day, the art galleries and boutiques were closed, and the Plaza was almost deserted. Now that the summer crowds of tourists had thinned, only a few people strolled along the early-evening streets, window-shopping and heading toward restaurants.

Driving up Bishop's Lodge Road and into Tesuque, Callahan passed the entrance to her renovated adobe home, set back from the road and secluded amid magnificent old cottonwood trees.

She continued on for another half-mile to Donny's house. He would be dying to discuss her encounter with Luke. Should she tell him about the mysterious birthmarks?

Donny didn't share her belief in the metaphysical. He'd dismiss the marks as just an odd coincidence. And he'd certainly chalk up the image in the mirror to an over-stimulated imagination—after which, he'd throw in a lecture about getting emotionally involved with a gigolo. She could already imagine him saying, *Whoa, Cal girl. Hit the brakes. A little recreational sex... sure, that's therapeutic. But you're going over the top!*

No, she'd best keep that part of the story to herself, until she had a chance to talk it through with Red Feather.

As soon as she parked in front of Donny's house, Mucho came loping down the dirt driveway, dancing in circles, barking joyously.

"Hello, baby boy." Callahan bent to hug his massive head and receive passionate licks on her cheeks.

"He recognized the sound of your Jeep before you pulled into the driveway," Donny said from the open front door. "Nearly knocked me flat on his way out."

She walked up the steps to give Donny a hug. Five foot four—exactly three inches shorter than Callahan—and proud of his trim, small-boned build, he was always a stylish, if somewhat flamboyant, dresser. This evening's outfit was a black silk Japanese kimono and matching velvet slippers.

Deathmark

She handed him his gift.

"You darling girl. A sour dough starter kit! Yum, I'll put this to good use. I'm touched that you made time to shop for me, with all that *you've* had going on." He flashed a devilish grin. "Well, come in. The bubbly is chilled and I'm all ears."

As they entered the house, Martha began screeching a welcome from her nearby floor-to-ceiling cage.

"Quiet! Quiet!" Donny said to the cockatoo.

"Quiet. Quiet." Martha echoed in a slightly subdued voice. After a short pause she spoke again. "B-o-r-i-n-g."

Callahan burst into laughter. "I didn't know she could spell!"

"She heard it on a television show, some silly sitcom. I'm afraid it's her favorite new thing. At least," he added in a whisper, "it's taken her mind off underpants."

They moved into the kitchen. "Now," Donny said, opening the refrigerator, "don't hold a thing back. I want all the details." He brought out a platter of marinated shrimp, skewered with jalapeño chilies and lemon slices. "A little welcome home treat," he said. "Get those little cocktail plates down, please, while I open the Veuve."

"We're having Champagne?"

"Of course." He lifted a bottle of Veuve Clicquot from a silver-plated cooler. "This is a celebration!"

"Why is it a celebration?" She carefully set the gold-trimmed Fitz and Floyd china on the kitchen table.

"For two reasons. Your season of celibacy is over, and you're home. I've missed you, girlfriend. Now, go sit at the table. You must be exhausted after all that time in bed." He chortled at his own joke. "How did you meet this mystery man? Wait, don't tell me yet. Let me get settled. Let's see, we need the flutes, napkins…"

"Here, let me help you."

"Sit, sit. No, not you, Mucho. I was talking to your mommy."

Callahan watched Donny expertly pop the cork and arrange everything at the table just so, before finally sitting down. He placed a napkin on his lap with a flourish and poured the Veuve into two Waterford flutes.

"A toast," he said, raising his glass with a smile. "To life, with all its surprises."

"I'll certainly drink to that!"

Donny savored his first sip. "Now, who is he?"

She hesitated.

"Cal! You're not going to hold out on me, are you? No fair. I just opened a bottle of fifty-dollar Champagne here!"

As always, he made her laugh. "Well, I think I told you about the escort Leda lined up for me?"

"I thought you'd turned down his more personal services."

"I did. But then I ran into him in Union Square yesterday. He asked me to lunch, and he came to the opening last night. Then he called from the lobby of the hotel after I got back from dinner, asking if he could come up, and…"

"And?"

She shrugged. "One thing led to another."

Donny clapped his hands. "Marvelous! I'm so envious. Here, have some shrimp. Now, tell me, what does he look like?"

"Well, he's tall, about six-two—just a minute…" She got up to retrieve the newspaper clipping from her purse. "I can show you."

"My, my," Donny said, peering at the photo. "He *is* a sweet treat. And you, my dear, look like you were caught with your hand in the cookie jar."

She swatted him with her napkin. "I knew you'd get a kick out of it."

Two hours later, Callahan drove in through the entrance to her property.

"Home, sweet home," she announced.

Mucho, taking up most of the backseat, barked in response. Callahan pressed the remote and watched the garage door roll up. She parked the Jeep and waited until she heard the door close behind them. Once inside the house, she quickly disarmed the security system and, with Mucho leading the way, carried her suitcases down the long, wide hallway that led into the living room.

Deathmark

She inhaled deeply, enjoying the familiar combination of smells—old wood, leather furniture, a hint of peach fragrance from her favorite potpourri. Her hacienda-style home had a cozy charm, in spite of its rambling floor plan. The original structure had expanded through the decades from a small, turn-of-the-century adobe to almost four thousand square feet. Various owners had added rooms, walled courtyards and patios, sometimes in offbeat locations. *Santa Fe Funky*, Donny called it.

Although she loved it, she would have been just as happy in a smaller, less expensive place. It was Brad who'd insisted she buy the property when it came on the market.

"This is the real deal," he had said, his face flushed with enthusiasm. "An authentic *hacienda*! Hand-rubbed plaster on adobe walls. Brick floors. And the woodwork! I'll bet that front door is part of the original house, it must weigh a ton. Babe, this is a great house for entertaining. Real class. I can already see the two of us here."

As she usually did in the early days of their relationship, Callahan had agreed, wanting to please him. It was certainly more house than the two of them needed. But, as the listing agent, Brad could get it for a good price. The property included three wooded acres and a rustic log cabin that was perfect for a studio. He'd convinced her it would be a great investment. And so, Brad got what he wanted.

She stood in the hall, feeling the bitterness that thoughts of Brad still evoked. At least he hadn't fought her on the terms of divorce. The property was all hers. After all, her money had bought and furnished it. Her lawyer had had a private talk with Brad, explaining that only by cooperating would he avoid charges of assault and battery. Not wanting the scandal, Brad had been agreeable. Now he was doing his entertaining elsewhere. According to local gossip, he had moved in with a wealthy widow who had recently arrived from Los Angeles. Callahan wished the widow luck. She'd need it.

Don't waste energy thinking about him. Just be glad you got out of that marriage in one piece. Other battered wives aren't so lucky.

She walked down the hall and into her study. After booting up her computer and checking her e-mail—already several messages from Leda—she sent a brief message to Patrick to report that she was home from a her successful trip, loved and missed him. What would her son say if he discovered that she'd spent the night with someone only slightly older than he was—and a professional escort, at that? She shook her head, not wanting to even imagine his reaction. The truth was she could hardly believe it herself.

Callahan removed the newspaper clipping from her purse, studied Luke's image, and then tacked it on her bulletin board. She stood staring at it for another long moment before forcing her attention to a stack of mail that Consuela had left on her desk.

An hour later, she was in her bedroom, unpacking. Mucho, having inspected everything, both indoors and out, was fast asleep on his super-sized sheepskin bed in the corner of the room. The security system was activated.

When the phone on her nightstand rang, she checked the caller ID, didn't recognize the number, and started to ignore it. Then something made her change her mind and lift the receiver.

"Callahan? It's Luke. I just wanted to make sure you got home all right."

"I did." She definitely felt fluttery. "The flight was uneventful."

"I just had to call. I needed to hear your voice and I'm trying to picture where you are. The newspaper article said you live on several acres. It must be really private. Do you feel safe there, all alone?"

"Yes. If you could see the size of my dog and how protective he is, you'd understand why."

"Good." There was an awkward pause. "I had an appointment tonight, but I canceled it. I just couldn't..." His voice trailed off. "The agency wasn't too happy, but to hell with them. I just want you to know I'm thinking about you. I can't *stop* thinking about you."

"I...I'm glad you called."

"I told you I would." He sighed. "Oh, Callahan, Callahan, Callahan. Just saying your name is a huge turn-on for me. I'll never call you anything else."

Callahan was taken aback. *Never call me anything else? Odd thing to say, as though we're in a long-term relationship.*

Deathmark

He continued, "I realized that I forgot to give you my cell."

She copied down the number. "Okay. Well…" She faltered, and then tried again. "Stay in touch."

"You can count on that. Goodnight, sweet Callahan. Have *happy* dreams." The phone went dead.

She stood for some time, staring out her bedroom window at the darkness beyond. She couldn't shake the feeling that something irrevocable was happening. Something that would change her world completely.

8

Callahan was sitting at the kitchen table early the next morning, eating a bowl of cereal and scanning the *Santa Fe New Mexican*, when she heard the front door open. Mucho leapt to his feet, barked once, and ran to investigate.

Consuela had used her key to enter the house.

She called out from the entryway, "*Señora* Callahan? I'm here. *Ay*, Mucho. *Basta*! Don't knock me down, *perro loco*." She came bustling into the kitchen followed by Mucho.

Just under five feet tall, Consuela exuded cheerful energy that belied her sixty-five hard-working years. A native of Mexico, she'd been working for Callahan for more than a decade, starting shortly after arriving in Santa Fe with her husband, three grown sons, and their families. There was little about her employer's life that Consuela didn't make it her business to know, or to comment on. Callahan appreciated the concern and had grown to dearly love her.

Deathmark

"*Bueno*, you're home." Consuela deposited a grocery bag on the countertop. "Your trip was good, no?"

"It was certainly interesting."

Consuela cocked her head. "Interesting is good?"

Callahan wasn't so sure, but she smiled and nodded.

"I make chicken with green chile tamales last night," Consuela said, unloading the paper bag and placing a plastic container in the refrigerator. "Here is some for you."

So much for the diet. Callahan thanked her and took a final sip of her lukewarm coffee. "How was everything while I was gone?"

"*No problemas.* I clean in your studio on Friday, since you were gone from it. Don't worry, I do not try to organize nothing, only dust, vacuum, and straighten a little. I hide the key back under our secret rock. Today, I wash windows and do laundry."

"Fine." Callahan hesitated, remembering Donny's comment about Consuela's husband being in *el* dog house. "How's Florencio?"

"That man, his brain is limping. Last week it was our anniversary. Forty-eight years since our wedding mass. And did he remember? Humph! He did not. But I give him a few reminders and no dinner, and he go hurrying to Walmart to buy me a new vacuum cleaner. A deluxe, easy-pusher Hoover," she added proudly.

"Well, happy anniversary." Callahan made a mental note to include an anniversary bonus in Consuela's weekly paycheck.

"*Gracias.* Should I unpack your suitcase?"

"I did that last night. But thanks, anyway. You take good care of me."

"Good thing, because you no take such good care of yourself." Consuela put Callahan's empty cereal bowl and coffee cup in the dishwasher. "*Abuela mia*, my grandmama—you know she was a *curandera*, a healer—had a saying: '*Viejo que se cura, cien años dura.*' He who takes care of himself lives to a hundred years. She herself lived through one hundred and three winters, God rest her soul." Consuela made the sign of the cross and began scrubbing out the sink.

"One hundred years, huh? Good goal. It means I'm not quite middle-aged." Callahan pulled a light jacket out of the coat closet and slipped it on. "See you later. Come on, Mucho. Let's go up to the studio and get some work done."

As she went to the door, Callahan could hear Consuela talking to herself.

"All she think about is work. Never fun. There is need for another good man in her life—like *Señor* Edwin, God bless and keep him. Not like that *no bueno por nada* jackass Brad."

Callahan sighed and closed the door behind her. Standing on her west-facing patio, she took a deep breath of crisp high-desert air. The few early morning clouds were already gone, dispelled by the sun now bathing the foothills in light. Callahan was especially aware of the magic of the light—intense, constantly changing light that had been drawing artists to this area for almost a century.

She unfastened the gate and walked beyond the walls, along a graveled path. The air was filled with birdsong. Winding through wild grass, fragrant piñon trees, and gnarled juniper bushes, the path continued for several hundred feet to a log cabin, surrounded by old cottonwoods that were now dropping golden leaves. The cabin was an ideal studio, secluded and spacious, with tall, well-placed windows. She retrieved the key from under the secret rock and opened the front door.

Sunlight filled the large room that had been partitioned off to include a small kitchen area and a bathroom. A comfortable leather sofa and chair filled one corner, accented by a large sheepskin rug and positioned opposite a small wood-burning stove. The rest of the room served as workspace, with a paint-splattered concrete floor. A long wooden table was laden with tubes and jars of acrylic paint, brushes in different sizes, as well as sticks of graphite and charcoal. Canvases in varying stages of completion leaned against the walls. Two large easels stood in the center of the room, one empty and the other holding a partially painted canvas depicting a young Native American man sitting in a forest beside a flowing stream, his face in shadow. Callahan had titled it *At One with the Forest*.

She flipped on her stereo and, as the eagle-bone whistle of Carlos Nakai filled the room, she set a large canvas on the empty easel. Then she closed her eyes, trying to recapture the dream she'd had that morning, just before awakening. *Natives wearing animal skins danced to a drumbeat around a campfire. Suddenly the face of a bear appeared—long brown snout in a great shaggy face, jaws open to expose deadly teeth.*

Callahan tensed, trying to bring the image into sharper focus. No, it wasn't a live bear. It was a man wearing a bearskin with the head still attached. As the dancer moved around the fire, his feet shuffling in imitation of a bear's movements, a large bear claw slapped against his chest. *Running Wolf's amulet! The dancer was Running Wolf.*

Callahan rubbed her forehead, wondering how best to transfer the dream onto canvas. *Don't try to force it, that never works.* She willed herself to relax, open up to the vision and allow the images to present themselves. After a few moments, she picked up a stick of charcoal and began to sketch a dancing bear figure. As she worked, her thoughts turned again and again to Luke's birthmarks. *Identical to the ones I've drawn—even the two slashes on the lower part of his chest! I have to talk to Red Feather.*

She put down the charcoal and grabbed the phone, a line that she kept private to avoid interruptions while working. Only Patrick, Consuela, and Donny had her studio number, and they knew to call only if absolutely necessary. Patrick rarely called, anyway, preferring to e-mail. She started to dial Red Feather but realized she'd have better luck reaching him around noon. He always had a full schedule. Mornings were usually spent working on his next book; afternoons were reserved for those seeking his help.

Callahan returned to her drawing. An hour later, the sketch was complete. She studied it from across the room. After a few minor changes, she was satisfied with the basic outline and began applying various shades of brown in quick sweeping brush strokes.

"Red Feather? It's Callahan."

"Good to hear from you, my friend." The deep, calm, voice on the phone was reassuring. "How are you?"

"Confused. I really need to talk to you."

"How about this afternoon? I have some free time around three o'clock."

"Great. I'll be there."

There was a pause, during which she heard the muffled sound of Red Feather talking to someone. Then he laughed. "Strong Heart says to bring Mucho. She misses her *amigo*."

Callahan smiled. Strong Heart was a small, brown and white, short-haired, big-eared mutt that Red Feather had found abandoned and starving beside a road in the nearby Jemez Mountains last spring. Mucho adored her.

"We'll both be there in a couple of hours."

She hung up the phone with a sense of relief. Red Feather had a way of seeing things from an elevated, spiritual point of view. Perhaps he could give her some perspective about Luke and the unlikely circumstances that had brought them together.

Callahan opened the small studio refrigerator and poured herself a glass of orange juice. Her stomach felt empty, but she wasn't willing to take the time for a real break. As she sipped the juice, she forced her attention back to her work, studying the canvas from different angles. This was the point in her creative process where she consciously made a shift from the intuitive to the pragmatic mind set. Did the painting work?

She added a few more details and color contrast to the canvas, pleased with how it was coming together. It had a haunting, surreal feel to it, one that reflected the mood of her dream. And it had a definite sense of movement. It was one of those pieces that seemed to be painting itself.

She glanced at the clock on the wall. One-thirty. She needed to leave in an hour. That left just enough time to check her phone messages, return some calls, and eat one of Consuela's tasty tamales.

"Hey, baby boy," she said to Mucho, napping on his foam-filled bed in a corner. Close by his head was a ragged, much-chewed sheepskin bunny, his favorite toy. He lifted his head.

"Want to go see Strong Heart? See your girlfriend?"

Rrrrumph! Mucho sprang to his feet, dancing in excited

Deathmark

circles around her. He grabbed the bunny in his jaws and ran to the door.

She took one last look at the almost-finished painting. Suddenly, as so often happened, the title of the piece came to her. *Dancing the Bear.*

Luke's words echoed in her mind. *"I've always had a thing about bears. They scare the hell out of me."*

Although the room was warm, Callahan felt a sudden chill.

9

The drive to Red Feather's house, thirty minutes south of Santa Fe, gave Callahan time to organize her thoughts. She was grateful to have the shaman in her life, both as healer and friend. He had certainly stretched her mind, or at least her concept of what was possible.

When she had first heard of him, shortly after moving to Santa Fe fifteen years ago, Callahan was impressed by his credentials but skeptical of his healing methods. Her new-found friend, Suzanne, a talented pianist and freelance photographer, was seeing him for crippling osteoarthritis in her hands and had given him rave reviews.

"He works miracles," Suzanne had insisted. "I've seen the best doctors in the country, and all they did was prescribe expensive drugs with all kinds of side-effects. After just four sessions with Red Feather, I can't believe the improvement."

"What kind of treatment does he use?" Santa Fe was full of

Deathmark

so-called spiritual healers, and Callahan, from a rather conservative background, was skeptical.

Suzanne described the treatment: "I sit on a Navajo rug and Red Feather sits across from me, holding my hands. After chanting to call in his spirit helpers, or 'allies' as he calls them, he goes into a trance. My hands start feeling warm, almost hot, and I get a tingling sensation in the joints of my fingers. Red Feather ends the session by guiding me through a meditation, teaching me to communicate with my pain and release the inflammation. I'm telling you, the swelling has disappeared and I have almost complete flexibility in my fingers now."

Callahan wasn't convinced, but she was definitely intrigued. Several weeks later, she had found herself seated next to Red Feather, at one of Suzanne's dinner parties. His quiet dignity and articulate manner impressed her. The shaman looked to be in his mid-to-late sixties, of medium height and build. He was dressed in a white western shirt and pressed Levis, both wrists encircled by turquoise and silver bracelets. His thick gray hair hung in a single braid halfway down his back.

During dinner, Callahan had learned that in addition to his doctorate in anthropology, Red Feather held a master's degree in Jungian psychology. He had explained that many of his own healing methods were borrowed from his Native American background, as well as other shamanic traditions. In the early 1990s, he had founded Ancient Wisdom, an international society dedicated to the support of time-honored shamanic healing practices.

"I was raised on the Northern Cheyenne Reservation in southeastern Montana," he'd explained, "but I'm a mixed-blood. My mother's mother was *Sahiyela,* or what white people call Cheyenne, and her father was Kiowa. My own father was French, Mexican, and who-knows-what-else. I draw from a blend of healing traditions, including Jungian psychology."

He graciously responded to another guest's questions about his experience. "I've studied and worked with native healers around the world, from Australia and Europe to the Peruvian Amazon. Shamanic traditions are remarkably similar the world over. A shaman

95

journeys outside of time and space, by entering into an altered state of consciousness. It's a time-honored and most effective means of retrieving information."

The words "altered state of consciousness" triggered alarm in Callahan. She'd seen enough of that sort of thing when she was married to Kevin.

"Do shamans use drugs to get into this altered state?" she'd asked.

"Some do," Red Feather answered. "I don't find it necessary. A trance can be achieved through the use of sound—a rattle or rhythmic drumbeat—combined with visualization. Besides, hallucinogenic drugs can be dangerous and cloud the way. Some don't find their way back from drug-induced journeys."

Callahan could certainly understand how one might become lost in another reality. She gave an involuntary shudder.

"Visiting other realities is nothing to play around with," Red Feather continued. "But with proper guidance and natural methods, trance journeying carries little risk. Your mind will take you only as far as you need to go."

"Interesting," another guest had replied. "How does this method of healing work?"

"By probing the subconscious. We all have answers to our problems deep within ourselves. Shamanic healing is largely a matter of tapping into that knowledge and bringing the body, mind and spirit back into balance."

During coffee and dessert, Red Feather had answered more personal questions, including how he got his name. "I was born Russell Martine Gautier. But during my graduate work with a native tribe in Belize, I was bitten by a coral snake and lay in a coma for two weeks. During that time, I was lost in a different reality, one where I met and interacted with animals and spirits. I eventually found my way back to physical consciousness by following a trail of bright red feathers up through a dark tunnel.

"The shaman of the tribe welcomed me back to the physical world by gifting me with a red macaw feather and calling me by my 'true' name, 'Red Feather.' That's the name the spirits gave me when they saved my life. After that, I knew I was meant to follow the shamanic path."

Callahan had been fascinated, by both the man and his work. Almost a year in psychotherapy had shed no light on her recurring dreams or the feelings of depression and anxiety they often triggered. Could Red Feather's approach offer some answers?

Several days later she had made an appointment, despite Edwin's outspoken skepticism.

"My dear," her ultra-conservative and protective husband had said, "of course you must do as you wish. But I can't help considering such things as superstitious nonsense. Please be very careful."

"Always," she had assured him, placing an affectionate kiss on his cheek.

During that long-ago visit, Red Feather had closed his eyes and undertaken a shamanic journey on her behalf. Callahan watched closely as his lips moved silently and his body occasionally jerked. When he came out of what appeared to be a trance, Red Feather had reported that her dreams involved unfinished business.

"You are still experiencing trauma from another lifetime."

She was surprised. "Another lifetime? I didn't realize that Native Americans believe in reincarnation."

"Not all of us do," Red Feather quickly pointed out. "Traditions vary greatly from tribe to tribe. But a belief in the ongoing journey of the soul in various bodies is common. I personally believe that many lifetimes are essential for spiritual evolution, just as many years are necessary for physical development. Each life is a learning experience, an opportunity for soul growth. Eventually, all souls reach a state of wholeness and are allowed to dwell in the love of the Creator, which is our true spiritual home."

He'd ended the session by guiding her to use her work as a means of healing.

"Try seeing your dreams as gifts. Welcome them into your art. In time, you will understand what your dreams are trying to tell you."

Although, after all these years, Callahan still didn't understand the reason for her dreams, she would always be grateful to Red Feather for his advice. She hadn't seen him professionally since that time, but they continued to connect at various social functions. In the last year or so of her marriage, as though sensing her unhappiness with Brad, Red Feather had taken to dropping by for short visits, accompanied by Strong Heart. In fact, he showed up, unannounced, the day after she threw Brad out.

When she tearfully confided what had happened, Red Feather performed a short ceremony designed to "move energy" into her cracked rib, as well as to purify and strengthen her spirit.

Whether it was the ceremony or simply Red Feather's emotional support, Callahan had felt an infusion of inner strength. She withstood Brad's desperate pleading and never wavered in her determination to file for divorce.

Red Feather was certainly a blessing in her life. He seemed to be looking after her, in his own mysterious way.

Callahan turned off the highway onto the historic Turquoise Trail and slowed down as the narrow two-lane highway neared the outskirts of the village of Cerrillos. The dirt road leading to Red Feather's house was easy to miss. Spotting the marker, a small wooden arrow nailed to a piñon tree, she made a left turn. After bumping along for half a mile on a rutted road, she saw the modest, brown stuccoed house where Red Feather had lived alone since the death of his wife several years ago. His well-traveled pickup was parked off to one side.

As she pulled into the driveway, a scruffy-looking sand-colored dog appeared from behind the house. Mucho, recognizing Strong Heart, barked a greeting from the backseat.

"Okay, okay," Callahan said, unbuckling her seatbelt. She got out of the car and opened the rear door. "Take it easy," she advised, as Mucho bounded toward the much smaller dog. Strong Heart held her ground with a soft, warning growl. An instant later, the two were exchanging intimate sniffs.

Red Feather grinned from the open front door. He was dressed in jeans, a gray sweater and worn black moccasins. As usual, his hair was gathered into a single braid. She handed him a packet of loose tobacco, the traditional gift when visiting a healer. Although Red Feather was opposed to smoking, she knew he used tobacco for ceremonial purposes.

Deathmark

He thanked her and then spoke to Strong Heart.

"Entertain your guest outside for a while. Don't go off the property." Strong Heart listened intently, appearing to understand each word. She gave a short bark and raced around the side of the house with Mucho close behind.

Red Feather ushered Callahan into his cozy, book-filled living room.

"Can I get you something to drink, water or tea?"

"Water, please."

"Make yourself comfortable. I'll be right back."

Callahan walked around the room while he was gone, admiring his collection of ancient Native pottery and baskets. As always, such items filled her with a vague feeling of nostalgia.

Red Feather returned with two glasses of water and motioned for her to sit on the sofa.

"Now, my friend," he said, settling into a chair across from her, "tell me what's troubling you."

She took a sip before speaking. "I just returned from a promotional trip to San Francisco. Something strange happened there. Really strange." She explained how she met Luke and spoke honestly about most of what had transpired between them.

Red Feather listened without interruption, but leaned forward as she described Luke's birthmarks.

"You're certain their location is the same as the wounds you see in dreams? The ones you paint?"

"Absolutely certain." Although she hadn't planned to, she found herself confiding that Luke had spent the night with her. When she described the vision she'd seen in the mirror that night, Red Feather's eyes narrowed.

"This warrior...was his face familiar?"

"I couldn't see his face. The room was too dark. But he was wearing a bear claw around his neck, the one Running Wolf wears in my dreams. Then the light came on, and it was Luke standing there. It was his reflection in the mirror! I know this sounds crazy. It was obviously Luke all along. It had to have been. But I swear to you I saw...someone else."

Red Feather closed his eyes, absorbing the information. Several moments passed before he spoke again.

"You obviously felt a powerful connection to this man."

"Almost from the moment we met."

"I can see this confuses you. But listen, my friend. When two souls experience such a powerful connection, it's like a spark jumping between two wires. It cannot be stopped. Age doesn't matter, race doesn't matter, even gender doesn't matter." He paused. "You must understand that the soul can wear any disguise—man, woman, beautiful, ugly, healthy, crippled… The particulars of any life are masks that souls put on and take off. In one life, you may belong to a certain race or nation; perhaps in your next life you belong to another. The language you speak, the age you happen to be when you meet, the color of your skin—they simply do not matter between souls. It's all just a distraction. You must learn to see more deeply, to use the eyes of Spirit."

And then Red Feather again closed his eyes. His lips moved silently, and from time to time he nodded his head. Callahan assumed he was communing with his spirit helpers and watched as beads of sweat broke out on his forehead. Several minutes later, he opened his eyes and reached for his water, draining the glass.

"This work always makes me thirsty." He wiped his brow with the back of his hand.

She resisted a nervous impulse to laugh, but Red Feather obviously wasn't joking. He got up for more water, and then sat silently, staring into space. At last, he turned his gaze back to Callahan.

"Well," she said, unable to stand it any longer, "what do you think? Am I jumping to crazy conclusions about the connection between Running Wolf and Luke?'

The shaman shrugged.

"The truth is never simple. There are many layers in all relationships and happenings. That is why we say, *mitakakuye oyas'in*, which means 'all my relations' in the Lakota language. All things are connected in ways that are invisible."

Callahan was frustrated by the vagueness of his answer, but she knew from experience that Red Feather processed information in his own way and couldn't be rushed. She let it go for the moment.

Deathmark

"I'm grateful for the artistic inspiration my dreams give me, whether they're dreams or memories. The problem is that I sometimes feel more than a little crazy, like I'm living in two different worlds."

Red Feather nodded. "In a spiritual sense, you are. We all are. Realize that no one is ever completely awake or completely asleep. Our waking life is filled with what we call 'daydreams.' Our night-time dreams affect us during the day, whether we consciously remember them or not. Your unusually vivid dreams are gifts, a way for the Great Spirit to contact and guide you."

"Guide me toward what?"

"I can't answer that. Just trust that these dream-memories are necessary for your spiritual development. A part of your psyche fled into exile during that lifetime, creating a hole through which illness and despair can enter. You are cut off from part of your personal power, and that's why you're continually drawn back. Apparently, you have lessons to learn from that lifetime."

"What lessons?"

He gave another shrug. "All things will become clear in their right time."

"Okay. I can accept that, but do you think there's a connection between Luke and Running Wolf?"

Red Feather hesitated. "The mark of a fatal injury—particularly if it was traumatic—*is* sometimes carried from one lifetime to another, as a so-called 'birthmark.'"

"So Luke's birthmark could be Running Wolf's..."

"Deathmark," Red Feather finished for her.

The word chilled Callahan to the bone. *Deathmark.*

"Serious psychological research is being conducted on this subject," Red Feather continued. "Other issues, such as phobias, depression, and recurrent physical ailments often respond well to trance journeying or other forms of past-life regression. Identifying the deep reason for such problems may help deal with and even eliminate them. "

"Yes, I've read that. But you haven't answered my question."

"The answers to all questions lie in the spirit world." Red Feather leaned forward. "Are you ready to journey *with* me this time?"

In spite of her trust in the shaman, Callahan felt a frisson race down her spine. Dreams were one thing, but the idea of deliberately plunging into another reality was something else. What if she couldn't find her way back? She took a deep breath and shook off her fear.

"Let's do it," she said.

Deathmark

10

Red Feather spread a vintage Navajo blanket on the floor.

"My traveling blanket."

Callahan watched as he assembled other items—a painted gourd rattle, an eagle feather, an abalone shell, dried sage, and a folded piece of deerskin that she recognized as his medicine bundle. The last things he placed on the floor beside the blanket were a tape player and cassette.

"In the old days, healers needed someone to drum for them while they conducted journeys to other planes of existence," he explained. "Modern technology has its advantages." He placed sage in the abalone shell and held a lighted match to it until it was smoking. "Take off your boots and socks and come stand in the center of the blanket, facing east."

When she was properly positioned, he passed the shell from

her head to her feet, front and back, using the eagle feather to fan the smoke toward her. He carried the smoking shell in a clockwise circle around the blanket, honoring each of the six directions—east, south, west, north, below, and above—and creating a sacred space for the work he was about to do. Then he handed the feather and shell to Callahan, indicating that it was her turn to "smudge" or purify him with the smoke.

That accomplished, Red Feather sat cross-legged on the blanket and gestured for her to do the same. He began shaking his rattle and singing in a soft voice. She remembered from the previous ceremony that this was the healer's "power song," secret words requesting the help of spirit allies during his journey. As the rattling and singing continued, Callahan sat silently, doing her best to center herself.

Red Feather's song finally wound down, and he put the rattle aside. He opened his medicine bundle and removed two small quartz crystals.

"Lie down with your head facing north. Then just relax."

Kneeling beside her, he placed one of the crystals on her forehead. He slipped the cassette into the tape player, lay down beside her, and put the other crystal on his own forehead.

"The crystals will connect our spirits," he said. "Now, when the drumming begins, I want you to close your eyes and imagine that you are entering a cave, a private entrance to your deep consciousness. Within the cave, you'll find a tunnel. Follow the tunnel, trusting that it will take you where you need to go. It is your own intention that will make this happen. Do you understand?"

"I…I think so."

"The sound of the drum will support you throughout your journey. Four loud, rapid drumbeats will be your signal that it's time to return to physical reality."

"But how?"

"The same way you left, through the tunnel. The drumbeats will carry you. Trust me. You will be protected."

Callahan lay very still. Was it her imagination, or was the crystal on her forehead beginning to feel warm? The drumming

Deathmark

began, a fast one-two, one-two cadence that matched her hammering heartbeats. Closing her eyes, she visualized herself entering a cave, walking down a long, dark and sloping tunnel, moving deeper and deeper, carried by the drumbeats to a mystical place within her own psyche.

She emerged from the tunnel into a densely forested landscape, a place bathed in an unearthly shimmering light. The air felt cool on her face. A loud whoosh-whoosh sound suddenly filled the air and an enormous eagle, its body larger than her own, landed on a nearby rocky outcropping. Golden eyes glared from the great feathered head, holding her in their unwavering gaze.

Come fly with me.

She understood the invitation without actually hearing the words. Approaching the eagle, she clasped her arms around its neck and swung herself up onto its back. With a mighty flap of wings, they were airborne, climbing up and up, high above the tallest trees. Her cheek pressed against sleek feathers, she viewed the mountain ridges below. The sky slowly changed from brilliant blue to indigo, as the eagle flew her into a thick dark cloud.

Suddenly the eagle was gone and she was falling, spiraling backward through time.

She sat, waiting, within the privacy of their tipi. With her were Dancing Bird, her younger sister, and Blue Rain, her father's second wife. Her heart pounded with excitement. People were gathering outside, she could hear soft laughter and murmurs.

Nervously, she rose to her feet and smoothed her wedding dress—a sheath of white doeskin, decorated with elk teeth and red-dyed porcupine quills worked in intricate sun-symbol patterns across her chest. The short sleeves were fringed, as were the cuffs of her new moccasins. A red line was painted in the center part of her waist-long hair, symbolizing her connection to Mother Earth and the abundance of life.

She felt a sudden yearning for her beloved mother, who had succumbed to coughing sickness two seasons ago, during the Moon of Frosting. Her mother would have radiated happiness, on this beautiful spring day.

A soft scratching at the entrance flap interrupted her thoughts, and her father entered the tipi. Although he had seen more than fifty winters, Spotted Antelope was still a vigorous man and greatly respected within the tribe.

"It is time, my daughter." His voice was gruff, but she knew the tone hid his love for her and his satisfaction with this union. He had accepted Running Wolf's bridal gifts of buffalo robes and six fine ponies, and he was obviously pleased that she had chosen such a proven warrior.

She took a deep breath to steady herself and then followed her father, ducking under the flap to face the assembled crowd. Her stepmother and sister positioned themselves behind her.

People made way as Running Wolf approached, riding the magnificent white stallion he had captured in a recent raid on an enemy camp. He swung down from the horse and tied it to a nearby tree. All eyes were on him as he approached, tall and proud, to take his place beside her. He looked so handsome, dressed in a new buckskin shirt decorated with his personal and clan symbols, a loincloth and fringed leggings. Two eagle tail feathers were positioned in the forelock of his oiled and braided hair.

She felt the blood rise to her cheeks. The moment she had yearned for was at hand.

Her father raised his hand for silence.

"I, Spotted Antelope, am announcing a happy occasion. These two before me, Running Wolf and Sun-in-Her-Face, have declared their wish to be as one."

Several women began a joyful trilling. The sound was instantly picked up by others and punctuated by shouts of approval from the men. After a few moments, Spotted Antelope again signaled for silence. Drawing his knife, he first slit Running Wolf's right thumb and then hers. Holding the two cuts tightly together, he raised their hands up for the tribe to witness the mingling of their blood.

Deathmark

"It is done," he announced. "In the name of the Great Mystery, Source of All, these two are now husband and wife. Running Wolf and Sun-in-Her-Face will, from this day forward, walk the path of life together. Two hearts beating as one."

She thought her own heart would burst with happiness as Spotted Antelope placed his hand over Running Wolf's heart, accepting him as his son. Blue Rain brought forth a cup made from a buffalo horn, containing honey-sweetened juice to promote fertility. Running Wolf took the first drink, and then offered it to her with a big smile. As she drank, a lusty shout of approval, followed by more trilling, rose from the tribe.

Her father waited for the noise to die down before he placed a hand on each of their heads and offered a blessing: "My children, may you never know hunger or thirst. May you never fear the cold. May you always be a shelter, each to the other. Go now and warm your new lodge."

Running Wolf took her hand and led her to the white stallion. He helped her mount and then, following tradition, handed her his shield and lance to carry as a symbol that she was proud to be his mate. She sat tall on the horse, believing she must be the most blessed among women as her new husband led the way to their freshly raised tipi, a short distance from the rest of the encampment. As the people followed behind, women sang an ancient wedding song:

Come together, come together.
Like minds, share your thoughts.
Let customs and traditions develop.
Let respect be the medium of exchange.
Love each other the way you love your own self.
Give your children paths to choose that can't go wrong.
Come together, come together.
Your life on earth is only so long.
Come together, come together.

As she sang along in her head, the familiar words struck her with new poignancy. "Your life on earth is only so long." Something within her went a little cold, as though a cloud had suddenly passed over the sun.

Running Wolf helped her dismount in front of their tipi, and they waved to their departing tribesmen. He crossed two branches—keep-out sticks—in front of the entrance flap, signaling their wish not to be disturbed.

Once they were inside and finally alone, he gently held her face in his hands.

"We belong to each other, my beloved," he whispered, his black eyes filled with a fierce love. "From this day forward, our souls are joined."

She felt herself spinning, being sucked upward through total darkness. Abruptly, she was back in the dark tunnel—lying on cool, hard-packed earth. Four fast drumbeats signaled it was time to return. They were repeated with an urgent tempo.

It took all of her energy just to pull herself to her feet. Help me! *The words were thought, rather than spoken. She felt invisible arms around her, supporting and moving her forward. The drumming stopped but she heard a voice calling her, urging her on, toward the light.*

Callahan returned suddenly to the present, feeling dizzy and disoriented. It took her a moment to focus on Red Feather's face as he knelt beside her.

"Good," he said. "You're back. Take deep, slow breaths. A few more. Now, relax while I breathe your missing spirit part back into your heart center and the crown of your head."

He cupped his hands over the middle of her chest and lowered his head. His breath was warm as he exhaled through his hands. He removed the crystal from her forehead and helped her to sit up. Then he knelt behind her and she leaned against him, still fighting dizziness as he blew hard against the top of her head.

"There." He helped her lie back down. "Stay still while I seal your spirit back into your body."

She watched as Red Feather took up his rattle and rose to his

Deathmark

feet. He circled the blanket several times, rattling and singing softly. Although her dizziness was receding, Callahan's mind was reeling. What had happened? Did she fall asleep, hypnotized by the drumbeat? The dream was one she'd never had before. *No, it wasn't a dream. I was actually there, living it! Living as Sun-in-Her-Face!*

As she closed her eyes, a vivid image came into focus. *Wide-set black eyes looked down at her. Prominent, well-shaped nose. High cheekbones set in a ruggedly handsome face. A small scar cut through his left eyebrow and a larger one ran from the right corner of his mouth to the middle of his chin.*

Her eyes flew open. *His face!* For the first time, she had seen Running Wolf's face.

Red Feather bent over her again. "How do you feel?"

"Weak." She pushed her hair back from her damp forehead. "My mouth is so dry."

"I'll get more water."

He returned in a moment with freshly filled glasses. She drank deeply, and then glanced at her watch. Almost four o'clock. The trance journey had taken less than half an hour, but Callahan felt as if she'd been gone for a lifetime.

"It was a successful journey," Red Feather said. "Are you ready to talk about it?"

She hesitated, trying to organize her thoughts. "It was bizarre. After I came out of the tunnel, I flew on the back of an enormous eagle. It seemed so real…" She broke off, remembering the feeling of feathers against her skin.

"It was real," he said. "Only a different reality. That eagle is a friend of mine."

Callahan stared at the shaman. "One of your spirit allies?"

Red Feather's smile answered her question.

"Where did Eagle take you?"

"To…to that life I dream about. I married Running Wolf. There was a short ceremony." She looked down at her right thumb, half expecting it to be cut. "Every detail was so vivid. And there's something else, something really exciting! I saw Running Wolf's face clearly in my mind for the first time. It's always been a blur to me after waking up."

"That's because you weren't asleep this time. You were in an altered state of consciousness. An altered state provides insights and sharpness of vision that the dreamtime can't." Red Feather paused. "Our spirits were connected through the crystals, allowing me to witness some of what you experienced as Sun-in-Her-Face. The sun-symbol quill design on your wedding dress was beautiful."

Callahan looked at him, astonished. "I didn't mention that. How did you know about the dress?"

"As I said, I traveled with you. Who do you think pulled you back through the tunnel?"

"Oh, my god…this is incredible."

"You still have doubts about me, don't you, my friend?"

"I trust you," she answered honestly. "But the rational part of my mind still has a hard time wrapping around this." She hesitated. "You said something about blowing my missing spirit part back into me. What did you mean?"

"Our journey was successful. I was able to locate the part of your psyche that splintered off in shock and grief during that lifetime."

She rubbed her throbbing forehead. "Does that mean my dreams will stop now?"

"I doubt it. They may even intensify for a time. But, gradually, you should feel more complete and grounded in the present. Be patient. Remember, everything happens in its right time."

Callahan was feeling anything but patient. She desperately wanted to make sense of all this. "Given that I *am* remembering an actual lifetime, why does it continue to haunt me? Why is it overlapping into this life?"

"In the Lakota language there is a word, *waki-ksuya,* for that special kind of remembering. It means to travel back into the past, to visit the spirits of those we have loved. Why that particular lifetime haunts you, I still cannot say. Except that you clearly have unfinished business."

Deathmark

"Is Luke a part of that unfinished business? Is he the reincarnation of Running Wolf?"

Red Feather closed his eyes and sat motionless for several moments. She watched him frown, move his lips, then frown again, as if listening intently. When at last he opened his eyes, they were full of concern.

"My spirit allies feel that you must be warned."

"Warned? About what?"

"It seems that you have, indeed, found your long-lost warrior."

It took a moment for Callahan to find her voice.

"If that's true, what do I do now? How do I handle this?"

He shook his head. "I don't have those answers, I can only remind you that all things have a purpose. We are drawn to those experiences that we need, in order to heal old wounds and to grow. You and your warrior obviously came together again for a reason. What that reason is, I cannot say." He leaned forward, his expression intense. "But, Callahan, you must use caution where this young man is concerned. There may be danger. Serious danger. My allies sense a growing darkness around him."

"What are you saying? Luke is in danger?' She swallowed. "Or do you mean that *he* is dangerous?"

"I'm not sure. I can only pass on the warning." He was quiet for a moment. "Do you know if Luke has any memory of the lifetime you shared?"

"No, not that he admitted. At least not consciously. He did say that he's always had a fascination with bears, and a great fear of them."

Red Feather nodded. "His body is carrying the memory and the marks—the deathmarks—of an encounter with that great beast."

"You're saying that Luke and I came together again to heal old wounds, but at the same time you're warning me of danger. I'm confused. Should I see him again or not?"

"I can only tell you that you must listen to your own intuition, use your own judgment, especially where this young man is concerned."

Red Feather rose to his feet and Callahan understood that the session was over. The shaman had done all he could do. She stood on legs that felt rubbery.

"Thank you."

"You are welcome, my friend." He walked her to her car and whistled for the dogs. An instant later, Strong Heart and Mucho raced up the road toward them.

"Just a moment," Callahan said. "I have something for you." She opened the Jeep's hatchback and removed a canvas wrapped in brown paper. "My gift to you."

Red Feather unwrapped the package. It was a portrait of an elderly man with long white hair blowing across and obscuring his face. Behind him was the ghost-like image of a great horned owl.

"I see him sometimes in my dreams," Callahan said. "His name is Night Flyer, and he's a medicine man. I call the painting *Keeper of the Power.*"

"It is well named, a most magical image. I am honored." Red Feather placed his hand on her shoulder. "This is a time of transition for you, an opportunity for great learning and growth. Such times are never easy. Take care of yourself, my friend, and keep in touch. Keep in touch," he repeated.

Callahan coaxed a reluctant Mucho into the Jeep. As she started down the dirt road toward Santa Fe, she glanced at her watch. Five-fifteen. She'd been with Red Feather for over two hours. And yet she'd traveled back in time more than two centuries. She felt the hairs stand up on the nape of her neck. Something deep within her knew that her journey was just beginning.

Deathmark

11

"**Until next week,** Luke dear?" the Countess spoke with a flirtatious lilt to her voice.

The Countess—she insisted he call her that. *What a joke. She's about as royal as I am.*

He forced a smile. "Next week, same time, Countess."

Following her expressionless butler to the front door, Luke breathed a sigh of relief. *That's over.* His sessions with the scrawny, overly made-up and perfumed old broad, while far from enjoyable, were at least manageable—as long as he closed his eyes and let his mind wander. Plus, she was generous. In addition to his fee, she'd tipped him two hundred dollars.

He stepped out of the Pacific Heights mansion and into the early evening air, headed for a well-earned Johnny Walker Red and water at the nearest bar. Two young women, one of them a redhead, gave him a flirtatious glance as they passed him on the street. The redhead immediately brought Callahan to mind, and Luke's spirits lifted. She'd sounded surprised but pleased to hear from him when he'd called the night before.

It was dark when a weary Callahan pulled into her driveway. The phone was ringing as she let herself into the house. She turned off the security alarm and rushed past Mucho, into her study. Checking caller ID, she recognized Brad's cell phone number.

"No fucking way!" Just the thought of talking to him made her stomach clench. She glared at the phone until it stopped ringing and then checked her voicemail. The only message was Brad's.

"Callahan. It's me. I need to talk to you. Please, pick up if you're there." He paused. "Just because things didn't work out with us doesn't mean we have to be enemies. I don't see why we can't at least be friendly. I mean…after everything we meant to each other."

There was another pause, during which Callahan was sure she heard him take a drink. *It's after six. He's no doubt on his second or third martini by now.*

"I left some of my things at the house," he continued, "and I need to come by and get them." After another pause, another obvious sip, his voice tightened with frustration. "Well, hell. I'll catch ya later."

No, you won't! She erased the message. *Tough shit, Brad. Everything belonging to you was bagged up and dropped in a dumpster months ago.*

Callahan fed Mucho and returned to her study. Checking her e-mail, she found yet another message from Leda: *Is the acrylic dry yet? Need more canvases ASAP! The Steinbergs just purchased* Evening Song *and want to see more! Also expect the Garretts from Houston to break out their fat checkbook. They've been in twice, considering* All My Relations. *The iron is hot, darling—let's strike!*

I'd like to strike you, Leda! she thought. *Do you think I have a staff of elves here, painting on an assembly line?*

She deleted that message and went on to the next, a typically

Deathmark

short note from Patrick: *Hi, my Mom! Glad the trip went well. I'm fine, putting in long hours at work. Re: your web site, I'm still waiting for those photos Suzanne took of the last six canvases. What's the hold up? Don't work too hard. Love you a bushel and a peck and a hug around the neck, P.*

Their special, customary goodbye, left over from Patrick's childhood, coaxed a smile from her. How she wished he was there to deliver that "hug around the neck" in person. She could sure use it. *He may be all grown up, but he's still my sweet boy.*

She made a mental note to call Suzanne regarding the photos. But not tonight. After the session with Red Feather, she wasn't up to talking to anyone. She turned off her computer and sat back in her chair. Her gaze went, as it so often did, to the framed photos of Patrick on her desk. There he was as a chubby-faced baby with a halo of red curls, then a skinny eight-year-old, striking a cocky pose in his Little League uniform. Next came a long-haired teenager leaning against his first car, his formal high school and college graduation pictures, and a fairly recent snapshot of him taken on a whitewater rafting trip with a now-ex-girlfriend. He was the greatest love of her life, but the images always made her a little sad. The years had flown by so fast.

Callahan took a deep breath, blinking back tears. She snapped off the light, walked through her bedroom, closely followed by Mucho, and unlocked the French doors that opened onto a courtyard.

"God, I'm tired," she said aloud, as she walked outside to turn up the temperature on the redwood hot tub. "It's been quite a day."

Mucho *rrrumphed* a sympathetic response and followed her back inside. A short time later, she was wrapped in a terrycloth robe and back outside. The large courtyard was a wonderfully peaceful spot, covered in flagstone and enclosed by eight-foot-high adobe walls. There was a sliver of a moon in the west and the clear night sky was filled with twinkling stars. Lights scattered in the shrubbery illuminated the area with a soft glow.

Callahan watched Mucho circle the courtyard, sniffing around the juniper bushes and the ceramic pots that held the last of the summer's geraniums. She slid the vinyl cover off the tub, dropped her robe, and eased herself into the heated water.

Her muscles began to relax, but her mind was still in high gear. Red Feather's words echoed in her head. *"You have found your long-lost warrior. All things have a purpose."*

What purpose? Where could a relationship with Luke possibly lead? *Talk about a good news/bad news scenario... The good news is I may have finally found my soulmate. The bad news is that he's a twenty-nine-year-old gigolo!*

Even though she accepted the concept of reincarnation, the idea that Luke was actually Running Wolf in another body was still a stretch. *And yet, he has those marks...Running Wolf's deathmarks.* She closed her eyes, reliving scenes from her trance journey: *the smell of food cooking over campfires, the sounds of trilling and singing, the sharp sting of a knife drawn across her thumb. Running Wolf's face, vivid and real.*

Callahan hugged herself beneath the hot water until her dream lover's visage faded. And then her thoughts moved to Red Feather's warning about the danger connected to Luke. *What did that mean? How is Luke dangerous? He seems so considerate, so sincere. But so did Brad, in the beginning.*

Still, if Red Feather was right—if Luke was a link to another lifetime—how could she not explore it?

A deep-throated, menacing growl shattered her reverie. She bolted upright in the water.

"Mucho? What is it, boy?"

The dog's teeth were bared. He growled again, sprang to his feet and ran to the wall, barking and lunging, trying in vain to get at something on the other side.

Callahan tried not to overreact. *It's just some animal. Probably a coyote.* Mucho's barking intensified. *Coyote or not, tub time is over.* She climbed out, yanked her robe on, and hurried to the bedroom door.

"Mucho! Come!"

Mucho held his ground, barking.

"Right now!"

He reluctantly obeyed, casting concerned looks over his shoulder at the wall. She pulled him inside the house and locked the door. Then she turned on the outside lights and set the security alarm.

Deathmark

Callahan heated one of Consuela's tamales for dinner and ate it standing over the kitchen sink. She then retired to her room, removed her robe and pulled on a pair of baggy cotton pajamas that Brad had always hated. Now she took satisfaction in wearing whatever she damn well pleased. She paused in front of her bookshelves, collecting some well-read books on reincarnation. Mucho, who had finally settled down, kept a protective eye on her from his bed by the fireplace.

Settling herself against two overstuffed pillows, she opened a book by a well-published psychologist and began to reread a passage she had previously underlined: *According to ancient teachings, souls travel together from lifetime to lifetime in groups, changing ethnic backgrounds, relationships, and gender. We are drawn to individuals with whom we have lived before... Remnants of traumatic past life experiences may surface as fears or phobias in this lifetime.*

Just as Red Feather said. She put the book aside and reached for another, one that dealt with past life regression. Two sentences caught her attention: *Physical conditions in current lifetimes often have origins in a previous life. Past physical trauma may even leave present physical residue.*

Physical residue... Birthmarks would certainly fall under that category. She read a little farther, before switching to a book on the meaning of dreams: *Dreams, the royal road to the unconscious, often contain clues about past lives. Some convey literal past life memories.*

Too tired to keep her eyes open any longer, Callahan piled the books on her nightstand and switched off the light. Luke's face instantly appeared behind her closed lids. Then, as sleep carried her away, she thought she heard Running Wolf's voice. It was just a whisper.

"We are one. Our souls are forever joined."

12

"Sun-in-Her-Face!"

She felt someone shaking her shoulder. "You cannot remain here any longer. The sun sinks and it is cold. You must come back to the camp, rest and take nourishment."

She opened her eyes and realized that she had fallen asleep on the hard ground, close to Running Wolf's burial scaffold. With an effort, she pushed herself up on one elbow.

"I must remain close to my husband."

Dancing Bird's face was pinched with concern when she bent close, and her voice was firm.

"Running Wolf's spirit has departed this place. He walks where you can no longer follow. Now you must say goodbye. If you have no care for yourself, consider your unborn child."

She felt her sister's arms around her, helping her up. The grief wounds on her own arms throbbed as she raised them to Dancing Bird's shoulders for support. At that moment, she felt a rush of warm

Deathmark

liquid run down between her thighs. She doubled over in excruciating pain as her belly began to cramp.

"No! It is too early. My baby..."

Callahan jerked awake in the darkness. She moved her hand across her stomach and lower, feeling a warm, sticky wetness between her thighs. Turning on the bedside lamp, she stared at her bloody fingers. Then she felt another cramp. Her period.

Throwing back the comforter, she swung her legs out of bed. As she stood, she felt stinging pains in her calves. Suddenly, another lower abdominal cramp hit—this one severe—followed by a wave of dizziness. Gasping, she dropped to her hands and knees and rolled into a fetal position on the floor.

What's happening? She had never experienced menstrual cramps like these. Another twisting spasm of pain. As she lay, eyes tightly closed, she thought she felt hands touching her, soothing her. *The dream! I'm back in the dream. And these cramps are labor pains!*

Mucho licked her face, grounding her in present time.

Callahan opened her eyes and lay very still. Gradually, the pain and dizziness began to subside.

"I'm okay," she whispered, trying to reassure herself as well as Mucho. She rose slowly and made her way into the bathroom. Mucho stayed close by her side.

She lay awake for some time after returning to bed, afraid to sleep and dream. Her menstrual cramps had subsided to minor twinges, but the memory of intense pain was still fresh. She'd had that terrible dream many times before, of going into early labor and losing her baby. But never had it been this realistic. *It must be a reaction to the trance journey. Red Feather said my dreams might intensify.*

Exhaustion finally overcame fear, and she drifted into a fitful sleep.

The next morning was chilly, with thick gray clouds spread like a blanket across the western sky. Although tempted to pull the

119

covers over her head and stay in bed, Callahan forced herself up and into her sweats. She had work to do. First on her list was to get Running Wolf's face on canvas, while it was still clear in her mind.

Mucho gobbled his breakfast and stood by the door, waiting for her to open it. She grabbed a bagel to eat later and followed him as he bounded up the path to her studio.

Winter is on the way. A feeling of heaviness settled on Callahan's shoulders like a cloak. For as long as she could remember, cold weather had depressed—even frightened—her. Especially snow. Her mother used to tell the story of Callahan's hysteria when she was three years old and they'd had a rare snowstorm on the ranch. Her father's idea to build a snowman was quickly aborted, as she'd screamed and fought to get back into the house. Although she'd gotten better at handling it through the years, her reaction to snow was still one of phobic dread. That was the only drawback to living in Santa Fe. Every winter there would be days when she thought longingly of southern California, but then the snow would melt and she'd fall in love with northern New Mexico all over again.

She stepped inside her studio and turned up the heat. Then she made a pot of coffee, turned on her Red Thunder CD, and began preparing her canvas. Her thoughts turned to Luke. Would he call again? And if he did, what on earth would she say to him?

She began to sketch the strong, masculine features she had seen during her trance journey. As the face took form, Callahan was hit with a confusing range of emotions—joy, yearning, grief. Tears blurred her vision and she turned away from the canvas. She poured a cup of coffee, hoping it would clear her head. As she sipped the strong brew, she stared at the emerging portrait. How strange that Running Wolf's face had been hidden in her subconscious for all these years. Meeting Luke must have brought it clearly, painfully into focus. She took a deep breath, lifted the canvas off the easel and leaned it against the wall. *I've got to get work finished for the galleries. I'll get back to this portrait later.*

Callahan forced herself to concentrate on *Dancing the Bear*, adding a few finishing touches. Then she turned her attention to another half-finished painting that was based on a recent dream-memory: a young Indian woman sitting by a mountain stream, her head bowed and her face obscured by long black hair. She called it *Contemplation*.

She lost track of time as she worked, only gradually becoming aware of an ache between her shoulders and a growling stomach that signaled time for a lunch break.

Work continued on *Contemplation*, but as the afternoon wore on, Callahan's thoughts kept returning to the sketch of Running Wolf. With some ambivalence, she replaced the canvas on an easel and stepped back to study it. After a moment, she picked up a piece of charcoal and began to draw.

His face… a little narrower, more sharply angled below the cheekbones. His eyebrows thicker… Wait. There was a thin scar running just above and through the left eyebrow, wasn't there? She drew it in. His mouth wider, the bottom lip a little fuller. She quickly made the corrections. *The scar on his chin from that encounter with the cougar he'd tracked and cornered…*

The thought stunned her. *Cougar? How did I know about a cougar?* She backed away from the canvas, her ears roaring, her head spinning with a sudden, vivid image—*Running Wolf riding into camp with a fresh cougar skin draped across one shoulder. A blood-crusted tear from the corner of his lip down to his chin…a wound that dripped fresh blood as he smiled and waved to her.*

She collapsed onto the sofa, shaking her head. *Dear god, am I losing my mind?*

The clouds had spread and now hung thick and low over surrounding hilltops as Callahan made her way back to the house later that afternoon. By early evening, the weather turned unseasonably cold and it started to snow.

She stood at her bedroom window, staring out. Big fluffy snowflakes, illuminated by the security floodlights, were coming down fast, striking the window and piling into drifts against the adobe patio wall. She fought against a wave of anxiety and quickly closed the wooden shades. *It's like being buried alive!* In spite of her heavy robe and the fire burning brightly in the small kiva fireplace, she felt chilled to the bone. Hurrying into the bathroom, she swallowed a Xanax.

The phone rang, causing her to jump. Caller ID indicated it was Donny.

"Hiya, Cal, just checking on you. I know the first snowstorm of the season always unnerves you. Are you all right?"

Callahan hesitated. It would be a relief to tell Donny everything, to express her confusion and fears. But she knew he would worry that she was having a major breakdown.

"Cal? Are you there?"

"I'm just tired. I put in a long day." She tried to steer the conversation away from herself. "How did your day go?"

"Most productive. I finished the final draft of *Poisonous Passion* about thirty minutes ago. Always a relief. I'll whip up some gorgeous French onion soup and chill a bottle of excellent Chardonnay, if you'll come over and help me celebrate."

"Oh, Donny, I'm sorry. I don't want to go out in this weather. Besides, I've already eaten. I'm in my jammies and ready for bed. But congratulations! You knocked this one out in record time, didn't you?"

"Six months. It took feather-brained Fiona Fontaine twenty-eight chapters to finally get fucked." He sighed. "Someday, when I can afford to retire Desiree Denton, I'll write something with substance under my own name. I'm considering an only slightly fictionalized version of my own life story. I've already got the title—*Unauthorized Autobiography*. What do you think?"

She smiled. "I like it."

"It would make a great B movie. Who do you think should play me? Matt Damon was brilliant in that HBO movie as Liberace's boyfriend. Or Rob Lowe—too pretty?"

"Hmmm. I'll have to sleep on it."

"Do that. You sound positively pooped. Off to bed with you; we'll talk again soon. Love you. Nighty night."

"I love you, too."

Callahan snapped off the light and climbed into bed. She snuggled under the heavy down comforter, grateful for its warmth

Deathmark

as she watched the flames from the fireplace create dancing shadows on the wall. Her thoughts returned, unbidden, to the vision she'd had while working on the portrait of Running Wolf.

I saw his facial scars during the trance journey. So, did I just have an unusually vivid daydream? Fantasize about a cougar to explain the scar across his chin? Or are past life memories breaking through while I'm wide-awake? What if it starts happening all the time? The idea was terrifying.

Stop it! She rolled over, trying to maneuver her stiff body into a comfortable position. *I'm stressed and exhausted, physically and emotionally. Stress can do strange things...*

Just as she was dozing off, an image formed in her mind. *The weather-lined face of her dream father, Spotted Antelope.* His voice seemed to reach her from a great distance. *May you always be a shelter, each to the other. May you never fear the cold...*

Callahan burrowed deeper under the covers.

The powdery snow was deep, up to her knees in places, but no matter... Nothing mattered now. She trudged on, barely feeling the bitter wind that stung her nose and cheeks. It would all be over soon.

"Running Wolf," she whispered, "I am coming, beloved. I will soon be with you and our baby son in the spirit world."

She reached an old, twisted cottonwood tree and leaned against its rough bark.

"Grandfather, I am so tired. Let me sleep here, beneath your branches." She removed the buffalo robe from her shoulders and spread it on the snow beneath the tree. Then she took off her dress, shivering as the wind hit her bare skin. Sitting on the robe, she removed her wet leggings and moccasins.

The sky to the west blazed with color as Father Sun sank behind the mountains. Gold, orange and red...red as Running Wolf's bloody wounds. Even when she closed her eyes, she could see the claw marks, the gashes in his once-smooth skin. Would death erase that terrible image?

She stared up through the tree branches at the darkening sky and willed her body to relax, to stop shaking and surrender to the cold. A lone raven circled several times, cawing loudly before landing on a branch overhead. A sign.

"Watch over me, brother," she whispered through numb lips. *"Guide my spirit on its journey home."* She closed her eyes and began to chant her death song.

Ni'hai'hi'hi, *My father*
Ni'hai'hi'hi', *My father*
Na'eso'yutu'hi', *I come to him*
Na'eso'yutu'hi', *I come to him*
U'guchi'hi'hi', *The raven*
U'guchi'hi'hi', *The raven*
Na'nisto'hewu'hi, *I cry like it*
Na'nisto'hewu'hi, *I cry like it*
Ga'!Na'hewu'hi, *Caw! I say*
Ga'!Na'hewu'hi, *Caw! I say*

Callahan opened her eyes. The strange words echoed in her ears. *Crying like a raven? My death song...* Gripped by the force of her dream, she lay motionless. Her body felt numb, frozen stiff. *Cold. I'm so cold.*

With difficulty, she moved her arms and legs, rubbed them vigorously until feeling returned. *That was no dream!* She lay shivering beneath the covers as the revelation hit her. *I died in the snow.*

124

Deathmark

13

Morning dawned bright and clear. During the night, the storm had moved out, leaving half a foot of snow. The view from Callahan's kitchen windows revealed a picture postcard landscape of snow-draped piñons, chamisa bushes, and gracefully sloping adobe walls.

She took no pleasure from the sight, an unwelcome reminder of last night's dream and the fitful insights that followed. Her snow phobia had never been worse. The Xanax she had swallowed upon awakening had done little to relieve her anxiety. By mid-morning, she was still in her flannel pajamas and warmest robe, reluctant—in spite of another slave-driving e-mail message from Leda—to venture out to the studio.

She kept going over the dream, reliving the feelings of hopelessness and despair she'd experienced as Sun-in-Her-Face. *The dreams were real happenings.* Any doubts she may have had were now gone. *These are actual memories. I once lived—and died—as that young Lakota woman.*

Her thoughts were interrupted by Mucho's sudden bark and wild dash to the front door. *Who the hell?* Callahan cinched her robe tighter and ran her fingers through uncombed hair. *It had better not be Brad.* She was relieved to see Red Feather's pickup truck in the driveway. Hastily, she unlocked the door and saw the shaman on her portal, stomping snow off his boots. Mucho shot past her to greet their visitor with his usual enthusiasm. Spotting Strong Heart perched in the cab of the pickup, his joy reached a fever pitch.

"Bring her in," Callahan said. "We'll put them in the courtyard where they can romp to their hearts' content."

After the dogs were taken care of, she led Red Feather to the kitchen table. "How about a cup of coffee while I get out of this robe and into some clothes?"

"Coffee would hit the spot, thank you." He took off his heavy sheepskin jacket and draped it across the back of a kitchen chair before sitting down.

"I'll be back in a jiff," Callahan said, handing him his coffee before hurrying down the hall.

Moments later she was sitting across from him, dressed in jeans, a sweater, and sneakers.

"You never cease to amaze me, Red Feather," she said. "How did you know I needed to talk to you, again?"

"An uneasy feeling. I was in town running errands and decided to stop by."

"I'm so glad you did. Are the roads bad?"

"Most have been plowed. Anyway, my truck has four-wheel drive." He studied her. "I see my intuition was right. You look exhausted. What's going on?"

"I really don't know. I'm walking a tightrope between two different worlds, and it's getting harder to keep my balance." In vivid detail, she described her visions and latest dreams.

Red Feather listened with his usual careful attention.

"The door separating the life you lived as Sun-in-Her-Face and this present life has never been completely closed, Callahan. Your dream-memories began, along with your feelings of depression, when you were just a teenager. Now that you have found this young man, this Luke, the door has opened wider. More memories are slipping through, even when you're awake."

"But how do I handle it? I'm losing control of my thoughts, my reality! I'm scared!"

"Yes, a change of consciousness is always frightening. Remember, nothing is accidental. Let me see what I can pick up...."

Red Feather closed his eyes and began softly chanting his power song. After a few minutes, his eyes opened, but they still held a distant look.

"Your dream of dying in the snow explains why you are still haunted by that lifetime. The feelings we have at death are so powerful they sometimes carry into another incarnation. This is especially true with suicide. When one chooses to abandon the body, much is left undone. Lessons remain unlearned. That learning must be continued in the next life."

"What lessons am I supposed to be learning?"

"That's for *you* to realize, my friend. Each soul has its own curriculum. Perhaps your lessons have to do with acceptance, accepting that all things happen for a purpose. We live in a world of duality, where joy must be balanced by pain. By accepting that pain, living through it and learning from it, we grow. You didn't complete your grieving process in that prior lifetime. As Sun-in-Her-Face, you didn't come to terms with the deaths of your husband and baby. You short-changed yourself and your tribe by ending your life to escape the suffering. I have no doubt that many of the feelings of loneliness and the depression you have suffered in *this* lifetime stem from that long-ago decision."

"But it happened hundreds of years ago! What can I possibly do about it now?"

"Trust in divine order. Answers come to us in their own time and in their own way. View and accept your memories as gifts, spiritual opportunities, and stay open to them."

Red Feather pushed back from the table and stood.

"I can see that your energy is sluggish. Blocked in places.

Come, stretch out on the Navajo rug in your living room. I'll help get it moving again. Your spirit could use some strengthening, too."

Callahan lay on her back, uncomfortably aware of hard bricks beneath the thinly padded rug. Red Feather knelt beside her, eyes closed, chanting. She watched him rub his hands together, briskly. *Concentrating the healing power in his hands*, she remembered. He moved his hands in circles above her face and chest, then lightly tapped the crown of her head several times and moved his fingers clockwise in a small circle on her scalp. He repeated the tapping and circling between her eyes and at the base of her throat. Moving to the upper part of her chest, his fingertips thumped a quick rhythm.

"I'm stimulating your thymus gland and boosting your immune system. Do this for yourself several minutes each day, especially when you're under stress."

He moved on, circling his hands above her torso. Finally, he swept his hands down the length of her legs to her feet, and then he sat back on his heels.

"Close your eyes. Visualize healing energy moving from the top of your head to your feet. Now, back up again. Keep it circulating. You do it yourself."

Callahan began to feel a warm tingling sensation move throughout her body.

"Take a deep breath through your nose, hold it for six counts, and blow it out through your mouth. Again... Again... Better." There was a note of satisfaction in Red Feather's voice. "That's much better. You can get up now."

Red Feather put on his jacket and placed his hands on her shoulders.

"You look much stronger. Feel that strength. *Own* it."

She stopped him as he opened the front door. "I can't thank you enough, but what you said before, about sensing danger where Luke is concerned. I don't know what to make of that."

He shook his head. "Neither do I. Spirit allies are not always specific. Just be alert and trust your inner wisdom. I'm here, if you need me."

Callahan gave him a quick, hard hug. She remained under the

Deathmark

portal as Red Feather freed the dogs from the courtyard and directed Strong Heart into his truck. Mucho, wet with bits of snow stuck on his nose, whimpered softly as they drove away.

"I know," she said, wiping the snow away. "But you'll see Strong Heart again soon. You had a fine time, didn't you, you big snow bunny?"

Mucho lifted his ears and cocked his head at her words and then trotted off down the hall. Seconds later he returned with his sheepskin bunny in his mouth.

"I said 'snow bunny,' not 'show bunny.'" Callahan laughed and bent to kiss the top of his head. Whether it was Red Feather's healing ceremony or just his reassuring presence, she did feel much stronger.

Now fully aware of the origin of her phobia, Callahan stared defiantly out the window. *Okay, that was then, and this is now. Feel your strength and own it. Bundle up, put on your snow boots, and get going before Leda arrives with her whip.*

The afternoon passed quickly while Callahan put the finishing touches on *Contemplation*. She made arrangements for the two canvases to be sent to Leda on Friday.

Somewhat reluctantly, she turned her attention to the portrait of Running Wolf. Placing the canvas on an easel, she steeled herself against any visions his picture might trigger and began sketching in the rest of the likeness. *Long hair blowing in the wind. Arms folded defiantly across a broad, muscular chest.* She held her hand over his chest as Red Feather had done for her. *His heart, brave and strong.* Her eyes blurred with tears. *Yes, that's it. I've captured his determined attitude. His confidence.* She focused on the face, highlighting his eyes and smudging shadows under his broad cheekbones. The charcoal moved quickly. *His lips, the corners upturned, that trace of a smile.* She drew a thin, jagged scar from the left corner of his lower lip and across his chin before stepping back to evaluate her work.

The power and familiarity of his countenance struck her like a blow. *Running Wolf...* Mita'wa higna, *my husband...* Callahan took a deep breath, and then another. She lifted the portrait off the easel and leaned it in a corner.

I'm okay. I'll just work on something else for awhile. She set up a clean canvas and started to sketch. As the moments went by, another figure took form. A lone Indian woman walking through a snow-covered landscape. Callahan felt a tightening in her chest.

"*The Last Sunset,*" she whispered, naming the painting.

Time to split. Luke didn't have to look at his watch to know that his two hours with Darlene were up. He'd gotten good at gauging the passing of time while on a job, especially with his regular clients. Usually he performed well for Darlene, a pudgy fifty-plus-year-old widow, but this afternoon had been bad. He was too tired to be at his best and had actually dozed off at one inopportune moment.

A call from the agency the evening before, just after he'd spoken to Callahan, had set him up with identical twin sisters—in the city from some hick town in Wyoming—come to celebrate turning twenty-one with some "big city action." *Those two may have been young, but they sure as hell weren't inexperienced.* It was after two in the morning when he finally made his escape and fell, exhausted, into his own bed. Then up at seven to make an eight o'clock Legal Ethics class. *An oxymoron?* He was becoming cynical enough to think so.

"Your mind is obviously elsewhere tonight." Darlene lit a cigarette and blew smoke in his direction, something she knew he hated. "And, frankly, I don't appreciate it."

Luke sighed. "I'm sorry. I…"

She cut him off. "At three-fifty an hour, honey, I expect performance, not apologies."

He clenched his jaw. *Demanding bitch. No wonder her husband dropped dead. Probably poisoned himself.*

"Perhaps I'll request someone else for next week."

Luke got out of bed and pulled on his pants. "You know, Darlene," he said in a deliberately neutral tone of voice, "that's probably a good idea."

She opened her nightstand drawer and casually withdrew

two one-hundred-dollar bills and tossed them on the bed. Abruptly, she snatched them back saying, "Forget the tip."

Moments later, Luke was on the street. He pulled the collar up on his leather jacket and quickened his pace. The air was damp and a little crisp. But the cold he felt went clear to the bone.

Callahan brushed snow from Mucho's face and legs before unlocking the kitchen door and following him into the house. The short walk from the studio through the twilight snowscape had left her unnerved. Only after she'd flipped on lights and turned up the heat a few degrees did she take off her heavy sheepskin jacket and push the sleeves of her sweatshirt up over her elbows.

She scrambled four eggs, mixed half of them with dried dog food for Mucho and put the rest on her dinner plate. She took a wine glass from the cabinet and uncorked a bottle of Pinot Noir. As she watched the glass fill with the crimson liquid, Callahan's ears began to roar. Time shifted, folded back on itself.

No! Blood rose from long, deep slashes in the smooth light brown skin of her forearms. It dripped...and dripped.... Mita'wa higna! *My husband! See how my blood flows for you! See how my heart breaks...*

The sound of Mucho's worried whine as he nudged her hip brought Callahan back to herself. With a gasp, she saw the wine spilling over the granite countertop and dripping onto the brick floor.

Later that night, feeling somewhat calmed by a couple glasses of wine, Callahan was in bed, trying to distract herself by paging through the latest issue of *New Mexico Magazine*, when Luke called. A thrill shot through her at the sound of his voice.

"How's it going in Tesuque? Are you alone?"

"Yes, except for Mucho."

"Right. I remember, your Great Dane. Well, I sure wish I could remedy that. I think about you, Callahan. All the time. Do you think about me?"

"Yes, I do." *Understatement there.*

"I wanted to call you last night, but I was too bummed out to talk. There was a drive-by shooting outside my apartment building. I was coming home and saw this guy—just a kid, really—lying in a puddle of blood in the street. Some gang-related incident, I guess."

"God, that's terrible."

"Yeah. I've about had it with everything here. That ranch in Montana is sounding better all the time. Or maybe a hacienda in Tesuque. I've been having these wild fantasies about just showing up on your doorstep and surprising you."

"Well, yes, that would surprise me." *Is he serious?*

"I had a dream about you last night. Like I told you, I don't usually remember my dreams. But this one was unforgettable."

Is he starting to remember, too? "Tell me about it."

"Better not. It was X-rated. You'll have to wait until I'm with you…in person."

In person?

Before she could reply, he said, "That's going to happen, Callahan." She could hear the smile in his voice. "You haven't seen the last of me."

What the fuck are you doing? Luke ran his fingers through his hair. Took a deep breath. *Can't let this woman get under my skin like this. Always big trouble when that happens.* He went into the bathroom and stared into the mirror. *Need to get a grip. I've got a sweet deal going here, and only one semester left.* He combed his hair. *Can't let my emotions screw me up. Not again! Never again.*

He threw on his jacket and slammed out of the apartment, merging into the cold but comfortingly familiar night scene.

Callahan awoke before dawn, flushed from a lovemaking dream, unsure whether it was with Luke or Running Wolf, but she was definitely disappointed to discover that she was alone. She rolled over

Deathmark

and tried to pick up the dream again. But the sleep that carried her away was a dark, lonely void.

Jann Arrington-Wolcott

14

The sun glinted off fast-melting snow as Callahan drove toward town the next morning. Turning off Old Santa Fe Trail, she found a parking spot near Kaune's Neighborhood Market, which, according to the sign over the door, had been in business since 1890. That alone was enough to guarantee Callahan's business. Cracking a window for Mucho, she locked him inside the Jeep and hurried into the store. She was picking through mushrooms when she heard Brad's voice.

"Well, hello there."

She turned to see his still-handsome, although definitely aging face. His skin was sallow and puffy under bloodshot eyes. The booze was obviously catching up with him. He was wearing a tan lambskin jacket and a cream-colored Stetson she'd never seen before.

"I saw Mucho in the Jeep and figured you must be in here."

"Well, you figured right." She put the sack of mushrooms in her shopping cart and started around him.

Deathmark

He blocked her escape. "It's good to see you." He flashed the lop-sided grin that used to charm her. "You're looking great. Lost some weight, haven't you?"

When she didn't respond, he pushed on. "I left a message on your phone a couple of nights ago. And then I dropped by. I could hear Mucho barking in the back courtyard, but you didn't come to the door."

So you went snooping around behind the patio wall? That explains Mucho's behavior when I was in the hot tub.

"I wanted to pick up the rest of my winter clothes and a few other things that are in the garage."

"Nothing of yours is there anymore. I did some major house cleaning. Try the dump."

Anger flashed in his eyes. "You threw my things away? Damn it, Callahan, you had no right…" He stopped short when an attractive, carefully made up middle-aged woman with spiky blonde hair walked up and stood beside him. She was wearing a jacket identical to his.

Ah, his latest well-heeled widow. Callahan felt a mixture of bitterness and pity.

Brad frowned but quickly recovered. "This is Anita Houghton-Reed. Anita, meet my ex-wife, Callahan O'Connor."

Anita offered an obviously forced smile. "Hello."

Callahan nodded in her direction. "Excuse me," she said, swinging her cart past them. "I'm in a rush." She hurried down the aisle, aware of Brad's eyes on her all the way.

She was in the Jeep, groceries loaded, when Brad tapped on her window. Swearing under her breath, she rolled down the window.

"What do you want?"

"Just to say hi to Mucho. Come over here, boy."

Mucho leaned his head protectively over Callahan's shoulder. Brad reached through the window to give the dog a brief, distracted pat, then shifted his eyes back to Callahan's. "I guess I can't blame you for getting rid of my things." He paused. "And I'm sorry if this upset you. I mean, the three of us running into each other."

She looked beyond him at the blonde, sitting alone in a red Mercedes illegally parked at the curb. "It's a small town," she said. "Unfortunately, that's bound to happen."

"Well, I just wanted to explain. I'm living with Anita now, but that doesn't mean…"

"Try to get this through your narcissistic skull, Brad. You are not part of my life anymore. I don't give a rat's ass *who* you're living with."

He looked a little taken aback, then chuckled. "I've always said you're especially beautiful when you're mad. Those flashing green eyes. " His voice took on that old, familiar, coaxing tone. "I was a fool to let you get away, Callahan. I still love you. I guess I always will. Can't we at least be friends?"

"You must be joking! I don't have to get restraining orders against my *friends*."

"Come on. That bad part's over."

"Go fuck yourself, Brad."

"Let's not argue."

"This *isn't* an argument. This is *adios*." She turned on the ignition, hit the window control, and pulled out of the parking lot.

"That bastard," she yelled and pounded the steering wheel with her fist. Always a smooth talker, ready to say whatever she needed to hear: "*I didn't mean to hurt you. I swear to god, it'll never happen again. You've got to give me another chance, babe. You mean everything to me.*"

Men like Brad should come with warning labels: *Toxic! Call 911 after exposure!*

Callahan felt sick at the memory of how desperately she'd wanted that marriage to work, at all the time she'd wasted smelling the bullshit and calling it roses.

"I'll get prints to you in the next few days," Suzanne said, putting her top-of-the-line digital camera back into its case. "I have to say, these paintings are just stunning. It's a treat to photograph them."

Deathmark

"Thanks. Oh, that reminds me, I got another e-mail from Patrick this morning. He's clamoring for photos for my website."

"He'll have them this afternoon." Suzanne brushed a strand of salt and pepper hair back from her face and gave Callahan a close look. "I wish you would reconsider dinner Saturday night. I think you'd enjoy meeting Paul. He's really a terrific guy. Maybe I've mentioned him before, he's an old college friend of Rob's."

Callahan shook her head, trying to hide her impatience. She was ready for Suzanne to leave so she could get back to work.

"Anyway, Paul's visiting us this weekend. He's been through a really rough time. His wife of almost thirty years died in a car accident two years ago, but he seems to be doing better now, starting to get on with his life. Actually, he's thinking of moving to Santa Fe. Turns out he saw your last exhibit in Chicago and loves your work. It would be a nice, relaxing evening, just the four of us."

"I really appreciate the invitation. But, as you can see, I'm up to my ears right now."

"All the more reason to join us. Remember what Red Feather says about balancing work and play."

"Frankly, Suz, I'm in no mood for a blind date."

"Then don't think of it that way. Just dinner with friends. I thought we'd go to La Casa Sena. Get one of those cozy tables by the fire. Come on, it'll do you good. You've done nothing *but* work for months." She hesitated, shook her head. "Look, we've known each other for a long time, and I feel I've earned the right to be honest. I'm worried about you. You spend too much time alone. It's just not healthy." She put her hands on Callahan's shoulders. "Besides, Rob and I miss you."

"Well, I…"

"No more arguments. Saturday night, seven-thirty."

Callahan sighed. "All right."

Suzanne gave her an enthusiastic hug. "We'll pick you up."

Callahan worked, unaware of the time, throughout the afternoon, finishing *The Last Sunset.* When she was satisfied with it,

137

she took a short break, stretching her shoulders and rubbing her stiff neck. Then she began sketching out a new canvas of two young Native lovers, lying with faces hidden and naked bodies entwined.

Only vaguely aware that night had fallen, she added color and shadows to the painting, until she happened to glance at the clock. Almost eight! Way past time to stop.

Fatigue hit in a wave as Callahan put away her paints. She pulled on her heavy jacket and snow boots, turned out the lights, and locked the studio. Using a flashlight, she followed Mucho along the path toward her house, cautiously avoiding patches of crusted ice. At one point, she almost slipped, but steadied herself by grabbing onto the rough branch of a piñon tree. She paused for a moment, caught her breath, and gazed up at the moon, almost half-full between two clouds in the night sky.

Between that instant and the next, Callahan again lost her balance. This time, the sensation was disorienting, an indescribable shift of reality. She gasped and reached again for the branch as her ears began to ring and the world around her went totally black. She heard the branch snap and felt herself falling...falling...in slow motion. Finally, her knees struck hard against the ground.

She shook her head, trying to clear it, rising slowly to her feet on trembling legs. Looking up at the sky, she stared at the moon in disbelief. It was perfectly round. *A full moon? How is that possible?* She gazed at the sky, a cloudless, black-velvet canopy sparkling with incredibly brilliant stars—more stars than she'd ever seen. *My god! This can't be...*

Her frantic thoughts were cut off by the realization that she was no longer on the path between her house and studio. Instead, she was standing beside a tipi, on the edge of a large encampment. Shock turned to panic as she looked down at her body. Gone were her jacket, sweatpants, and snow boots! She wore a short-sleeved, buckskin dress that hung down to her small, moccasin-covered feet. In that instant, her sense of herself as Callahan O'Connor vanished, along with her fear.

Deathmark

The night breeze was warm and fragrant with the delicious aroma of meat roasting on open fires. Drumbeats echoed through the noisy encampment like thunder before an approaching storm. Her heart pounded in rhythm with the drums. The dances were starting!

Running Wolf ducked through the flap of their tipi and came to stand beside her. He took the traditional stance of a warrior—legs apart, shoulders back and chin held high, arms folded across his chest—silently awaiting her approval. His buckskins and moccasins were freshly stitched, and his tomahawk and favorite knife were fastened around his waist.

The Great Spirit had truly blessed her. She felt a surge of pride to be the bride of such a man—fearless in battle, yet gentle and loving beneath their sleeping robes.

She smiled and nodded at him. "You look good, my husband."

Her tongue spoke true. Earlier, she had tended his battle wound, applying warm poultices of willow bark to the cut an enemy warrior's lance had inflicted high on his right outer thigh.

When he insisted he was well enough to perform his victory dance, she had helped him prepare, taking great care in the grooming of his long, thick hair. First, she smoothed it with a brush made of stiff prairie grass, and then oiled it with warm buffalo fat. She carefully wove his protective amulets—an eagle talon, a string of wolf teeth, and the jawbone of a weasel—into thin braids that hung in front of his ears and framed his face. Finally, two golden eagle tail feathers were positioned and secured in his hair. The effect was most pleasing.

"I wear this shirt, made by my wife, with honor." He took her hand and placed it against the quill-decorated buckskin covering his chest. Her fingers lightly touched the bear claw—long, curved, and deadly sharp—that Running Wolf always wore tied around his neck. He had killed the bear during his fourteenth summer, using only two well-placed arrows. The achievement had marked his coming-of-age as a hunter, and he wore the claw as tribute to the mighty beast.

Running Wolf caressed her cheek. "My heart soars like a hawk to have such a beautiful wife dance my scalps on this night." He reached for his war lance, from which three scalps hung—the black hair long and caked with dried blood—and handed it to her.

She gripped the lance firmly and rose on tiptoes to press her mouth against his. Their tongues touched, and the kiss deepened. She felt him harden beneath his loincloth.

"Your war lance is not the only shaft that wishes to dance tonight," she teased, reaching down to stroke him.

He groaned and pulled her closer. "Would Sun-in-Her-Face have her husband miss his turn in the dance?"

She laughed softly. "Would Running Wolf promise not to spend all of this night stomping around a fire? There are other ways to celebrate his safe return from a raid."

"I give you my promise." He stepped back, attempting to subdue his yearning for her. "But for now, the drums call."

Laughing together, they hurried to the ceremonial grounds. A crowd had already gathered around a huge, blazing fire. Her gaze was drawn to a nearby tipi where spoils of the recent raid were held captive—three young women, an infant, and a small girl child.

The infant's wails rose above the sound of the drums. Pity welled up in her heart. Were the scalps of their husbands, fathers, or brothers decorating her husband's lance this night? She forced her heart to harden by remembering an unfortunate cousin—one of five women stolen by the same enemy during the last Moon of Falling Leaves. There was a long history of bad blood between the two tribes.

Running Wolf touched her arm, indicating she should take her place in line with the other women participating in the scalp dance. She hurried to do so, feeling a fresh wave of pride that the lance held by her friend, Little Squirrel, carried only one fresh scalp. In fact, out of all the proudly assembled spears, only Running Wolf's was adorned with three scalps, the bloody trophies of his valor.

The old medicine man, Night Flyer, held his hand up for silence, and the drumbeats stopped. He was an impressive sight, his face framed by a pair of owl wings tied in his still-thick white hair, and with a silver wolf skin covering his bony shoulders.

After throwing a handful of sacred sage into the fire, Night Flyer offered thanks to the Great Mystery for the successful raid.

"Many enemy horses now graze outside our camp. Many warriors have proven themselves strong of heart. All who left on this

140

Deathmark

war party returned safely to their lodges. Now, we will witness the stories of how this good thing occurred."

Smoke from the fire rose high into the clear, star-filled night and a chorus of cheers greeted her husband, the first and foremost warrior to step into the circular space. The drums started up again, the cadence louder and stronger. Running Wolf let loose a full-throated war whoop and began to dance, reenacting the battle. As he stomped and whirled, he raised his tomahawk high and brought it down on an imaginary foe, again and again. Then, to the cheers of the men and the high-pitched trills of the women, he pulled out his knife and stabbed the air—jabbing left, slashing right—all the time dancing in perfect rhythm to the drums.

She danced in place with the other women, trilling her encouragement and shaking the lance so that the long black hair of the scalps fluttered wildly.

Another warrior joined Running Wolf and began dancing his story. More cheers and trilling. Yet another warrior, unable to contain himself, jumped into the circle, and then another. The drumbeats were louder now. They seemed to come from the earth itself and travel up her legs to match the pounding of her heart. The sound filled her, became her, as she lost herself in the wild movement and magic of the dance.

Then, suddenly, she was falling, spinning weightlessly through a black void, flying through a tear in the shifting fabric of time.

Callahan opened her eyes and found herself lying on the frozen ground.

"Running Wolf!" She screamed his name in a desperate lament. But only Mucho stood beside her. He whined and licked her cheek, then nudged her shoulder with his head. Feeling numb with cold, Callahan pulled herself up and somehow managed to stand on legs that felt too weak to support her.

The moon, glimpsed between clouds that raced across the nighttime sky, was once again less than half full. She stared at it, her heart pounding. After bending to retrieve the flashlight that had rolled several feet ahead of her, she slowly made her way to the house, with Mucho close beside her.

Callahan left her clothes where they fell on the floor and pulled a flannel nightgown over her head. Leaving the bedside lamp on, she climbed into bed, examined her red, already swelling knees, and yanked the comforter up under her chin. Her body was shaking, her teeth chattering—whether from fear, shock or cold, she couldn't tell. Probably all three.

She glanced at the clock on her nightstand. Eight-forty! The short walk from her studio to the house had taken more than thirty minutes. *How could that be?* Her mind reeled as she recalled looking at the moon, relived the feeling of falling, of being sucked into a waking dream in which she was herself, and yet *not* herself. Into a dream she'd had before—the scalp dance, the captive women and children. She'd even painted it. *But this was no dream. This was real. I was actually there!*

I may have fallen, but I didn't hit my head. There would be a bump or a bruise, some evidence.... No, I have to face it. Whatever's wrong with my head wasn't caused by a fall.

Deathmark

15

Callahan opened bleary eyes the next morning and pushed herself up in bed, trying to make sense of what had happened the night before. The more she tried to rationalize the irrational, the more frightened she became.

The phone on her nightstand jarred her out of her thoughts.

"Uh-oh," Donny said. "Sounds like I woke you."

"No... I was awake, just not ready to face the day."

"Sorry for calling so early, honey, but I had to catch you before you got to work. I wanted to sure that you *are* aware tonight is Halloween?"

"Actually, I wasn't. I've...sort of lost track of time.*" To put it mildly!*

"You're not prepared for trick or treaters?"

"You know we never get them out here."

"Well, you may get a couple tonight. I was hoping Curtis and

I could stop by. I know I've mentioned him, he's that great colorist at The Hair Affair."

"Oh, right."

"Darling boy, not the sharpest pencil in the tray, but he does lift my spirits. He's read every one of my books—can you believe that?—and he insists that they're inspired literature. Of course I've never dared ask him what else he's read. I mean, besides *See Spot Run*. Anyway, he's invited me to a Halloween party. I've decided to go as a cowboy vampire, but I'm fresh out of eye shadow and lipstick. May I raid your supply?"

"Of course," she said, making an effort to sound normal. Donny would be over in a flash if he knew how very far from normal she actually felt.

"Fabulous! We'll just pop in for a Halloween drink and a makeover. Would six-thirty work for you?"

"Fine. It'll force me to knock off work at a reasonable hour."

Mucho padded over, yawning, and gave her arm an affectionate lick. She scratched his head as she talked.

"Oops, gotta go, Mucho needs attention."

"Hey, wait…why don't you come to the party with us? You could come as a straight Santa Fe artist."

"Good one! But I'll pass. Thanks, anyway."

"OK, Party Pooper. But feel free to change your mind."

"See you tonight." She hung up the phone and eased out of bed. Every muscle in her body felt sore, and both knees were bruised. She pulled on a clean pair of sweats and wrote Consuela a note saying that she was already at work and would see her at lunchtime. Although she'd eaten almost nothing the day before, the thought of food held no appeal.

Following Mucho up the path, she hesitated as images of the previous night flooded her mind. *Dancing to a pulsing drumbeat beside a roaring fire, trilling high-pitched sounds as she shook Running Wolf's war lance, enemy scalps waving above her head.*

A crow scolding Mucho brought Callahan back to the present. She took a deep breath and continued on to her studio. Inside, she made a pot of coffee, turned on the stereo, and was soon immersed

Deathmark

in both her art and *Songs of the Indian Flute* by John Rainer, Jr. She decided the new painting would be titled *Timeless Love*.

I've been really productive since returning from San Francisco...as though the creative force has been fueled by meeting Luke. Leda would have escorts flown in for me daily, if she ever made that connection!

Callahan walked through the patio door into the freshly cleaned kitchen.

"Consuela?" No answer. "Go find Consuela," she commanded Mucho. He started off at a trot, down the hall. "But be a good boy," she yelled. "No jumping!"

She had just opened the refrigerator when she heard screams from the back of the house. *"Ay! Basta! Basta!* I'll be falling!"

Callahan hurried to the rescue.

Consuela, face flushed, stood on a chair in the back guest room, swinging a broom at Mucho who was running in excited circles around her, dodging blows.

"Mucho!" Callahan shouted. "Stand still!"

He came to a sudden stop, looking puzzled.

"I was cleaning cobwebs from the *vigas*," Consuela explained as Callahan helped her down. *"Que milagro* he didn't knock over the chair. I could have broken my bones! *Perro loco!"* She took a final swat at Mucho, who began running in a wide circle again.

"He thinks it's a game," Callahan explained. "Mucho! Sit!" He obeyed, sitting on the floor with his head cocked expectantly to one side.

Consuela suppressed a giggle. *"Payaso."* She shook her finger at him. "That's what you are, a big, *loco* clown." She turned to Callahan. "Some flowers, very beautiful, came this morning in a delivery truck. I put them in *la sala."*

"Flowers? For me?"

Consuela just grinned.

As she walked out of the room and into the hall, Callahan could hear Consuela talking to herself.

"From a man, I hope. A *good* man; that would be a blessing."

Sitting on the living room coffee table was a gorgeous bouquet of two dozen long-stemmed red roses. Callahan opened the small envelope that was stuck between the blooms and read the card: *You rocked my world, one week ago tonight. Luke.*

"Trick or treat!" Donny burst into the entryway dressed in an ankle-length, black woolen cape, snug black Levis and red, silver-toed cowboy boots. His face and neck were talcum-powdered white. Long fangs protruded from beneath his thin upper lip, and perched on his head was a black Stetson with a rhinestone-studded band. Behind him came a taller, gym-toned young man, similarly white-faced and fanged, wearing a long blond wig, Daisy Duck eyelashes, and blood red lipstick that extended an eighth of an inch beyond his natural lip line. A full-length, faux-leopard coat and white fuzzy snow boots completed his outfit.

Mucho came running, but stopped when Callahan yelled, "Sit!"

"Aren't we the cutest couple since Thelma and Louise?" Donny asked as he whipped off his cape to reveal a white sweatshirt decorated with a picture of a horse. Underneath the horse in bold black letters was the message *SAVE A HORSE—RIDE A COWBOY.*

"My latest cause. You know how I love animals," he said with a wink as he removed the fangs. "Can't talk with these damned things. Could you spare a drink for a gay vampire *caballero* and his lady friend? Oh, excuse me. Cal O'Connor, this is Miss Kitty, also known as Curtis Roybal."

"Hi, Curtis. Excuse me, I mean Miss Kitty."

"Kitty Curtis!" Donny exclaimed triumphantly. "That's it! The perfect name for my new heroine. God, what a relief. I've been wracking my brain all day. Now, with that creative dilemma solved, I can enjoy the evening."

Callahan smiled at her outrageous friend. She tried not to laugh out loud as Curtis removed his coat and snow boots, revealing a red satin off-the-shoulder dress that exposed a hairy chest and the tips of falsies positioned at slightly different angles. The hem stopped just above his knees, exposing unshaven calves.

"Let me get my shoes on…" He took a black stiletto pump from each coat pocket. "…so you can get the full effect." In a moment, he was four inches taller, but struggling to maintain his balance.

"Stunning," Callahan said, with all honesty. Mucho's tail beat the floor in agreement.

Donny and his date followed her into the living room.

"What do you drink, Curtis?"

He removed his fangs and stuck them down the front of his dress, between the falsies. "Uh, rum and coke, if you have it."

Callahan walked to the wet bar and put a bottle of Meyers on the counter, along with a can of coke. "What about you, Donny?"

"Diet tonic, with just a whisper of vodka," he said, fixing Curtis's drink. "I'm driving. What about you?"

"You can pour me a glass of wine. There's a bottle of Pinot Noir open." Callahan carried a bowl of salsa and tortilla chips to the coffee table. "Try some of that, if you dare," she said, when the three of them were seated. "It's Consuela's secret, shock-and-awe recipe. She brought me a pint of it today."

Curtis tentatively dipped the tip of a chip into the salsa and took a nibble. "Yikes!" He fanned himself with his hand. "That's *lethal*. I hope it doesn't grow more hair on my chest."

Mucho, who had positioned himself close to Curtis's high-heeled feet, gave his hairy ankle a loving lick. Curtis screeched, and then reached down to pat Mucho's head.

"We just met, you naughty boy. What kind of girl do you think I am?"

Callahan laughed and then winced, as she crossed one painful knee over the other. She reached for a sofa pillow to place behind her sore back.

Donny frowned. "You okay?"

"Yeah, just a little banged up. I slipped on some ice last night, coming back from the studio."

"You were working after dark? In this weather? Honey, what were you thinking? That's dangerous!"

"I'm okay. Just a little bruised." She avoided his eyes. "Really, it's no big deal." She took a healthy gulp of wine, wishing she believed her own words.

"Well, please be more careful. You owe it to me. Best friends don't grow on piñons." He took a sip of his drink and changed the subject. "My, what beautiful roses!" He reached for the card on the coffee table.

Uh-oh, I meant to put the card and flowers out of sight.

Donny read the message and his expression grew even more worried.

He turned to Curtis. "Would you excuse us for a moment? I must get my makeup on. Just sit here with Mucho and finish your drink." He shot a glance at Curtis's empty glass. "Oh, goodness. You must be thirsty. Well, fix yourself another. Better take off your heels, first, before you trip and break something."

Curtis giggled. "You silly! I've been practicing in these shoes all day." He stood and wobbled toward the wet bar.

Callahan braced herself as they walked down the hallway to her bedroom. She knew that look on Donny's face, his Serious Mother Hen expression.

"Help yourself," she said, flipping on the light in her bathroom. "My makeup is in that drawer on the left."

"I don't like this, Cal," he said. "I mean, a phone call, fine. That's flattering. But two dozen long-stemmed roses? That set him back a pretty penny. And a note saying, 'You rocked my *world*?' What the hell's this guy up to?"

"Why does he have to be 'up to' anything? Maybe he just likes me."

"Of course he likes you." Donny applied a thick swipe of gray eye shadow around his eyes. Then he went to work with an eyebrow pencil. "But seriously, Cal, look at the facts here. He's a working boy. You've got money. And let's face it, honey, you've got quite a few years on him."

"I'm well aware of that," she said in a flat voice.

He covered his lips with a smear of red lipstick, and then turned to her.

148

"I hate to burst your bubble, sweetheart. God knows, you deserve a little fun, and I support that one hundred percent. Just keep your eyes wide open, that's all I'm saying. There are plenty of opportunists out there...looking to prey on vulnerable people, especially single women."

"Who says I'm vulnerable?"

Donny raised one of his just-darkened eyebrows at her.

"Well, okay, I suppose I am. But I'm not stupid. And I'm telling you, Luke's not like that."

"How do you know what he's like? He's a professional, and you only saw a side of him that he wanted you to see. Just be careful, that's all I'm saying. Bastardly Bradley kicked your ego around the corral, repeatedly, before you finally gave him the boot. That would take its toll on any girl."

She gave a short nod, fighting back sudden, unexpected tears.

"I'm sorry." Donny put his arms around her. "I didn't mean to upset you. I love you and would fight tigers for you—well, small ones, anyway."

She nodded again. "I know you would. I love you, too."

"Okay." Donny gave her a quick hug. "Now, let's go check on Miss Kitty. She's probably face down in the salsa by now."

Callahan cleared the coffee table after Donny and Curtis left.

"Sorry, baby," she said to Mucho, who'd been eyeing the leftover chips.

She sat back on the sofa, staring at the roses. Donny's words made sense, and the rational part of her brain had to agree with him. But the connection she felt to Luke went beyond anything she could logically explain. *Red Feather insists that everything happens for a reason. If that's true, meeting Luke was no accident. I have to see where all of this is leading, no matter how it might look to anyone else.*

She bent toward the roses, inhaling their fragrance. Then, shadowed by Mucho, she carried the vase into her bedroom and placed it on her dresser. With a loud sigh, Mucho collapsed on his sheepskin bed and closed his eyes. Seconds later, he was snoring.

Callahan sat on her bed, reread the card from Luke. A few minutes later she decided to give him a call and, after several rings, heard his taped voice.

"Leave a message. I'll get back to you."

"Hi, it's Callahan. Thank you for the beautiful roses. It was a special surprise. I'll look forward to talking to you soon."

She hit the off button and replaced the phone on its charger. She undressed, easing her Levis over the extra-large band-aids on both knees, and put on her flannel nightgown, warm robe, and slippers. Although she tried to walk quietly past Mucho, he awoke in mid-snore, yawned, and scrambled up to follow her down the hall and back into the living room.

"You are absolutely the world's best watch dog." She kissed him on the head and poured herself another glass of wine. She gave Mucho a doggie biscuit and the two of them went into her study. She checked her computer, scrolling through a long list of e-mails—two more from Leda, one from the Dallas gallery, several from neglected friends, and the usual junk-mail offers to enlarge her penis, grow her hair and nails longer and increase her libido with an exotic miracle juice. *Don't need any of that.* She jabbed the delete button repeatedly, took a sip of her wine and settled into answering her important messages.

The dance floor of Rocca Pulco was crowded, and the music was hot.

"Where did you learn to dance like this?" asked Linda Morelli, one of Luke's semi-regular clients. She clung to him awkwardly, having just completed a double spin. Then she gave a husky little laugh and touched her tongue to his ear. "One of your many talents, hmmm? Much as I enjoy your vertical moves, I think it's time for some horizontal action. Let's go back to the hotel."

"Whatever you want." *You're the one calling the shots, lady.*

She made a purring sound. "You always know *exactly* what I want."

Deathmark

Callahan turned off the computer and settled into her comfortable office chair with a stack of magazines. She flipped through the latest *Newsweek* and *National Geographic* with no real interest, realizing she was doing her best to distract herself from thinking about the night before. But unable to banish Luke from her thoughts, she kept glancing at the phone, willing it to ring.

Finally, she tossed the magazines in a box to be recycled, and headed back to her bedroom, Mucho at her heels. A hot soak would no doubt relax her tense, sore muscles. As the bathtub filled, she stripped, and stood critically before the full-length mirror, studying her figure as she would one of her paintings.

Her full breasts hung lower than they used to, no doubt about that. And her thighs could definitely use some toning. If she put a treadmill in her studio, she could take exercise breaks during the day. She touched the thin white lines on her belly, stretch marks from her pregnancy with Patrick. *Oh, hell, who am I kidding? I have stretch marks as old as Luke.*

"Hey, hot stuff." Linda Morelli's voice was post-coital husky as she snuggled closer to Luke. "You aren't asleep, are you? Come on, wake up." When he didn't answer, she continued. "That was great, but my engine is still running." She made a deep-throated growling sound. "How about another spin around the track?"

Luke kept his eyes closed and gritted his teeth, fighting an urge to push her away. *Christ! She's insatiable—been in overdrive all night. What the hell is she on?* He grunted and opened his eyes as she elbowed him hard in the ribs.

Linda's badly smeared eye makeup made her resemble a demented raccoon.

"Hi," she purred. "Nice to have your attention again. Come on, baby. I'm leaving the country in the morning." She snuggled under his arm and ran her tongue inside his armpit.

Luke forced a small, practiced smile as she stroked his flaccid penis and pressed a wet kiss on his lips. Her breath was stale from booze and cigarettes.

"I've got you for the whole night, let's make the most of it. I can sleep tomorrow on the plane."

Horny bitch. I have an eight o'clock class.

"Hey, I know," she said, releasing his unresponsive penis. "Let's have more Champagne. There's still another bottle iced in the bathroom sink."

"Your wish is my command." *Maybe it'll knock her out and I can get a little sleep.* He got out of bed and walked into the bathroom. Squinting in the harsh light, the man he saw in the mirror looked rough and desperate. *I don't know how much longer I can do this. Something in me is unraveling...*

"Hey, hot stuff!" Linda's called. "What's keeping you? Forget the Champagne just get yourself back to bed."

For another moment Luke remained transfixed by his reflection.

Callahan pinned up her hair, added a liberal splash of perfumed bath oil, and lowered herself into the tub. *So Luke's younger...so what? No one thinks a thing about a fifty-year-old man involved with a woman half his age. Edwin was old enough to be my father. And Donny, for all his concern, is dating Curtis, who can't be a day over thirty. How did Red Feather put it? "When two souls are connected, it's like a spark jumping between two wires. The age you happen to be when you meet doesn't matter."*

She sank deeper into the soothing hot water. *Maybe nothing else matters.*

Feeling considerably better by the time she got out of the tub, Callahan headed straight to bed. Within moments, she fell into a deep, oblivious sleep.

Oh, Jesus! Luke frantically collected his clothes from the floor and pulled them on. The voice in his head was screaming. *Get out of here! Get out of here!*

Deathmark

He started for the door and then stopped, staring at a black leather briefcase lying on the blood-splattered hotel bed. He hesitated for a second, and then grabbed it and bolted out the door. Not daring to wait for the elevator, he ran to the exit and down five flights of stairs.

16

The next day, Callahan got an early start and went right to work, putting finishing touches on *Timeless Lovers*. She had another image in her head that she was eager to get started on—a warrior on horseback, his face obscured as he leaned forward to speak into his pony's ear. Visual impressions were coming to her faster than she could get them down.

She had to force herself to take a break around noon. The phone rang as she was fixing a salad.

"Hi, Callahan, it's Leda. I need more canvases! *Sacred Ritual* just sold to a couple from Sonoma. You are *hot*, girl!"

"That's very good to hear. I shipped two paintings to you yesterday, you should get them on Monday."

"Any chance I could have a few more? I mean, like soon? My gallery in Tucson is running low, too."

Callahan hesitated. She'd promised two pieces to Santa Fe

Deathmark

Visions, and the manager of a gallery that represented her in Chicago had left a message two days ago, saying they needed more.

"I'll do my best. I'm working seven days a week right now."

"Ah, the price of success. I know it doesn't leave much time for fun."

"Painting *is* fun to me."

"You know the kind of fun I mean. That reminds me, I saw your boy toy last night."

Callahan slumped against the counter. "Who?"

"Don't be coy, darling. You know who. Tall, dark, and gorgeous from the escort agency."

She tried to sound nonchalant. "Oh, Luke... Where did you see him?"

"At Aqua, a four-star restaurant on California Street. He was having dinner with a bleached blonde who was getting her money's worth. She couldn't keep her hands off him."

Callahan felt like hanging up. But, as usual, there was no stopping Leda.

"He really is quite a hunk. I'm definitely going to request him for myself one of these days. I usually ask for Antonio, who is unbelievably..."

"Leda," she cut in, "you'll have to excuse me. I'm in the middle of something."

"Okay. I'll be expecting more canvases ASAP. Keep cranking them out!"

Cranking them out? Like I'm some sort of machine? Insensitive, greedy bitch. Callahan took a deep breath.

"Will do. Goodbye." *So that's where Luke was last night. With a paying blonde.* She felt irritated with herself for letting it bother her. After all, she knew what Luke did for a living. She'd certainly known *that* from the start.

Her appetite gone, she nibbled at the salad. *At least I'm losing weight.* She gave up and shoved most of it back into the refrigerator. Wishing she hadn't let Suzanne talk her into dinner tonight, she hurried out of the house and back up the path to her studio.

Luke gazed from his hotel window, looking with unfocused eyes at the bumper-to-bumper traffic on the Las Vegas Strip. *Shit. Everything is fucked now. Forget a career in law. The only way I'll ever be in a court room now is wearing handcuffs...if I'm lucky enough to survive that long.*

He pulled the drapes closed and sat on the bed, his head in his hands. *What now? Where can I hide? I'm fucked. Just fucked...*

A visage formed in his mind—green, searching eyes and tousled red hair—and the muscles in his shoulders relaxed a little. *Callahan...*

The doorbell rang at seven thirty-five.

"Sit," Callahan warned Mucho as he charged down the hall. "Stay right there."

Suzanne, elegant in a black velvet tiered skirt, matching tunic and a stunning silver concho belt, swept into the entryway.

"Hi," she said, giving Callahan a hug.

Right behind Suzanne was her husband, Rob, a nuclear physicist who'd recently retired from nearby Los Alamos National Laboratories.

He kissed Callahan's cheek. "Delighted you could join us."

"And this is Paul Kramer."

Suzanne grabbed the arm of a tall, amiable-looking man standing behind Rob. He stepped forward with a reserved smile. Callahan thought he vaguely resembled the middle-aged Jimmy Stewart.

"Paul and Rob were fraternity brothers at Stanford."

"Nice to meet you, Callahan," Paul said. "I'm a big fan of your work." He walked over to Mucho, who studied him for a moment and then licked his hand. "Hi, big fellow. What's your name?"

"Mucho," Suzanne answered. "Appropriate, isn't it?"

"I had a Great Dane when I was a boy," Paul said. "They're terrific dogs. Intelligent and very protective."

Deathmark

Rrrrumph, Mucho said, in solemn agreement.

Paul grinned. "How old is he?"

"Almost three." Callahan had a sudden flash of Mucho as a big-footed, gangly puppy with a red bow tied around his neck. He was her gift from Brad, the first Christmas they were married. She remembered sitting beneath the tree, cuddling him like an over-sized baby. "I love you," she'd said. "I love you, mucho." And so he was named. She had to hand it to Brad; Mucho was a perfect gift—the only good thing to come from that marriage.

Suzanne's voice broke into her thoughts. "We'd better get going. We have eight o'clock reservations."

The atmosphere at La Casa Sena, originally a seventeenth-century family compound built around a charming Plaza, was one of understated Southwestern elegance. A fire burned in the main dining room and candles cast a romantic glow from the tables. It was one of Callahan's favorite restaurants. She and Brad had gone there fairly often for dinner. She nervously glanced around as the *maitre d'* escorted them to their table. The last thing she wanted was to run into her ex-husband.

Paul pulled a chair out for her then sat next to her. During the drive into town, he had seemed polite but a bit withdrawn, saying little. Suzanne had mentioned that he took his wife's death very hard. Callahan's heart went out to him. *He's nice. There's something refreshingly old fashioned and courtly about him.*

"Is this your first visit to Santa Fe?" she asked.

"No. We—Alice, my late wife, and I—used to come here every chance we got. Especially in the summer. She loved the opera."

Callahan could see the grief in his eyes.

"I understand that you're an architect. I've always thought that would be fascinating work."

"It is. Of course, I had illusions of being an artist when I was young. Then, in college, I decided I'd better channel those impulses into something practical." He suddenly looked embarrassed. "I didn't mean that artists are impractical. I just…"

157

Callahan smiled as his voice trailed off. "You're right. Any of the arts can be a rough way to make a living. I've been fortunate, especially in recent years."

"I was in Santa Fe Visions today, and one of your paintings in particular really touched me. It's the figure of an Indian woman, reaching toward a man's outstretched hand."

"*Commitment.* It's one of my favorites, too."

"Good evening," a dark-haired, good-looking, thirty-ish waiter interrupted. "May I start you off with something to drink?"

Callahan found herself watching the waiter as he took their orders. Something about his confident smile reminded her of Luke, and she realized how disappointed she was that he hadn't returned her call. *Maybe he's still with that bleached blonde.* Her stomach tensed at the thought.

"Callahan?" Suzanne was staring at her.

"I'm sorry, were you talking to me?"

"I was just saying that Paul might be moving to Santa Fe."

"We're trying to talk him into it," Rob added.

"Well, I'm retiring," Paul said. "I think I need a change of scene from the Midwest. My daughter and her family live in Albuquerque, and it would be nice to be close to them. I could do some freelance work here, maybe even try my hand at painting again." He smiled at Callahan. "I've been practical long enough."

She returned his smile. When the handsome waiter reappeared, bringing wine and appetizers, Callahan tried not to look at him.

"I plan to be back in a couple of weeks," Paul said, walking her to her front door. "I'd really like to see you again."

"That would be nice," Callahan said, reaching into her purse for her key. "But I have to warn you, I'm not very social." She could hear Mucho barking behind the front door. "It was a lovely evening." She held out her hand.

Paul clasped it. "It was a real treat for me. I'll be hoping to catch you in a social mood one day soon."

Callahan gave him a quick smile and withdrew her hand.

Deathmark

"Goodnight."

She unlocked the door, slipped inside, and quickly disarmed and reset the alarm system. Mucho greeted her as though she'd been gone for days rather than a couple of hours.

"You're my guy, aren't you?" She rubbed her cheek against his. "The one I can always count on."

She walked into her study and checked her voicemail. No messages. *Luke must be having a great time.* She took the San Francisco newspaper clipping from her bulletin board and spent a moment staring at the photo. Just looking at Luke's face brought back all the emotions he had awakened in her—the intense soul connection, knee-buckling passion, and a truckload of confusion. *The reincarnation of Running Wolf? Or am I just caught up in a crazy fantasy, trying to justify a case of middle-aged lust?* She was still debating the question when she climbed into bed and turned off the light.

The air was filled with dust and triumphant shouts. She knelt in the grass, her hands and lower arms covered with warm, sticky blood. The strong scent of it filled her nostrils as she slashed her knife through the tough hide of the freshly killed buffalo.

"We must work fast," she said to Dancing Bird, beside her. "The Great Spirit has smiled on this hunt. Many buffalo brothers have given their lives. We will have meat enough to dry and last through the winter."

She swatted at a camp dog that had sneaked up to lick the blood from her arm.

"Get back! There will be plenty of bones for you to gnaw, greedy little one. But first there is work to be done."

Expertly pulling the hide back to expose the meat underneath, she began to butcher the large bull, first hacking off the fat-filled hump, the most succulent part.

"Did you see Running Wolf kill this one with only one well placed thrust of his lance?" she asked Dancing Bird, who had forced open the beast's mouth and was slicing out its tongue.

"Your husband is a fearless hunter." Her sister hesitated

before speaking again. "Some say he is too fearless for his own good."

She frowned, annoyed to hear Dancing Bird voice her own secret fear. Running Wolf's bravery did lean toward recklessness. Watching the hunt from the safety of a nearby hill with the elders, children, and other women, she had hidden her eyes when he rode in so close to those dangerous horns.

"Some say that bravery should be balanced with caution and a cool head," Dancing Bird continued, placing the severed tongue in a large, leather basket. "A man with courage can be called Naicinji, *a defender of the People. But one who lacks good judgment brings danger upon himself and others. Such a one dances with death."*

"*...dances with death... dances with death..."* Callahan moaned, rolled over, but continued sleeping. It was just after dawn when she jolted out of the familiar dream of Running Wolf's body being brought back to camp. But this time, the body had *Luke's* face! Fear flashed through her. She sat up in bed, shivering and hugging herself. *Luke... Oh, dear god, has something happened to Luke?*

Deathmark

17

Concern for Luke still weighed heavily on her mind as she hurried to her studio later that morning. She needed to be reassured that he was all right. If he didn't call by tonight, she'd try his number again.

Throwing herself into her work, Callahan pushed her worry aside and lost track of time until a hunger-induced headache reminded her that she needed a break. She set paint brushes to soak in a can of water and followed Mucho back to the house for something to eat. After a quick sandwich, she checked her phone messages. Still nothing from Luke. She gave Suzanne a call to thank her for dinner.

"So, what did you think of Paul?" Suzanne asked, obviously settling in for a long chat.

"I liked him. It was an enjoyable evening."

"It was, but you seemed a little preoccupied. Are you sure you're okay?"

"I'm working hard… and have a lot on my mind these days. Sorry if it showed."

"I'm sure no one noticed but me. You're certain you're all right? Brad isn't causing any trouble, is he? I heard through the grapevine that he's hitting the bottle hard these days."

"Nothing new there. Don't worry. I'm staying clear of him."

"Good idea. So… Paul left for the airport early this morning, but he'll be back before long. I think he's serious about moving here; there's a great property north of town that he's considering. Sweetie, I hope you don't mind, but I gave him your phone number."

Callahan felt a stab of annoyance. There was a reason she had an unlisted number. She expected her friends to respect that.

"Suzanne, Paul seems to be a very nice man, but…"

"He's more than *nice*. He's intelligent, reliable, and lots of fun, when you get to know him."

"I'm sure he is all those things. It's just that I'm not ready."

"I know, I know. And Paul isn't the type to push. He's hesitant himself about venturing out socially. But he liked you, I could tell. I'm sure you'll be hearing from him."

"Well, I've got to get back to my studio…" Callahan was eager to end the conversation. "Thanks again for the night out."

At seven that evening she dialed Luke's number. After several rings, she heard his taped voice. Should she leave another message?

"Hi," she found herself saying. "It's Callahan, again. My roses are still beautiful. I'd like to talk to you. Please call when you have a chance."

She undressed and settled into bed with the latest Michael McGarrity novel, one she'd been looking forward to reading. The fast-paced story distracted her, but not enough to prevent her checking the clock at regular intervals. By ten-thirty, she decided Luke probably wasn't going to call. She put the book aside, snapped off the light, and stared into the darkness.

What's the matter with me? Why do I feel so damned anxious? Her thoughts turned to their last telephone conversation, when Luke

Deathmark

described a drive-by shooting outside his apartment building. It was obviously a dangerous neighborhood. Red Feather's voice echoed in her head. *"My spirit allies sense danger around him..."*

Callahan rolled over and closed her eyes. But sleep refused to come. After more than an hour of tossing and turning, she looked at the clock. Midnight. An hour earlier in California. Before she could stop herself, she dialed Luke's number again. When it went to voicemail, she hung up. *Where is he? Why isn't he answering—or returning my calls?* Suddenly, it was as though the emotions she was feeling weren't hers alone. Someone else—young, frightened, desperately in love—had invaded her consciousness. *Please, let him be safe. I couldn't bear losing him again.*

Panic gripped her. "What the hell? I can't let this happen!" she said out loud. "I can't lose myself! I'm Callahan, Callahan O'Connor, *not* Sun-in-Her-Face!"

The next couple of days passed in a fog of work and worry. Callahan tried repeatedly to reach Luke, hanging up when she got his voicemail. There was no doubt in her mind now, something was wrong. She decided she would call Dream Dates. They would know if he was all right. She got the number from information and punched it in.

"Dream Dates," a smooth, masculine voice answered. "How can we make your dreams come true?"

Callahan almost dropped the phone. Luke *had* made her dreams come true!

"I...I'd like to make an appointment with Luke Bennett."

"I'm sorry. He isn't available, right now. But we have other..."

"Is Luke still working for you?"

There was a slight pause. "I can only say that he's unavailable."

"Is he all right?"

"I'm sorry, ma'am, I didn't get your name. Are you a client?"

Realizing that she was getting nowhere, Callahan hung up, more alarmed than ever.

Late the following afternoon, Donny knocked on the studio door.

"Sorry to burst in on you, but I got worried. It's not like you to ignore your best buddy's phone calls."

"Oh, Donny, I'm sorry. I've just been working like a madwoman." *And feeling like one, too.*

"I can see that. Frankly, honey, you have serious shadows under your eyes. Doesn't she, Mucho?"

Mucho cocked his head and whined.

"Okay." Donny took Callahan's arm and led her to the sofa. "Sit. Yes, you, too, Mucho. Everybody sit. Now, tell Uncle Donny. What's *really* going on?"

She sighed. "I'm way behind in my work schedule. Leda is pushing me to the limit, the Dallas gallery wants more paintings…"

He cut her off. "No girlfriend, it's more than that. I've seen you overworked before, many times. I mean it, I'm not leaving until you come clean. I'll borrow one of your nighties and sleep over, if necessary. Do you have anything in lavender silk? You know lavender is my favorite color—part pink and part blue."

As always, Donny could tease a smile out of her.

"Would white flannel work?"

"No way. I'm too old to pass for a virgin." He paused for a moment. "It's the escort, isn't it?" When she didn't answer, he moved closer and draped an arm around her shoulder. "Honey, don't even try to put on an act with me. I know lovesick when I see it."

Callahan's eyes welled with tears.

"Has he been calling?"

"Not for almost a week."

"Ah," Donny said. "Sweetheart, you have to understand how it is with guys like him. Sweet-talk and sex are just tools of the trade."

"No. You don't understand." She pulled away and stood up.

"What don't I understand?"

"I'm *worried* about Luke. I have this terrible feeling that something has happened to him."

"Why? Because he stopped calling you?"

"Yes. He hasn't answered my calls and…"

"*You've* been calling *him*? Oh, mercy. This is worse than I thought. Break out the white flannel, this feels like an all-nighter. For starters, let's close up shop here. It's almost five o'clock, quitting time in the civilized world." He stood. "We'll go back to the house and get you cleaned up. I can't take you out all speckled with paint."

"Take me out where?"

"To Maria's—voted Best Margaritas in Santa Fe for the past twenty years! Trust me, Margaritas are an ancient remedy for affairs of the heart, brought to this area by the conquistadors. We'll order blue corn chicken enchiladas with guacamole and gobs of sour cream. And we won't worry about the calories, because tequila dissolves them." He held up his right hand. "The truth—told to me years ago by a sinfully svelte bull fighter in Mexico City. So, let's get a move on! I'll help you tidy up."

Donny stopped, staring across the room at the still-unfinished portrait of Running Wolf that leaned against a wall.

"Wow. That's a show-stopper." He walked closer. "Are you taking your work in a new direction?"

"Not necessarily…" Callahan tightened the lids on several jars of acrylic. "It's just a face that…broke through."

"Impressive. You didn't use a model?"

"You know I never do."

"Too bad. I would have loved to meet him."

The phone was ringing as they walked into the kitchen. Although she'd almost given up hope that it might be Luke, she rushed to get it.

"Callahan?"

Her knees went weak with relief.

"Luke. I'm so glad to hear your voice."

"That's good, because I'm calling to invite you to dinner."

"Dinner? Where are you?"

"In Albuquerque and just about to head towards Santa Fe.

How far is it? It looks like maybe fifty miles on this map I picked up."

She felt dazed. "It's closer to seventy. Tesuque is on the north side of Santa Fe. I can't believe you're here." Out of the corner of her eye, she saw Donny roll his eyes and sag into a kitchen chair. He sat there, shaking his head.

"It was a sudden decision. Is it all right? I mean, are you free for dinner?"

"Yes. I'm free." She shot an apologetic look at Donny.

"Make reservations somewhere special."

After giving him directions to her house, Callahan hung up the phone.

"I take it you got a better offer for dinner?" Donny said.

"I'm sorry. But Luke's here—or he will be soon. He was calling from Albuquerque."

"So I gathered," he said dryly. "Just a little surprise visit? A quick in and out sort of thing? The pun is intended."

"You do understand? About dinner, I mean."

"Of course, I understand. Only too well, I'm afraid. I've gone head-over-hunk myself a time or two." He started toward the door and then turned back. "Have a nice evening, girlfriend. But keep your head screwed on where this guy is concerned. Please. I've said it before, and I'm saying it again. I think you're playing with fire here."

"Donny, give me some credit. I'm a big girl."

"And big girls can't get burned? You should know better. Just don't let it happen again."

Deathmark

18

Callahan hurried into her bathroom and turned on the shower. Standing under the spray of hot water, she tried to collect her thoughts. She'd been wrong. Luke was fine, apparently. But she couldn't ignore the apprehension that lay beneath her relief and excitement. What was he doing here in the middle of the week? He must be missing classes. More to the point, how was she going to handle seeing him again?

After quick deliberation, she dressed in a denim dress and cowboy boots. She blew her hair dry and then peered into the magnifying mirror on her dressing table. *Donny's right. I look like I've been ridden hard and put away wet.* As she smoothed makeup on the dark circles under her eyes she noticed that her hands were shaking.

Mucho, not understanding her excitement, but sharing it nonetheless, paced between the bathroom and bedroom, *rrrrumphing* nervously.

"Okay," she said out loud, stepping away from the mirror. "That's it. I'm presentable." *And nervous as a teenager dressing for the prom*!

She carried Luke's wilting roses back into the living room and placed them on a corner table. Then she called The Pink Adobe and made dinner reservations, asking for a secluded table near a fireplace. Within moments, she saw a flash of headlights in the driveway and heard Mucho bolting down the hallway, barking all the way.

Callahan grabbed his collar, and opened the door. And there stood Luke, dressed casually in a beige sweater and slacks, smiling and looking even more handsome than she remembered.

"Hello, Callahan."

She took a deep breath. "Hello, yourself."

At that moment, Mucho lunged forward, straining for a sniff.

"Sit," she ordered without taking her eyes from Luke and was relieved when Mucho obeyed.

"He's friendly, just enthusiastic. Come in."

Luke stepped into the entryway and, without another word, took her into his arms and lowered his mouth to hers in a gentle kiss that quickly grew more intense.

Callahan's physical response to him was as natural and strong as ever, maybe stronger. She felt lost in him—the smell of him, his taste, his familiar touch.

Mucho whined and then let out his pay-attention-to-me bark. They released the kiss and stood with their arms around each other.

"Is he jealous?" Luke asked. "I wouldn't blame him a bit."

"He's just waiting to be introduced. Luke," she said formally, "this is Mucho, my housemate and the best doggie in the world. Mucho, this is Luke."

Luke bravely knelt until he was face-to-face with Mucho. He was rewarded by a chin-to-cheek lick.

"Hey, that's the second best kiss I've had all day."

"You should feel honored," Callahan said, surprised by Mucho's ready acceptance of Luke. "Great Danes aren't overly expressive with strangers."

"He must sense that I'm no stranger." Luke rubbed Mucho's

head, and then stood to look around. "Wow. This is quite a place. A true hideaway, where no one could ever find you."

She looked at him closely. His face had a strained look—tension around his eyes that hadn't been there when she'd last seen him in San Francisco.

"You must be tired from your trip. Can I get you something to drink?"

"Scotch if you have it. On the rocks."

Callahan nodded, a little surprised. *Hadn't he said in San Francisco that he wasn't much of a drinker?* Following her into the living room, he stood staring out at the lighted patio while she poured his drink, along with a glass of wine for herself.

"To our reunion." He clinked his glass to hers and took a healthy swallow of Scotch. "I apologize for not giving you more warning. This trip was a sudden decision."

"No need to apologize. I'm really glad to see you. I left a couple of messages on your voicemail, thanking you for the roses. As you can see, they're a little wilted, but still beautiful." She sat on the couch and Luke joined her, sitting sideways to face her. He glanced at the roses and sipped his drink.

"To tell the truth, I was concerned when you didn't answer my calls. I was afraid something bad might have happened." She paused. "I mean, after what you told me about your neighborhood."

"Yeah, well… I lost my cell phone… somewhere." He fixed her with a questioning look. "You were concerned? It's nice to know someone cares." He put his drink down, leaned in and gave her another kiss, his tongue soft and tasting of Scotch. The kiss deepened, and she found herself responding with a mindless passion as his hand moved up her leg, under her skirt. He pressed her back until she was lying under him on the sofa.

At that moment, Mucho sprang into action. With a sound that was half-whine and half-growl, he threw his upper body on Luke's, pinning him, along with Callahan, to the sofa. Luke drew in a quick, alarmed breath.

She had to laugh. "Mucho! Get off! Off."

Mucho hesitated. Then, with a confused and still-worried half-growl, he dropped to the floor. He pushed his face against Callahan's, giving her cheek a possessive lick.

Luke sat up. "I'm sorry, but this three-way isn't going to work."

"I told you I was well protected." Callahan gave Mucho's head a reassuring pat and pushed herself up. "Come on, sweetie. You're going outside for awhile."

She put Mucho in the courtyard and returned to sit by Luke, not sure if she was disappointed or relieved that the mood had been broken.

"Should I bring my bags in from the car? What I mean is... would it be all right if I spend the night?"

Callahan hadn't thought that far ahead.

He saw her hesitation and said, "If it's an imposition, I can find a motel."

She quickly made up her mind. "No. Stay here. As you see, I have plenty of room."

He smiled, reached out and gently stroked the side of her cheek.

Callahan's breath caught. "Why do you do that?"

"What?"

"Touch my cheek like that."

"I don't know. It just seems like a natural thing to do. You don't like it?"

"I do. I like it very much."

He gave her a quick kiss and rose to his feet.

"I'll get my things out of the car." He went out the front door and returned moments later carrying a large, well-used suitcase and a beautiful ostrich-skin briefcase. "Where should I put these?"

"Follow me."

As they moved down the hall, Luke paused to stare at her collection of American Indian artifacts hanging on a wall.

"Is that a real Indian spear?" He put down his suitcase and touched the six-foot-long wooden shaft.

"Yes. It dates back to the early seventeen-hundreds. I bought it at a Native American antique show several years ago, along with that buffalo hide shield and Lakota war club."

"This is an arsenal. That spear point looks wicked."

Deathmark

"It was chipped out of obsidian, sharp as a razor. I was told it was actually used in battle. See those marks cut into the shaft? There are twelve of them. According to the dealer, each one represents an enemy killed in battle."

"Like notches on a gun handle. Stuff like this fascinates me. It must stir my Indian blood."

Callahan shot him a startled look, before realizing what he meant. *His Cherokee grandmother... Of course.*

He lingered, staring at the artifacts for several more seconds, before following her down the hall.

"You can put your things in here," she said, showing him into a guest room.

He set his suitcase and briefcase on the floor by the bed.

"That door leads to a bathroom." Out of the corner of her eye, Callahan saw him push the briefcase under the bed with his foot. The gesture struck her as odd, but she dismissed it. *Probably just a habit from living in a dangerous neighborhood.*

"Where's your room?" he asked.

"There, across the hall."

He stepped inside her room and looked around. "Very nice. This is the room I want to spend time in." Taking her in his arms, he planted warm, wet kisses along the side of her neck. Then he started moving her toward the bed.

Don't fight it, you know it's what you want.

"But, what about dinner?" she heard herself asking. "Aren't you hungry?"

"Starved, but not for food."

An hour and a half later, they arrived at The Pink Adobe. Luckily, it was a slow night, and they were able to be seated immediately. The atmosphere was romantic, with a candle flickering on the table and a fire burning in the nearby fireplace. Luke leaned back in his chair.

"I can see why you like living here. Santa Fe has such an Old World feeling to it, almost like another country."

"My parents brought me here for Fiesta when I was thirteen years old," she said. "I loved it. I can remember standing in the Plaza and thinking that someday I might live here."

His smile looked a little sad. "It must be nice to feel at home somewhere."

She couldn't avoid the question any longer. "What made you decide to make this trip?"

"Things got a little… crazy. I needed a change of scene. And I wanted to see *you*. So I flew to Albuquerque, took a cab to a used car lot and bought some wheels."

"You bought the Nissan you're driving? I assumed you'd rented it."

He shrugged. "I needed something to get around in."

"So you'll be driving it back to San Francisco?"

"I'm not sure what my plans are. Like I said, I need a change of scene."

"What about law school?"

"I dropped out."

"Just like that?"

"Just like that."

"But why? You're in your last year, so close to…"

"I told you I was having second thoughts about practicing law." He clenched his jaw and she saw a muscle twitch. He took a deep breath, reached for her hand and gave it a squeeze. "Look, I'd rather not talk about it tonight."

His eyes held hers with such startling intensity it took a moment to find her voice.

"Okay."

Another squeeze to her hand and he picked up his menu. "This all looks good. What do you recommend?"

After dinner, they walked arm-in-arm toward the Plaza. Callahan pointed out landmarks—La Fonda, the historic hotel at the end of the Santa Fe Trail where Billy the Kid supposedly once washed dishes, and the Palace of the Governors, the oldest government building in the United States. Luke seemed eager to take it all in. After looking in the shops and art gallery windows that surrounded the Plaza, they sat on a bench and he pulled her close.

"You're cold. Let's go home and build a fire...in the bedroom fireplace."

Home? Callahan couldn't ignore the warning bells that went off in her head, but she did her best to rationalize them away. *Just a figure of speech.*

He rose and pulled her up with him. They made their way in an unspoken urgency back to Luke's car. He opened the door for her and as she settled into the passenger side, Callahan noted the soft, leather seats and loaded music system. *It may be used, but this car wasn't cheap. I guess escorting pays better than I thought.*

"You can park in the garage," she said, as they pulled into the driveway fifteen minutes later. "There's plenty of room." She gave him the code for the outside garage-door control. After punching it in, he parked his car beside hers. The heavy door rolled down, securing them inside with a final-sounding thud.

Sometime during the night, Callahan awoke with a start. The fire in the hearth had burned down to glowing embers. She sat up in bed and stared at Luke, sleeping soundly on his back beside her. He moaned softly and muttered something in his sleep. Again, she marveled at how natural it felt being with him. Her body responded to his as though they'd always been lovers. She touched the birthmarks on his chest with her fingertips. *Beloved. Soul of my soul.* The voice in her head was just a whisper.

She slid back under the covers, close to him. Softly, so as not to wake him, she pressed her lips against his shoulder. How long did he plan to stay? She realized that she hadn't asked. She sighed and closed her eyes. Just as sleep claimed her, the voice whispered: *We're together again. That's all that matters.*

19

The doorbell rang at nine o'clock the next morning. Mucho galloped down the hall, barking. *Damn!* Callahan finished brushing her teeth and followed after him. From the entry window she saw Donny's BMW parked in the driveway. *Oh, great. Just great.*

"Goodness," Donny said, sidestepping Mucho's welcoming lunge when she opened the door. "You're still in your robe. It must have been a late night. Hello, poocho. Yes, yes. I'm glad to see you, too." He returned his attention to Callahan. "Forgive my just popping in, I'll only stay a minute. I'm on my way to the gym to work out—got an appointment with a new trainer, a blond Adonis with abs you would *not* believe—and I just couldn't stand it. I had to stop by and see how it went last night."

"It went...fine."

"Well, are you going to let me in?"

174

"Oh. Sure. I was just about to make some coffee."

He talked his way into the kitchen.

"I'd love a quick cup. And, of course, all the details. Where did you and lover boy go for dinner?"

Callahan put her index finger to her lips. "He's asleep. Or at least he was. Mucho's barking probably woke him."

"Well, silly me. When I didn't see a car in the driveway, I just assumed he had a hotel room."

"His car's in the garage."

"I see." Donny perched on a stool at the counter. "It obviously *was* a good night. So tell me. How long is he going to… " Donny's voice trailed off as his gaze shifted over Callahan's shoulder.

She turned to see Luke standing in the doorway, dressed in a long-sleeved, black teeshirt and jeans.

"Sorry," he said. "I didn't mean to interrupt."

"No, I'm the one who's interrupting," Donny said, rising. "Good morning, I'm Cal's neighbor and very best friend, Donny Denton."

Luke's eyebrow shot up for a second, before he offered his hand. "Luke Bennett," he said with a big smile. "Nice to meet you, Mister Denton."

"Please," Donny said, giving his hand a quick shake. "That makes me feel ancient. Call me Donald."

"Callahan's mentioned you."

"Really?" Donny's mouth twisted in a little smile. "Well, that makes us even. She's mentioned *you*, too."

Luke's face flushed and he looked away. Callahan could have kicked Donny. She put water and ground coffee in the coffeemaker and turned it on.

"Coffee will be ready in a minute," she said, breaking the heavy silence. "In the meantime, why don't we sit at the table?"

"By all means," Donny said, leading the way. "Tell me, Luke, what brings you to Santa Fe?'

"I needed a break from the city. I've been living in San Francisco."

"So I understand. One of my favorite American cities. I lived there for a time in the seventies. My wild, hippie days. Ah, the naughty memories." There was another uncomfortable pause before Donny said, "So, Luke, how long will you be visiting our little City Different?"

Callahan saw Luke shift uncomfortably in his chair and answered for him.

"Long enough for him to get a feel for it, I hope." She gave Donny a warning look. "We're doing some sightseeing today."

"You mean you're actually taking a break from work? I applaud that." Donny turned his head toward Luke. "Cal has been working herself to an absolute frazzle. She could use a *brief* distraction."

"Then I'll do my best to distract her," Luke answered, with a pleasant smile.

Donny frowned, started to reply then obviously thought better of it. He glanced at his watch and pushed back from the table.

"Heavens, I didn't realize the time. Better pass on that coffee. Glad I got to meet you, Luke. If you're going to be here for another day or two, I'll probably see you again."

Luke stood, exhibiting his usual good manners. "I hope so, Donald. Nice meeting you, too."

"I'll walk you to the door," Callahan said.

"Well, you were right about one thing," Donny said in a low voice when they reached the entryway. "He *is* gorgeous. But he didn't answer my question. How long is he staying?"

"I don't know. But I'm asking you to please back off."

Donny bent his face close to Mucho's. "I'm leaving you in charge here," he said in a loud whisper. "Keep a close eye on your mom. She has obviously taken leave of her senses."

Callahan returned to the kitchen to find Luke standing with his back to her, staring out the window.

"He knows, doesn't he?" he said without turning around.

"What?"

He turned to face her. "How we know each other."

"Yes. I told him."

"No wonder he doesn't like me."

Deathmark

"He doesn't *dislike* you. He doesn't even know you."

"He knows what I was doing for a living. That's enough for most people to pass judgment."

"Well, Donny isn't most people. He has a very open mind. He's just protective of me."

"Does he know about my birthmarks, too?"

She shook her head. "I saw no reason to divulge that."

Luke managed a strained smile. "Okay. Well, I could use some of that coffee."

After breakfast, they walked up the path to the studio. "I can't get over this place," Luke said, stopping to watch two ravens circle high above the trees. "It's so private and peaceful. Tesuque. I like the sound of that."

"It means 'The Village in the Narrow Place of the Cottonwood Trees' in the Tewa language. Some of the trees on this property are well over a hundred years old."

"No kidding? Hey!" He pointed off to the right. "Did you see that rabbit? Mucho did. Look at him go! Think he'll catch it?"

She laughed. "If he did, it would be a first. And he'd probably try to tame it for a playmate. He's only aggressive when he thinks I'm threatened."

"So I noticed. Apparently, he's decided I'm trustworthy."

"Apparently."

"Donny's another matter. He's going to take a little work."

Another alarm went off in Callahan's head. *He's planning to be here long enough to change Donny's mind?*

"I've never seen a sky this blue," Luke continued. "It's been gloomy as hell in San Francisco." He looked away, but not before she saw something darken the light in his eyes.

"Luke, is something wrong?"

"Nothing is wrong—now that I'm here." He grabbed her hand. "Come on. I can see the cabin through the trees. You weren't kidding. It's a *real* log cabin."

Once inside, Luke walked around, studying her sketches

and paintings. Callahan leaned against the wall, watching him. The truth was she found it difficult to take her eyes off him. The way he moved... and stood, like right now, with his arms folded in front of his chest—so familiar.

"Do you always work on several paintings at one time?"

"No. But lately the ideas have been coming to me so fast I can't wait to get them down."

"They're really great, all of them."

He walked to the half-finished portrait of Running Wolf, leaning against a wall, and knelt to study it. "Is this the Indian—*Native American*—guy in your dreams?"

Callahan swallowed hard. "It is."

"I thought you couldn't remember his face."

"I couldn't... until I went to see Red Feather last week."

Luke stood. "The medicine man?"

"Yes. I did tell *him* about your birthmarks."

"Oh, yeah? What did he say?"

"He took me on a trance journey to the spirit world, to look for answers."

"The *spirit* world?"

"Red Feather believes that the physical and spirit worlds are interconnected, and that it's possible to travel from one to the other by inducing an altered state of consciousness."

"Really? You did that? What do you use to induce this state?"

"Red Feather doesn't use drugs. He relies on natural methods like drumming, rattling, singing, dancing. Native ways. It's something you have to experience to understand."

Luke's expression was clearly skeptical. "I suppose so... Go on."

"Well, during the trance, I had a vision of Running Wolf. When I came out of it, I could still see his face. So I decided to paint it. It's not finished yet..."

"What did Red Feather say about my marks?"

She hesitated, not sure Luke was ready to accept the possibility that he'd been looking at his own past life portrait. "He said that we—you and I—have a powerful connection."

Luke smiled his irresistible smile.

"I don't need a medicine man to tell me that." He put his arms around her. "Anything else?"

"That we have some unfinished business."

"My thoughts, exactly." He backed her to the wall and pressed himself against her.

Callahan knew they would have to have a serious conversation about this. But feeling his growing hardness through his jeans, and her own immediate response, she decided this was not the time. When he removed a condom from his pocket, there was no question. The conversation could wait.

"I have something to confess to you," he said, sometime later. They were lying on her studio sofa, bodies entwined and naked beneath a soft woolen throw.

"Hmmm?"

"Our running into each other at the bookstore on Union Square—it wasn't an accident."

Callahan raised herself out of her post-coital euphoria.

"What do you mean?"

"Okay…here goes. From that first night, when I took you to the party, I was just knocked out by you. I went to the hotel expecting to pick up an eccentric, middle-aged artist. Somebody's grandmother. Then you opened the door, looking drop-dead gorgeous. But it was more than that—I know a lot of beautiful women. By the end of the evening, it was like I'd *always* known you. I could hardly sleep that night. I knew I had to find a way to see you again. The next morning I went back to the Fairmont, sat in the lobby, trying to decide whether or not to call your room. I wasn't sure what to say. I was afraid if I admitted my feelings, it would scare you away." He shifted his weight and pulled her even closer.

"Then I saw you step out of the elevator and leave the hotel. So… I followed you."

Callahan pushed back to look at him. "You *followed* me?"

"It wasn't like I was stalking you or anything. I just wanted to spend more time with you. I waited across the street from the coffee shop until you came out. I was really nervous in Saks, afraid you'd turn around and spot me. I didn't think you'd believe that I just happened to be browsing in the ladies section."

She suppressed a smile. "You're right. I wouldn't have."

"Then, in the bookstore, I thought it might work. I pretended to just run into you." He paused. "I wouldn't blame you for being upset. Perhaps I shouldn't have told you."

"Yes, you should have."

"You're not angry?"

She looked away, trying to sort through her feelings.

"I'm more surprised than angry. I certainly don't like the idea of being followed."

"I had to see you again." He cupped her chin and turned her face so that he could look into her eyes. "Please, Callahan, try to understand. And forgive me for finding you so damned irresistible."

She almost laughed. *Charming devil.*

"Well, I appreciate your leveling with me. Now, I want you to continue. What made you decide to drop out of school and come here?"

"I've already told you. I couldn't stop thinking about you— and the Indian you'd painted with wounds that match my scars. Things you said, like thinking you'd lived before... Everything about you haunted me—your smile, your touch, the way you studied me when you thought I wasn't looking. It was like an obsession." He paused, biting his lower lip. "Then things got really crazy. The life I was leading was just too freaking much. I knew the time had come for a serious change. And, strange as it sounds, I knew I had to come *here.*"

Callahan drew a shaky breath. *He feels it, too. This powerful bond between us. He doesn't understand it, but he feels it.*

"*What* things got crazy?"

He shook his head. "I want to just leave the past behind. Okay? Please, let that be okay."

She took a deep breath and nodded. Although she allowed him to draw her close again, his evasiveness didn't sit right with her. *Am I expecting too much too soon? Emotional intimacy takes time.* His roaming hands quickly brought all logical thoughts to a halt.

Deathmark

20

"What a fabulous lunch." Luke leaned back in his chair at Geronimo on historic Canyon Road. "That lobster and shrimp enchilada really hit the spot. Excellent choice. I don't know when I've felt this relaxed."

Callahan smiled, feeling pretty good herself. *I've had more sex in the last—what? eighteen hours?—than I had in the last year with Brad.* She resisted the urge to stretch like a pampered cat.

"Ready?"

She gave him what she knew was an outrageously flirty look.
"For what?"

He chuckled. "You are one hot lady. Do you know that?"

"I didn't until I met you." *Now I know what Leda meant by that special glow.*

"Shall we go home?"

There's that word again—'home.'

"Not yet," she said, trying not to read too much into his choice of words. "Canyon Road is famous for its art galleries and boutiques. Let's walk a bit."

Luke signaled for the check and paid with cash. Callahan had an instant of concern for his finances. It had been a pricey lunch, and she'd planned to pick up the check. They'd certainly eat at *home* tonight.

"Legend has it that this was a prehistoric trail leading over the mountains to Pecos Pueblo," Callahan said, as they strolled along the narrow street, holding hands. "We know for sure that it was a burro trail in the seventeenth and eighteenth centuries. These centuries-old adobe buildings were once private haciendas. And did I tell you that Santa Fe is the third biggest art market in the country?"

"You did." Luke stopped suddenly. "Hey! Isn't that one of your paintings in that window?"

"Yes. Santa Fe Visions carries my work."

"I'd recognize it anywhere. Come on." He guided her across the street. "Let's go in."

"Callahan!" A white-haired, anorexic-looking woman dressed all in black suede, her flat chest covered in multiple strands of turquoise and coral, hurried across the room toward them. "I just left you a voicemail. We sold *Evening Shadows* yesterday to a couple from Chicago. Now I'm down to only three of your paintings."

"I have another almost ready for you."

"Splendid." She turned her attention to Luke. "Is this handsome young man your son?"

Callahan felt her smile freeze. "No." She struggled to keep her voice light. "Louise Roberts, this is Luke Bennett."

"I'm a close friend," Luke said, putting his arm around Callahan's waist.

Louise's surgically-widened eyes went even wider. "Well... how nice." She fingered her necklace for a moment, obviously at a loss for words.

Luke steered Callahan over to the wall featuring her work and leaned his face in closer to her. "These are just incredible," he whispered in her ear. "I can't believe I'm sleeping with the artist."

Deathmark

Louise, her composure obviously recovered, appeared behind them. "May I offer you two something to drink? Coffee or iced tea?"

"No," Callahan said. "Thanks, anyway. We'll be going now."

"Well, it's always such a pleasure to see you, Callahan. Give me a call when the new painting is ready and I'll send the truck over for it." Her long, thin fingers returned to her necklaces. "Nice meeting you, Mister... "

"Bennett," Luke finished for her. "Nice to meet you, too." He kept his arm firmly around Callahan's waist as they walked to the doorway.

Out on the street, they continued on in silence for a few minutes. Callahan's spirits had taken a nose dive. *Well, what do you expect? He's Patrick's contemporary. You keep trying to forget that.*

Luke stopped in front of El Farol.

"I could use a cappuccino. How about you?"

"Fine," she said, avoiding his eyes.

They were seated at a small table in a dark corner of the back room.

"This place has seen a lot of history," she said, keeping it cool, trying to shake her depression. "It's the oldest restaurant on Canyon Road and has been a favorite hangout of local artists since the twenties when five East Coast painters, called *Los Cinco Pintores* by the locals, settled here and... "

"You don't have to pretend with me," he interrupted. "I know you were embarrassed by what that old biddy said." He covered her hand with his. "Look, we need to talk about it. Is this age thing an issue with you? I need to know, because it isn't with me."

She sighed. "Of course it bothers me."

"Why?"

"Because I'm twenty years older than you are! That's a huge gap. A whole generation."

"Do I seem immature to you?"

"Definitely not."

"And you don't seem one bit over-the-hill to me. So, what's the problem?"

"There isn't a problem when we're alone. But other people..."

"Screw other people! What matters is *us*...how we feel about each other."

"Is it that simple?"

"It is if we decide it is."

Callahan thought about his words, wished she could believe them. But she knew there was nothing simple about their relationship.

He reached out and stroked her cheek in that special way, then touched a faint, quarter-inch scar just under her right eye.

"I've never noticed that scar before. What happened?"

She hesitated, reluctant to bring up the unhappy past. But, on the other hand, she wanted to encourage honesty between them.

"It's a souvenir from my ex-husband, Brad. He can turn into someone very ugly when he's drinking. He lost his temper one night and threw a glass. It hit the wall right beside me and shattered. Fortunately, it missed my eye."

Luke's eyebrow went up and his face went hard. "He was abusive to you?"

"Until I threw him out."

The sound that Luke made was almost a growl. "Lucky for him I didn't know you then."

Callahan rubbed her forehead, trying to erase all those painful memories.

"It's hard for me to talk about him. It brings up all kinds of feelings—anger, shame, mostly disbelief that I tolerated his drunken tantrums for as long as I did."

"I understand those feelings. My father was a mean drunk, too. Worse after my mother disappeared. He used me for a punching bag for years. Then, when I was sixteen, I started lifting weights. He didn't seem to notice—rarely noticed *anything* I did. One night he came home from the local dive, mad at the world and ready to take it out on me. He punched me and... well, let's just say I finally got his attention. I dropped him off at the ER a little later." Luke paused for a moment, his eyes narrow and hard-looking at the memory. "I moved out of the house after that and he never messed with me again."

"You were on your own at the age of sixteen? How did you live?"

Deathmark

"My best friend, Kevin, had a great family. They took me in. I worked nights at a 7-11."

"How did you go to college?"

"A scholarship. And I worked part-time as a waiter. After I graduated, I bummed around for a few years, getting some life experience, trying to decide what I wanted to do."

Callahan laid her hand on his arm. It hurt her to imagine him growing up mistreated and alone. If she'd known him then... *What would I have done? Adopt him?*

"My childhood left me with zero tolerance for bullies." He sipped his cappuccino. "Your ex-husband, what's his name?"

"Brad."

"Brad what?"

"Hamilton."

"He's still here in Santa Fe?"

"I'm afraid so."

"What does he do?"

"He's a real estate broker."

He looked thoughtful for a moment and then abruptly changed the subject. "Better drink your cappuccino, it's getting cold."

They browsed through a few more galleries, and then stopped at the grocery store on their way home.

"What are you in the mood for?" Callahan asked, as they pushed the cart past the vegetable section. She was struck by how good it felt to be planning a meal with someone again.

"Besides you?" Luke grinned. "How about pasta?"

"Good choice. I make a mean lasagna. It's Patrick's favorite."

"Patrick?"

"My son." Again, she was struck by the age thing. Then she remembered Luke's words and immediately felt better. *What matters is us—how we feel about each other.*

They ate dinner by candlelight in the dining room. Mucho lay sprawled on a rug close by the table.

"Dee-licious," Luke said, finishing his second helping. "Keep this up and I'll never leave."

Callahan gave him a quick look. *He is joking, isn't he?*

"Well, it's pretty quiet here. You'd soon be missing all of that big-city excitement."

"I don't think so. I've had enough excitement to last for the rest of my life."

"But dropping out of school is a huge decision. I'm afraid you'll regret it."

He shrugged. "So, I lose this semester. If I have a change of heart, I can finish up and take the bar somewhere else."

"Would you have any problems getting into another law school?"

He shook his head. "I graduated from college with almost a four-point average." He grinned. "Why? Did you think I was just another pretty face?"

She laughed. "No, I never thought that." She poured herself some more wine. "San Francisco is a beautiful city, though. Is that why you chose to go to school there?"

He was quiet for a moment, staring at the flickering candle. "Actually, I applied to Hastings to please my fiancée." Seeing the surprise on Callahan's face, he quickly added, "Guess I haven't mentioned her... Monica."

"No, you haven't."

"Well, we met right after college and were together for several years. She traveled around with me—had a trust fund, which was nice. Monica was the first person in my life I felt I could truly rely on and trust. She loved San Francisco and wanted to settle down there. I wanted whatever Monica wanted."

"So what happened?"

"It doesn't matter now. Let's just say it all fell apart—unexpectedly. She just... disappeared from my life." He shrugged.

"That must have been a terrible blow."

"You could say that." He took a deep breath. "But I survived.

Deathmark

And I went on to San Francisco, alone." He sighed. "You know the rest of the story."

Do I? She took a sip of wine, studying him over the rim of the glass.

He looked away, and when he again met her gaze, his eyes were filled with pain.

"Sorry, it's still hard for me to talk about… that time."

Callahan's heart softened and she put her hand on his arm.

"I understand." She hesitated before continuing. "This might sound strange to you now, but Red Feather says that everything happens for a reason. That there are no mistakes, no coincidences. Everything that happens is really a blessing, given to us to learn from."

He gave her a skeptical look. "Then we should be *grateful* to the people who hurt us? Consider the bruises a blessing? Give me a break. That's crap. I mean, are you *grateful* to your ex-husband for beating on you?"

She removed her hand. "No. I haven't reached that point yet. Maybe I never will. But I do know that we can't see where life is leading us. I need to believe that things happen as they're supposed to. I have to trust in that."

Some of the tenseness left his face.

"So, you think me being here is part of some big plan?"

She hesitated. Was this the time to tell him everything that Red Feather had said about his birthmarks?

Before she could make up her mind, he spoke again.

"Well, speaking of plans, I have one for tonight." He put his hand behind her neck and drew her close. "You cooked, I'll clean up. Why don't we meet in the bedroom in half an hour or so?"

Callahan drew a bath and settled in. Her muscles relaxed in the hot, perfumed water, but her mind refused to follow suit. It was good having Luke there. She couldn't deny it. But she needed to know what his plans were. Although she wanted to be with him as much as possible, learn all she could about him, her work couldn't be neglected. Tomorrow morning would have to be spent in her studio.

She came out of the bathroom a short time later, wrapped in a warm chenille robe, to find flames from a burning piñon log gently crackling in the bedroom fireplace. She walked down the dark hallway, in search of Luke. Suddenly, she saw something out of the corner of her eye. In the shadowed alcove leading to the kitchen stood a figure with a long spear raised above his head.

Without warning, the room tilted. Time stopped, changed gears, and spun backward.

Running Wolf, wearing only a loin cloth, his black hair hanging loose past his shoulders, raised his war lance and threw it at the buffalo hide target he used for practice. She watched the lance fly through the air and pierce it dead center.

He let out a whoop and turned to her, laughing. "Do I get a gift from my wife for that?"

Her heart overflowed with love. 'A gift' was their special code for lovemaking. "Many gifts!" she said. As she started toward him, the ground beneath her feet seemed to dissolve and she was falling—everything around her spinning...

Callahan regained consciousness, lying on the cold brick floor in the hallway. Luke was pushing Mucho aside to kneel beside her.

"Oh, my god! Callahan, are you all right?"

With his help, she sat up, still feeling dizzy.

"Just give me a minute..."

"God, I'm sorry... I didn't mean to scare you. I was just checking out that old spear, testing its balance."

Mucho let out a concerned whimper.

"Calm down, boy," Luke said as he carefully helped her to her feet.

She was grateful for his strong arm around her as they walked back down the hall to the bedroom. And when, sometime in the middle of the night, she came half-awake, whispering his name... *Running Wolf...* she was relieved to find him there, asleep beside her.

Deathmark

Luke eased out of bed and moved toward the bathroom. In the faint glow of a nightlight, he saw Mucho raise his head.

"Shhh, big boy, it's just me. Go back to sleep." Mucho groaned, thumped his tail once, and rearranged his long limbs on his sheepskin bed.

The numbers on Callahan's bedside clock glowed 3:05. *Shit. Terrible night. Old memories, old yearnings. Talking about the past stirred them up.* He softly closed the bathroom door, turned on the light and relieved himself. Then he studied his reflection in the mirror. His son-of-a-bitch father always said he looked like her—same blue eyes and dark, wavy hair. *"Can't stand to look at you, you little shit."* His father's voice and words came back, clear and sharp as glass shards. *"Spitting image of that two-timing whore. Hope she rots in hell. She didn't give a damn about you or me, you know that? Packed her bags and snuck off with some jerk—didn't even leave a note. Take my advice, Lukey boy. Never trust a woman. Whores, all of them."*

A time-blurred memory broke through his consciousness—a face framed by long, brown, wavy hair, eyes as blue as the sky, red lips smiling. *Mommy.* And then another face, this one crystal clear—dark hair fanning across a pillow, fine-featured face, bright blue eyes, full lips with the corners turning up in that special smile. *Monica.*

Luke didn't realize he was crying until a teardrop hit his hand where he was holding onto the rim of the sink. *Never trust a woman. Whores, all of them.* He made a fist and slammed it hard into the palm of his other hand—several times. Then he took a deep breath. *Get a grip. Get a fucking grip.*

He opened the medicine cabinet where he'd earlier spotted Callahan's prescription bottle of Xanax and dry-swallowed two of them. Then he turned off the light and crept back to bed.

21

Callahan was awakened by Mucho's bark and the sound of him running down the hall. She disengaged herself from Luke's sleeping embrace and sat up, peering at the clock. Almost eight. *Oh, hell. This is Friday!*

"*Ay, Mucho! Buenos dias.*" Consuela's voice floated down the hall. "*Basta*! Enough with the licking. *Señora* Callahan?"

She slid out of bed and snatched her robe from the floor. Tying it around her, she closed the door to her bedroom and hurried down the hall.

"Good morning, Consuela." She ran her fingers through her disheveled hair. "I...I overslept."

"*Bueno*. You work too hard. Sleep is good."

Mucho began pushing his empty bowl around the kitchen floor with his nose, a not-so-subtle hint for breakfast. Callahan filled the bowl with dog food and then set up the coffeemaker.

Deathmark

"Coffee will be ready in a minute, Consuela, would you like a cup?"

"*Sí*. But first, I start the laundry." She headed down the hall.

Still groggy, it took Callahan a moment to realize that Consuela intended to strip her bed.

"Wait!" As soon as the word was out of her mouth, she heard a scream. Then the slamming of a door. Hurrying down the hallway, she found Consuela standing outside her bedroom door, eyes wide in her flushed face.

"*Dios mío!* There's a man!" she whispered urgently. "Standing by your bed. Wearing no clothes!"

Callahan struggled not to smile. "It's all right, he's a… friend."

Consuela's expression changed from fear to embarrassment, and then to shocked disapproval as she grasped the significance of Callahan's words. Her face turned an even darker shade of red.

"I'll be cleaning…somewhere different," she said, hurrying away.

Callahan sighed and walked back to the kitchen. Placing two cups of coffee on a tray, she returned to the bedroom.

Luke, dressed in the jeans and sweater he had worn the day before, was sitting on the edge of the bed, putting on his shoes.

"I just scared the hell out of some old lady."

"That was Consuela, my housekeeper. She comes on Fridays."

"I was headed into the bathroom, buck naked." He grinned. "Afraid I made a lasting first impression."

She chuckled. "You certainly did."

His smile faded. "Look, the last thing I want to do is cause you problems. But I have to ask you something. It would really help me out if I could stay awhile, a week or so, just until I can figure out what to do. Would that be all right?"

Callahan hesitated. She certainly wasn't ready for him to go. Far from it. But still, she couldn't go on ignoring the feeling that something was very wrong in the way he'd just bolted from school and his life in San Francisco. *What is he hiding?*

He turned away.

"Forget it. I can see that I'm asking too much."

"No," she heard herself saying. "You're not asking too much.

191

That would be fine. However, as much as I enjoy your company, I truly must get some work done today."

He nodded, his relief obvious on his face.

"Of course. I thought maybe I'd just take off, explore the area. I'll be back in time to take you out for dinner."

"No…you don't need to do that. As you no doubt have noticed, this is an expensive town. We can eat here."

"I insist. You choose the place. Money is no object."

"It isn't? What did you do, rob a bank?" Suddenly, Callahan was hit with the thought that what she'd said in jest might not be so far off the mark.

Luke's smile faltered—for just an instant. Then he laughed.

"Right. I'm Clyde and hoping you'll be my Bonnie. No, scratch that—they didn't come to such a happy end." He pulled her close and kissed her. "I know you have questions, and it means the world that you aren't pressuring me. Please, just give me more time. Will you do that? Just trust me?" He pulled back and looked into her eyes. "We have to trust each other. Without trust, there's nothing—just a big, black hole."

Callahan nodded. She felt close to tears.

"Deal?" The pleading in his eyes nearly broke her heart.

"Deal."

He kissed her again before releasing her. "Now," he said with a grin, "let's see if I can make a better impression on Consuela with my clothes on."

They were in the kitchen, fixing breakfast, when the phone rang. Callahan saw that it was Donny, so she picked up.

"Hey, Cal girl, what's going on?"

"Luke and I are about to sit down to breakfast."

"How cozy. Well, that answers my real question. He's still there. Any idea how long he's staying?'

"Not exactly."

She could feel Donny's disapproval oozing through the phone.

"Look, honey, we need to have a private chat. Any chance

you could pry yourself away from Lover Boy this morning, for half an hour or so?"

She glanced at Luke, who was dishing up the eggs. "I'm going to be in my studio, working all day," she said, reluctantly.

"Great. I'll be by in about an hour." Donny hung up before she could object.

At that moment, Consuela came into the kitchen, carrying cleaning supplies. She stopped cold at the sight of Luke.

"Consuela, please let me introduce my friend, Luke Bennett."

Luke put the frying pan in the sink and held out his hand.

"It's nice to meet you. I'm sorry I frightened you earlier."

Consuela hesitated, blushing furiously, before shaking his hand.

"Luke will be visiting us for awhile," Callahan said.

Consuela gave a little nod and moved the frying pan so that she could fill a bucket with water and cleaning solution.

"There's no need for Consuela to clean in the guest room, is there?" Luke placed their plates on the table. "I mean, my things are… spread out all over."

"Well, she…"

"I'd rather she didn't." He smiled quickly at Consuela, who was looking at him with an indignant expression.

"I no bother your things, *Señor* Bennett," she said stiffly.

"I didn't mean to imply that you would. It's nothing personal, just one of my little quirks. I'm used to cleaning up after myself."

"*Bueno.*" Consuela's face was rigid. She picked up the bucket and marched out of the room.

"I didn't exactly win her over, did I?" Luke said, buttering a slice of toast. "But give me time. I will."

Donny knocked softly and opened the studio door. Mucho was thrilled to see him, even if Callahan wasn't.

"Hello, hello," he said. "How's my timing?"

She put a finishing touch on *The Last Sunset*.

"Not bad. I'm about ready to call this one done." She stood back to examine it. "What do you think?"

"A knockout. That sunset background is visual opera. And the Indian woman walking through the snow… I sense heavy symbolism here. Was this inspired by a dream?"

"Yes, it was." She examined the canvas from another angle.

"Want to talk about it?"

"Not now. But thanks, anyway."

"What great visualizations you have! I'm jealous. My dreams, when I can remember them, are in boring black and white. I find that surprising for someone of my colorful mindset, don't you? Oh, good…" He headed toward the kitchen area. "… brewed coffee. I prefer espresso, but you know what they say about desperate times calling for desperate measures. I was up half the night."

"I thought you were taking your between-books vacation."

"I am. Just couldn't sleep." He poured a cup, made a face as he took a sip, and parked himself on the sofa. "Where's Luke?"

"Out exploring. He understands that I have work to do."

"Practical of him. We need to keep that money coming in."

"All right," she said, coming to sit beside him. "Out with it. Let's get this over with."

"Cal, I'm worried, *really* worried. And I couldn't live with myself if I didn't speak my mind. What do you actually know about this guy? I mean beyond the fact that he's a great lay."

"I appreciate your concern, but…"

"No buts about it. Let's review the facts. You, a successful, divorced and extremely attractive middle-aged woman, hire a savvy young stud for a night on the town. Then you just happen to run into him the next day in a crowded bookstore on Union Square. Do you honestly think that was a coincidence?" Before she could respond, he continued. "Yank off the blinders, girlfriend. He set you up. That 'chance meeting' was carefully planned, as was the romantic little bistro lunch. That *besos*-for-*pesos* boy knows a meal ticket when he sees it."

"For your information, Luke has admitted that he followed me to the bookstore. He wanted to see me again. That doesn't mean that he saw me as a… meal ticket."

"Honey. He's a hustler."

Deathmark

"Look, he was doing some escorting on the side to help him through law school. Is that really such a big deal? He was just smart enough to get paid for doing what unattached men do anyway."

"Ted Bundy was a law student. I'll bet you didn't know that."

"What? What does that…"

"This guy could be a sociopath! I mean, he follows you in San Francisco. He shows up here. You don't have any idea what you're getting into. Luke could make old Bradley look like a choir boy. Are you sure Luke Bennett is even his real name? Sounds like a stage name to me. Have you seen his driver's license?"

"No, I haven't gone through his wallet. Damn it, Donny, I understand your concern, but…"

"Just try to look at this objectively for a minute. Pretend it's me that's gotten involved with a big-city hunk-for-hire. He calls. He sends flowers. Then he's on my doorstep. Moves his jammies into the master bedroom."

"I'm not an idiot, Donny. And I didn't just fall off the turnip truck. I know how it looks. But there's more to this than you understand." She stood up, snatched a tissue from her work table and blew her nose. "There's a bond between Luke and me. Something really… special. And I want to enjoy it, for as long as it lasts. Is that so terrible? Just because he's younger…"

"Sweetheart, it's not his age that's the issue with me. I date younger men, and more and more women are opting for passion over security. As a romance writer, I keep up with these things. An article in *Vanity Fair* said there's been a one-hundred-percent increase in the last ten years of older women involved with younger men. No, it's not about his age. It's his background. And his intentions. But let's start with the background. Now, sit back down and tell me what you actually know about him."

She chewed on her bottom lip. Donny's opinion was important to her. Maybe if he knew what a struggle Luke's life had been, he'd be less judgmental.

"He hasn't had it easy." She filled him in on the details she knew.

Donny was quiet for a minute, his forehead wrinkled in thought.

195

"Okay, that story confirms what I could already see. He's smart and he's a survivor. But there's something missing here. Doesn't it seem strange to you that a good-looking, ambitious guy like that has no young woman in his life?"

"He was in love, after college, and planning to get married."

"What happened?"

"I don't know the details. She was going to San Francisco with him, but the relationship fell apart. He was devastated."

"Fell apart, huh? That doesn't reassure me. What's the *real* story?"

"Don't make another mystery out of this. She apparently just changed her mind, that's all. Don't you see? Everyone Luke ever counted on let him down—his mother, his father, and then his fiancée."

"And you'd like to make it all up to him."

"I know I can't do that. But everyone deserves a break— someone they can count on."

Donny sighed. "Cal, what do I have to do to get past your hormones here? This guy is damaged goods! Listen, I saw a feature on a news show the other night about anti-social personalities."

"Oh, please. Don't start with that again."

"Just let me finish. Studies have shown that children with no lasting emotional ties often become sociopaths. Take Jeffrey Dahmer, John Wayne Gacy, Ted Bundy. None of them had close ties, and none of them developed a conscience."

"But the majority of people from rough backgrounds turn out just fine." Luke's words replayed in her mind. *We have to trust each other. Without trust there's nothing.* "I have to go with my instincts here, Donny. And from what I've seen, Luke is a brilliant, sensitive…"

"Yeah, yeah. Okay. I guess I have no choice but to bow to your 'instincts.' For the moment, anyway." He sipped his coffee, studying her. Then he exploded. "Fuck it! The moment is over. I've known you too long and love you too much to just waltz away. There's obviously more to this than you're telling me, and I'm not budging from his sofa until you do."

Callahan threw her hands in the air.

"You are such a bulldog. All right, damn it, there *is* something I haven't told you. Something really amazing."

Deathmark

"I knew it! My feminine intuition is rarely wrong."

"Luke has birthmarks that match exactly the claw marks I've seen on Running Wolf, the warrior in my dreams. You know, the grizzly wounds that inspired the *Fallen Hero* series."

Donny stared at her. "Oh-kay," he said slowly.

"He even has one on his back that I've dreamed about, but never painted." She saw the incredulous expression on his face. "Donny, you know I've been dreaming about Running Wolf since I was a teenager. I understand that you don't believe in reincarnation, but..."

"Holy shit. Is this leading where I think it is?"

She met his horrified gaze with silence.

"It is, isn't it? Yikes. It's all falling into place. You went running out to see Chief Featherhead the day after you got home. What did he say about all this? No, don't tell me; let me guess. You and Hiawatha shared some previous life, until he tried dancing with a bear. Now, several hundred years later, who should you encounter in San Francisco—working as a hooker, no less—but Hiawatha himself in a brand new body. Of course! It makes perfect sense."

Callahan groaned. "This is why I didn't tell you about his birthmarks earlier. I knew you would just turn it into a bad joke."

"You're dead wrong. I don't see this as a joking matter. I see my best friend going off the deep end. You've let that creative imagination of yours run amok, confusing this Luke character with your dream lover. You've got to start thinking straight, honey, and return to the real world." He put his head in his hands for a moment and then looked up. "Would you do something for me? Would you see a therapist? A *real* therapist? Please! I know a good one."

"No!" She shook her head. "Damn it, Donny. I resent your making fun of my spiritual beliefs. Many intelligent, educated people believe in reincarnation. Most of the population of the world does, in fact. Just because *you* don't, doesn't make it crazy. And another thing, don't you *ever* ridicule Red Feather again, not in my presence. He's someone I genuinely admire and respect."

Donny looked down at the floor, his lips pursed.

"Okay. I went too far. I apologize. But you have to admit, this is a damned weird situation."

"Yes." She felt her anger fading. "I certainly do admit that. But I have to work it out myself."

He held his hands up. "Do it your way. But just remember, I'm here for you, honey. I'm on your side." He paused. "I take it Consuela met Luke?"

"Yes. She surprised him in my bedroom this morning. Or I should say he surprised her." Callahan couldn't help but smile a little at the memory. "She's probably still in shock. Did she say anything?"

"No. But she was out on your bedroom patio, shaking rugs with a vengeance and jabbering to herself when I came up the path."

"What was she saying?"

"Something that roughly translates to '…out of the frying pan and into the fire.'"

Callahan and Luke had just been seated at the Santacafé that evening when she heard an unmistakable voice.

"Well, well. Look who's here."

She turned in her chair to see Brad standing behind her, his face flushed and his eyes bloodshot. Bad signs, Callahan knew from hard experience. The martini in his hand obviously wasn't his first.

"Saw you come in," he slurred and moved closer to lean against the table between Callahan and Luke. "Decided to come over and say hello. Meet your friend."

Callahan saw the spiky-haired widow sitting alone several tables away, pouting and spilling out of a low-cut red dress. Obviously, her evening wasn't going well. Callahan felt a stab of pity for the woman. Her hair would probably be standing on end even more by the time the night was over.

"Well," Brad said, "aren't you going to introduce us?" When Callahan didn't answer, he continued, "Fine. I'll just introduce myself." He turned to Luke. "Hi, I'm her ex. One of 'em, anyway."

"Go away, Brad," she said in a low voice.

"Hey, that's not very friendly. Like you said, this is a small town. We're bound to run into each other. We might as well be civil."

Luke rose to his feet. "You were just told to move along."

Deathmark

"Who the hell are you to tell me what to do?" Brad looked away from Luke and back down at Callahan with a smirk. "What's the deal, babe? You robbin' the cradle?"

Callahan pushed her chair back, grabbed her purse and stood. "Let's go, Luke."

Brad caught Callahan's arm. "Wait a goddamn minute. You can't treat me like…"

Before he could finish his sentence, he was pinned against the wall, with Luke's forearm under his chin in a choke hold. Brad's martini glass shattered on the tile floor.

"It's lucky for you that we're in a public place, asshole," Luke said in a soft voice, his mouth an inch from Brad's ear. "Real lucky. If you're smart, you'll stay far away from Callahan. And from me." He released his grip and backed away from Brad. Then he turned and cupped Callahan's elbow, steering her past the tables of staring people and out the front door of the restaurant.

Callahan was so mortified by Brad's behavior and shocked by Luke's that she couldn't think of anything to say. They sat silently in Luke's car for a few tense moments before his furious expression began to relax.

"Let's pretend that didn't happen," he said.

"I really don't think I can do that."

"I'll help you. I've had a lot of practice pretending bad things didn't happen. That creep isn't going to ruin our evening. So, let's start by finding another restaurant."

Although Luke appeared able to put the incident behind him, their encounter with Brad had taken its toll on Callahan. They were back home and in bed by ten o'clock. Callahan lay with her head on Luke's shoulder, her arm across his chest, willing herself to relax. He shifted a little, pulling her closer. Moments later, his deep breathing told her he was asleep. She couldn't stop thinking about the cold rage he'd displayed at the restaurant. For a moment there he'd looked fully capable of breaking Brad's neck. Her weary mind backed away from the thought and moved toward the world of dreams.

199

Jann Arrington-Wolcott

*The sun felt warm on her back as she knelt on the ground,
picking tender green sprouts. They would add flavor to the elk stew she
planned for Running Wolf's evening meal. Just the thought of pleasing
him, her husband for almost a moon now, made her smile.*

*"Sun-in-Her-Face!" She looked up to see who called her
name and then waved at Little Fox, the youngest daughter of her
father's sister, on the top of the ridge.*

*"Cousin!" she answered. "Join me. The greens are plentiful
here by the stream."*

*She straightened for a moment, savoring the peaceful late
morning. A herd of ponies, several belonging to Running Wolf,
grazed contentedly nearby on the new grass. Looking up, she
watched a red-tailed hawk circling high above in the cloudless sky.
Her spirit soared with the winged one. Who would not be happy on
such a day? This was, after all, the Moon of New Grass, a joyous
time after the long, harsh winter, a time when Mother Earth brought
forth new life.*

*Sensing movement behind her, she turned to greet Little Fox,
but her voice died in her throat. A small band of strange men stepped
from behind a nearby stand of trees. Crow! Enemy warriors!*

*She let out a shrill scream before a hand roughly covered her
mouth. Another scream shattered the stillness—Little Fox! Her mind
reeled in shock and terror, but still she took note of things—the bad
taste of dirty buckskin tied across her mouth, the alarmed snort and
whinny of a captured horse, the jagged scar across the cheek of the
cold-eyed man who roughly tied her hands behind her. Then she was
lifted and flung, face down, across the back of one of the horses. Her
captor leapt on behind, securing her with the hard pressure of his
naked knees and they were off at a full, jolting gallop.*

*Blood pounded in her temples and dust filled her nostrils as
she watched the ground fly past beneath her. She closed her eyes and
sent a frantic prayer.* One Above, spare me!

*She had no idea how long they had been riding when they
finally came to a sudden stop. Rough hands pulled her from the horse*

Deathmark

and flung her to the ground. She shook her head to clear it and counted her abductors. Five seasoned warriors. No...six. She saw Little Fox lying on the ground, her forehead bleeding, her eyes wide with shock.

The scar-faced one was kneeling at the stream, drinking water from his cupped hand. One of the others, his forehead and right cheek painted with two thick bands of red paint and his hair plucked bald except for a long greasy top-knot in the style of the Crow, came to her and pushed her hair out of her eyes. He said something and then laughed. His laughter turned to a strange, gurgling sound as an arrow pierced his neck. He made it to his feet and was instantly impaled by a second arrow in the center of his chest.

The air was thick with shouts and fierce war cries. Her heart leapt to her throat as Running Wolf burst into the clearing, followed by two more warriors from their band. Before she could draw another breath, Running Wolf's war club felled one man, and his knife slit the throat of another. In a matter of moments the six Crow lay dead.

Running Wolf knelt beside her, removed the filthy buckskin that gagged her, and freed her wrists. With a rasping sob, she threw her arms around him. He held her close.

"You are safe, beloved. No one will ever harm you and live."

She watched numbly as Running Wolf and his fellow warriors hacked off the dead enemies' scalps and gathered the stolen ponies. Her husband vaulted onto the back of the white stallion he had recently tamed, the one he called Stands Firm, and then reached down to pull her up behind him. She clasped both arms around his waist and pressed her face against his broad back. As they rode, his words echoed in her head, "No one will ever harm you and live..."

22

Callahan was sipping coffee and reading one of her metaphysical books when Luke walked into the kitchen the next morning. She smiled at Mucho's obvious delight to see him. One thing was certain, she thought as she watched the two of them roughhouse, her dog shared none of her best friend's reservations when it came to Luke.

"That's enough, boy," Luke said, after a few minutes. "I'll throw the stick for you after breakfast."

Mucho settled back down by Callahan's feet.

"Good morning," she said. "How did you sleep?"

"Okay." He poured himself a cup of coffee. "Better than I ever did in San Francisco, anyway. It's such a relief to wake up and find myself here, instead of in that crummy little apartment. I'm not going to miss that place."

"What do you mean? You're giving up your apartment?"

Deathmark

"As far as I'm concerned, I already have. I'm never going back there."

"But don't you have a lease?"

He shrugged, stirring cream into his coffee.

"Guess I'll lose my deposit."

"What about your things? You must have belongings…"

"Whoa," he snapped. "What is this? An interrogation?"

She drew back, stung by the sharpness in his voice.

"No, I'm just surprised. Why wouldn't I be?"

"I told you it was a sudden decision. Okay? I needed to get out of there, so I did. End of story."

She stared at him. "End of story? I don't think so."

He exhaled an impatient breath. "Oh, hell. I'm sorry, Callahan. I didn't mean to jump on you like that. I can be a real jerk sometimes. Guess I didn't sleep so well after all. Will you forgive me?"

She nodded a little stiffly. *What's going on with him? What is it he's not telling me?*

He sat down at the table beside her. "What are you reading?" Without waiting for an answer, he picked up the book and read from the jacket: *Who Were You? Remembering Past Lives.* Looks interesting." He took a sip of coffee, before meeting her gaze. "You were moaning and talking in your sleep last night. Were you having one of your Indian dreams?"

She noticed that he didn't bother to correct the term "Indian," as he'd always done in the past.

"I had a restless night, and one dream in particular that I've never had before." She flashed on Running Wolf's furious face and remembered his vow: *No one will ever hurt you and live.*

"Want to talk about it?"

She shook her head. "I'm still trying to think it through."

"I've thought a lot about the things you told me in San Francisco," Luke said, "especially since I've been here. I mean, I see you staring at my marks and I can't help wondering what you're thinking."

Callahan decided it was time to level with him. And time for him to open up to her.

"We do have things we need to talk about. So... let's do it." She held his gaze across the table. "I told you I visited Red Feather, and that we talked about you and your birthmarks. We discussed the fact that there is serious research connecting birthmarks with wounds inflicted when someone died in a past life."

Luke put his cup down. "What are you saying?"

"Red Feather believes that you were Running Wolf in that lifetime, and that's what drew us together again."

"Is that what *you* think? Is that the reason you're letting me stay here?"

"I guess that's part of it. But, suppose that we all do live many lives, that each lifetime is just a chapter in a long book. Wouldn't we be affected—spiritually, emotionally, even physically—by those past identities?"

He ran his hand through his hair. "If that's true, why wouldn't I have memories of that life, too?"

"Maybe you do but just accessed them. Red Feather says that few people consciously remember past lives. Those that do... they have the opportunity to consciously work on unresolved issues and trauma from a previous life that are affecting their growth and development in this one."

"And you think I could be part of your unresolved issues?"

"Not just mine. That lifetime would have been traumatic for you, too. And you would need to heal from it. That would explain your birthmarks—to remind you of the wounds you suffered as Running Wolf. You said in San Francisco you had dreams that upset you, dreams you can't remember. Maybe they're about that life."

She picked up another book and turned to a page she'd marked.

"There's serious medical research being conducted on the healing effects of past life regression. Listen to what this Stanford-educated psychiatrist has to say: *In my past life regressions I have found a definite correlation between the injuries, diseases, and phobias that we have in this life and what has occurred in other lives. Birthmarks often mark an injury that occurred in a previous lifetime.*"

Luke let out a long breath. "Shit. This blows my mind."

Deathmark

"Would you like to talk to Red Feather about this? You told me in San Francisco you'd like to meet him."

He shook his head. "No. I said I'd like to meet a medicine man someday—not get involved in a past life pow wow. I have enough shit I'm trying to deal with right now. I don't need this."

"Exactly what 'shit' are you trying to deal with?"

He looked away. "Can we just change the subject?"

"No! Not any longer. We keep dancing around this conversation. Look, we're in a relationship here! I've taken you into my home and my bed. That isn't a casual thing for me. I need for there to be honesty between us. As you said, we have to be able to trust each other."

His eyes suddenly clouded. "Honesty and trust," he said in a flat voice. "Yeah, wouldn't that be great?"

She waited for him to continue. Instead, he grabbed her hand.

"What do you say we get out of here? Take a drive into the mountains. We could have a picnic." He looked down at the floor. "Mucho, you can come, too!"

Mucho jumped to his feet, his wagging tail whacking against Callahan's leg like a whip.

"Damn it, Luke! Why can't we just deal with this—whatever *this* is?"

"I need time. I'm asking you—begging you—to give it to me."

She studied him, saddened by the look of desperation in his eyes. *A little more time. I can give him that.*

"Okay. A picnic would be nice, for all three of us. But I need to spend the morning in my studio, finishing up a few things."

Luke pushed back from the table. "I'll go to that Tesuque Market we passed yesterday and put together a picnic lunch. Let's meet back here around noon."

Shortly after one, they were in Callahan's Jeep, Luke at the wheel, headed up Hyde Park Road into the forested and snow-capped Sangre de Cristo Mountains. Although the sun was shining and the temperature was in the mid-forties, the weather forecast said possible late-afternoon snow flurries. Callahan had thrown a couple of down jackets into the back of the Jeep, along with gloves and an old blanket. Mucho, overjoyed by the outing, let out frequent whines of excitement from the backseat.

Luke seemed determined to keep the mood light. He wouldn't let Callahan look inside the picnic basket, insisting that its contents be a surprise.

"Do you know what I really love about this part of the country?" he asked.

She shook her head, thinking he was driving too fast. *A lot of accidents happen on this mountain road.* She was about to tell him so, when he continued.

"There's such a feeling of freedom. Like you could just start all over, wipe out your past and reinvent yourself."

"Look over there," she said, pointing to a picnic area just ahead. "Let's park and we can walk back in to a little creek that runs through the woods."

"Great. Looks like we're the only ones up here." He slowed and pulled off the road. "Does this road lead to the Santa Fe ski basin?"

"Yes." She silently resolved to drive home.

"When do the runs open?"

"Not until after Thanksgiving. But another early storm and the cross-country skiers will be out in force." Her already nervous stomach gave a little lurch at the thought of a snowstorm.

"I did some skiing after college and loved it."

His words triggered another memory—Thanksgiving weekend, last year. Brad, dressed for a day of skiing, glowering at her over the breakfast table.

"I wish you'd get over this stupid hang-up you have about snow. You know what I think? It's just an excuse. You'd rather be up in that damn studio of yours than spending a little quality time with your husband."

"It wouldn't be quality time for me, Brad. I'd be miserable. I don't like snow..."

"Fine. You can expect me when you see me then."

He'd stalked out of the kitchen.

Deathmark

Luke opened the door on her side of the Jeep, bringing her back to the present. Released from the backseat, Mucho ran ahead to explore the new territory.

They walked a short distance into the woods and spotted a weathered picnic table and benches. Nearby was a gently flowing creek. Luke unfolded the blanket and laid it across the bench.

"Sit down and close your eyes. Don't open them until I tell you to."

Callahan did as he instructed. Turning her face up toward the warm sun, she felt some of her tension release. After a few minutes, Luke sat down beside her and whispered in her ear.

"You can look now."

She opened her eyes to a spread of grilled salmon, artichoke hearts and red potato salad, chocolate-covered strawberries, and a chilled bottle of *Moet & Chandon*. He'd packed two of her Champagne flutes, her good silverware, and linen napkins.

"Wow," she said, surprised and pleased by the effort he'd made. "This is quite an elegant feast."

"Nothing more than you deserve, my lady." He kissed her gently, and then more deeply. His hand slid under her jacket and cupped her breast.

A sudden crashing through the bushes interrupted them, as Mucho appeared and ran in circles around the picnic table. Luke laughed and pulled some doggie biscuits out of a sack.

"This is your picnic, too, big boy." He gave Mucho a biscuit and opened the Champagne.

After they'd eaten, Callahan leaned her elbows on the picnic table and watched Luke play fetch with Mucho. Neither of them seemed to have a care in the world. But she knew something had caused Luke to leave California abruptly, something he refused to discuss. Much as she wished to ignore it, her inner voice kept breaking through, urging her to take a good, hard look at what she was reluctant to see.

Danger! It was Red Feather's voice.

They strolled, hand-in-hand along the bank of the creek. Mucho ran on ahead, reveling in the adventure. After a while, they stopped by a long, flat rock that protruded out over the water. Callahan brushed away remnants of snow and sat on the edge of it. Luke stretched out beside her and closed his eyes.

The sun slipped behind a bank of clouds that had moved in from the west, casting a soft, almost luminous glow across the wooded meadow beyond the water. A strong breeze seemed to come up out of nowhere, making a musical rustling sound as it moved through the aspens. She watched a yellow leaf swirl in the moving water, caught in a whirlpool, going around... *and around...*

In that moment, Callahan felt a familiar dizziness, a sense of falling. *No! Not now!* Pitching forward, she gripped the rock—just as everything around her was swallowed up by a swirling blackness. But then the feeling passed and she opened her eyes. The sun seemed brighter and felt warm on her bare arms. She stared at her naked brown limbs, confused. Her eyes were drawn to the stream in front of her. It was much wider than it had been and deeper. And the meadow beyond was sprinkled with red and yellow wildflowers.

"Sun-in-Her-Face!"

Running Wolf's voice brought her to her feet. Then she saw him, motioning to her across the stream.

"Over here! I have a gift for you."

Giggling, she slipped off her moccasins and stepped into the flowing water.

A shocking sensation of cold brought Callahan back to herself. She heard Luke's voice.

"What are you doing?"

She lost her footing and fell, splashing into the frigid water. An instant later, strong arms lifted her up and carried her back to the flat rock.

"Are you all right? Callahan! Say something!"

Her teeth were chattering too forcefully for her to speak. *It happened again! I'm wide awake... I slipped back!*

Deathmark

"What were you doing wading into that freezing stream?"

I was trying to reach Running Wolf. She began to cry as the realization hit her. *That's what I've been doing for most of my life!*

23

"Champagne in the middle of the day was a bad idea," Luke said, as he drove them down the mountain. "Especially at this altitude. You must have dozed off and woke up disoriented."

Stripped of her wet clothes and wrapped in a blanket, Callahan stared numbly out the window. Best to let him assume the drinks had gone to her head. She didn't have the energy to tell him the truth just then, and besides it would probably send him packing. She just wasn't willing to take that chance. Not yet.

When they got back to the house, she took a long, hot shower, trying to fight off a chill that went beyond her physical body. Mucho, always sensitive to her feelings, paced nervously outside the bathroom door. When she came out, wrapped in a robe, her hair still damp, Luke was turning down the bed. Dropping the robe, she slid gratefully under the warm covers. Mucho *rrrrrumphed* and nuzzled her with his nose before plopping down on his own bed, nearby.

Deathmark

"Rest now." Luke pulled the covers up over her shoulders. "I'll be right back with some hot tea." He gave her cheek a loving caress before leaving the room.

The gesture moved Callahan to tears. *Running Wolf...Luke... they're blending together in my mind. I'm not sure what's real anymore.* She slid farther under the covers. *Maybe something is physically wrong, some kind of sleep disorder. Or a brain tumor. I should call a neurologist.* She took a deep breath, tried to calm herself. *I want to talk to Red Feather. But what can he say that he hasn't already said?*

Luke returned, carrying a steaming mug. "Here you go. Chamomile tea. It'll warm you up and help you relax. Take a nap now. We'll have a quiet night here at home." He pressed a warm kiss on her cold lips and left the room.

She took several sips of tea and set the mug down on her bedside table. Her mind was still churning, but she couldn't hold a thought long enough to examine it. Leaning back against the pillows, she closed her eyes.

Callahan sat up in bed, startled to find herself in darkness. She looked at the clock. Seven-thirty! She'd been asleep for almost three hours. Security lights illuminated the courtyard and revealed occasional snowflakes outside the bedroom window. Her chest tightened with dread.

She made a quick trip to the bathroom, brushed her teeth and tried, with little success, to do something with her sleep-matted hair. Dressed in robe and slippers, she walked down the hall in search of Luke and Mucho. She located them in the kitchen, where Luke was stirring a pot of fragrant soup.

"How are you feeling?" he asked.

"Better. I'm amazed I slept so long. What are you cooking?"

"One of my specialties." He ladled soup into two bowls and carried them to the already set table. "Potato soup—my old standby as a kid. My father wasn't exactly reliable about keeping food in the house, and I learned to be creative with whatever I could find. I thought soup would be good for you tonight."

She was touched by the gesture and the thought of him as a neglected child fixing his own meals touched her heart.

"It smells delicious. And the bread looks wonderful."

"I bought it this morning. Mucho already helped himself to several slices while I was setting the table." He pulled Callahan's chair out for her, then sat down across from her.

"Mmmm, delicious."

"Not bad… My original recipe improved when I discovered spices." He buttered a piece of crusty bread and bit into it.

"I can't help thinking about your childhood," Callahan said, "and how difficult it must have been for you. Do you have any contact at all with your father?"

"I heard from my friend, Kevin, that he's dead. Drank himself to death a few years ago. I didn't shed any tears, the world's a better place without him. But you know something? In a weird sort of way, I'm grateful to him. He taught me a lot about living, about doing whatever it takes to survive." He paused. "And he showed me something else. Something I've thought about a lot."

"What's that?"

"The dark side of human nature. It's one thing to read about it, it's something else to experience it on a regular basis, especially from someone who's supposed to be taking care of you. It put me in touch with my own dark side, and that scared the hell out of me."

She put down her spoon. "What do you mean?"

He was quiet for a moment, staring down at his soup. Then he shook his head and looked up at her.

"Sorry. Sometimes old demons surface."

She nodded. "I know."

"No, you don't." His voice was unexpectedly sharp. "No one can really know someone else's demons."

"That's true. I was referring to my own." She hesitated. "What do you mean about your dark side scaring you?"

"Nothing you want to hear. I shouldn't have brought it up."

Callahan refused to let the subject drop, not this time.

"Damn it, Luke, talk to me! I've certainly confided in you."

He gave her a searching look.

Deathmark

"Okay…but it's not a pretty story. I told you a little about the last time my father beat me." His eyes narrowed, remembering.

"He came home from the local bar, belligerent as usual. I had just gotten my driver's license, and we got into an argument about me using the car the next night. He threw me against a wall and punched me in the stomach. I got away from him, but he came after me again. I slugged him, and he fell to the floor. When he got up, he said, 'I should kill you, you little son-of-a-bitch.' I really thought he might. I grabbed my baseball bat and started swinging. I fractured his arm in a couple of places."

Luke stopped and took a deep breath before continuing. "Then, after I dropped him off at the ER, I just completely lost it."

She managed to hold his gaze.

"I went back to the house and started breaking everything in sight—dishes, furniture, windows, even smashed the doors to kitchen cabinets. I wanted to obliterate every bad memory in that house."

"Dear god."

"A neighbor heard the racket and came over. He called the police when he saw the mess. They apparently had a hard time calming me down. I barely remember parts of that night—guess I was in shock."

Callahan's mouth went dry. "What…what happened after that?"

"I was in juvenile detention for awhile, until I could be properly evaluated. They gave me a battery of psychological tests. Sent a social worker to interview my teachers and friends. My dad was nowhere to be found. Just left the hospital and disappeared.

"Finally, the authorities determined that I wasn't a menace to society, so I was put on juvenile probation, forced to take an anger management class, and released to the custody of Kevin's parents. They were good to me. I supported myself with part-time jobs and filed for a Petition of Emancipation when I was seventeen."

"Did you ever see your father again?"

"Nope. Never did." He looked toward the window, where outdoor lights illuminated the patio. "Hey," he said, his voice losing some of its edge. "Look at that snow coming down."

Callahan didn't want to look, feeling chilled to the bone as it

213

was. She forced herself to swallow a little soup, although her appetite was gone. Luke was right, it wasn't a pretty story. He couldn't be blamed for defending himself against an abusive father. She probably would have used a bat on that bastard herself. *But smashing up the house? Getting that out of control?* Now she knew what he'd meant by fearing his own dark side. His rage—she'd seen it at the Santacafé, unleashed on Brad. He'd rather quickly gotten it under control, but she'd seen it. And now it scared her, too.

They had finished dinner and Luke was building a fire in the bedroom fireplace when the doorbell rang. Mucho bolted to his feet, barking.

"Who can that be?" she asked.

"I'm sure not expecting anyone," Luke said.

Reluctantly, Callahan followed Mucho down the hall. She opened the front door and froze, staring at her son.

"Patrick!"

"Hi, Mom." He quickly stepped inside. Setting his suitcase down, he shook snowflakes out of his red hair, opened his arms wide, enveloped her in a big hug, and kissed her cheek. "I got off to a late start. Hope you weren't worried."

He released her and turned his attention to an overjoyed Mucho, who rose up and placed his paws on Patrick's shoulders.

"Hey, there, pooch." He rubbed the dog's head. "Calm down. It's good to see you, too."

Mucho's response was a big lick across Patrick's face.

Callahan's mind was racing, trying to think how to handle this unexpected development.

"I…I wasn't worried. I didn't know you were coming."

"Didn't you get my e-mail? I have a meeting in Albuquerque Monday and Tuesday, so I thought I'd spend part of the weekend with you. Give us a chance to catch up."

"Well." She forced a welcoming smile. "That's great! I'm just surprised because I haven't checked my messages for a couple of days."

Deathmark

"I called the house and studio a couple of times en route, but all I got was your machine. Of course, calling your cell was a waste of time. I thought you must be out shopping for a welcome home dinner."

"I *was* out, but…well, it doesn't matter. You're here! It's wonderful! Come in."

He laughed. "I am in, Mom." He looked at her robe and disheveled hair. "Did I get you out of bed? Are you sick?"

"No."

"Really? You look exhausted."

"I'm okay, sweetheart." She gave him another hug. *Oh, dear god. How am I going to handle this?* "I'll bet you're hungry. I'm so sorry. Of course, you were expecting me to have dinner ready."

"You know me, always hungry but not picky. Whatever you have on hand will be fine. Maybe a couple of fried egg sandwiches. Let me put my suitcase in the guest room first."

Before she could detain him, Patrick walked down the hall toward the room where Luke had put his bags. Close behind him, Callahan watched him stop, staring through the open door of her bedroom, which afforded a clear view of the unmade bed—and of Luke, still tending the fire in the fireplace.

Callahan realized there was nothing she could do but make introductions.

"Patrick, honey," she said, avoiding her son's eyes, "this is my friend, Luke. We met in San Francisco. He decided to come to Santa Fe for a visit. Luke, this is my wonderful son."

"Hi, Patrick," Luke said, coming forward with a smile. "Nice to meet you."

Patrick—with a look of absolute shock on his face—hesitated before shaking Luke's outstretched hand. Callahan broke the uncomfortable silence.

"Why don't you put your bag in the back bedroom?" She took Patrick's arm and led him down the hall.

"I'm clearly interrupting something here," Patrick said.

"No, honey. It's okay."

"Mom, you have a right to a personal life. But how *old* is that guy?" he asked in a emphatic whisper.

When she didn't answer, he looked away, busied himself opening his garment bag and hanging a few things in the closet.

Callahan, at a loss for a response said, lamely, "There's some leftover soup, I'll go reheat it."

Luke found them in the kitchen, all charm. "May I join you?"

"Of course," Callahan said, bracing herself.

He took a seat across from Patrick at the kitchen table. "Your mother's told me a lot about you."

"Really?" Patrick's normally out-going manner was tense. "She hasn't said a thing about *you*. What do you do in San Francisco?"

"Luke's in law school," Callahan answered quickly, setting a bowl of soup in front of Patrick. "We met at my opening." That was as close to the truth as she was willing to go.

Luke met her eyes and then looked away. "Actually," he said, "I just dropped out, decided law wasn't for me. I understand you're a computer expert."

"I'm a software designer," Patrick corrected. He buttered a piece of bread and didn't speak again until he'd eaten it. "So," he said, giving Luke a level look. "How long are you staying?"

Luke did his eyebrow thing. "I'm not sure. Until I get some things figured out."

There was another uncomfortable silence. Patrick picked up his spoon and started eating his soup. "This is good."

"Thanks," Luke said.

Patrick shot him a surprised look.

"Luke made it," Callahan said, again avoiding her son's eyes.

Patrick's face flushed bright red, as it always did when he was upset.

Callahan tried to steer the conversation back to Patrick's work, but got little more than "yes" and "no" answers from him.

"So, tell us about your meeting in Albuquerque."

"It's just a two-day conference. I'll be driving straight back to Denver as soon as it's over." He finished his soup and pushed back from the table. "Well, I think I'll turn in now. It's been a long day."

Deathmark

"I'm sure it has, honey. Get a good night's sleep. We'll talk in the morning. Is there anything you need? I'm sure Consuela put fresh towels out in the back bathroom. There are extra blankets in the closet..."

"Mom—I'm not exactly the guest here. I know where everything is." He gave her a peck on the cheek and left the room without a word to Luke.

Callahan dropped her head into her hands. *God, he's beyond shocked. Should I go after him and try to explain? Explain what? That my young lover is actually an old lover? Very old...*

Luke sighed. "Well, chalk up one more great first impression for me."

When she didn't answer, he leaned forward and stroked her cheek. "I'm really complicating your life, aren't I? Would it be better if I left?"

She shook her head. The damage was already done. No matter how complicated things might get, she couldn't let Luke walk out now.

"You're wiped out," he said softly. "Come on. Time for bed."

She let him help her up. "You're going to have to sleep in..."

"I know," he said. "I'm relegated to the guest room tonight." He pulled her close. "But just for tonight."

Luke lay alone and frustrated. It was hard to know that Callahan was just down the hall and he couldn't be with her, touch and hold her. He wanted to comfort her, assure her—and himself— that things would be all right. *Patrick. Shit. Hadn't given him much thought. Should have realized he'd be an obstacle. A big obstacle.* He turned over, pulling a pillow to his chest for comfort. *I can work around that priss Donny, and find a way to soften up Consuela. But Patrick...*

For a few seconds Luke tried to imagine having a mother as devoted and loving as Callahan. Introducing him as "my wonderful son." What kind of a difference would that have made in his life? *Does Patrick realize how fucking lucky he is? Had everything just handed to him. How much influence does he have over Callahan? Maybe not as much as he thinks. After all, he hadn't stopped her from marrying that asshole, Brad. And he'd better not try to keep her away from me. He'd better not...*

Luke took a deep breath and released it as a sigh. *I'll get around Patrick. There's a way. There's always a way.* He clutched the pillow tighter as his conscious thoughts began to drift away.

Deathmark

24

Callahan stretched and groaned the next morning, reluctant to face the day and her disapproving son. She looked at the clock—7:35—forced herself out of bed and opened the window shades. Although they'd gotten several inches of snow during the night, the sky was clear. She hoped that was a good omen.

Mucho was nowhere to be seen. Dressing quickly in jeans and a warm sweater, she hurried down the hall to the kitchen, where she found Luke loading last night's dishes into the dishwasher. Mucho, lying nearby, leapt to his feet to greet her.

"Hi, guys," she said, accepting Mucho's kisses and then turning to Luke. "Your door was closed, so I thought you were still asleep."

He gave her a kiss and continued cleaning up. "I've been up for about an hour. Mucho came in to keep me company."

She poured herself coffee, noting that orange juice, cereal, and the Sunday morning paper were on the table. Luke had obviously already eaten and worked the crossword puzzle. She was glad Patrick was still asleep, he didn't need further evidence of Luke making himself so at home.

"How did you sleep, all alone in your bed?'

She shrugged. "Not well."

"I know how upset you were. Does Patrick often drop in like that, unannounced?"

"No. He thought I was expecting him."

Luke put his arms around her. "I sure missed you last night." He nuzzled her neck.

At that moment, Mucho gave a welcoming little bark. Callahan looked over Luke's shoulder to see Patrick standing in the doorway. She pulled away, feeling her cheeks burning.

"Good morning," Patrick said in a tight voice.

"Good morning, sweetheart," she said cheerfully, determined to somehow defuse the tension. "How about some coffee?" Without waiting for an answer, she poured him a cup.

Luke moved over to the window. "Looks like it's going to be a beautiful day." His enthusiasm rang false. "That sun should melt the snow on the roads in no time. I just read in the paper they got more than a foot on the mountain. Maybe I'll get in a little cross-country skiing this week."

"Or you could take a hike."

Patrick's barb obviously hit home. Luke's jaw clenched, but his voice remained neutral. "You know, I think that's a good idea—a nice long walk in the snow."

Hearing the word "walk," Mucho went wild, barking and dancing around Luke.

Luke took Mucho's leash off its hook inside the coat closet, and the two of them wasted no time getting out the door. Callahan took a reinforcing deep breath and turned to her son.

"Patrick, honey, we have to talk about this."

He nodded. "Sorry if I was rude to your boyfriend. But I wish I'd had some warning here. I mean, I walk in and find this...dude I

220

never even *heard of* acting like he owns the place. Please, tell me he isn't going to be my new stepdad!"

She ignored his comment. "It was a surprise visit. He just arrived a few days ago."

"And you opened the house to him? Someone you just met? 'I'll be staying until I get some things straightened out.' What the hell does that mean? God, Mom… I know last year was a rough time for you, and you're lonely. But can't you see what this guy's up to?"

"I know how it looks, honey. But, there's more to this." How could she tell Patrick the truth? He didn't even know that she believed her dreams weren't really dreams. She'd never discussed that with her left-brained, down-to-earth son. She'd always planned to someday, but this certainly didn't feel like the time.

"More to what? Mom, you can't be seriously involved with him!"

When she didn't answer, Patrick sighed and leaned back in his chair. "I don't want you to take offense, but this looks like a classic mid-life crisis. A woman in my office—she's about your age—suddenly started acting really weird—I mean totally out of character. She sold her car and bought a motorcycle. And then she got her nose pierced. She came within an inch of getting canned when she told the boss to screw himself, but now she seems back to her old self again, thanks to some kind of natural hormone therapy. She's really up front about what the problem was."

Callahan suppressed a smile, realizing that a woman approaching fifty has a built-in excuse for erratic behavior. *Blame it on hormones. Mid-life dementia.* She decided to go with it.

"I have an appointment with Dr. Rodriguez for a checkup in a couple of weeks," she replied honestly.

Patrick looked somewhat relieved. "Can't you get in sooner? Tell him it's an *emergency.*"

Callahan felt a wave of intense love for her son and grabbed him in a hug.

"I'll do my best. Meanwhile, please, my sweet son, don't worry about me."

"It's Luke I'm worried about. And *he* should be worried about *me*. I mean it, Mom. I won't just sit by and let him take advantage of you. I watched Brad do that, and it's not going to happen again!"

"Luke's not taking advantage of me."

Patrick acted as though he hadn't heard her. "I had a strong gut feeling about Brad, right from the get-go, but I didn't say anything. I didn't want to spoil your happiness. I feel really guilty about that, Mom. Maybe if I'd spoken up…"

"Honey, you're my son, not my guardian. I appreciate your concern, but I'm responsible for my own decisions." She kissed his cheek. "Speaking of decisions," she said, determined to regain her role as parent, "do you want pancakes or French toast for breakfast?"

His expression relaxed into a grin. "No one makes French toast like my mom."

Callahan returned his smile, relieved that the tension between them had broken.

"So," she said, assembling the ingredients, "tell me about this new girlfriend of yours."

She was cleaning up the breakfast dishes when Donny called.

"I've been doing my best to stay out of your hair, but you didn't answer my call yesterday, and I'm dying of curiosity. Are you still playing hostess?"

"You have no idea. Patrick is here, too."

"Omigod! How did *that* happen? Can you talk?"

"For a few minutes. Patrick is in my study, checking his e-mails. Luke is walking Mucho. I'm having a nervous breakdown."

"No doubt. So, hurry. Fill me in."

Callahan gave Donny an update, including the incident with Brad at Santacafé.

"I wish I'd seen that! Perhaps I've misjudged Luke. Anyone who manhandles Bradley wins points with me." He paused. "Any update on Luke's plans for the future?"

"No. He said he decided to drop out of law school, give up his apartment, and sort things out."

"Alarm! Alarm! Hello? Can't you hear those bells going off?"

Deathmark

Callahan sighed. "You might as well know. I said he could stay here for awhile, until he decides what to do next."

"You didn't. Cal, honestly…"

"Stop right there, Donny. I've had enough lectures for one morning."

"Well, keep in touch, girlfriend—with me *and* with reality."

Luke returned with a wet but happy Mucho a short time later. "Where's Patrick?"

"Working in my study."

"So, how long is he staying?"

Funny, he was just asking the same thing about you.

"Early afternoon. He's meeting co-workers for dinner tonight in Albuquerque to strategize for tomorrow's conference. He'll drive straight through to Denver late Tuesday afternoon."

"I'll make myself scarce until he leaves—take a drive into town." He grabbed her and gave her a quick but passionate kiss. "See you later."

The rest of Patrick's visit went smoothly. He joined her in the studio to see her latest paintings, and they talked about his work, friends, and love-life. They both avoided the subject of Luke until they were saying goodbye.

"Please, take care of yourself, Mom. I'll try not to worry about you."

"There's no reason to worry."

"You can't convince me of that. I have a really bad feeling about this guy, and I'll be happy when he's gone."

She avoided responding by giving him a big hug.

"Drive carefully, honey. You know how much I love you. You've always been the center of my life."

"I know, Mom. Love you, too."

After Patrick left, Callahan sat on a bench under the covered portal with Mucho by her side. She was exhausted and near tears.

"Oh, poocho, what am I going to do? Everyone thinks I'm nuts to be involved with Luke. Am I?"

223

Mucho answered the rhetorical question with a sympathetic *rrrrrumph* and nudged her chest with his head. She put her arm around him.

"You're the only one who likes him, aren't you, boy?'

He answered by licking her cheek.

Callahan smiled. "Well, I definitely feel better. You've always been an excellent judge of character. A smoocho for my Mucho." She planted a kiss on the top of his head. "Come on, baby boy, let's go to the studio and make good use of this time alone."

At four o'clock she was about ready to call it a day. She put aside a new sketch she'd titled *The Rescue*—an Indian maiden riding horseback behind a long-haired warrior, her arms tight around his waist—and paused to study the still-unfinished portrait of Running Wolf. Setting it on an easel, she began fine-tuning his face. *The nose should be slightly wider at the bridge. A little more flare to the nostrils. More definition under the cheekbones. It's almost there—more curve to the upper lip.*

She stood back, her eyes narrowed in concentration. Although the shape of Running Wolf's face and his features differed from Luke's, there was a similarity in the set of their eyes that she hadn't noticed before. She examined it from another angle. *Is that true? Or am I just seeing what I want to see?*

Mucho barked and Callahan heard the clunk of the garage door closing.

A few minutes later, Luke's voice rang out, "I'm home."

She cringed, at the same time thankful Patrick wasn't there to hear *that* announcement.

"I'm in the bedroom," she called out to him.

He came in carrying skis, poles, and several large shopping bags, obviously filled with clothing.

"Hey," she said. "It looks like you've been shopping."

"That big sports store south of town is amazing." Luke leaned

Deathmark

the skis and poles against the wall and tossed the bags on the bed.

"Wait right here," he said, hurrying out of the room. "There's more." Moments later he was back with another large bag.

"Wow," she said, trying to hide her surprise. She'd assumed that he would rent ski equipment for a few days, not make an expensive investment. He pulled out two jackets—one down, the other a lightweight Gortex—ski pants, a day pack, two heavy sweaters and several pairs of insulated socks.

"And last but not least—the finishing touch." He pulled a red woolen cap over his dark hair. "What do you think?"

He looked so excited, she had to smile.

"Looks like you're all set."

"Oh, wait—I'd better get the groceries out of the car. I picked up king crab at Whole Foods. And fixings for my special Caesar salad. I'm going to fix you a dinner you won't forget."

After he left the room, Callahan looked at all the stuff strewn across her bed. He'd certainly spent a lot of money. And that wasn't inexpensive Champagne they'd had on the picnic. Although they had never really discussed his financial situation—beyond his saying that 'money was no object' before they went to dinner, and he was just being a considerate guest then, wasn't he?—she had assumed that his budget was tight. After all, he'd been in school, now had car payments, and he hadn't escorted for almost two weeks. A receipt from the sporting goods store lay among the items on the bed. $2,576.50.

And he'd paid for everything with cash.

25

"*Buenos dias*," Consuela shouted from the entryway. "*Ay,* Mucho. No licking on me!" She came into the kitchen, pushing him away and giggling. Her smile vanished when she saw Luke sitting with Callahan at the kitchen table.

"Good morning, Consuela," he said, in between bites of a blueberry bagel. "Nice to see you again."

She gave a quick nod, her dark eyes averted. "I'll start cleaning at the back of the house."

"Don't you want a cup of coffee first?" Callahan asked.

"*No, gracias.*" She disappeared down the hall.

"Well, it's time for me to get out of your hair." Luke pushed back from the table. "I've decided to exchange my skis for another brand that the salesman recommended. They're more expensive, but what the heck. You only live once." He shot her a quick glance and grinned. "Oops. Just an expression."

Deathmark

Callahan again felt concern for his finances, and then tried to shrug it off. *How he spends his money is his own business, I'm not his mother.*

He leaned toward her. "On second thought, maybe I'll really scandalize Consuela by ravishing you here in the kitchen. Or I could sweep you up and carry you screaming back into the bedroom. Lock you in and show you no mercy."

Callahan laughed. "You are outrageous. What am I going to do with you?"

"I'll help you think of something tonight." He kissed her, long and deep, pulled back to look into her eyes, then kissed her again. "Have a productive morning, gorgeous. I'll see you later."

Callahan sat at the table after he left, smiling and shaking her head. *Face it, O'Connor, you're crazy about him. Or maybe just crazy, period.*

Consuela came down the hall and paused at the kitchen door. "Is it permitted for me to clean in your bedroom today?" she asked, with uncharacteristic stiffness.

"Of course," Callahan said, dismayed and a little irritated by Consuela's disapproving attitude. It was, after all, *her* house and *her* life.

"Consuela, I know you're uncomfortable around Luke. And I'm sorry about that. But you have to understand he's someone very special to me."

Consuela's mouth tightened. "He'll be staying for longer?"

"Yes. Maybe for a couple of weeks."

"He is *muy guapo*, very handsome." Consuela hesitated, obviously weighing whether she should say more. "I don't mean to be the busybody. But you're a good woman. You don't deserve more hurt." When Callahan didn't answer, Consuela continued. "Some men are not what they act to be. As my grandmama would say, '*No es oro todo lo que reluce.*' All that glitters is not gold."

Callahan had just walked in the kitchen door, a couple of hours later, when she heard Luke's voice, raised in anger.

"You were told to stay out of this room! I said I'd clean up after myself."

Consuela's reply was muffled. Callahan hurried down the hall toward the guest room, an equally alarmed Mucho at her heels.

"This door was closed," she heard Luke continue. "What were you doing in here?"

Consuela stood beside the vacuum cleaner, her stout body rigid with indignation. They both turned to face Callahan as she entered the room.

"What's going on here?"

"I came back and found her snooping around, moving my things."

"I just move that little case from under the bed so to vacuum under it." Consuela's voice shook and tears shone in her brown eyes. "Monday is my vacuum day!"

Callahan saw Luke's briefcase lying on the bed. "I'm sure Consuela didn't mean to…"

"I don't like people messing with my things," he said in a soft voice. Snatching up the briefcase, he left the room.

"*Señora,* I do nothing wrong." Consuela shook her head adamantly, then burst into tears. Mucho whined and licked her arm.

"Of course you didn't." Callahan gave her a hug. "I'm so sorry. Don't worry. I'll straighten this out."

Luke was in her bedroom, staring out the window with his back to her. The briefcase was still in his hand. She slammed the door shut behind them.

"Listen, here," she said, making no effort to hide her own anger, "there's something you'd better understand. Consuela has been with me for years. She's more than just my housekeeper; she's my *friend*. She has a key to this house and is the most trustworthy person in the world. She would *never, ever* bother your things, and I *will not* have you speaking to her like that! Do you understand?"

He turned to face her. "Okay. I blew it." His voice was soft, but his blue eyes looked darker, as though a storm brewed somewhere behind them. He put the briefcase down and moved toward her, his expression contrite. "Please forgive me." He wrapped his arms around her, ignoring her lack of response. "Oh, Callahan," he whispered into her hair, "I wish I could just…" His voice trailed off.

"What?"

He held her tighter. "Nothing."

Callahan was out of patience. She pulled back and gave him a hard look. "*Tell* me. What were you going to say?"

"Just that I wish I could learn to think before I act. That's an old problem with me."

It was Callahan's turn to speak before she thought. "Perhaps a lot older than you know."

"What's that suppose to mean?"

"Running Wolf was hot-headed and acted without considering the consequences…"

"Oh, Jeez." He ran his fingers through his hair. "Can we please not get off on *that* right now? Can we just focus on the here and now? It's a beautiful day and I'm looking forward to trying out my skis for a few hours. Please, Callahan."

"It's just that I've had it with you being so damned secretive."

"I can't expect you to understand. But if you'll just…"

"I understand that you have trouble trusting, Luke. And now I understand why. But you can trust *me*. I deserve to know what the hell is going on with you."

"Nothing's going on. I'm just used to living alone and I acted like a jerk. It won't happen again, I promise. I'll apologize to Consuela for my rudeness." He took her in his arms and nuzzled her neck. "Forgive me?" As always, she felt herself respond to his touch.

Then he abruptly glanced at his watch and released her.

"Hey, I'd better get going. The salesman at that ski shop yesterday told me about a trail that starts just below the ski runs and loops along the west side of the mountain. The Norski Trail, I think he called it. I can follow it for awhile and take off exploring from there."

Callahan remembered that the Norski Trail was one of Brad's favorites, but immediately suppressed the thought.

Luke pulled on his new ski pants. "I know you need to work, but I wish you were coming with me."

"I don't ski."

He pulled his new wool sweater over his head. "Maybe someday you'll give it a try."

"Don't count on it."

He winked. "I can be pretty persuasive."

"I've noticed."

He picked up his briefcase. "Do you mind if I stash this on one of the back shelves in your closet? Just to get it out of the way."

She shrugged. "Go ahead."

He briefly disappeared into her walk-in closet. When he came out, he collected his ski equipment and flashed a cocky grin. It was hard to believe he'd been so upset only moments before.

"Okay, here I go. How about a kiss for luck?"

As she closed her eyes and accepted his kiss, a familiar dream-image moved across the canvas of her mind. *Running Wolf, seen from a distance, galloping his horse up behind and then close beside a stampeding buffalo, his spear held high.* Her eyes flew open and she pulled back to stare at Luke.

"Careful..." She heard the warning before she realized she had spoken. "Be careful."

Luke's confident grin reappeared. "No way. That would take all the fun out of it."

Callahan sat on the bed for a few minutes after he'd left, shaken by the image. *Why did I remember that dream, just now?* She took several moments and deep breaths, willing herself to relax.

Then her mind jumped to Luke's briefcase. Why is he so protective of it? She got up and went into her closet. It was on a top shelf, lying on its side, pushed into a corner. Near the handle she saw small silver initials. She moved closer. LM. *M?* She stood on tiptoes to make sure of what she was seeing. *Luke—what the hell does 'M' stand for?* She heard Donny's voice in her head: *"Are you even sure Luke Bennett is his real name? Sounds like a stage name to me."*

For a moment, she considered taking the briefcase down and opening it. *No, that would make me just another person he can't trust. But I'm not going to let this go by. We're having this out, tonight. For god's sake, if I don't even know his last name, what else don't I know?*

Heading down the hall on her way out of the house, Callahan

Deathmark

heard Consuela's voice in the kitchen, talking to herself in an impassioned tone.

"He's trouble, that one. Eyes like blue ice. To say to me that I am *snooping*, moving his things... *Que loco hombre!*"

Callahan shook her head. Consuela had a memory like an elephant. She would never forgive Luke.

"I would say to him a thing or two," Consuela said, furiously scrubbing the countertop. "*Cree el ladron que todos son de su condición*, the thief thinks everyone's a thief." She fell silent when she saw Callahan standing in the kitchen doorway.

"Consuela, Luke is sorry he upset you. Did he apologize before he left?"

"No, *señora.*" Her expression turned hopeful. "He has left?"

"For the day. He knows he owes you an apology, and I'll make sure you get it."

Consuela's brown eyes filled with tears. "To be accused of *snooping* in a house where I have work for so long, is no fair! It was my day to vacuum rooms. Dust hides under beds."

"Of course. You were only doing your job. I can assure you nothing like this will ever happen again. Try not to let it ruin your day," she added, knowing that she was wasting her breath. "I'll be in the studio for a few hours. There's sliced turkey in the fridge. Make yourself a sandwich when you get hungry."

As Callahan pulled her down jacket out of the coat closet, she could hear Consuela's voice continuing her solitary conversation.

"Strutting like *el gallo*, he comes down the hall. Like he's master of the *hacienda*! Apology? Humph! That one has feelings for himself only!"

231

26

Callahan was working on *The Rescue* when Mucho ran to the window and let out his oh-boy-someone's-coming bark. She was surprised to see Donny hurrying up the path. Mucho lunged to greet him as she opened the door.

"You great, over-sexed beast!" Donny staggered backward, Mucho's paws on his shoulders. "Can't we just shake hands?"

Mucho gave Donny's mustache a juicy loving lick before backing off.

"He *has* had all his shots, hasn't he?" Donny wiped his mustache with the back of his hand. "We must be very careful in these days of dangerous sex." Then he patted Mucho's head. "Just kidding, poocho—you know Uncle Donny loves you. But you could use a breath mint."

Callahan laughed. "I do my best, but have you ever tried brushing a Great Dane's teeth?"

Deathmark

"You know, that's one experience I've missed." He and Callahan exchanged air kisses.

Donny shrugged out of his tan leather jacket. "Don't you just love this?" He stroked the jacket before laying it carefully across the top of the sofa. "It's my gift to myself for finishing that last book." He looked around the room. "Where's Lover Boy?"

"Skiing."

"Good. Please don't bother offering me any of your ghastly coffee. I know I'm intruding on sacred work time, so I'll get right to it. I've just come from my dermatologist's office—that charming Bob Thomsen. I needed emergency Botox to soften the lines between my eyes—a professional hazard, all those hours peering at a computer screen. The point is—god, I'm out of breath from dashing up here. I must sit." He plopped himself on the sofa. "The point is I talked to the doctor about Luke's so-called birthmarks..."

"You *what?* And what do you mean, 'so called?'"

"Don't get excited. And don't frown like that..." He waggled his finger at her."...or you'll be visiting Doctor Bob, too." He gently pressed the red puncture marks between his eyes. "He's now removing tattoos with a laser. Apparently there's a big demand— tatter's remorse, I suppose. If I'd tattooed the names of all my past lovers on my body, I'd look like an ink pad!" He pressed between his eyes again.

"Donny! Get to the point."

"So, I told him I was doing research for a book and asked if a *tattoo* could be made to look like a birthmark. He said it certainly could." Donny sat back with a self-satisfied expression. "Don't you see, Lukey boy knew you were coming to town, did his homework, and got ready to get your attention. A con artist *par excellence!*" He gave her a sympathetic look. "I guess this punches a hole in your past life theory."

She shook her head. "No, it doesn't! The night in San Francisco when Luke showed me his birthmarks, he also showed me photographs of himself as a baby and a young child. The marks were already there."

Donny clearly wasn't going to give up.

"He could have doctored the photographs, too! Photoshopped them. There has to be a *rational* explanation."

"And then there's the mark on his back. I never painted that, never even told anyone about it."

"Maybe he just threw that one in for effect and got lucky."

"No. It's too perfect. In exactly the same place, the same shape. Jagged like huge bear teeth would make…"

Donny threw up his hands in defeat. "You're absolutely *blind* where this guy is concerned. What's he done? Hypnotize you?"

She thought about the initials on Luke's briefcase, briefly considered talking to Donny about it but decided against it. She wanted to confront Luke directly, as soon as he returned.

"I don't really have the energy to go into this right now. I told you that it's complicated between Luke and me."

"Looks pretty simple to me. Luke's a sexy con artist, taking advantage of your crystal-packin'-mama spiritual beliefs and generous nature. Have you set up a trust fund for him yet?"

Callahan's anger flared.

"Stop! I can do without your sarcasm. Besides, you're hardly the one to lecture about relationships."

"Okay, okay. I've kissed a few frogs myself—that Brazilian tango teacher on the cruise last summer certainly comes to mind—but, sweetheart, this escort of yours takes the prize. Now, calm down. I'm not here to fight with you. I'm on your side, remember?"

She sighed, her anger dissolving.

"I appreciate your caring, Donny. I really do. This is a difficult, confusing time for me. But it's something I'm just going to have to work through, in my own way."

He stood up. "All right, girlfriend. I'm off. Rather not be here when Luke returns. I might end up challenging him to a duel or something. Swords at dawn." He paused. "Hmmm. Not a bad title. Now, all I need is a plot."

She gave him a weak smile. "I love you. Thanks for coming by."

"Love you, too. Yell if you need me. I'll go home and sharpen my blade, just in case."

Deathmark

Callahan worked until almost five. On her way to shower, she stopped to check her voicemail.

"Hello, Callahan…it's Paul Kramer. Just hoping to catch you in. I have exciting news, exciting for me, anyway. I'm about to be a Santa Fe homeowner. My offer on a property northwest of town was accepted today. It's everything I hoped to find—a comfortable house, several acres, and stables for a couple of horses. I'll be moving, as soon as I can. In fact, I'll be in Santa Fe next Monday to finalize some things. How about having dinner with me? I can't think of a better way to celebrate. Hope to hear from you soon." He gave her his cell phone number, and then repeated it.

She saved the message, planning to call and decline later. Paul was an attractive man, but she had no intention of seeing him again. Her life was complicated enough. He'd certainly have no trouble finding female companionship in Santa Fe. The town was filled with unattached women.

By five-thirty, Callahan was anxious. It was dark and Luke wasn't back yet. *Is he lost? It's easy to lose your way on the mountain, if you get off the trail.* She remembered it happening to a couple of seasoned cross-country skiers last year, and they weren't found for days. Both suffered serious frostbite, one nearly died from dehydration and exposure. *If only Luke hadn't lost his cell phone. He should have gotten another one when he was out buying all that ski equipment.* With relief, she heard the garage door open and close. Mucho ran to investigate.

"Hello, boy." Luke's voice in the hall sounded subdued. A moment later, he walked into the kitchen. His sunburned face and tousled hair made him more handsome than ever, but his smile looked forced.

She prepared herself for a confrontation. "We have to talk."

"Not now, please." He took her in his arms. "Just let me hold you for a minute."

She did, and then pulled back. "Luke, what's happened?"

He avoided her eyes. "Nothing. I'm just beat. It was incredible skiing. Beautiful country. I saw some deer tracks, but no deer." He sniffed the air. "What do I smell cooking?"

"Consuela made a pot of green chile stew before she left." She studied his face and saw the tension there. "Listen, Luke, we really have to talk."

"Okay, okay. But first, I need a long soak in the hot tub." He turned and left, without asking her to join him.

When Luke didn't reappear after forty-five minutes, Callahan found him asleep in her bed. She shook his shoulder. He groaned and rolled away. *What the hell is going on with him?* Then she saw her bottle of Xanax, open on the bedside table. *Holy shit! How many did he take?* She poured them into her hand. It didn't look like many were missing. She shook him again, this time hard.

"Luke! Wake up!"

His eyes fluttered open. "Callahan … my love," he whispered.

She shook him again. "How many Xanax did you take?"

"I dunno. Just a few. So tired... No worry. Just need to sleep." His eyes closed again.

For the second time that day, Callahan made an effort to calm herself. He couldn't have taken enough to kill him—probably no more than three, fifteen milligrams. *Okay, no need for 911. No need for panic. But by god, I'll have answers tomorrow. He won't put me off again.*

The shades on the window were open, and the security lights outside cast a soft light across the bed. Lying beside him, Callahan could see the marks that ran across his chest. *Donny's wrong. I'm afraid there is no easy, "rational" explanation for any of this.*

She awoke sometime in the night, feeling Luke's hand on the curve of her hip.

His voice was sleepy, barely coherent. "Are you awake?"

Deathmark

"Sort of."

"I… want to thank you… for something."

"What?"

"Not being frightened by what I told you… about my father… about wrecking the house. You…trust me. Thank you." He snuggled closer, and before she could respond, he was asleep again.

Did she trust him? How could she? And yet…somehow, in spite of everything, she felt that she knew him, on a far deeper level than she could explain.

Mita'wa higna, my husband. The voice whispered in her mind as she closed her eyes and drifted into oblivion.

27

"**Time to hit** that mountain again!" Luke rushed into the kitchen where Callahan sat at the table, drinking her second cup of coffee. He bent to kiss her. "I'll just take a couple of these bagels with me, finish getting my things together, get an early start."

"Not so fast, Luke. Sit down."

"Uh-oh, that sounds like an order." His tone was teasing, but his eyes had lost their sparkle. He pulled out a chair and sat.

"Look, I know I owe you an apology for just numbing out on you last night."

"Is that what you call getting into my Xanax?"

"I was tired and stressed out. I didn't want you to see me like that. I just swallowed a couple to take the edge off. But I guess on top of all the exercise and the hot tub, they knocked me out. I'm sorry about dinner."

"*Dinner* isn't the issue."

"Borrowing a couple Xanax is?"

Deathmark

"You said last night that you took 'a few.' That's more than two."

He shrugged. "Why are you making such a big deal about this?"

She leveled her gaze at him. "What's your real name, Luke?"

He jerked as if she'd slapped him. "What?"

"You heard me."

"What are talking about? You know my name."

"I saw the initials on your briefcase. LM."

"Shit. Is that what you're so upset about?" He paused, staring at the table. "My old man's last name was Moore. Bennett is my middle name, my mother's maiden name. I legally dropped the Moore. I wanted to erase everything that came from him. Can you blame me?"

"No. But that briefcase looks brand new."

"It looks new because it was a Christmas gift from Monica and I've taken good care of it. I keep important papers in there and didn't want to leave it behind when I left. Okay? So is the interrogation over?"

"This isn't an interrogation! We're not exactly casual friends, you know. I'm tired of all this mystery surrounding you. I'm tired of being patient, waiting for you to open up. I care so much about you, and yet there's so much about your life I don't know." Her voice cracked, as anger gave way to frustrated tears.

"Oh, Callahan." He came around to pull her to her feet and hold her tight. "I know I haven't been fair. There are reasons…" He took a deep breath. "I can't begin to tell you what you mean to me. You've shown me how it could be, between two people. I would do anything for you. Anything."

Tears of exhaustion, relief, confusion were spilling from Callahan's eyes. He caressed her left cheek and then the other, wiping the tears away.

"If you don't believe anything else about me, believe that." He held her face in his hands, looking hard into her eyes. "It *is* time to be honest—past time. It's just so hard… I need more time alone today, out in the fresh air, getting my head back on. Okay? Will you give me that? Let's order dinner in tonight, and we'll talk. Meanwhile, I want you to carry this around with you all day." He kissed her, long, deep and thoroughly. "You have no idea how much you mean to me."

He released her, walked to the counter and helped himself to the bagels.

"See you tonight." Then he blew her another kiss as he left. "Wish me luck."

Callahan stood frozen in place.

"Good luck," she whispered, not knowing if she was talking to Luke or herself.

She was about to head off to the studio when the phone rang. It was Suzanne.

"Oh good, I'm glad I caught you! If you haven't already heard, I felt you should know about Brad. He was in a car accident last night."

"Is he all right?"

"From what I've heard, he's pretty banged up. Noreen talked to Anita earlier this morning. Apparently, he has a concussion and a couple broken ribs. They were worried about spinal damage for a while, but tests show he's just badly bruised."

"What happened?"

"He was cross-country skiing. And, apparently, really hitting his flask. A witness said he got into a heated argument with some guy in the Norski Trail parking area, before leaving the mountain."

Callahan's stomach clenched. She pulled out a kitchen chair and sat down.

"He had no business driving," Suzanne continued. "Thank god no one was riding with him. His blood alcohol level was point-one-two when they got him to the hospital, around six-thirty last night."

"Where? Where did the accident happen?"

"On Hyde Park Road. He completely totaled his car, lost control of it on one of those tight curves. Fortunately, he ran into a tree or he'd have gone over into a deep ravine. According to Anita, he's insisting that the accident wasn't his fault—that someone deliberately ran him off the road."

Luke's words to Brad at Santacafé rang in Callahan's ears: *You're lucky we're in a public place, asshole.*

"Typical of Brad, isn't it?" Suzanne continued. "He was never one to take responsibility for his actions. Anyway, that's the story."

"But he's going to be all right?"

"Unless one of the nurses kills him. Anita told Noreen that he's raising holy hell. Threatening to hire a private investigator."

"Oh, my god."

"Are you all right, dear? Frankly, I didn't expect you to be this upset."

"This just... took me by surprise."

At that moment, the doorbell rang. Mucho scrambled to his feet, barking. *Probably Donny. News of Brad has traveled fast.*

"Listen, Suzanne, I have to go. There's someone at my door."

"Wait. You *do* know that Paul's buying property here? It's a great house, but it needs a woman's touch. He's coming next week..."

"Yes, he called and left a message. Talk to you later." She hung up and hurried to the front door. A glance through the entryway window revealed an unfamiliar white Ford Taurus in the driveway. She held Mucho by the collar and opened the door.

"Ms. O'Connor?" The gray-haired, heavy-set man standing in the doorway wore a trench coat over a suit and tie. *Definitely not from around here.*

"Sit, Mucho. Yes?"

"Callahan O'Connor?"

"Yes."

"I'm Detective James Silvo." He flashed an ID. "I'm working with the Santa Fe County Sheriff's Department on a special investigation, and I need to talk to a friend of yours."

She gave him a questioning look.

"Luke Bennett? I understand he's staying here with you."

Callahan felt a sharp rush of adrenaline. "Well, yes."

"May I speak with him?"

"No. I mean, he isn't here."

"When do you expect him back?"

"May I ask what this is about?" *As if I didn't know. Damn you, Brad!*

"I'd rather speak to Mr. Bennett, ma'am."

"I just told you, he's not here."

"Do you know where he is?"

"Actually, I don't. " *Not exactly a lie. Luke could be anywhere on that mountain.*

"When do you expect him back?"

"I'm… not really sure."

"Well, perhaps I could just wait here, until he returns."

"That could be quite a while. He said something about exploring the area."

"In that case, ma'am, you and I definitely need to talk. May I come in?"

Callahan hesitated, her mind racing. She knew she could get in trouble for being evasive. *What was it? Obstructing justice?* But Brad was just trying to cause trouble for her. No doubt if Luke and Brad had run into each other, they *did* quarrel. That would explain why Luke was upset when he came home. *But that doesn't mean Luke had anything to do with Brad's accident. The bastard was drunk! Still… why didn't Luke tell me about it?*

The detective handed her his badge and ID.

"Ms. O'Connor, please examine my credentials to be sure you have no questions regarding my authority."

She looked at them more closely. Detective James Silvo, San Francisco Police Department. *San Francisco?* She frowned and shot him another look, carefully comparing his face to the one on his ID before handing them back. *What is this about?*

"It's smart to be cautious," the detective said. "Never a good idea to let a stranger into your house. Not these days. Of course, you do have that big watch dog. What is he… a Great Dane?"

"Yes. Just a minute. Sit, Mucho. Over there. Stay." She moved back from the doorway. "Come in."

He stepped into the entryway, looking around. "Nice place you have here."

"Thank you." She gestured toward the living room. "We can talk in there."

He took off his coat, laid it across the arm of the sofa.

She sat facing him, hoping she appeared calmer than she felt. *Why is a San Francisco detective looking for Luke? This isn't about Brad's accident!*

242

Deathmark

The detective took out a pad and pencil. He studied her.

"How well do you know Mr. Bennett?"

"He's a friend."

"You've known him for some time then?"

"No... I met him in San Francisco a few weeks ago, when I was there promoting my work. I'm an artist."

"And a good one." His smile changed his deeply lined face, made it seem younger. "I'm familiar with your work, Ms. O'Connor. You show at a gallery in Ghirardelli Square, don't you? What's it called? Bay Gallery?"

"Gallery on the Bay," she said, surprised.

"My wife majored in art history in college. Her idea of a great Saturday afternoon is visiting galleries. We were in Gallery on the Bay a couple of weeks ago."

"I don't understand. If you live in San Francisco..."

"I live in Burlingame, actually. About thirty minutes south of the city."

"I'm sorry, Detective...Silvo is it? But I'm confused. What is this about?

"It's about a murder, Ms. O'Connor."

Callahan stared at him in disbelief. "A *murder?*"

"A woman by the name of Linda Morelli was killed in San Francisco on October thirty-first. Halloween night. We have reason to believe that she was, shall we say... *involved* with Luke Bennett. In fact, they had dinner together earlier that night. He may have been the last person to see her alive. He obviously left her hotel room in a big hurry. H was seen running down the stairs."

Callahan felt the blood drain from her face. *The woman Leda said couldn't keep her hands off Luke—dead?*

"I can see this is a shock."

She swallowed hard. "Look, there must be a mistake. Luke couldn't be involved in..."

"Murder, Ms. O'Connor. The victim was shot. Two bullets to the head. The crime appears to have been drug-related. Bennett and the dead woman may have been dealing in drugs."

This can't be happening.

"Do you live alone here?"

"What?"

"Do you live in this big house alone?"

She nodded.

"No live-in help?"

"Why are you asking these questions?"

"Because I'm concerned for your safety. If you know where Luke Bennett is, you need to tell me."

When she didn't answer, he continued.

"Did you know that your *friend* works for an escort agency in San Francisco? I mean, he hires out his *services* to women. He's a prostitute. The woman who was killed was apparently a regular client. His name and work number were in her address book." He paused, watching Callahan.

She waited in horrified silence for him to continue, to say he knew that *she, too,* had been a client.

"Now," he continued, after a moment, "if Mr. Bennett is innocent, he has nothing to worry about. But the sooner he's located and questioned, the better." Silvo reached into his pocket and pulled out a business card. "This has my cell phone number. I'm staying in a motel on the south side of Santa Fe. My expense account doesn't allow enough to stay near the Plaza. A shame, because the downtown area is really charming." His expression softened. "I'll have to bring my wife here someday. She'd be in heaven with all the art galleries."

When Callahan didn't respond, he stood and put his notepad back in his pocket.

"Thanks for your time. Contact me as soon as you hear from Mr. Bennett. Please."

Sick to her stomach, she walked him to the door. As he put his trench coat on he asked, "How long has Mr. Bennett been here in Santa Fe?"

"He arrived sometime last week. I think it was Wednesday."

"And he's been staying here with you the entire time?"

She nodded.

"You're certain he's planning to come back here?"

"I… Actually, I'm not certain." *Of anything, right now.*

244

Deathmark

"Did he take his things with him?"

"Some of them."

"But… some of his belongings are still here?"

Aware that the detective knew she was being evasive but unwilling to out-and-out lie, she nodded. *I won't let him examine Luke's bags without a search warrant. Luke and I are going to have it out tonight. I have to hear his side of this.* Another part of her brain was screaming *Are you crazy? What makes you think he won't kill you?* And then, the soft whisper, *Mita'wa higna, my husband. Soul of my soul.*

The detective was talking. Callahan could see his lips moving, but the voices in her head drowned out his words. She felt light-headed, and then struck by a serious wave of nausea.

A strong arm gripped her and led her back to the sofa.

"Steady, Ms. O'Connor. Now, put your head between your knees."

She did what he said. Mucho was close by her side, whining.

"Breathe deep. You almost fainted on me."

After a long moment, Callahan sat back up. "I'm sorry… I just…"

"Completely understandable. You're in shock. Stay right here, I saw where the kitchen is, and I'm getting you a glass of water."

Mucho looked torn between staying with Callahan and keeping an eye on the detective. He trotted into the kitchen. Moments later, they both returned, the detective carrying a glass of water.

"Drink this, and try to breathe normally." After a few moments, he said, "Just a couple more questions. What was Bennett driving?"

"I really didn't pay attention." *Why am I protecting him?*

"Was it a rental car?"

She shrugged, as if she didn't know. *Just go, please go!*

The detective took out his pad and made some quick notes.

"Okay, thanks for your help, Ms. O'Connor. Don't get up yet. I'll let myself out. No, on second thought, you'd better come and make sure the door is locked behind me." He turned at the door. "My wife will be thrilled that I met you. And remember, you have my cell number. I'll be expecting to hear from you. Soon. Time is of the essence in getting this matter cleared up."

245

She started to close the door.

"Take care of yourself, ma'am. I mean that."

Before getting into his car, she saw him scrutinize the courtyard, as though he expected to see Luke lurking behind a bush. Finally, he drove away.

Deathmark

28

Callahan braced herself, walked into her bedroom closet, grabbed Luke's briefcase and carried it to the bed. The latch wasn't locked and opened easily, revealing stacks of hundred dollar bills. *Oh, my god!* With trembling hands, she counted the stacks. Twelve. And ten bundles per stack. She estimated that each bundle contained about fifty tightly packed bills and did a quick calculation. *Six hundred thousand dollars! Drug money?* She didn't want to believe that—couldn't bear to believe that—but what other explanation made sense? *Why else would he be carrying around this much cash?*

She saw a slip of paper sticking out from a side pocket of the briefcase. It was a bill of sale from Monty's Used Cars, Las Vegas, Nevada. Signed by Luke B. Moore, for a 2012 Nissan Pathfinder, Four-Wheel Drive. $18,000. Paid in Cash. The sale was dated November 1. *Luke B. Moore! He said he legally dropped Moore.*

Fuck! Can I believe anything he says? He bought the Nissan in Las Vegas, not Albuquerque. He was in Vegas when I was trying to reach him, to thank him for the flowers. What was he doing there? Dealing drugs?

Callahan closed the briefcase, shaken to her core. Images filled her mind: *Luke with the murdered woman—eating dinner, having sex...and then...* Overcome by another wave of nausea, she ran to the bathroom. After a few minutes of dry heaves, she lay on the bed. Then she grabbed her phone and punched in Red Feather's number. Her heart sank when she got his recording. She knew he didn't carry a cell phone, preferring to stick to the old ways as much as possible.

"Red Feather, this is Callahan. I desperately need to talk to you. Please call me as soon as you can."

She tried to relax her body, as the shaman had taught her. *Pull energy through the top of your head and down your body. Now back up. Again, slowly. One more time. Now, go deep inside. Connect to your inner knowing.* She repeated the exercise, more slowly. *What does my 'inner knowing' tell me?*

The rational side of Callahan's brain started screaming! *It tells me that I'm a complete idiot for trusting Luke. It tells me that I'm fucking lucky to still be alive!*

More deep breaths. Then Red Feather's voice, *"You have found your warrior. Trust your instincts to guide you."* Then Running Wolf's voice, *"We are one, my beloved. From this day forward, our souls are joined."*

At that point, Callahan's head began to spin. She dug her fingers into the blankets and closed her eyes. Suddenly, her consciousness opened and she was back in the other lifetime, preparing Running Wolf for burial, tying his bear claw amulet around his neck and kissing his cold lips. *My heart is yours, for all time. For all time. This I swear.*

Callahan drifted—was it sleep or just a shifting from one physical reality to another? When she opened her eyes, half an hour later, she had no idea. But she did have a sense of certainty: Luke did not kill that woman. *I don't know what the real story is, but I know in my gut that he didn't do it. There's another explanation.*

She looked again at the briefcase beside her on the bed.

Deathmark

LM. Did the detective say the murdered woman's name? Her whole body went cold as ice. *Linda. Linda...Morelli. LM.*

Walking to her bedroom window, she stared out with unseeing eyes. *Red Feather warned me about a darkness around Luke. Have I been the world's biggest fool?*

Callahan knew it would be impossible to focus on work. It was almost noon and she needed something in her stomach, but the thought of food brought back the nausea. Not knowing what to do with herself, she took Mucho for a long walk.

They hadn't been back long when the doorbell rang. Glancing through the window, Callahan's heart sank. The white Taurus was parked by her courtyard gate.

"I'm sorry to bother you again, Ms. O'Connor." Detective Silvo's expression was noncommittal, but his eyes looked concerned. "Any sign of Mr. Bennett yet?"

"No. Stay, Mucho."

The detective studied her. "Are you all right?"

"I'm fine."

His gaze scanned the entryway. "May I come in?"

"Luke's not hiding behind the door, if that's what you think." She opened the door wider. "Look for yourself. I haven't heard from him since he left, early this morning."

The detective gave her another studied look, and then stepped back, apparently convinced.

"Okay. Keep my number close at hand. I'll be waiting to hear from you."

It was almost five o'clock when Callahan heard the garage door roll open and then close. Mucho ran to meet Luke in the hall and then the two of them, still roughhousing, came into the living room, where she was waiting.

"What a terrific day." Luke pulled off his cap and smoothed his hair down with his fingers. "I saw two deer! They stood not twenty yards away, they just stared at me. Beautiful! But it gave me the oddest feeling—like that had happened to me before. *Déjà vu*, right?" He removed his jacket and tried to pull her up into his arms.

She refused, her heart heavy as stone.

He pulled back to look at her. "What's wrong?"

"You tell me. I had a visitor this morning. A Detective Silvo from San Francisco."

Luke's face lost its ruddy color.

"He wanted to talk to you. About a woman who was murdered in San Francisco."

"Oh, shit."

"He said that you knew her. She'd been a client of yours."

"What did you say to him?"

"I was evasive. Said I didn't know where you were or when you'd be back."

"Callahan, I…"

"There's something else." She fought to keep her voice steady. "I know about the money in your briefcase. If it *is* your briefcase."

"You opened it?" He took a deep breath. "It isn't what you think. Oh, Jesus. Jesus. I've got to get out of here." He started toward the bedroom.

She ran behind him. "Wait a goddamn minute! You can't just leave without explaining…"

He turned to face her, his eyes brimming.

"I didn't mean to bring you trouble. You have to believe that. I didn't want you involved in this. I have to go now."

"Go where? Tell me what the fuck is going on! Is that drug money in your briefcase?"

He looked stunned. "What made you say that?"

"The detective said the murder might be drug-related."

"Shit!" He grabbed the briefcase out of the closet and hurried into the guest room.

"Where are you going?" she yelled, following behind him.

"I don't know." He threw a few items of clothing into his suitcase and hurried into the bathroom to gather his toiletries. "I can't let the police find me. Not yet. I need to think. Make some decisions. I'll call you…"

"Just like that?" Furious tears ran down her cheeks. "If there's a contest somewhere for a woman who can keep her head in the sand the longest, I'm sure as hell a top contender! How could I have been such a fool about you?"

He put his bags down and grabbed her in a hard embrace.

"Don't say that. I'm so sorry. Don't cry. I…I thought I could just start over here. A clean start. You mean so much to me. It was so perfect."

"I don't understand…"

"I'm leaving for your sake! I don't want you involved in this!"

"For god's sake, I'm already involved! Have I been harboring a fugitive? Are you a murderer?"

"No!" His eyes were bright, looking feverish and frantic. "I swear to you. It isn't the way it looks. I didn't kill anyone. Please, you've got to believe that."

"I want to…I…"

"I'll call you; I promise. You'll hear from me soon. Take care of her, buddy," he said to Mucho as he hurried down the hall.

An instant later, Callahan heard the garage door open and close. She stood in the entryway and watched the lights from his Nissan pull out of the driveway and disappear into the night.

29

Detective Silvo rang the doorbell early the next morning, before Callahan was dressed.

She opened the door in her bathrobe. "Luke's not here," she said abruptly.

"You haven't heard from him?"

She forced herself to meet his gaze. "Not since he left yesterday," she said. *Technically true.*

The detective sighed.

"Do you think I could bother you for a glass of water? I usually carry a water bottle with me, but I left it in the motel room. My blood pressure medicine makes me thirsty all the time."

Callahan groaned inwardly, recognizing his obvious ruse, but how could she refuse the man water?

"All right. Mucho, stay."

"I can see that he's a good watchdog."

Deathmark

He stepped uninvited past Mucho and into the entryway.

"What did you call him? Moochie?"

She tightened the sash on her robe. "Mucho."

Detective Silvo chuckled and scratched Mucho's head.

"Appropriate name. He *is* a lot of dog. Real protective of you, too. That's good. A woman alone can't be too careful." He followed her into the kitchen and looked around as she filled a glass with water. "Beautiful place you have here. I told my wife on the phone last night that it looks like something out of one of those Southwestern magazines she gets."

"Thanks." She handed him the glass, hoping he would gulp it down and be on his way. With a stab of irritation, she watched him pull a stool up to the counter and sit down. "Look here, Detective…"

"My wife, her name's Betty, wanted to know if you had a lot of your own paintings on the walls. I told her I didn't really get a chance to look around. Unfortunately, it wasn't a social call." He paused. "Which brings me back to Luke Bennett."

"I've told you everything that I…"

"You said he arrived last Wednesday. And he's been staying here with you the whole time."

"That's right."

"Does he have any other friends in town?"

"Not to my knowledge." She hesitated. "How did you know Luke was visiting me?"

"Figuring things out is my business, Ms. O'Connor. When we searched his apartment we found a note he'd written to himself at the bottom of a grocery list. 'Send flowers to C,' it said. You'd be surprised how many florists there are in San Francisco. It took awhile to find the right one and get your last name and address. But, like I said, that's my business."

Callahan's throat tightened. "I really don't have any more to say to you. I'll tell Luke you want to talk to him, if and when he returns."

"*If* and when? You think he may have skipped out?"

She shrugged.

"You said he left some of his things here."

"Did I?"

The detective reached into the pocket of his trench coat and pulled out a newspaper clipping. "I think you ought to see this."

She stared at the words **Woman Found Dead in Hotel Room,** written above a photo of a striking blonde with large eyes and a movie star smile. Callahan's knees went weak. She lowered herself onto a barstool and forced herself to continue reading.

> *The body of Linda Morelli, 46, owner of Morelli*
> *Interiors, a San Diego decorating service, was*
> *discovered yesterday morning in a suite of the*
> *Mark Hopkins Hotel. According to authorities,*
> *Morelli was shot twice in the face at close*
> *range. Witnesses report having seen her with a*
> *male companion in the hotel lobby and elevator*
> *shortly before midnight. Police are investigating.*

Callahan's hand was shaking, as she returned the clipping to Detective Silvo.

"Beautiful woman, wasn't she? Recently divorced. Apparently visited San Francisco regularly. Her assistant said she went on frequent *buying* trips. We think her business included some pretty shady deals. And that she had more than *one* reason to meet with Luke Bennett." He set his glass down on the counter. "I'll be on my way now. Unless you've thought of something else you want to tell me."

Callahan could only shake her head, as she followed him to the door.

"I'll be waiting for your call. Remember, you can reach me any time." The detective paused. "You know, Ms. O'Connor, sometimes even the smartest people let their feelings get in the way of their better judgment. And that can be very dangerous. Deadly, in fact. I see it all the time in this business."

She nodded, frantic for him to leave.

"Thanks for your time," he said.

254

Deathmark

Callahan closed the door and leaned against it, reeling from the shock of the newspaper clipping. Seeing the dead woman's photograph made it real. *Shot twice in the face. At close range.*

The wall of denial concerning Luke was collapsing. *He knew that woman—knew her intimately. He was with her the night she died. And he has all that money.*

Luke's voice spoke up, echoing in her confused head. *"I didn't kill anyone. You've got to believe that..."*

Callahan's head felt like it was about to explode. She rushed into the bathroom and swallowed a Xanax. Her thoughts swirled as she waited for the medication to take effect, curb her mounting panic. *Do the San Francisco police have a list of Luke's clients? If they do, my name is on that list!*

In her studio, some time afterward, the unfinished portrait of Running Wolf drew Callahan to it. She picked up the canvas and set it on an easel. Again, she was struck by the portrait's resemblance to Luke. *It's more than just the set of the eyes, it's the slope of the shoulders...the lift of the chin...the head cocked to one side with a hint of defiance.*

Callahan heard a roaring in her ears. She watched the dark eyes in the portrait lighten, and then change to a piercing blue. As she continued to stare, the whole face began to shift—alternating back and forth between Luke's features and those of Running Wolf. Moments passed before the roaring in her ears stopped and her vision returned to normal. She leaned against a wall, shaking and gulping air like someone who'd been held underwater. *Another vision? Or am I just sliding into dementia?*

Callahan turned the portrait toward the wall and forced herself to work on another canvas throughout the afternoon. *Focus on something else...*

The sun was low in the west when she locked the studio and followed Mucho back to the house. She quickly checked her voice messages. A call from Donny, eager to gossip about Brad's accident. Another from the gallery in Dallas, asking if she would do a show in the spring. One from Leda, wanting to schedule the photo shoot with *Art Scene* magazine. Nothing from Luke.

The phone rang just after midnight, jerking Callahan from a fitful sleep.

"It's me," Luke said. "Sorry to call so late."

"Where are you?"

"It's better if you don't know. Has that detective been back?"

"Yes."

"What did you tell him?"

"The truth. I don't know where you are or if—or when—you're coming back."

"I'm coming back. I can only imagine what you're thinking. I won't blame you if you never want to see me again. I shouldn't have come to Santa Fe. I'm so sorry for all the trouble I've caused you."

"If you care about me at all, you'll tell me what's going on. Now."

"Not on the phone. Please, Callahan, don't give up on me." The line went dead.

Callahan slept intermittently, floating between anguished dreams and wakefulness. Sometime during the night, she awoke from the familiar dream of kissing Running Wolf's lifeless lips.

Mita'wa higna, my husband. The voice still ringing in her head was higher pitched, much younger than hers. *How do I live without you?*

Deathmark

30

After a quick trip to the grocery store the next morning, Callahan was sickened to see the now-familiar white Taurus parked outside her front courtyard—empty. The wooden gate to the courtyard was open. *Damnation!* She pulled into the garage and closed it. Moments later, she unlocked and yanked open the front door. Detective Silvo sat on a bench under the covered portal.

When Mucho greeted him like an old friend, he laughed and patted the Great Dane's head.

"Hi, there, Much Dog. You're a fine fellow, that's for sure." He rose to his feet. "Good morning, Ms. O'Connor. I hope you don't mind my sitting out here. It's so pleasant. This is such a private, beautiful spot."

"I'm afraid I *do* mind, Detective. I'm very busy, and I have no new information for you."

"Well, then, I'll just impose on you for another glass of water."

"Forgot your water bottle again?" She didn't bother to keep the sarcasm from her voice. *Do I look stupid? You just want to check for signs of Luke.*

He smiled and moved toward the door.

"I'm afraid I did. Boy, the altitude here is something else. Makes me feel my age. How high above sea level are we? About seven thousand feet?"

She nodded and opened the door. *What the hell? If I refuse to let him in, he'll be suspicious. Probably get a search warrant.*

He followed her into the kitchen. Taking the glass she handed him, he plopped down on the same bar stool he'd occupied the morning before. Callahan lost it.

"Detective Silvo, I don't have time to chat with you. I'm a busy woman! I have groceries in the car…"

He was instantly on his feet. "I'll help you bring them in."

"No! That's not necessary."

"I don't mind. In fact, I insist."

She gritted her teeth and started down the hall, Detective Silvo right behind her, making small talk. *Who the hell does he think he is? Columbo?*

"Your house is so interesting. It's hard to take it all in." He came to a stop, staring at the wall. "Are these real weapons?"

Callahan curtly acknowledged that they were.

"Well, what do you know? This place is a regular museum. A spear, tomahawk, and what do you call that?"

"An Apache war club." She was itching to use it on him.

"Wait 'til I tell Betty," he said, still studying the display. "She's crazy about Indian stuff. Bought one of those 'dream catcher' things at a trading post in Arizona last summer. Hung it right over our bed to trap nightmares." He chuckled and then obviously saw the impatience on her face. "Okay, let's get those groceries."

They returned to the kitchen, the detective lugging a fifty-pound sack of dried dog food. Callahan shoved things into the refrigerator and then turned to face the detective.

"I think you can see by my meager provisions that I'm just

Deathmark

shopping for myself and my dog. Luke Bennett isn't here, and I don't know that he'll ever be back."

"I know you're in an uncomfortable position, Ms. O'Connor. But the fact is I have a job to do. Right now, you're my strongest link to Bennett."

"I've told you everything I can. And now I'm politely asking you to leave. I have work to do."

"I'm sure you do. Being an artist takes dedication, no doubt about that. By the way, I dropped into that gallery on Canyon Road that shows your work. What's it called? Santa Fe Visions, that's it. And I talked to the manager." He pulled out his note pad and consulted it. "Mrs. Louise Roberts. She had nothing but good things to say about you and your work. She also said that you'd been in the gallery a few days ago with Luke Bennett."

Callahan stared at him, aghast. "You're investigating *me*? You have no right to be asking…"

"I'm afraid I do have that right, ma'am. A killer is running around loose. It's my job to catch him before he kills someone else."

His words hit her like a fist.

"Someone else? What are you saying? That Luke might be a…a serial killer?"

"Let's just say I believe he's someone who takes what he wants. He preys on women and then shows them no mercy." His expression hardened. "You have to understand the danger here, Ms. O'Connor. Linda Morelli got her head blown off. Whoever did that is *not* a nice person. You've got to stop protecting him."

"You have no proof that Luke killed her!"

"We know that he was with the victim the night she died. Then he disappeared." He stood. "We've put out an APB on him. In the meantime, let me know immediately if he contacts you or shows up here again. I don't want to have to view your body, too."

Donny called a little after eight that night.

"Hi, Cal. I'm doing my best not to pout, but you didn't return

259

my call last night. What are you trying to do, give me a new crop of worry wrinkles?"

"I'm sorry. I was wiped out."

"You have been wiped out for quite a while, kiddo. Is Luke there? Are you free to talk?"

Callahan would have given a lot to confide in Donny, but she didn't dare involve him. He'd go bonkers and call Detective Silvo in a heartbeat. She was still praying that Luke would come back—and with a damned good explanation.

"He's... gone. I mean, he left for a few days."

"Really? Where did he go?"

"I don't know."

"But he's coming back?"

"I think so."

"You don't know for *sure*?" He paused. "Okay, girlfriend, level with me. Something big is going on. I can feel it."

Callahan's head was splitting.

"It's nothing you can help me with, but I appreciate and adore you. You're the dearest friend in the world."

Another pause, this one longer.

"Yes, I am. And if this continues I'm going to do something drastic. Like come after you with a straitjacket."

"Let's hope that won't be necessary." She changed the subject. "What's the latest on Brad's condition, have you heard?'

"Suzanne said he's been released from the hospital. Apparently the concussion didn't help his disposition any. I understand Anita is fed up and planning to kick him out, soon as he's well enough. I think his broken ribs are poetic justice, after his farewell present to you. As they say, 'What goes around comes around.' Oh, and by the way— Suzanne said that you had a blind date a couple of weeks ago. Need I say that I'm seriously wounded that you didn't bother to even mention it to me?"

"Oh, Donny, I'm sorry. I've been so preoccupied with Luke, it just slipped my mind. Anyway, it was no big deal."

"Suzanne would be disappointed to hear that. She went on and on about the guy—what's his name, Paul? Said he was really impressed with *you*. I have to say, available and financially secure meets *my* dreamboat qualifications. Too bad he's straight."

Callahan stifled a yawn. "I have to go. I'm dead on my feet."

"I can hear it in your voice. Get some sleep, girlfriend. And remember, I'm always here for you."

"Thank you. I count on that."

She climbed into bed, trying to ignore the empty space beside her, and pulled the covers up over her head. *Am I absolutely certain that Luke's innocent? I'd better be. I'm betting my life on it.*

31

Consuela rang the doorbell before using her key to open the front door the next morning, a formality she'd abandoned years ago. "*Señora* Callahan? It's me. I'm arriving now," she announced from the entryway. Mucho ran to greet her. She came into the kitchen, a guarded expression on her face.

"Good morning," Callahan said, pouring herself a cup of freshly brewed coffee. She was still in her bathrobe and exhausted from lack of sleep.

"*Buenos días.*" Consuela bustled about, taking cleaning supplies down from a cupboard and arranging them on the kitchen counter. "Is it okay I go to your bedroom, to change the sheets?"

"Yes, of course."

"*Señor* Luke, he's not sleeping?"

"He's not here."

"*No está aquí?*" Consuela's face lit up. "His visit is over?"

Deathmark

"I don't know. He may be coming back."

"Today?"

"I said, I don't know!" Callahan felt instantly contrite at Consuela's injured look. "Sorry… I didn't mean to snap at you. I just have a lot on my mind this morning."

"*No problema.*" Consuela helped herself to a cup of coffee.

Callahan gave her a brief, distracted smile and left the kitchen to dress.

The studio phone rang just as Callahan was beginning to sketch out a new piece, a portrait of a young Indian woman, her head bent in sorrow. Assuming it was Patrick, she answered and was surprised to hear Consuela's voice. Although the studio number was written on the kitchen bulletin board, it was rare for Consuela to use it.

"*Señora*, a man is here—a detective he says—he wants to talk to you."

"Oh, hell! I'll be right there." She swore under her breath all the way to the house. *Is that damned Silvo just here to drive me up a wall, or has something happened? Has Luke been arrested?*

The detective was settled on his usual stool at the counter, talking in a low voice to Consuela, whose face was almost as bleached out as the dish cloth she was clutching.

"Ms. O'Connor," he said, rising, "sorry for the interruption. I was hoping you might have some information for me."

"Well, I don't. Nothing has changed."

"That's disappointing. I'm sure ready to wind this investigation up and get back home. I don't sleep worth a darn in motel beds." He looked at Consuela. "I was just about to ask Mrs. Borrego here if she happened to notice Mr. Bennett's luggage."

Callahan's heart sank as she thought of the incident with the briefcase. Consuela, obviously thinking the same thing, gave her a worried glance and looked down at the floor.

"When you were cleaning, Mrs. Borrego, you must have seen his bags."

Consuela remained silent.

"Are his bags still here, Mrs. Borrego?"

Callahan exploded. "Don't say anything, Consuela! I've had enough of this! Detective Silvo, I won't have you just dropping by here, interrupting my work and upsetting my housekeeper. Unless you have a search warrant..."

"I hoped I wouldn't need one, but if I do it won't be a problem." He sighed, "You're understandably upset, ma'am. But you're taking it out on the wrong person. I'm just trying to protect you. As I was explaining to your housekeeper, Luke Bennett is looking more and more like an *extremely* dangerous man."

He paused to let his words sink in, before turning to Consuela. "Thank you for your time, Mrs. Borrego." Giving Mucho a pat on the head, he headed toward the door. "I can see myself out. I'm afraid we'll be speaking again. Soon."

Consuela stared at Callahan after the front door closed, her eyes wide with shock.

"*Madre de Dios!* I can't believe what my ears have heard. *Señor* Luke killed a woman?"

"There's no proof of that."

"But the detective, he told me *Señor* Luke was with this woman in San Francisco when she was killed! Murdered!" Consuela's voice rose. "Then he comes here! *Ay, Dios!*" She crossed herself.

"Just calm down!" Callahan said, although she was feeling far from calm herself. "We don't know what happened and neither does Detective Silvo. Just because Luke had dinner with the woman doesn't mean he had anything to do with her death. I don't believe that he did."

Consuela didn't look at all convinced. "Where did he go to?" She looked around as though he might spring out at her at any moment.

"I don't know."

"That detective, he say that the woman—*pobricita*—was shot two times in the head. In *cold blood*, he say." She crossed herself again.

Callahan turned away.

"That detective say he is worried that something happens to you, too." Consuela grasped Callahan's hand. "*Cuidado, Señora*, be

Deathmark

careful. Maybe you be too trusting. Remember, *Donde hay humo, hay fuego*—where there is smoke, there is fire."

Shortly after noon, Callahan took a break from her distracted attempt at work and returned to the house. Mucho trotted through the kitchen and down the hall, looking, she supposed, for Consuela. The dishwasher was open, partially filled with dirty dishes, a few more were still in the sink. Bottles of cleaning solutions sat on the counter, and a broom and mop leaned against it. Working around the mess, Callahan put together two chicken sandwiches. She regretted having been short with Consuela earlier. A shared lunch would help make amends.

Mucho returned a few moments later and sat back on his haunches, eyeing the sandwiches.

"Where's Consuela?" she asked. Mucho cocked his head, looking puzzled.

"Let's go find her." They walked through the dining room and into the living room. "Consuela?" she called. "Take a lunch break with me."

No response. Stepping around the upright vacuum cleaner standing in the hallway, she continued on to her bedroom. Throw rugs were in a pile by the French patio doors, ready for shaking. The bed was stripped and a stack of clean sheets were on the dresser. No Consuela.

She heard Mucho bark. Stepping back into the hall, she saw him standing in front of the closed guest room door. Mucho let out another bark, followed by a whine, and then bounded through the door when she opened it. He pawed at the closed closet door. With a feeling of cold apprehension, Callahan yanked the door open. Consuela was sprawled out face down on the closet floor.

"My god! Consuela!" Kneeling beside her, Callahan saw blood trickling through Consuela's gray hair and across her cheek to form a crimson pool on the Saltillo tile.

32

Callahan frantically called 911 as Mucho stood next to Consuela, nudging her gently with his nose.

"I need an ambulance! My housekeeper has been badly injured. She's breathing, but unconscious. Hurry, please!" She gave directions to her house and hung up.

Consuela gave a little moan. Callahan dropped to her knees beside her and examined the source of the bleeding—a two-inch gash in Consuela's scalp and an egg-sized lump that had formed around it.

"Consuela, open your eyes," she pleaded, afraid to try moving her. *Hit on the head. Closed in the closet.* "Consuela! Who did this?"

"*El me hirio,*" she whimpered. "*…me hirio.*"

"Who? Who hurt you?"

No response.

"Consuela!"

266

Deathmark

The ten minutes it took for an ambulance to arrive seemed like forever. Callahan sat by the unconscious Consuela, her mind reeling. *Who could have done this? A burglar? Could someone still be in the house? Not without Mucho knowing it.*

An ambulance, fire truck and two Santa Fe County Sheriff's cars pulled into her driveway, sirens blaring. She rushed to open the door and led the two paramedics to Consuela.

"Serious blow to the head," said one of the paramedics after a quick examination. He went on to check Consuela's vital signs. "How long has she been unconscious?"

"I don't know," Callahan said. "I found her here in the closet less than fifteen minutes ago. She came to for just a moment, but lost consciousness again."

"Was she lucid?"

"She said someone had hurt her. I can't imagine who." Callahan suddenly flashed on Luke's angry face after Consuela had moved the briefcase from under the bed. *No. Surely not...*

Moments later, they had Consuela strapped onto a gurney. Callahan grabbed the senior medic's arm as they started down the hall.

"Is she going to be all right? Please, tell me she's going to be all right."

"We'll do all we can. It looks like a skull fracture, but we'll know more after x-rays."

The words "skull fracture" horrified Callahan, instantly taking her back to her father's fatal encounter with that untamed horse. After Consuela was loaded into the ambulance, she turned to one of the officers.

"I want to go with her!"

"I'm afraid not," he said. "We have to question you. If this was a burglary, it has to be checked out."

"I...guess it was a burglary."

"Wait outside while we check the house."

Within ten minutes, the inspection was complete and Callahan was allowed to re-enter the house.

"If you'll come with me, we'll see if anything is missing," a deputy sheriff said.

After a thorough search, she could find nothing amiss. *Not a burglar. So who attacked Consuela?*

The deputy questioned Callahan while the guest room and closet were being photographed and vacuumed, and the house dusted for fingerprints.

"Now, let me verify a few things. Who else lives here?"

"Just my dog and me."

"But neither of you were here when the incident occurred."

"I was working in my studio, behind the house. My dog was with me. We came back a little after noon."

"Through which door?"

"The kitchen."

"Was the door unlocked?"

"Yes. I don't bother locking it when Consuela's here."

"There's no sign of forced entry. Was the front door unlocked, as well?"

"Probably. Consuela came in through it earlier." Her voice caught. "And she usually shakes rugs on the portal."

"So, anyone could have just walked in."

"I'm afraid so."

The deputy made more notes. "Have you noticed anything out of the ordinary lately? Anything that might have struck you as strange or suspicious? Unknown visitors or cars parked nearby?"

The question jolted her. *Detective Silvo! He's working with the County Sheriff's Department, so they'll make the connection with Luke—if they haven't already. But Luke didn't have anything to do with this. He's not even in town. At least as far as I know...*

"Ma'am?"

Callahan's head was reeling. She still felt an irrational need to protect Luke, but Consuela needed protecting, too. *Who would be mean enough to do this?* Brad's angry face suddenly surfaced in her mind. *He's out of the hospital, maybe still seething about his things being dumped, so he sneaked in to help himself to some of the art. Consuela would have done her best to stop him. She hated Brad and*

Deathmark

the feeling was mutual. But he couldn't be angry or drunk enough to do this. Could he?

Callahan shook her head, more in reaction to her tangled thoughts than to answer the deputy.

"Okay. Since nothing appears to be missing, we can probably rule out burglary. How long has Mrs. Borrego worked for you?"

"Almost ten years."

"Does she have any enemies that you know of, anyone she might be having trouble with? Anyone in her family?"

Callahan stared into space.

"Ma'am?" The officer was watching her closely.

She took a deep breath. "Consuela is a wonderful, kind-hearted person. As far as I know, she has a very close relationship with her family."

The deputy put his notepad back in his pocket. "Well, we've made a thorough check of the house and property. Everything is secure. Keep your windows and doors locked and your alarm system activated. We'll be questioning your neighbors to see if they saw anything, and we'll be in close touch with you." He handed her his card. "Don't hesitate to contact me directly if you think of anything else."

"Florencio...Consuela's husband! Has he been contacted?"

"My partner talked to him. He's on his way to the hospital."

"Well, so am I. I assume we're finished here?"

"For now."

Callahan cracked the Jeep window for Mucho, locked him in, and ran through the ER entrance at the hospital.

"Consuela Borrego was brought in with a head injury about an hour ago," she said to a receptionist just inside the door. "What can you tell me about her condition?"

The woman quickly accessed the information on her computer.

"Are you a relative?"

"No."

"In that case, I'm not allowed to give out information."

"But she's a very close friend. Please, we're like family."

"Go to the ICU waiting room. I'll let the security guard know that you're there."

"Security guard?"

"As an attack victim, Mrs. Borrego is under police protection."

"Florencio!" Callahan jumped from the waiting room sofa to greet the obviously distraught man. "How is Consuela?"

"Not so good. Her skull is broken, and she can't wake up." His red-rimmed eyes brimmed with tears. "The doctors, they don't know. The pressure of her blood is better. But maybe her brain swells."

Callahan put her arms around his thin shoulders and gave him a hug.

"I'm so sorry. I can't believe this happened."

"Who would do such a thing to my Consuela?"

"I don't know. But the police will find out."

Although Callahan wasn't allowed in the ICU, she remained at the hospital throughout the afternoon, drinking bitter machine coffee and offering what little comfort she could to Consuela's family and friends. From time to time she checked on Mucho, bringing him water. The only word they received was that nothing had changed. Finally, they got word that although Consuela was still unconscious, her vital signs were stabilizing. The prognosis was "guarded." There was nothing to do but wait and pray.

The sun was down by the time Callahan got home. If it weren't for the comfort of Mucho, she would have been wary about entering the dark house. She turned lights on, inside and out, and then called Donny.

"This is the Denton residence," his recorded voice announced. "I'm not available to take your call." There was an ear-piercing screech in the background. "Martha is also unavailable, having flown the coop. Leave your name and number and one of us might get back to you."

Deathmark

"Donny, it's me. Are you there? Please, pick up."

No response.

"I left a message earlier from the hospital. I'm home now, and I really need to talk to you…about everything that's been going on." Her control broke and she started to cry. "Please, come over as soon as you can."

She was in the bathroom, splashing cold water on her face when Mucho barked. Grabbing a towel, she rubbed it across her face. *Donny! Thank god!* She was just out of her bedroom when she saw the door leading to the garage open. She froze, her scalp prickling with fear, as a tall figure stepped into the dark hallway.

Mucho's bark turned joyous and Callahan flipped on the hall light. "Luke!"

33

" Hi, boy." Luke patted Mucho's head. "It's good to see you, too." He turned to focus on Callahan. "I didn't mean to startle you. I just parked in the garage without thinking." He thrust a small box toward her. "I missed you so much. I bought something for you."

She backed away, ignoring the gift.

"What's wrong? Why are you looking at me like that?"

"Something terrible has happened."

"What?"

"Consuela's in the hospital."

His face seemed to register genuine surprise.

"Really? God, that's awful. I noticed her car parked in the driveway," he continued, coming closer, "and thought it was odd she'd be working so late. Was it a heart attack or something?"

"Someone hit her on the head, and hard enough to fracture

her skull."

Luke looked horrified. He set the box on the entry table next to him.

"Are you saying someone broke in and attacked Consuela?"

"Yes! That's what I'm telling you."

"A burglar?"

She shook her head. "Nothing seems to be missing. Not even my jewelry box, which was sitting in plain sight on my dresser."

"Oh, Jesus." The tone of Luke's voice chilled her. "He's tracked me down."

"What? What the hell are you saying? Who…"

His eyes widened with alarm. "Are all the doors locked?"

"Of course."

"And the windows?"

"Yes. The police checked all the doors and windows. They were all over the property! Luke, answer me! Who tracked you down? Do you mean Detective Silvo? I told you that he'd…"

But Luke was already running down the hall. "Turn on all the outside lights," he yelled, over his shoulder.

She ran behind him, followed closely by Mucho. "They're on. For god's sake! What's happening?"

He rushed into the living room, checked the locks on the doors and pulled the shades. When he turned to her, his face was shockingly pale.

"Okay… I'm going to tell you everything. That's why I came back, to tell you in person. You deserve that. I should have told you when I first got here. I wanted to. But I kept putting it off. I was afraid…"

"Tell me *what*?" Callahan stared at him, vaguely aware of the metallic taste of fear in her mouth.

He sat on the sofa, his head in his hands.

"I should have known he'd find me. I've been kidding myself…"

She sat beside him and grabbed his arm.

"Damn it! Look at me! What the hell are you talking about?"

"I'm talking about my stupidity!" He lifted his head. "My

fucking reckless stupidity..." He turned to face her. "I did something I shouldn't have done. Did it on the spur of the moment, without thinking. And then I panicked. I'm so sorry, Callahan. I've put you in terrible danger—and Consuela in the hospital."

She felt the blood drain from her face. "Luke, you're not making sense!"

"What that detective told you was true. I was with Linda Morelli on Halloween night. She'd been using the agency, hiring escorts, for over a year. Every couple of months, each time she came to town. And she usually requested me. She was an interior designer, had her own business in San Diego. At least that's what she said. She was good-looking...fun to be with. And she always had lots of money to spend." He stood suddenly. "I need a drink. Can I get you one?"

Callahan shook her head impatiently and watched him walk to the wet bar and pour a healthy slug of Johnny Walker Red, before returning to the sofa.

"Linda was a client, certainly never anything more." He took a gulp of his drink. "I picked her up at her room in the Mark Hopkins and we went to dinner. She seemed unusually wound up. Said she was flying out early the next morning for an extended trip to Europe. She didn't volunteer any more information, and I didn't think anything of it. Most of my clients are guarded about their private lives. Still, there was...I don't know..." He searched for the right word. "I mean she was *edgier* than I'd ever seen her. I remember wondering if she was on drugs. After dinner, we went dancing. Then we went back to the hotel." He hesitated.

"Go on!"

"Okay. We had sex. Then I went into the bathroom. It must have been around 2:00 a.m.. The bathroom door was slightly open. All of a sudden the light in the bedroom went on. I heard voices—a man's and Linda's. I don't know how he got in, he must have stolen a key or something. He sounded furious. I heard him say, 'Did you really think you'd get away with it? You stupid bitch. Where's the money?' Linda was crying and pleading with him. I peeked through the crack in the door and saw her get out of bed. She took a briefcase out of the closet,

Deathmark

put it on the bed and opened it. 'Take it,' she said. 'It's all there. Just take it and go. Please!'

"I saw him give the money a quick check and snap the briefcase shut. Then he screwed a silencer on a hand gun—god, she was pleading with him!—and he shot her. Two times! In the face. It happened so fast! I couldn't believe it. It was horrible—blood and brains sprayed everywhere. I must have made some sort of horrified noise, because all of a sudden he turned toward the bathroom. I knew I had to act fast. There was an unopened Champagne bottle, iced in the sink. I grabbed it and stepped behind the door. When he pushed it open, I brought the bottle down on his arm and knocked the gun out of his hand. Then I swung the bottle back up and caught him under the jaw. He went down, and I hit him again on the head—knocking him out. I jumped over him, yanked my clothes on, and headed for the door. As I passed the bed, I saw Linda's briefcase—I don't know what made me do it. I just grabbed it and ran."

Callahan sensed that Luke was finally telling her the truth. That belief was followed by a range of wildly conflicting emotions— relief that he hadn't killed anyone, anger at his involvement in the horrific scene he'd just described, and a steadily building fear.

"I grabbed a cab," he continued. "And somehow managed to lose my cell along the way. I was in deep shock—shaking like crazy— especially after I saw how much money was in the briefcase. It's got to be drug money. Linda must have been some kind of courier. She was apparently trying to sneak it out of the country.

"I threw some things into a suitcase and took another cab to the bus station. I didn't want my name on an airline passenger list or to leave an easy-to-follow trail. I jumped on a bus to L.A. and then transferred to one headed for Las Vegas. Didn't care where I went, I just wanted to get the hell out before that guy caught up with me."

He gulped the Scotch, almost draining his glass.

"The next day I bought the Nissan at a used car lot. Paid cash. I gave the salesman a false address and told him I would register and license it back in California. That way, I got temporary dealer tags to be street legal. I didn't know what to do next, or where to go. But your face kept coming into my head." He looked at her wistfully and managed a smile. "You probably won't believe this, but it was like I was being drawn to you. I made the drive to Albuquerque in less than ten hours, got a motel room and slept for fourteen hours straight. Then I called you."

She stared at him as though seeing him for the first time.

"All the time you've been here, you've hidden this! Weren't you afraid?"

"It's been horrible, knowing the police would be looking for whoever was with Linda that night. Not to mention the killer. But I convinced myself no one could track me here."

"Well, you were wrong! Detective Silvo found you."

"I'm afraid the *killer* has found me, too."

Callahan's lips were almost too numb to talk. "The man who shot the Morelli woman—that's who tried to kill Consuela?"

"He must have come looking for the money."

"Then he'll be back!" She jumped to her feet. "He could be out there right now!" She started for the phone. "We have to call Detective Silvo."

"I guess you're right." His voice was flat and resigned.

"I'll get his number." As she passed a window, she saw the lights of a car pulling into her driveway. "Someone's here!"

Mucho let out a loud bark, and Luke was instantly on his feet, moving protectively toward her. "Get away from that window!"

"Wait. It's probably Donny. I called him…" She broke off as the gate to the courtyard opened and she caught sight of Detective Silvo hurrying up the walkway.

"It's okay," she said over her shoulder to Luke as she unlocked and opened the front door. "Come in." She grabbed Mucho by his collar. "We were just going to call you. Luke, this is…"

She heard Luke's quick intake of breath as the detective stepped inside. In that instant Callahan knew that she'd made a terrible mistake. She knew it, even before she heard Luke's voice—"You!"—and saw the look of shocked recognition on his face.

Deathmark

"About time you showed up, Bennett." Detective Silvo stepped inside and withdrew a compact pistol from inside his trench coat.

Callahan gasped and drew back. Mucho, whose tail had been wagging in happy greeting, instantly sensed her alarm. His body stiffened. He made a deep-throated growl of warning, showing his fangs and placing himself in front of Callahan. When the detective took another step forward, brandishing his weapon, Mucho lunged at him.

"No!" Callahan screamed, just as Silvo pulled the trigger. Twice.

With a strangled sound of disbelief and horror, Callahan bolted forward to grab the Great Dane as he fell, blood spurting from his head and chest.

She screamed again—"No! Oh, my god! No!"—and threw herself across Mucho's body, trying to stop the flow of blood.

"Give me any trouble, Bennett, and your girlfriend's next." The words, spoken in a detached, chilling tone, barely penetrated Callahan's consciousness. "Get her up. I want both of you against that wall. Move!"

She felt herself being lifted. Her shock exploded into blind rage, and she struggled in Luke's arms, trying to get at Silvo.

"You son-of-a-bitch!" The words ripped from her throat. "You killed Mucho! You killed him! How could you?"

Luke restrained her, holding her firm against his chest as she sagged and wailed.

"Too bad he was so protective," Silvo said in a thoughtful tone of voice. "I kinda liked that dog."

"You're a monster!" Callahan screamed through her tears.

"Now that sort of talk hurts my feelings." His voice changed suddenly, becoming as sharp and merciless as broken glass. "And I tend to get a little ugly when my feelings are hurt. Now…where's the money?"

"In my car," Luke said. "I'm parked in the garage."

"I know. Saw you arrive. About damned time. I was getting real impatient." He turned to Callahan, who was sobbing uncontrollably.

"Knock it off, cookie. Hysterical women try my patience. Like that stupid maid of yours, interrupting my *investigation*"—he said the word with a small twisted smile—"of the bedroom closet. I warned her she was getting on my nerves, but she kept crying and rattling on, calling on one saint after another. Had to shut her up. Christ, I hit her hard enough to kill her, but the gal at the hospital info desk bought my 'detective' line and said she's still hanging on. Must have a head made of cement. Goes to show you, always use the shooting end of a gun." He prodded Luke with his pistol. "Now, let's go. Out to the garage. All three of us."

"Don't hurt her," Luke pleaded. "I'll give you the money. Listen, you can do whatever you want with me. Just don't hurt her."

Silvo sneered. "My, what a gentleman. You're in the right line of work, Romeo. Now, move!"

With his arm still protectively around Callahan, Luke turned and started down the hall. They were halfway to the garage when the front door burst open.

"Cal? Where are you? I came as soon as I got your…"

"Donny!" she screamed. "Run!"

In that moment, time took on an elastic, slow-motion quality. Callahan saw Donny stop, staring at the three of them, his mouth hanging open. He turned, just as Silvo raised his gun.

"No!" Twisting from Luke's grasp, Callahan started forward. There was a sharp crack from the pistol—just as Donny slipped in Mucho's blood, tripped over his body, and fell to the floor.

"Oh, god! No! No!" Out of the corner of her eye, Callahan saw Luke reach for the spear that hung on the wall. Silvo turned and raised the gun, pointing it at Luke.

"Watch out!" She shouted the warning and saw that Luke had drawn back the spear. With a wild, piercing shout—a sound that some deep part of her recognized—he hurled the spear at Silvo.

She watched the spear penetrate Silvo's right shoulder. The gun went off and then dropped from his hand as he stumbled backward.

Reacting automatically, Callahan sprang forward. Grabbing the gun from the floor, she held it steady with both hands—pointed at the center of Silvo's chest.

278

Deathmark

"Stay back!" she warned.

Silvo gripped the spear with his left hand and, with a loud grunt, yanked it from his bleeding shoulder. He stood, hunched over like a wounded animal, his breathing loud and ragged. She was vaguely aware of the sour smell of his sweat as they stood facing each other. Their eyes locked. Then, with a low, growling sound, he lunged toward her.

Callahan pulled the trigger. She saw a look of surprise on Silvo's face as he staggered several steps backward, a bright red stain spreading across his chest. But he was still standing—and coming back at her. She fired again. This time Silvo's chest seemed to explode in blood and he crumpled to the floor. His body jerked violently a few times, and then was still.

She turned at the sound of Luke's groan. He was leaning against the wall, holding his right inner thigh. Blood seeped through his fingers, covering his hand and spreading across his tan slacks. He looked at her in confusion.

"Luke!" she screamed, realizing he'd been shot.

With another soft groan, he slid down the wall.

Callahan dropped the gun and knelt beside him. Casting a frantic glance down the hall, she saw with enormous relief that Donny was on his hands and knees beside Mucho's body. Then he was standing over Silvo's blood-soaked, lifeless body. He choked back a scream and rushed toward her and Luke, his face ashen with shock. He opened his mouth, but no sound came out.

"Are you all right?" she asked.

He nodded. "I…I guess so. Mucho—I fell over him. He's…" He broke off with a sob. Then he glanced back at Silva's body. "Who the hell…?"

Callahan turned her attention back to Luke, frantically pressing the flat of her hand against his wound, trying to stop the flow of blood. "Quick, Donny! Call an ambulance!"

Donny ran to the phone in the kitchen.

"You shot it…" Luke sounded dazed. "You're sure it's dead?"

Covered with blood and still pressing hard on his wound, she gave him a quick, surprised look. "What do you mean—*it*?"

"The bear," he whispered. "I saw a bear! I saw a huge bear…
when I threw the spear…" His voice trailed off.

She felt the hair rise up on her neck. *That cry he gave. Running
Wolf's war cry!*

"Callahan?"

It took her a moment to find her voice. "I'm here," she
managed to say. "I'm right here."

He squeezed his eyes shut, then opened them again in alarm.
"Are you hurt?"

"No, I'm all right. But if you hadn't thrown that spear, he
would have killed all of us."

"But I didn't kill the bear," he mumbled. "My aim was off…
again." He shuddered, and his eyes closed.

"Luke! Stay awake!" Feeling his warm blood pulsing up
through her fingers, she fought to control her panic.

Donny was yelling in a high-pitched, hysterical voice into
the phone. "Help! We need an ambulance! There's been a shooting!
Lots of shooting! A maniac broke in here! You have to hurry! What?
Tesuque! We're in Tesuque!" He gave them directions. "Hurry!"

Luke opened his eyes. "Sorry, Callahan," he whispered.
"So sorry."

"Shhh. Don't talk." She hoped he wouldn't hear the terror in
her voice. A fast-spreading puddle of blood was forming on the bricks
between his legs. "Help is on the way."

Donny dropped to his knees beside her, babbling. "Christ,
Cal! What the. . . ? Who is that man? Oh, my god! Oh, my god!"

"Help me. Quick! I need something to stop this bleeding!"

Donny scrambled to his feet and returned seconds later with
an armload of bath towels.

"Your arm!" She noticed blood seeping through a small rip in
Donny's jacket.

"I think the bullet just grazed me," he said, his voice high and
shaky. "Holy shit! I can't believe any of this!"

Luke, visibly paler, was shivering. Callahan grabbed a towel
and pressed it hard against his thigh.

"A tourniquet! We need something to use for a tourniquet!"

she shouted. "And blankets! Get some blankets. I think he's going into shock."

Luke's blood seemed to be everywhere—covering the floor, her arms, her shirt. Her knees slid in it. Her nostrils filled with its coppery scent.

"Please, hang on! You're going to be all right. Do you hear me, Luke? You *have* to be all right!"

Donny ripped off his jacket and shirt and helped her tie the shirt tightly above the wound. The bleeding slowed only marginally. Callahan continued to apply all the pressure she could muster, as Donny brought blankets and tucked them around Luke's upper body. Luke's skin was clammy, and he lay still and unmoving.

Callahan's vision was blurred with tears. "Don't go!" she pleaded, although she wasn't sure he could still hear her. "Please, don't die." For an instant, as she stared at Luke's ashen face, she flashed on Running Wolf lying lifeless on his burial fur.

Luke's voice, scarcely more than a whisper, made Callahan focus on the present. "I love you, Callahan. Love you so much. I didn't… deserve…you." He took a long, shuddering breath, and then slowly let it go. His eyelids fluttered shut.

"Luke! I love you, too. Do you hear me?" She was sobbing. "I love you!"

His lips hinted a faint smile, and his eyes opened—held hers—for just a moment. And then they closed.

Callahan heard sirens in her driveway. The sound barely registered. She was somewhere else.

"They're here!" Donny jumped up and ran outside in his undershirt, yelling from the portal. "Hurry! Hurry! In here!"

Uniformed men entered the house and bent over Silvo's body. Paramedics behind them moved Callahan firmly out of the way and began to examine Luke. She watched as they placed an oxygen mask over his face, took his blood pressure and pulse.

"Is he going to be all right?" she asked frantically. "Is he?"

"You're going to have to move back, ma'am," a medic said. She heard the pity in his voice.

34

The paramedics worked steadily to save Luke's life. Finally, Callahan heard one say, "It's no use. He's bled out."

Her sense of time and reality blurred. *No! It cannot be! One Above, don't let it be!*

She pushed her way through those who surrounded her beloved and dropped to her knees onto blood-soaked towels beside him. She touched his eyelids, traced the strong line of his jaw with her fingers, and kissed his lips. Pulling him closer and cradling his head in her lap, she began to wail.

Someone patted her shoulder saying. "Cal... Cal, honey."

The voice was vaguely familiar, but the words had no meaning. She was falling into an abyss, to a place of refuge where unbearable pain could no longer reach her. The voice seemed to be coming from farther and farther away...

"She fainted!" Donny yelled. "Help me, somebody! Carry her to the sofa."

Deathmark

Gradually, reluctantly, Callahan awoke and moved back into the present nightmare.

"Ms. O'Connor?"

She tried to focus on the stern-faced man in a sheriff's uniform bending over her.

"I'm Sheriff Miguel Jaramillo. Can you sit up? I'm very sorry, but I have to ask you some questions."

"Can't that wait?' Donny's voice was thick with tears. "She's obviously in serious shock. Leave her alone!"

"I'm sorry, but we have a double homicide here."

"Callahan acted in self defense. A maniac broke in here! He killed Luke, and Mucho—the most splendid dog…" His voice choked, and it took him a moment to continue. "And he shot at *me*—the bullet tore my jacket and nicked my arm. Look, it's still bleeding."

"We'll have a medic tend to it. Detective Daniels will take *your* statement in the kitchen."

"Actually, I'm feeling a little faint, myself." Donny collapsed into a chair and leaned forward, his head between his knees.

Sheriff Jaramillo sat on the sofa by Callahan, armed with a legal pad and small cassette recorder. A deputy sheriff, two detectives, and several crime scene technicians were in the house—photographing, videotaping, and taking measurements. A woman from the Office of Medical Investigation had just arrived to examine the bodies. Someone had put a box of tissues in front of Callahan.

"You have the right to remain silent," Jaramillo said. "Anything you say can and will be used against you in a court of law. You have the right to an attorney, and to have the attorney present during questioning. If you so desire and cannot afford one, an attorney will be provided for you without charge. Do you understand each of these rights?"

She stared at him through a thick fog of shock. *This can't be happening!*

283

"Do you understand each of these rights, Ms. O'Connor?"

"What are you saying? Am I…under arrest?"

"No, you're in protective custody. But you *are* involved in a homicide, and I'm advising you of your rights. Do you wish to give up your right to remain silent?"

Her lips felt numb. "I don't know. I…don't know… "

The Sheriff repeated his question.

"I…yes, I guess so."

"Do you wish to give up your right to speak to an attorney?"

"Why…why do I need an attorney?"

"You shot and killed a man, ma'am. Isn't that true?"

"Yes…but I had to. It was self-defense." Her voice rose in confusion and broke. "Don't you understand? He…he was going to kill all of us!"

"So you do wish to give up your right to speak to an attorney?"

"Okay. Yes. Whatever. Just get this over with."

"Please state your full name."

"Callahan Maxwell O'Connor."

"And you live here. Is that right?"

She nodded.

"You'll have to speak up, for the recorder."

"Yes. This is my home."

"Who else lives here?"

She looked across the room to the entryway, where Mucho's body lay in a pool of blood. "Just… my dog." She started to sob, deep, rasping sounds.

Sheriff Jaramillo handed her a couple of tissues and waited until she regained some semblance of control.

"I'm sorry. I know this isn't easy. Now, what happened here tonight? Start at the beginning."

Callahan tried to force her mind past the numbing sense of unreality that engulfed her. *The beginning?* Running Wolf's face flashed into her mind. *You don't know what you're asking.*

"Ms. O'Connor?"

"We…Luke and I were here. He had just told me…" She hesitated, then realized that she had no choice but to tell the whole

284

Deathmark

story of Luke's involvement with Linda Morelli—her death and the stolen money. It was all going to come out now anyway.

"You say the man who shot Luke Bennett claimed to be a police detective from San Francisco?"

"He said he was Detective James Silvo and showed me his identification. It looked authentic. I had no reason not to believe him."

"And he admitted attacking your housekeeper, Consuela Borrego, here in your home, this morning?"

"He bragged about it. Said she interrupted his search for the money."

"I need you to tell me again exactly how the shootings occurred."

"Why? Oh, god. Why do we have to go through it again?" She wiped at tears running down her cheeks.

"Routine procedure."

Callahan felt an involuntary clenching of her stomach muscles, followed by a strong wave of nausea.

"I feel sick. Give me a minute." She bowed her head.

"Do you need to go the bathroom?"

Callahan didn't move or answer for a moment. Then she shook her head as the nausea ebbed. Swallowing hard, she stumbled through the story in as much detail as she could remember.

"I shot him. But he kept coming at me. I shot him again. And he finally went down." Her voice caught. "That's when I realized that Luke…" Her throat seemed to close, and it took her a long moment to continue. "He was shot in the leg when Silvo's gun went off. I tried to stop the bleeding." Wracking sobs tore through her. "I tried…oh, god, I tried."

The Medical Investigator signaled to Jaramillo, who turned off the tape recorder and stood.

"Thank you, ma'am. That's all, for now."

She saw that the bodies were about to be removed and sprang from the sofa.

"No! Where are you taking Luke?"

"To Albuquerque, ma'am. That's where we perform autopsies."

285

She let out a harsh cry and covered her face with her hands. Donny, his bloody undershirt visible under his jacket, hurried out of the kitchen, where he had spent the last thirty minutes being questioned by a deputy sheriff. He put his arm around Callahan and led her back to the sofa. She buried her face in his shoulder, wailing, as they carried Luke out.

"This is a nightmare," she moaned. "Please, please, let me wake up!"

"What are you doing with Mucho?" Donny asked the two paramedics zipping the dog into a body bag.

"We have to take him, too. They'll need to extract the bullets for evidence. Then his body will be returned to you, if that's what you want."

"Wait!" Callahan tore out of Donny's embrace and went to kneel beside Mucho, heedless of the blood surrounding him.

"Poor, sweet baby," she moaned, hugging him through the bag. "I love you, Mucho. I love you. I'll miss you so much. You were so brave. Oh, god, no. No!"

Donny helped her up and they held each other, both sobbing, as Mucho was carried from the house.

Sheriff Jaramillo approached them. "I'm sorry, but we're going to have to take you both in to make formal statements."

"What?" Donny wiped at his red and swollen eyes. "That's inhumane after all we've been through. We've already told you what happened!"

"I'm afraid we have to go through it again."

Donny glared up at Jaramillo. "This is an outrage!"

"This is a double homicide, Mr. Denton."

"Are you arresting us? Hold on, here! We need a lawyer!"

"Calm down, Mr. Denton. You may certainly call a lawyer, if you wish. But no charges are being made. At least not at this time." Jaramillo turned his attention to Callahan, and his expression softened a bit. "You'll have to change out of those clothes. We'll need to take them for evidence."

"I'm going with her," Donny said. "She might faint again."

"We'll both go," Jaramillo said. "I can't allow you two to

Deathmark

speak alone until we take your official statements."

"Oh, for pity's sake!" Donny put his arm around Callahan and helped her down the hall to her bedroom. Jaramillo was right behind.

Callahan looked down at the blood that had dried on her sweater, jeans, and hands. Spots danced before her eyes. *Luke's blood... Running Wolf's blood...* She felt the floor moving beneath her and, for an instant, feared that she was sliding back into that long-ago time.

Donny's grip tightened around her waist. "Help me here! She's about to faint again."

"No," Callahan whispered, as the dizziness slowly passed. "I'm...okay. Just give me a minute."

Donny turned to Jaramillo. "You surely don't plan to watch her change clothes!"

"Of course not." Jaramillo turned his back, as Donny stepped in the closet and then helped her to change. He handed the bloody clothing to Jaramillo.

Callahan held onto the bathroom counter. Her reflection in the mirror above the sink was shocking—blood smeared across her chin, right cheek, and forehead. *The ochre on Running Wolf's face... his hide-wrapped body lying on his burial scaffold.* Callahan held her cold hands under the flow of warm water and watched in numb horror as it turned bright red.

35

The drive to the Santa Fe County Sheriff's Department passed in a blur for Callahan. Donny was being transported in a separate vehicle, and there she was, alone in the backseat of a patrol car, caged in by the heavy, iron mesh bolted to the seat in front of her, feeling like a prisoner. She shivered in spite of her sheepskin coat and the hot air blasting out from the heater. The scanner blared static-coated phrases that made no sense. Nothing about the last twelve nightmare hours made any sense.

Luke is dead! How can that be? And Mucho—my poor, sweet Mucho. An anguished wail tore from her throat.

Finally, the patrol car turned off Highway 14, drove past the New Mexico State Penitentiary, onto Camino Justicia and into a parking lot directly across the street from the jail. Callahan stared numbly at the sign on the one-story plastered building—Santa Fe Public Safety Complex. Sheriff Jaramillo helped her out of the car and escorted her up a short sidewalk. She was hurried through a reception area, relieved of her coat, and checked for gun powder residue.

Deathmark

Callahan was then ushered into a small room marked INTERVIEW. An officer rose to his feet as she stepped inside.

"Detective Harris," Jaramillo said by way of introduction.

She gave the detective a distracted nod as Jaramillo seated her in an uncomfortable straight-backed chair and positioned himself on the other side of a small table. She noticed the video camera Detective Harris was positioning, pointing it directly at her. A red light suddenly flashed on, indicating that the camera was running.

She turned to Jaramillo. "You're recording this?"

"Standard procedure." Jaramillo's tone permitted no argument. He proceeded to place a tape recorder on the table between them as well, before repeating her rights. "Do you give up your right to remain silent?"

"Yes! I've already told you exactly what happened."

"Do you wish to give up your right to speak with an attorney?"

"I really don't see why I need one. The man I shot was a murderer. He killed… Luke… and my dog." She began to sob.

"All right, Ms. O'Connor. Let's go through it again. Starting with when you found Consuela Borrego in the bedroom closet."

Callahan stared at the video camera with its red light. It reminded her of a television interview she'd done in Albuquerque—a local noon-time talk show that focused on the arts—the week before she left for San Francisco. That seemed like a hundred years ago.

After she told the horrible story again, Jaramillo leaned back in his chair.

"How long did you say you've known Mr. Bennett?"

"About three weeks. Why do you keep asking me the same questions?"

Jaramillo ignored her question. "So, less than a month… you must admit that's a short time to become such *close friends,* especially given Bennett's profession."

Callahan didn't miss the sheriff's insinuation. He clearly saw her as a fool for trusting Luke. *What would he think if I said that I've known him for centuries?*

Jaramillo was watching her closely.

"Do you believe the story he told?"

289

She met his skeptical gaze head on, steadied her voice.
"Yes. I do."

"Ms. O'Connor, do you visit San Francisco often?"

"Once, sometimes twice, a year. My work is represented by a gallery there."

"The man you shot was from San Francisco. Are you sure you never met *him* there?"

"No! Of course not."

"You'd never seen him before he came to your house…when did you say that was?"

"Early this week. Monday was the first time. Then he came back, several times."

"Each time he was looking for Mr. Bennett?"

"Yes! I told you that. Don't you believe me?"

Again, Jaramillo ignored her question.

"Is there anything else you would like to add at this time?"

"I've told you everything I know. Over and over again." She put her elbows on the table and rested her throbbing head in her hands. "Please. Isn't this over?"

Jaramillo leaned back and studied her for a moment. Then he pushed his chair back and stood.

"I guess that's all for tonight. But I may have more questions for you later."

"More questions?"

"You have to understand the seriousness of your situation, Ms. O'Connor. You shot and killed a man tonight and withheld information earlier today when you were questioned concerning the assault on Mrs. Borrego. That could make you the target of a grand jury investigation. "

She stared at him. "A… grand jury investigation?"

"I just mentioned it as a possibility. One more thing: don't leave town." He paused. "Okay, that'll do it for tonight. Deputy Burns will drive you home, or wherever you want to go."

Callahan rose on shaky legs and walked out of the room. Someone handed her her coat.

"Cal!" Donny rushed toward her from a small waiting area

just down the hall. "You're coming home with me, honey. For an indefinite stay. No arguments."

Exhaustion, shock, and grief encased Callahan like a shroud. She lacked the energy to speak, much less to argue.

Yellow crime scene tape was strung across the two adobe posts that marked the entrance to Callahan's house, which was ablaze with light. Police cars were still parked along the road. As they drove past, Callahan clutched Donny's arm for support and looked the other way.

Safely inside Donny's guest bathroom, Callahan undressed and took a long, hot shower.

"Here…" Donny opened the door a crack and handed her a gray silk nightshirt. "This should fit. There's a new toothbrush and toothpaste in the right-hand drawer."

As she came out of the bathroom Donny, freshly showered himself and in pajamas, was turning down her bed.

"Now, climb in."

She did as she was told, and Donny carefully tucked the covers over her shoulders. Her numbness had lifted a bit and she broke down, guttural sobs coming from the deepest part of her being.

He sat with her, holding her and sharing her tears until she lay spent, with no more energy to cry.

"Mucho… he died trying to protect me."

Donny handed her a fresh tissue and then blew his own nose. "Bless his sweet heart," he said, in a choked voice. "He was an absolute prince of a dog." He shook his head. "That thug must have been the same one that broke in this morning and attacked Consuela. Why didn't he take whatever he was after then? What made him come back?"

Callahan suddenly realized that Donny still didn't know the whole story. How could he? They'd been questioned separately.

"He wasn't your ordinary burglar," she said.

"What do you mean?"

When she didn't answer, Donny's eyebrows shot up.

"Omigod! He had some connection to Luke! Am I right?"

She nodded. "I didn't know the whole story myself, until Luke came back tonight." She took a deep, shaking breath and forced herself through the story one more time.

Donny listened in silence, his eyes wide behind his glasses. "Holy shit," he said, when she was finished. "What a shocker. It beats anything *I've* ever written." He paused. "I knew Luke was hiding something…"

"I knew it, too. But I didn't want to force the issue. I didn't want to lose him." She started to cry again. "Now I've lost him for good—and Mucho, too. Consuela's in intensive care… and it's a miracle you weren't killed. I brought this nightmare into our lives. Oh, Donny, how can I live with that?"

"You can't shoulder the blame for this, honey." He handed her another tissue. "It was one of those crazy twists of life. But… I have to hand it to Luke—it was quick thinking on his part to grab that spear off the wall. If he'd missed…"

Luke throwing the war lance. That image would be forever burned into her mind.

"Your arm," she asked Donny, after a moment, "does it hurt?"

"Just a scratch. The only real damage the bullet did was to my new jacket."

"I'll buy you another."

"You'll do no such thing. Now, listen to me, you've *got* to get some sleep." He leaned down and kissed her cheek. "I'm giving you one of my use-in-emergency sleeping pills. This certainly falls under that category."

After she swallowed the pill he leaned down and kissed her cheek.

" You were really something tonight, Cal girl. Brave as hell. If your daddy had had his wish and you'd been born a boy, I'd ask you to marry me."

Deathmark

36

Walking toward the kitchen the next morning, Callahan heard Donny talking on the phone.

"I can't begin to tell you what a nightmare it was! Blood everywhere! I was dodging bullets; I kid you not. If I didn't have such finely-toned reflexes—I was a professional dancer for a brief time in my youth, you know—I'd be dead now. Callahan saved both of our lives. It's a good thing she was raised around guns. I'll never forget her standing up to that thug… "

He broke off when Martha screeched a jarring greeting to Callahan.

"Quiet, sweet beak! Okay, Callahan's up now. On her feet, if not fully awake. No, I'm sure she doesn't feel like talking just yet. Yes, I will. Bye." He hung up. "That was Suzanne. She's beside herself. Like the rest of the town, I'm sure. This phone has been ringing off the hook since seven o'clock. When Red Feather couldn't reach you, he called Suzanne. She was still in bed and hadn't read the paper yet.

So you can just imagine…"

"It's in the papers already?"

"Front page." He pointed to a copy of the *Santa Fe New Mexican* lying on the snack bar.

Callahan picked it up and stared at a smiling publicity photo of herself and a picture of a body being removed from her house, under the headline: **Two People Dead in Shootout at Tesuque Home of Well Known Artist.** Feeling kicked in the stomach, she read on:

> *Santa Fe County police were called to the Tesuque home of award-winning artist, Callahan O'Connor, shortly after six o'clock last night. The artist admitted to shooting and killing an armed intruder, whose name has not yet been released. Also dead at the scene was O'Connor's houseguest, Luke Bennett, 29, from San Francisco, California, and her Great Dane. Local author, Donald Denton, was reportedly treated at the scene for a superficial gunshot wound.*

> *Police had been called to the O'Connor estate just after noon yesterday to investigate a break-in and assault on Consuela Borrego, O'Connor's housekeeper. Mrs. Borrego, wife of Florencio Luis Borrego of Espanola, is listed in critical condition at Christus St. Vincent Hospital The incident is under investigation. No charges have been filed at this time.*

Callahan's hands shook as she put the paper down.

"Omigod, Patrick! I have to talk to Patrick."

"It's okay… I called him first thing this morning." Donny handed her a steaming latte in a delicate white porcelain cup. "He's on his way."

"Did you tell him everything?"

"Just the highlights. I didn't want him reading it first in the papers."

"How did he take it?"

"Once he was convinced that you're okay, he calmed down. He'll be fine. He's strong, his mother's son. I insisted that he stay here, too."

The phone rang.

"Here we go again," Donny sighed. "Anyone you want to talk to?"

"Just my lawyer."

"Right. First order of business. But there's one small problem. You look great in that nightshirt, but it might be a bit over the top for legal counsel."

"Oh, god. I can't think straight. I don't have any clothes here, except what I wore to the police station. I don't even have my car."

"You can use my car this morning, after I pop over to your house and pick up some more clothes for you."

"Would you? I don't think I can face…"

"Of course. Let's see, I have all the toiletries you might need, but you'll need your anti-depression pills. Are they in your medicine cabinet?"

She nodded.

"You know you can't skip days on those things or your brain starts giving little buzzes. Most unpleasant. Let's see, what else? Your cosmetics…"

"Don't bother. I probably have a lipstick in my purse. That's enough."

He shook his head. "You need a little concealer. And blusher—definitely. You're pale as a ghost." He bit his lip. "Sorry. Poor choice of words."

Fearfully, Callahan dialed the hospital's ICU. She didn't know if she could handle any more bad news. A nurse informed her that Consuela had been moved out of intensive care, into a private room.

"Then she's better?"

"She's been upgraded from critical to serious-but-stable."

"Has she regained consciousness?"

"Yes. She spoke a few words to her husband this morning."

Tears of relief filled Callahan's eyes.

"Thank you," she said, speaking as much to God as to the nurse.

Donny returned forty-five minutes later, carrying her small travel case and garment bag.

"It's still an absolute madhouse over there," he reported. "Police doing their CSI stuff, reporters snooping around... By the way, the entrance is being guarded by a stunningly attractive officer of the law—picture Enrique Iglesias in a uniform. I had to explain who I was and why I needed to get in before he finally let me pass. And I was cornered by a reporter from the *Albuquerque Journal* at the entrance to your driveway who insisted on an impromptu interview. And a photo. Damn. I wish I'd been wearing black. It photographs so well against adobe walls..." He stopped, looking horrified. "Oh, Jeez. Please forgive me for babbling on —I'm just in complete overwhelm. My mouth is disconnected from my brain."

He unzipped the garment bag.

"I grabbed a denim skirt, your black snakeskin boots, and that apricot-colored cashmere sweater you bought in Dallas last year. Apricot warms the complexion. Also some sweats and bedroom slippers for you to relax in."

"Thank you, Donny. For everything."

He patted her arm. "I just wish I could do more."

"So... the reporter. What did he ask?"

"Everything but my shoe size. And yours." He sighed. "Mostly, he was after inside info on you. Where you were—I just said you were in seclusion, period—how long we've been friends, what kind of a person you are, your relationships..."

Her stomach knotted. "Did he ask about Luke?"

"Of course. I said I'd met him only briefly and found him to be a personable young man."

"Nothing said... you know, about being an escort?"

"No. I don't guess that information has been released yet. But you better brace yourself, honey. It will be. And the media will go wild."

Deathmark

Donny looked worried as he handed Callahan his car keys.

"Are you sure you don't want me to drive you?"

"I appreciate the offer, but I'm sure. It's only a few miles. My attorney's on Marcy Street."

"Did you take a Xanax this morning? You know you shouldn't drive or operate heavy machinery…"

"No, I didn't take a pill, but only because I need every brain cell I have left in working order. And yes, I'm okay to drive."

"If you're sure. I'm just so worried about you that the mother hen in me is flapping all over the place. You know my personal motto: When in confusion, fear, or doubt, run in circles, scream and shout."

She managed a small smile. "I love you."

Callahan drove south, past her house and the many vehicles parked along the road, including a white van with Channel 13 News emblazoned on its side. She clenched her jaw and accelerated.

Soon she was in Vonda Kramer's office. Slender, with perfect skin, delicate features, and long dark brown hair, the attorney could easily have passed for a fashion model. Dwelling beneath her ultra-feminine exterior, however, was a brilliant legal mind and a ferocious dedication to justice. She'd also been a friend since buying one of Callahan's paintings several years ago.

"Professionally, I should just shake your hand, Callahan," she said, "but you look like you could use a hug."

Callahan accepted her embrace, struggling to maintain her composure.

"Thanks for working me in this morning."

"I'm just sorry I wasn't there last night. Want some coffee?"

"No, thanks. I'm about to jump out of my skin as it is."

"Okay, just sit back and give me the story. I know the newspaper version," she said, indicating a folded newspaper on her desk. "Now I want yours."

Callahan related the events of the past few weeks, omitting only Luke's marks and how they tied into her art. When she finished, the attorney leaned back in her chair.

"Two people killed in your house, one of them by you. The man you shot was trying to recover drug money that had been stolen by a male escort you'd hired in San Francisco, who then came to Santa Fe to stay with you. You cover for this escort after finding the money, even after your housekeeper is assaulted. I have to be honest, that makes you look either naïve as hell or involved in this drug thing. You have to understand what you're up against." She paused. "How old was Bennett?"

The word "was" sliced through Callahan's heart like a knife. "Just… twenty-nine. Way too young to die."

"A twenty-nine-year-old hooker. That won't play well for us if the DA decides to prosecute." Vonda drummed thoughtfully on the desk with a manicured fingernail. "Mr. Denton's statement about the shooting will support yours, right?"

"Yes, of course."

"Okay. So… whenever there's an unnatural death, there's an inquiry. All information will then be turned over to the DA, to make a determination as to whether or not the shooting was justifiable homicide. You haven't been charged with anything at this point. With luck, you won't be. Let me put in a call to the DA's office and see what the mood is there. I'll get back to you as soon as I know anything."

"Sheriff Jaramillo said I could be the target of a grand jury investigation."

"Well, you deliberately pulled the trigger. Twice. And, prior to that, you withheld evidence. You could be looking at a charge of second-degree murder."

Callahan's breath caught in her throat.

"My god!"

"That's a worst-case scenario. Personally, I think that bastard got exactly what he deserved. Anyone who would shoot a dog like that…" She shook her head. "Okay, leave this to me. Get some rest. And don't talk to *anyone* about this case, especially the press."

Deathmark

Callahan returned to Donny's, feeling ready to collapse. When she opened the front door, Martha let out a mind-jolting screech. Callahan was tempted to join her.

"I thought I'd fix garlic-sautéed Portobello mushroom sandwiches, made with my special sour dough bread, for lunch," Donny said.

"No, please—the thought of food makes me feel sick."

He shot her a concerned look and assumed his don't-argue-with-me tone.

"Well, you've got to eat *something*. I have some lovely cream of asparagus soup I made and froze a couple of days ago. I'll just heat it up and put it on a bed tray. Get back in the nightshirt, honey. You need a nap before Patrick arrives."

She had no intention of arguing. Moments later, she was between the covers.

"Here you go." Donny put the tray with its fragrant soup and a cup of tea in front of her. He had even added a small vase containing one perfect white rose he'd plucked from the floral arrangement on his dining room table.

"You are truly the *best* friend," she said.

"Oh, I'm just your reward for something you did right in a past life." He grimaced. "Forgive me—another unfortunate choice of words. That reminds me," he said, sitting on the chair beside the bed, "Red Feather came by while you were gone. He wants you to call when you feel like seeing him. And goodness, girlfriend, he is one impressive-looking man. That long braid and obviously first-rate, old-pawn turquoise jewelry… I'd certainly sign up for one of his trance journeys, except I wouldn't have a clue what to pack."

Callahan managed a small smile and several sips of the soup.

"I also arranged for a professional cleaning service to go to your house tomorrow morning, tidy things up. Jaramillo said they should be finished up by ten."

The soup she had just swallowed threatened to come back up. *All that blood…*

"I'm sorry. You just turned the same shade as the soup," Donny said. "Let me take that tray."

"Promise to wake me the minute Patrick arrives, all right?" She was asleep before Donny was out of the room.

Staring through eyes blurred by crying and lack of sleep, she sat at the scaffold where Running Wolf's body lay. The freezing wind did nothing to numb her pain. Nor the pain in her slashed arms and legs or her ruined cheeks. They were nothing compared to the pain in her heart. "Mita'wa higna, my husband," she wailed in a hoarse voice. "The pain is too great!"

She wrapped her thin arms around her swollen belly in an only half-conscious attempt to comfort her unborn child and rocked back and forth in her misery. As she rocked, she sang her song of grief:

A'nea'thibiwa'hana, *This is the place where crying begins*
A'nea'thibiwa'hana, *This is the place where crying begins*
Thi'aya' he'naa'awa, *I see the crying*
Thi'aya he'naa'awa, *I see the crying*
Na'hibiwa'hunna, *then I begin to lament…*

"Mom?"

Callahan heard the word, felt someone shaking her shoulder, but couldn't seem to pull herself out of the dream. *Na'hibiwa'hunna…*

"Mom!" The voice was more insistent. "Wake up."

She forced her eyes open. "Oh, sweetheart… Patrick. Thank god you're here."

"I got in about an hour ago. Donny and I agreed to just let you sleep. But then I heard you doing it—your 'sleep talk' that used to freak me out when I was a kid. It still does." He gripped her hand. "Are you okay?"

She sat up and threw her arms around her son, pressing her face into his neck, inhaling his familiar, comforting scent.

"I'm better, now that you're here with me."

Deathmark

Although Callahan still had no appetite, she forced herself to eat small helpings of the poached salmon and garlic mashed potatoes that Donny served for dinner.

"Comfort food," he said.

Patrick attacked his plate, accepting second helpings while making constant sounds of approval.

"I rarely get a home-cooked meal these days," he said between bites.

Donny beamed. "Then you must come home more often, dear boy. You're a pleasure to cook for. For dessert, we have a medley of fresh berries marinated in Amaretto."

After dinner, they moved into the living room, where Martha, obviously delighted to have company, did her best to enter into the conversation.

"I'm a bitchy bird," she screeched. "Sex. Sex. Sex. It's a good thing."

Patrick choked on his coffee. "Where did she learn *that*?"

"From Curtis, my boyfriend. A pity... now I can never invite her namesake, Martha Stewart, to dinner."

The conversation soon moved onto serious matters.

"I hate to bring this up, Mom," Patrick said in a tight voice, "but have you made any plans for Mucho?"

Callahan felt a band of grief tighten around her chest and just shook her head. "I haven't... been able to... No. No plans yet."

Donny sighed. "The Office of the Medical Investigator still has his body. I talked to them this afternoon. They removed the bullets, did all the tests... said we can pick him up tomorrow." He paused. "Of course it's hard to even think about right now, but I would recommend cremation. He's an awfully large dog to bury."

Callahan could only nod her agreement.

"I'll call the OMI and make the arrangements," Donny said.

After a long silence, Patrick asked, "What happened to the money?"

Callahan realized that she hadn't given the money a thought.

"I have no idea."

"Well, I do," Donny said. "It's in custody—tagged as evidence so they can check for fingerprints, note the serial numbers on the bills, and whatever else they do. The Feds have been called in because it's apparently drug money and an interstate situation."

Patrick nodded. "So, who gets it?"

"I asked that very question when they were through with me last night. I suggested some of it be donated to the Santa Fe Animal Shelter in Mucho's name. I was informed that it would probably go into a Federal fund that finances undercover drug busts." He shook his head. "Who knows where it will actually end up?" Donny shifted in his chair. "Well...I usually catch the late news at this time. But I'm wondering if it's such a good idea, tonight."

"Go ahead," Callahan said. "I need to see what I'm up against."

A smiling, young anchorwoman was reporting local news on an Albuquerque channel, something about the governor's latest plan to promote New Mexico tourism. Her expression and cheerful voice changed only slightly when she segued into the next story.

"The body of a man alleged to have broken into the Tesuque home of nationally acclaimed artist Callahan O'Connor last night has been positively identified as James—better known as Jimmy—Silvo, a San Francisco businessman with suspected Mafia connections. Silvo is also suspected of the Friday afternoon assault on Consuela Borrego, an Espanola resident and O'Connor's housekeeper. Borrego remains in serious condition in Christus Saint Vincent Hospital in Santa Fe.

"Also killed during the encounter was Luke Bennett, age twenty-nine, an employee of Dream Dates, a San Francisco escort service."

"What?" Callahan heard the disbelief in Patrick's voice. She closed her eyes, no longer so happy to have her son sitting beside her.

The announcer continued. "According to the police report, Bennett was a witness to the October thirty-first murder of San Diego interior decorator, Linda Morelli. Sources at the Santa Fe County Sheriff's Department say that Bennett took an undisclosed amount of money from the San Francisco hotel room where Morelli was murdered. The money is believed to be payment for Colombian drugs. According to the same reports, the drug money was recovered at O'Connor's Tesuque home, where Silvo was fatally shot by O'Connor. O'Connor's neighbor, Donald Denton, a best-selling author of romance novels, sustained a minor gunshot injury in the incident. No charges have been filed at this time…"

Donny hit the remote control, and the television went black. Almost as black as the mood in the room.

Jann Arrington-Wolcott

37

The newspaper headlines jumped out at Callahan the next morning:

**San Francisco Mobster Identified
in Tesuque Killings
Santa Fe County Sheriff's Department
Investigates Possible Drug Connection**

And there was another photo of her, smiling during a showing of her work at Santa Fe Visions last year, and one of Donny, posed in front of the walled entrance to her driveway. The story offered one new piece of information:

According to official police sources in San Francisco, James (Jimmy) Silvo was convicted in 1983 of a

Deathmark

gang-related killing in Chicago, for which he served fifteen years in a federal prison. In 1999, he moved to Los Angeles, where he was later arrested on suspicion of drug trafficking. The case was dismissed, due to the disappearance of a prime material witness.

The story ended with a comment from Donny:

"I'm not supposed to talk about the case, but Callahan O'Connor is a heroine. She grabbed the gun from that maniac and shot him before he could kill us all. I'm an eyewitness. It was self-defense, pure and simple."

O'Connor was not available for comment. No charges had been filed in the case, as of ten o'clock last night.

Callahan felt bile rise in her throat. She braced herself against the kitchen counter, taking deep breaths. When Donny came in, he took one look at her and shook his head.

"I meant to hide that, at least until you'd had a good, stiff latte. Sit down and I'll make you one. Did you get any sleep?"

"Some, thanks to your little pill. Where's Patrick?"

"At your house, checking on things. I'm impressed by how well he's handling everything. You obviously did a fine job raising him." Donny paused while his espresso machine foamed milk. "Sheriff Jaramillo called about thirty minutes ago to read me the riot act for talking to the press. I told him that the reporter caught me in an unguarded moment. He was still pissy about it, but this *is* America, after all. I believe I have a constitutional right to speak up and tell the truth—out of fashion as that may be."

He sniffed indignantly and sat down on a stool beside her.

"Anyway, Jaramillo had an update for us. It seems that Silvo was a silent partner in Linda Morelli's decorating business—which was also a front for big-time drug distribution. Apparently, Morelli had been skimming the profits."

Callahan sat at the kitchen table and took a sip of her coffee.

Luke was just in the wrong place at the wrong time. Or was he? Red Feather says there are no accidents. Everything is connected.

"There's something else we need to discuss, honey." Donny hesitated. "I had another call from the OMI. They're ready to release Luke's body."

Callahan closed her eyes, feeling as though she were falling into a deep, dark well.

"I told them we'd get back to them. Does he have family?"

She couldn't stop the tears. *God, help me. I'm so tired of crying.* Donny handed her a tissue.

"None that I know of. His mother may be alive, but they've been out of touch since he was a child."

Donny put his arm around her shoulders, and she leaned into him as she phoned the OMI. As no kin had been found in their investigation, they allowed her to make arrangements for cremation of Luke's body.

The good news of the day was that Consuela was alert enough to receive visitors. Since she knew Patrick would want to accompany her to the hospital, Callahan checked her voicemail as she waited for his return. The first message was from Red Feather, followed by one from a stunned Suzanne and two casual friends. Next came a gruff, unfamiliar male voice. "I'm a features writer for *The Southwestern Inquirer*, trying to reach Callahan O'Connor—" She erased the call, cutting him off. *How did he get my unlisted number?*

The following voice was easily recognizable. "Callahan, darling! It's me, Leda. I'm speechless! There's a story in this morning's *Chronicle*—I can't believe it. Did you *really* shoot that guy? I'm looking at his picture right now, and I'm positive that he was in the gallery just last week, asking all kinds of questions about you and your work. I talked to him *myself*, thinking he was a prospective buyer!" There was a breathless pause. "I nearly *fainted* when I realized that you'd lured that escort back to the boonies with you! Please don't tell anyone you met him through me. Oh, and don't worry. This publicity will do nothing but increase sales…"

Deathmark

Disgusted, Callahan deleted the message.

Next came Paul Kramer, calling from St. Louis. "I just spoke to Suzanne…she told me about the hell you're going through. I want to say how deeply sorry I am. I'll be in Santa Fe tomorrow for a couple of days and back permanently the second week of December. In the meantime, if there's anything I can do, or if you ever just feel like talking, don't hesitate to give me a call." He repeated his number. *Nice man,* Callahan thought, not for the first time.

The final message was from Vonda. "I'm glad you aren't answering your phone. The DA's office doesn't want to make their move too soon. No indictments, so far. Stay put. I'll let you know the minute I hear from them."

Consuela managed a slight smile when Callahan and Patrick walked into her hospital room. Her appearance was shocking. A nasty-looking, blue-black bruise spread from her right temple across her swollen eyes.

"The doctors say she will be fine." Florencio smiled wearily. "Her brain has shrinked back down to its right size."

"*Senora.*" Consuela's voice was little more than a whisper. "The police, they came to ask me… I tell them Detective Silvo—*un hombre muy malo*—should be fired from his job. He came back in the house with no invitation and he hit me…with his gun."

Callahan took her friend's hand. "I know. And I'm so very sorry. I never imagined that you were in danger." She hesitated. Consuela was clearly not in any condition to hear the whole story.

"I think…I won't be able to clean for you tomorrow."

Callahan stroked her hand.

"No, you certainly won't."

"But the floors, they need… " What little energy Consuela had was clearly waning.

"Don't worry about the house." Callahan kissed her forehead. "Don't worry about anything, my dear friend. Just rest and get well."

As Callahan and Patrick waited for the hospital elevator, a young man hurried up and pointed a camera in her face.

"No!" Callahan brought her hand up.

"Callahan O'Connor? I recognize you from your photographs. I'm a freelancer on assignment with *What's Happening?* I just need a…"

Patrick knocked the camera to the floor. "Get away from her!"

"Are you okay?" Patrick peeked around the half-open bedroom door of Donny's guest room later that afternoon.

Callahan sat in an upholstered chair by the window, watching thick gray clouds move in from the mountains, her feet on a matching ottoman.

"It's going to snow." Her voice was soft, expressionless. *How appropriate.*

Patrick sat near her on the edge of the bed, holding her hand.

"The weather channel said it's just a small storm front. Should move out by tomorrow night."

Vivid images flashed in Callahan's mind. *Snow. Deep drifts of snow. A hawk circling an old, twisted cottonwood tree, landing on a high branch. A small voice: "Grandfather, I'm tired. Let me rest here beneath your branches."*

"Mom?" Patrick's voice jerked her back. His eyebrows were pulled together in a worried frown. "I keep trying to think of something I can say—or do—to make this easier for you."

"There's nothing." She shook her head. "I'm all right, sweetheart."

"Like heck you are. Don't do that brave act for me. I'm a grownup, remember?"

"Yes. You certainly are. More levelheaded than I am, that's for sure. You always have been. Even when you were a little boy, and I was going from boyfriend to boyfriend, you usually pointed out their weak points before I saw them. It wasn't a very stable life for you."

"But then you married Edwin. He was a really good guy, a terrific stepdad."

"Yes, he was." Grief welled in her chest—grief upon grief

308

upon grief. Edwin. Her father. Her mother. Luke. Mucho. Consuela. Running Wolf. Sun-in-Her-Face.

Callahan buried her face in her hands and cried for all of them with indescribable heartache.

Patrick pulled her into his arms. "Oh, my poor mama."

Callahan was struck by the word. Patrick hadn't called her "Mama" since he was ten years old. She clung to him. When her sobs subsided, she blew her nose and took a long, deep breath before speaking.

"There's something I want to explain to you, an important aspect of my relationship with Luke. It'll help you to understand how I got involved with him—and the depth of what was between us." And so she described Luke's marks, how they tied into her dreams of Running Wolf's death.

"You really believe..." Patrick broke off, his expression incredulous. "You think that Luke could have been the reincarnation of an Indian you dream about?"

"I'm convinced of it."

"I... don't quite know what to say."

"You don't have to say anything. I just wanted you to know the full story."

"Wow..." He shook his head. "This is a lot to take in."

"I know. I feel so bad for you."

"For me?"

"To have your mother mixed up in something like this. And it may get worse. There could be criminal charges brought against me."

"I don't think so."

"I killed someone."

"In self-defense." Patrick's eyes were bright with unshed tears. "There's something *I* want to say, Mom, and I want you to *really* hear it. Are you listening?"

"I'm listening."

"It's true that you've never been an ordinary, predictable, cookie-baking mom. But it's also true that there's never been a time in my whole life when I wasn't proud as heck to be your son. Including now."

Not trusting herself to speak, Callahan held him in a tight embrace.

Snow was falling by bedtime. Callahan stood at the window, watching the fat flakes illuminated by Donny's patio lights. For the first time in her memory, the sight triggered no fear. Rather, it was strangely comforting.

Sleep. Escape the pain. Find peace. The thoughts floated like wisps of smoke through her exhausted mind. Without bothering to close the draperies, she climbed into bed and closed her eyes.

She was tired, so tired. But she forced herself on, walking through the knee-deep snow. Not much farther. She could see the cottonwood in the clearing just ahead. The Grandfather tree, under whose sheltering, full branches they had spent such happy times.

Running Wolf, I am coming.

Snow blanketed everything, changing the familiar landscape and burying rocks and bushes. As it would soon bury her body. The thought consoled her. At last she reached the tree and began to disrobe. Her fingers were blue, almost numb—as numb as the heart that, for just a short time longer, beat in her breast. I wish to die. I wish to die.

Cold terror bolted Callahan awake.

"Dear god," she spoke the words aloud—needing to hear her own voice. "What's happening? Is Sun-in-Her-Face taking over my mind... *and* my body?"

She shivered and chanted to herself. "I don't want to die. No, no, I don't want to die."

Deathmark

38

Callahan watched the clock the next morning, putting off making the call until six o'clock. She picked up the guest room extension. "Red Feather, am I calling too early?"

"No, I'm always up to greet the dawn. I'm glad you called; I've been very concerned. Are you still staying with your friend?"

"Yes." Tears choked her voice. "I need to see you."

"I'll be there in an hour."

"We got a lot of snow last night. I'm not sure about the roads."

"No problem for a shaman with four-wheel drive."

She hung up and climbed back into the warm bed. Shivering, she pressed her face into the pillow to stifle her moans. If it were not for Donny and Patrick sleeping nearby, she would have howled her grief.

Donny was still in his robe and looking a bit flustered when he ushered Red Feather into the guest room. Callahan was wrapped in a blanket over her sweats and huddled in the chair by the window.

"Work your magic, Red Feather," Donny said. "She's barely eating or sleeping." He gave her a worried glance as he closed the door behind him.

The shaman put his canvas bag on the floor, and Callahan went straight into his arms. His comforting embrace unleashed a fresh torrent of tears.

"I still can't believe it… it's a nightmare I can't wake up from. Luke is dead. *Dead!* And Mucho—I keep expecting him to come running in…"

Red Feather held her quietly for a long moment.

"Grief is the price we pay for loving. It's a high price, but what would life be without love?" He patted her back and continued, "I want to remind you of something you already know, on a deep level. Life and death walk hand-in-hand. They dance back and forth, like summer and winter. So, you see, death is just an illusion. The bonds of love can never be broken. The spirits of our loved ones remain with us, always."

He pulled back and looked into her tear-filled eyes.

"Take a slow deep breath. Follow it deep into yourself. Now, exhale slowly through your mouth. That's right. Like you're blowing away dark clouds of grief. Good. Another."

When Callahan regained some semblance of control, Red Feather led her back to the chair. "I know what I read in the newspapers and what Suzanne has told me." He sat on the edge of the bed. "I'd like to hear your words."

And so Callahan went through the events again, but this time—for the first time—she included what Luke had screamed as he threw the lance. "It was a war cry—the same cry Running Wolf made when he rescued me from those Crow warriors." She clutched Red Feather's hands. "Did you hear what I just said? When he rescued *me*."

"Sun-in-Her-Face is still a part of you."

"Last night…" Callahan tightened her grip, as though Red

312

Deathmark

Feather were a lifeline to sanity. She took a deep breath. "Last night, before I went to sleep, I felt so strange. I could easily imagine walking out into the snow and just lying down... giving up. Some part of me *wanted* to do that. Then I had the dream again. I *relived* it again. And when I woke up, the yearning to just give up was still there."

"Remembering is part of healing, but *reliving* old, traumatic events is not. We must re-establish your boundaries. You need to live totally in this body now." Red Feather paused. "As I said before, the door between the life you lived then and your present life has never been completely closed. Friday night, that door swung wide open— for Luke as well as for you."

"That's true. Before he died, Luke said something I'll never forget. He said, 'It's dead? You're sure it's dead?' Red Feather, he was talking about a *bear!* He saw a huge bear—not Silvo—when he threw that spear."

The shaman nodded. "The moment of great danger combined with the feel of the war lance in his hand... it must have triggered the memory for Luke. A violent death gets imprinted on our soul memory and we unconsciously carry it into our next lifetime. Luke's birthmarks were spiritual, as well as physical.

"He carried those character traits—recklessness and lack of judgment—that killed Running Wolf. He took the money from the hotel room that night. So, once again, he had to face 'the bear'—this time in the form of Silvo. The Creator is generous. Life on the physical plane is a testing ground, always presenting us with opportunities to learn and to grow. Maybe even become wise. Perhaps in his *next* earthwalk, Luke will pass that test."

"But he was so young. He had so much to live for." Deep painful sobs escaped from Callahan's chest.

The shaman nodded. "Life often appears tragic, but that's because we can't see the complete picture. Each lifetime is just one chapter in a very long book."

She wiped her face with her sleeve. "Help me to believe that."

"It is the teaching of many great spiritual masters throughout the ages, from many different cultures." He paused. "This may sound strange to you right now, but grief is always an opportunity for transformation, for growth. Go into the fire of it. Let it cleanse and strengthen you. It won't be easy. Growth never is."

Callahan tried to take in his words. Closing her swollen eyes, she breathed deeply, heard him chanting quietly. Unaware of time passing, she had a startling realization.

"It just came to me..." She opened her eyes and looked at the shaman's kind face. "... the karmic parallel between losing Luke and Mucho in this life and the deaths of Running Wolf and my premature baby in that life!"

Red Feather nodded. "Very good. Once again, you're at a crossroads. You're being given another chance, an invitation, for soul growth. It's up to you. It requires that you accept what has happened, that you experience grief fully and fearlessly—something that Sun-in-Her-Face was unable to do."

"I don't know if I can. I feel so utterly depleted. Sick to my very soul."

"You're still in serious shock. Not only your grief for Luke and Mucho, but the effects of killing Silvo. To take the life of another, even in battle, is a terrible insult to the spirit. If the spirit is not cleansed and brought back into balance, illness—emotional and or physical— often results. This is a great problem with soldiers in our American culture. Years after Vietnam, I worked with many veterans who were still suffering." He sighed. "Now I'm doing the same with soldiers returning from Iraq and Afghanistan."

In that moment, Red Feather looked far older than his age. Callahan saw in his eyes the heavy price he paid for trying to hold the pain of others, in addition to his own.

"Native peoples use different methods, such as sweat lodges and healing ceremonies, to correct the soul-damage caused by war. Some Plains tribes used to do a ceremonial mourning in which the slayer of an enemy in battle was expected to mourn for thirty days, blackening his face and wearing his hair loose. While it was considered no sin to take the life of an enemy, this public display of mourning demonstrated a reverence for the departed spirit and, by extension, for all life."

Callahan imagined Patrick and Donny's faces, if she emerged

from the room with a blackened face. She resisted a wild impulse to laugh.

"I'm losing my mind," she said, not realizing she'd spoken the words aloud.

"No, your mind is intact, my friend. But your energy—on all levels—is fragmented." He took a blanket from the foot of the bed and spread it on the floor. "Lie down and I'll work on it."

Red Feather repeated the cleansing and strengthening ceremony he had performed three weeks earlier. When apparently satisfied that a healing light was moving through her body, he moved into a more elaborate ritual. Opening his canvas bag, he removed his medicine items—dried sage and the abalone shell, eagle feather, two quartz crystals, tape recorder, and drumming cassette.

After they were both "smudged" in clouds of fragrant sage smoke, he said, "Now I'm going to sweep your body with an eagle feather, removing any negative energy that may still be attached to you."

She lay still as he tapped his medicine feather around her head and face then flicked it from her forehead to her chin. This action was repeated several times, the feather moving from neck to waist and down her entire body, until she had been "swept" from head to foot. He placed one of the crystals on her forehead.

Red Feather put on his drumming tape and stretched out on the tiled floor, a short distance from her.

"Close your eyes and relax. Try to empty your mind and just absorb the healing while I journey. You need another soul retrieval to collect those psychic parts that were scattered by the shock of all you've recently been through."

The repetitive drumming soothed Callahan and within minutes she was overcome by a warm drowsiness. All sense of time disappeared as she drifted in and out of sleep, only vaguely aware of Red Feather kneeling beside her and blowing a long, warm breath against her chest. Finally, he removed the crystal.

"I'm going to sit you up now, but keep your eyes closed."

Only half-awake, she leaned against him as he blew on the crown of her head. Then he helped her up and into bed.

"You will sleep now. A long, restorative sleep."

"Thank you," she whispered as her eyes closed.

It was late afternoon when Callahan awoke, feeling rested and more like herself than she had in the past few days. She had to agree with Suzanne, Red Feather appeared to work miracles.

She found Donny in his study, typing furiously on his computer keyboard. He held up a hand.

"Just a sec, let me finish this bit of dialogue."

She curled into a nearby recliner, Donny's high-tech Christmas present to himself the previous winter. With the push of a button, the chair would deliver a vibrating massage. Callahan resisted, deciding that her body had been jolted enough for one day.

Donny hit the "save" button and swiveled to face her.

"The idea for a new plot just came to me. Listen to this: my heroine, a Santa Fe journalist, interviews a sexy, mysterious medicine man and gets more of a 'treatment' than she bargains for. I think I may have a movie here!"

Callahan mustered a little smile. "Sounds like it."

"Well…" Donny studied her. "I'm delighted to say that you look one-hundred percent better. Dare I ask what went on in my guest room this morning?"

"Not the kind of treatment your heroine undoubtedly gets."

"Pity. Well, whatever Red Feather is distributing, it should be bottled."

Callahan suddenly felt a desperate need for her son.

"Where's Patrick?"

"He said he was going to visit an old classmate and then stop to pick up something for dinner. I was planning to cook, but the sweet boy insisted. He should be back soon." Donny paused. "You won't believe who called while you were sleeping. Bradley! He was polite as could be and absolutely oozing concern for you. Wanted to know if he could come by for a visit."

"You're kidding."

"I told him, also politely, that you were *not* receiving visitors."

Deathmark

"Thank you."

"Here's another update. When Suzanne called to check on you this morning, she reported that there are eye-witnesses to Brad's accident. A couple of teenagers were parked on the other side of the road and saw the whole thing. They said no other vehicle was involved. Brad was weaving all over the place and lost control on a curve."

Callahan felt a wave of relief and gratitude. The final doubt was removed. Her faith in Luke was justified. He may have been impulsive and reckless, but—like Running Wolf—he had a good and loving heart.

39

Callahan and Patrick, stood in Donny's driveway late the next morning, saying goodbye. She swallowed hard, trying to control her anxiety, her reluctance to let her son out of her sight.

"Are you sure the roads are all right?"

"Positive, Mom. They've all been plowed. Once I get over Raton Pass, it's clear sailing all the way to Denver. Look, the sun is shining. The storm has moved out." He gave her a long, hard hug. "You know I hate to leave you, but I have to get back to work. We have an important staff meeting in the morning. Are you sure you'll be able to manage?"

"Of course. As you know, I'm blessed with a great support system." *Life goes on.* She took both of her son's hands in hers, surprised at how large they were. *How did he grow up so fast?* She put on her bravest face. "So don't worry about me. I *mean* it. I'm going to be fine. Besides, you'll be back soon for Thanksgiving."

Deathmark

He grinned. "Donny was working on his menu this morning. Red chile-crusted Cornish game hens, mussels on saffron rice, something called a papaya and cactus pad salad, piñon nut torte—there's more, but I didn't retain it. I can't believe he's going to all that trouble for just the three of us."

"Six, actually," Callahan said. "Curtis will be joining us, as well as Suzanne and Rob."

"It's sure to be memorable." Patrick hesitated. "Keep me posted about any developments with the DA's office."

"I will. I love you, baby."

"Love you, too, Mom—a bushel and a peck."

"And a hug around the neck," they finished together. She planted a kiss on his cheek and hugged him once more, as tightly as she could, wishing she could keep him beside her forever. *Life is so fragile. In just a moment, it can be gone.*

Callahan stood outside in the cold for few minutes after Patrick left. She was overwhelmed with emptiness. She felt her grief as a cold, dark force washing over her—trying to flatten and suck her under. Then Red Feather's words came back, and she clung to them like a life raft. *Accept the pain. Live past it. Grow through it.*

The next couple of days at Donny's were quiet and relatively uneventful. Still no word from the DA's office. Several friends, including Suzanne, dropped by for visits. Although Callahan appreciated their concern, she had to force herself to make even short appearances. After a few minutes, she would excuse herself and escape to the sanctuary of Donny's guest room.

Other than Donny, the only person she felt comfortable with was Red Feather. She accepted his call early Friday morning.

"I knew this would be a difficult day for you," he said.

"Yes. I woke up thinking that it was a week ago today..." She broke off. "I just told Donny that I've accepted his hospitality long enough. I'm going home."

"Your house must be cleansed before you spend time in it."

"A cleaning service has been there. Patrick said they did a thorough job."

"I mean it needs a psychic cleaning. I'll pick you up shortly after noon. For a purification ceremony."

With Red Feather close behind her, Callahan unlocked the front door and stepped inside her house. Her eyes went immediately to the spot where she'd last seen Mucho, lying in a puddle of blood. The brick floor was spotlessly clean, as though the terrible night had never happened. A soft, strangling sound escaped her and she felt Red Feather's hand on her shoulder.

"Reach deep inside for your strength. Envision yourself wrapping that strength around you like a warrior's cloak."

Callahan did her best to follow his instruction. *Wrap myself in strength.*

Red Feather pulled some white candles from his canvas bag and positioned them on the floor in the entryway and on down the long, wide hallway.

"Candles expel negative energy," he explained, lighting them.

Next, he placed a bundle of dried sage in the abalone shell and put a match to it. Once the sage was burning, he and Callahan took turns smudging each other with the smoke.

"Show me where each body lay."

Carrying the shell, chanting in his deep voice, and fanning smoke with his eagle feather, the shaman stopped at the three locations she indicated. He paid particular attention to the spots where Mucho and Luke had fallen. Callahan stood beside him, her vision blurred by tears.

Red Feather put his strong hands on her shoulders, as though transferring his strength to her.

"I've done all I can do, my friend. Now it will just take time. Keep candles burning for several more hours. Eat. Rest. Keep your strength wrapped around you. I'll be in close touch."

320

Deathmark

Callahan thanked him and closed the door. Standing in the entryway, she was struck by the utter quiet. She had not been alone in the house since Mucho's arrival. He had always been there, her faithful companion, filling an otherwise empty place in her life.

And then she saw a box sitting on the entry table. *Luke's gift! I'd forgotten...*

"Native Arts and Antiques of Taos" was printed on the lid. Her hand trembled as she lifted it. Inside was a note, with small, precise handwriting: *Callahan, I was drawn to this and felt you should have it for your collection of Native American (note that I wrote it correctly!) antiques. The gallery owner told me it's at least two hundred years old. With all my love, Luke.* Under the note, nestled on a bed of cotton, was a large bear claw, its base wrapped with a strand of time-worn rawhide.

An image of Running Wolf, bear claw hanging around his neck, flashed into Callahan's mind. Holding the claw to her chest, she remained with her eyes closed—until she saw him no more.

Jann Arrington-Wolcott

40

The morning was cold and cloudy, with a forecast for snow that night. Callahan put on her thick down jacket and, with a heavy heart, picked up the metal box containing Mucho's ashes. He'd been such a large animal, yet the box weighed less than five pounds. *His essence—the loyal, joyful, spirit that was Mucho— still exists. Someday, in this life or another, we'll be together again.* She believed with all her heart that it was true.

She picked up a similar box; this one covered in brown vinyl and only slightly larger. She held it to her chest for a moment. Luke's ashes. With the two boxes carefully situated on the passenger seat of her Jeep, she started the drive up the mountain. Both Red Feather and Donny had offered to go with her, but Callahan needed to do this alone. Mucho and Luke had loved the mountain and each other. It seemed right to scatter their ashes there, together, near the creek where the three of them had picnicked.

Deathmark

She found the spot and parked. As she carried the boxes past the picnic table, to the clearing where Luke and Mucho had played—throwing and retrieving a stick—the bittersweet memory squeezed her heart until she could barely breathe. She removed the lids and stared through tear-blurred eyes at the fine gray ashes and small bits of bone that lay within plastic bags. *They were both so beautiful, so alive. And now this is all that remains of their physical bodies.*

She took a deep breath, and then another, summoning all of her inner strength. Handful by handful, memory by memory, she scattered Luke's ashes—in the clearing, the nearby woods, and along the side of the creek. She did the same with Mucho's. Her chest ached from sobbing when she tossed the last handfuls into the air.

At that moment, sunlight broke through a cloud. The drifting ashes were struck by its brilliant rays, transforming them into a shimmering golden haze that caught a breeze and drifted upward. Callahan felt deeply comforted by the sight and recalled Red Feather's words: *Bonds of love can never be broken. The spirits of those we love are with us, always.*

As she walked slowly back to the Jeep, she heard the echo of Luke's laughter, followed by a joyful bark.

Vonda called late that afternoon. "I have good news. You're in the clear. The DA just ruled justifiable homicide. You're also cleared of any connection to drug-dealing or the death of Linda Morelli."

Callahan went weak with relief. As she thanked her attorney, she silently included any spirit allies or guardian angels that might have influenced the decision.

Callahan got into the habit of not answering her phone, preferring to just check her messages. The number of calls had tapered off dramatically. Still some from the press, but that was about it. Stories in the tabloids—such as **Dream Dates Escort Leads to Nightmare for Award-Winning Artist**—had obviously left many of her so-called friends speechless.

One morning, a message elicited a small smile. "Callahan, this is Paul Kramer. Suzanne just called with the great news about the DA's ruling. I'm back in St. Louis, wrapping up some final business before I move. I look forward to being in Santa Fe permanently, in about two weeks. I'll keep calling and hope to talk to you in person one day soon. I know this must be a very rough time. Take care of yourself."

A really special man. He'll make some lucky woman very happy.

Donny was in a celebratory mood. He had set the table for two, using his best linens, china, and Waterford crystal. He'd also cut out the front page headline of the *Santa Fe New Mexican*— **DA Rules Tesuque Shooting Justifiable Homicide. O'Connor Cleared of all Charges**—and taped it across his refrigerator door.

They sat in his living room by a cozy fire, sipping chilled flutes of Veuve Clicquot. Callahan reached for another warm Medjool date, stuffed with goat cheese and pistachio nuts—her third.

"I'm delighted to see that your appetite is making a comeback. You haven't been much fun to cook for lately." Donny raised his almost-empty glass. "I propose another toast: To the future…may it bring all good things."

Callahan clinked her glass to his, although the future was something she tried not to think about. She was just taking it one day at a time.

"I could kiss that District Attorney," Donny continued, "although he really isn't my type. Of course, there was never any real doubt about your being cleared. No way could you wear inmate orange with your coloring." He grinned, stood, and offered her his arm. "May I escort you into the dining room, my dear? I've prepared an elegant salad with fresh spinach, candied walnuts, and gorgeous colossal shrimp."

Callahan took his arm. "You are absolutely the greatest. Are you sure you won't go straight and marry me?"

"What? And spoil a perfect friendship? Not a chance. But we will be best buddies forever."

Deathmark

"Buddies forever!" Martha screeched, as they walked past her cage. "It's a good thing!"

Jann Arrington-Wolcott

Epilogue

Callahan stepped back from the canvas, the fourth in a new series featuring contemporary women. She studied it with approval. The image, a woman half-rising from her bed, had just the right expression of eagerness on her face. Callahan added a little more color to the lips and cheeks. *Perfect.* She would title this piece *Awakening.*

A soft whine broke through the strains of a Mozart Horn Concerto. She turned to look at her three-month-old, black-and-white puppy, a gift from Red Feather. When the scrawny mixed-breed had turned up at his front door on Christmas day, Strong Heart had greeted and comforted the shivering puppy like an old friend. Red Feather suggested naming him Mato—the Lakota word for bear. Since bears

Deathmark

symbolize introspection, healing, and strength, the name felt exactly right to Callahan.

From the moment little Mato had entered Callahan's house, he seemed completely at home. Romping down the hall, he headed straight for her bedroom and his new bed in the corner beside the fireplace. After giving it a few good sniffs, he investigated the box where she had placed new puppy toys. He pulled them, one by one, onto the floor. Finally, his head and upper body emerged from the box one last time. When Callahan saw what he held in his mouth, she caught her breath. Mato dragged Mucho's beloved sheepskin bunny to his new bed and, cuddling it close, promptly fell asleep.

The spirits of our loved ones remain with us, always.

She smiled, remembering Red Feather's words, and returned to her painting, excited about the new direction her work was taking.

Jann Arrington-Wolcott

Deathmark

Acknowledgments

This book, has traveled a long, winding path from conception to publication. Without the support, patience, and constant encouragement of my husband, Dr. John H. Wolcott, it would never have made it. The same is true of my fabulous, old-soul, daughter and fellow writer/editor, Janna Szalay Bunnell. Great encouragement goes to my son, Jeffrey Gerard Szalay, who has his own stories and the talent to tell them.

In addition, many fellow-writers and treasured friends contributed to *Deathmark's* completion. They are listed, certainly not in order of importance, but as they dance through my head. I am blessed, awed, and humbled to be traveling with such an impressive group of souls.

Arlena Markinson, talented writer and editor in her own right, sister-of-my-soul and godmother to this book, who somehow understands my tales better than I do and always encourages me to "reach deeper."

David Dorwart, a true Renaissance man: writer in many genres, musician, scholar, philosopher, teacher, and compassionate confidant. I've reached out to you through distance and darkness, David, and you've always been there. I can never thank you enough.

Kimerick Hayner, who has more talent in every direction than is legal, and has been my much-loved and always supportive soul-friend since that long ago time when we thought we had all the answers, even if we didn't understand the questions.

Bobette Perrone, my talented, beloved, and loyal friend "for the long-haul" who writes/edits and lives with great honesty, integrity, compassion, and love. We'll spend more enchanted time with that river, dear heart.

Stepfanie Kramer, beautiful, ferocious friend, beyond-talented actress, singer, writer of screenplays and fiction, true psychic who always sees the "big picture" and literally saved my life. (Oh, honey, didn't we laugh in Italy?)

Richard Stearns, who contributed hugely to both my life and work and meant so very much for so long. Here's to all the wonderful memories, Richie.

Hector Amezquita, faithful friend since childhood, opera aficionado, true artist when it comes to styling hair and conscious living. During the hardest of times you have comforted me and used your wicked wit to make me smile. *Gracias, amigo.*

Dr. Stephen Blumberg, movie-star-handsome, eagle-eyed editor and treasured, long-time friend.

Wendy Wolf Blumberg who awes me with her poetry, sustains me with her prayers, and encourages my writing with her goose-bumps.

Bliss Kelly-Loree, witness to our real-life stories and "keeper of the memories," for the past fifty years. Kid, in many ways, you know me better than anyone could. Thank you for continuing to love me, anyway.

Jim Gautier, top-of-the-line photographer, poet, story-teller second-to-none, and his wife, Peggy Gautier, scientist and artist who succeeds at anything she puts her mind to. You two are "family" in the truest sense of the word. You've read, critiqued, and encouraged my writing from the earliest days, and have, in all of life's seasons, walked shoulder-to-shoulder with me.

Michael McGarrity, award-winning author and generous friend, for his expert advice and knowledge re: crime and psychology, and for threatening that if I didn't get back out into the world, he'd send his "cop friends to get me."

Mimi McGarrity, talented artist, gourmet cook, and rock-solid (through giggles and tears) girlfriend, for her fearless honesty, compassion, wisdom and support.

Peggy van Hulsteyn, brilliant author, constant inspiration,

Deathmark

witty and brave forever-friend (next time around, my dear, we'll make those changes!).

Forrest Fenn, art connisseur, author, adventurer, and collector of treasures, who read an early draft of this book and offered darn good advice.

Dr. Kenneth Tankersley, who generously shared his expertise in Lakota language and customs, as well as supplying me with authentic prayers and songs.

Amy Stein, whose internationally acclaimed art adds beauty and joy to my home, and whose time-tested friendship never falters.

Nancy Fay, whose editing and literary skills are equal to her legendary sense of humor.

Dr. Robert Thomsen, an exceptional poet and friend, who offered encouragement and medical advice.

Dan McBride, multi-talented artist, musician and soul-brother. Through the years, we've laughed until we cried, and cried until we could laugh again.

Michael Stanchie, for his basic goodness, laser insight, constant strong shoulder, and understanding of soul connection. I love you, Michael.

I must also thank my exceptional grandchildren, Christopher Keene, Kayla, Krista, and Kyle Szalay, Savanna and Michael Bunnell, who are awe-inspiring and surprised (as well as slightly shocked) by what their Mimi knows and writes.

Listed near the bottom so they'll stand out, Liz Trupin-Pulli ("Big Little Sis"), my agent/editor/great support on all levels, who boosts me up and calms me down.

And Annette Chaudet, author, editor, multi-talented artist and publisher of Pronghorn Press, whose versatility, writing and intuitive understanding blows me away. Thank you for embracing this story. There are no coincidences. I was a Lucky Girl to reconnect with you.

I'm sure I've left out some important people and will kick myself around the corral, when I remember.

Jann Arrington-Wolcott

Deathmark

Photo by John Wolcott

About the Author

Jann Arrington-Wolcott feels that she's lived many lifetimes in one body, playing different roles at different times: fashion model, actress, high school teacher, magazine writer, public speaker, author of fiction and non-fiction, and world traveler. Her most important roles, however, are wife, mother, grandmother, and fortunate friend to some of the most amazing people on earth.

A third-generation New Mexican, Arrington-Wolcott was raised on a cattle ranch near the Mexican border. Her colorful family background includes a Cherokee great-grandmother, a Harvey Girl grandmother, a frontier sheriff, a Methodist minister, and an infamous

train robber. As with the former, contemporary family rascals and outlaws shall go unnamed.

Arrington-Wolcott's first fiction, *Brujo*, was filmed as a USA Cable movie titled *Seduced by Evil*, starring Suzanne Somers. She is currently working on a sequel to that story. A lifelong spiritual seeker and student of many paths, she has studied shamanism with teachers in the United States, Mexico, Hawaii, Ireland and England. She lives in Santa Fe, New Mexico, her favorite place on the planet, with her retired physicist husband, John, and dog-angels, Lola Bella and Federico Mateo, aka Rico the Tongue.

Visit her on her Facebook page and at her website: JannArringtonWolcott.com

Deathmark

Discussion Questions

1. The main theme of *Deathmark* is that true love never dies. Arrington-Wolcott uses reincarnation to carry the theme from two Native Americans who lived centuries ago to two contemporary Americans who meet by chance. Do you feel she made a convincing case for this connected spirit of love? If so, why? If not, why?

2. As a follow-up to the preceding question: do you believe things happen by chance? Are there moments in your life that seemed to be coincidence, but now feel as though they were meant to be?

3. Callahan reacts negatively to the concept of arranging for a "date" to escort her to the gallery opening, but is over-ruled by the gallery owner who has already made the arrangements. Discuss how you would feel about using such an escort service.

4. Arrington-Wolcott portrays Callahan as a successful, hardworking painter who derives her inspiration from a deep, instinctual level that often taps into dreams. Did this approach to art interest you? If so, why? If not, why?

5. Callahan is a woman of a certain age who has been through a lot in her life, including a difficult divorce from a difficult man. Does the author successfully breathe life into Callahan?

6. Arrington-Wolcott develops Luke as a character who provides multiple elements to the storyline. Discuss these elements and how successful, or not, the author is in breathing life into Luke.

7. Callahan's best friend, Donny, is an important character in *Deathmark*. Discuss what Donny provides to the overall impact of the story. Do you feel Donny is a believable, well-rounded character?

8. *Deathmark* is a novel that combines elements from several different genres—suspense, romance, mystery, paranormal. Discuss whether this was satisfying to you. What was your favorite aspect? What, if anything, did not work for you and why?

9. Were you surprised by the true villain?

10. Many readers might react negatively to the fate of Mucho, Callahan's devoted protector and valiant Great Dane. Do you feel this choice was the right one? If so, why? If not, why?

11. Shamanism is an important element in *Deathmark*. Did this aspect of the story intrigue or resonate with you?

12. At the end of the story, Callahan didn't feel the need to rush into another romantic relationship. Were you surprised? Was the ending emotionally satisfying to you?

Deathmark

Recommended Reading

There is no shortage of excellent books about reincarnation and shamanism. The following are among those I consider to be most important:

Journeying: Where Shamanism and Psychology Meet, Jeannette M. Gagan, Ph.D.

The Way of the Shaman, Michael Harner, Ph.D., founder of The Foundation for Shamanic Studies

Soul Retrieval: Mending the Fragmented Self, among others by Sandra Ingerman

The Woman in the Shaman's Body, Barbara Tedford, Ph.D.

Reincarnation: A New Horizon in Science, Religion, and Society, Sylvia Cranston and Carey Williams

The Universe in a Single Atom: The Convergence of Science and Spirituality, His Holiness, the Dalai Lama

No Death, No Fear: Comforting Wisdom for Life, Thich Nhat Hanh

Old Souls: The Scientific Evidence for Past Lives, Tom Shroder

Life After Life, Coming Back: A Psychiatrist Explores Past-Life Journeys, and others by Raymond A. Moody, M.D., Ph.D.

Jann Arrington-Wolcott

Soul Journey: Many Lives, Many Masters, Tapping Into Past Life Memories, and Only Love is Real, among others by Brian Weiss, M.D.

Speaking From the Heart: Ethics, Reincarnation & What it Means to be Human, Joan Grant (edited by Nicola Benett, Jane Lahr and Sophia Rosoff)

Experiencing the Soul: Before Birth, During Life, After Death, insights and wisdom from The Dalai Lama, Elisabeth Kubler-Ross, Ram Dass, Joan Borysenko, Stephen Levin, Jean Houston, and others

Shamanism: An Expanded View of Reality, Compiled by Shirley Nicholson

Secrets of Shamanism: Tapping the Spirit Power Within You, Jose Stevens, Ph.D. & Lena S. Stevens

The Shaman: Voyages of the Soul—Trance, Ecstasy and Healing From Siberia to the Amazon, Piers Vitebsky

Shaman, Healer, Sage: How to Heal Yourself and Others with the Energy Medicine of the Americas, Alberto Villoldo, Ph.D.

Shamanic Voices: A Survey of Visionary Narratives and *Shaman: The Wounded Healer,* Joan Halifax, Ph.D.

Kahuna Healing: Holistic Health and Healing Practices of Polynesia and *Urban Shaman,* Serge Kahili King

Fire in the Head: Shamanism and the Celtic Spirit, Tom Cowan

CPSIA information can be obtained at www.ICGtesting.com
Printed in the USA
LVOW12s0258010714

392365LV00003B/4/P